"Powerful . . . a morality tale for modern times, and Parrish fleshes it out with carefully drawn, empathetic characters."—*Booklist*

"Parrish expertly blends deadly intrigue and courtroom drama."   —*Tulsa World*

"Powerful legal suspense . . . a vivid, surefire winner that provides a brilliant insider's exposé into the behind-the-scenes events that occur during the judicial process."
          —*Internet Bookwatch*

"A carefully built thriller of revenge. . . . Parrish tells a good tale."
          —*Sunday Advocate* (Baton Rouge)

"A shocking thriller."   —*MLB News*

"Excellent . . . a well-written, very realistic miscarriage of justice that keeps you involved."
          —*Ellenville* (New York) *Press*

"Tough . . . thought-provoking"
          —*Scottsdale Progress Tribune*

Richard Parrish

ABANDONED HEART

AN ONYX BOOK

ONYX
Published by the Penguin Group
Penguin Books USA Inc., 375 Hudson Street,
New York, New York 10014, U.S.A.
Penguin Books Ltd, 27 Wrights Lane,
London W8 5TZ, England
Penguin Books Australia Ltd, Ringwood,
Victoria, Australia
Penguin Books Canada Ltd, 10 Alcorn Avenue,
Toronto, Ontario, Canada M4V 3B2
Penguin Books (N.Z.) Ltd, 182–190 Wairau Road,
Auckland 10, New Zealand

Penguin Books Ltd, Registered Offices:
Harmondsworth, Middlesex, England

Published by Onyx, an imprint of Dutton Signet,
a division of Penguin Books USA Inc.
Previously published in a Dutton edition.

First Onyx Printing, September, 1997
10 9 8 7 6 5 4 3 2 1

Grateful acknowledgment is made for permission to reprint the following:

"I'm So Lonesome I Could Cry," by Hank Williams, Sr., copyright © 1949, renewed © 1976 by Acuff-Rose Music, Inc., and Hiriam Music for the U.S.A. World outside U.S.A. controlled by Acuff-Rose Music, Inc. All rights reserved. International rights secured. Used by permisssion.

"Ain't That a Shame," words and music by Antoine Domino and Dave Bartholomew, copyright © 1955 (renewed) EMI Unart Catalog, Inc. All rights reserved. Used by permission.

 REGISTERED TRADEMARK—MARCA REGISTRADA

Printed in the United States of America

PUBLISHER'S NOTE
This is a work of fiction. Names, characters, places, and incidents either are the product of the author's imagination or are used fictitiously, and any resemblance to actual persons, living or dead, events, or locales is entirely coincidental.

In the definition of "murder," the words "malice aforethought" long ago acquired in law a settled meaning: where the person committing the act which causes death does so with the actual intention to kill and from the dictate of an abandoned, depraved, and malignant heart.

—from 1 Russ. Crimes 641, and
State v. Pike, 49 New Hampshire
399, 6 Am. Rep. 533

A woman of valor, who can find?
Her worth is far greater than rubies.

—Proverbs 31:10

· PART ·
ONE

She weepeth bitterly in the night, and her tears are on her cheeks; among all who love her she has none to comfort her. All her friends have dealt treacherously with her, and they are become as enemies.

—LAMENTATIONS 1:2

· ONE ·

Donna Alvarez woke up drenched in sweat after a short, restless sleep. What the hell time was it? She squinted at the red LCD dial of the little electric clock. Almost one o'clock. Only an hour and a half of sleep. Shit! Another horrible night. She sat up slowly in bed, and her nine-year-old sister Janet moaned softly next to her and rolled over. The swamp cooler was clattering, and a wispy breath of moldy-smelling moist air came out of the vent, but it was still at least eighty-five degrees in the squalid bedroom.

She got out of bed, nude as she always slept, steadying herself against the wall. It felt clammy and hot to her touch, but she realized that even her tingling hands were wet with sweat. She needed a fix *now*. She'd be fighting off pink and blue gargoyles flying around her head if she didn't get some heroin fast. Her belly hurt the way it did when she was on the verge of withdrawal, spasmodic pains wrenching her stomach and guts and hurting all the way to her crotch.

She went into the bathroom and turned on the light. It was a twenty-five-watt bulb hanging from the ceiling, and she could barely make out her face in the reflection of the filthy medicine cabinet mirror. She turned on the faucet and splashed her face and armpits. The only towel was a soiled hand towel with SAFARI RESORT stitched in red script along the bottom.

She dried herself with it and peered into the medicine cabinet. There was a little bottle of Nina Ricci *L'air du Temps Parfum* she had stolen from Bullock's last week, and a big bottle of Chanel No. 5 toilet water that she had shoplifted from Neiman-Marcus. She loved doing her "shopping" at the Scottsdale Fashion Square. She sprinkled some toilet water into her hand, rubbed her hands together, and massaged the fragrance into her armpits and the silky brown hair between her legs. Then she took the dove-shaped Lalique crystal stopper out of the Nina Ricci perfume and touched it behind her ears. The tiny little bottle had come in a small yellow box with a four-hundred-dollar price tag, but the sweet savor almost made her vomit. She grimaced with the increasingly severe cramps in her gut. She doubled over the sink and dry-heaved several times, and the pain slowly receded. Her older sister Louise had swiped her last paper of heroin yesterday and hadn't even paid her for it. Bitch.

Big Gun Pete would have some papers. He always did. He lived up Thomas Road about a half mile in a dilapidated tool-storage shed that had been abandoned years ago when the Indians on the Salt River Pima-Maricopa Reservation started getting paid more money for leasing their huge fields to corporate cotton farmers in Phoenix than growing their own cotton. Pete would want her to do him for the H, maybe even slap her around for the hell of it, but tonight she needed junk too bad to worry about it.

Donna's first pimp, Bobby Sanders, a big, tall white guy, had always taken half her money, but the leftover was enough for her to buy plenty of smack and a few nice clothes. Then Sanders had been arrested and sent to prison for dealing cocaine, and Big Gun Pete had become Donna's "old man." He was vicious and unpredictable, and she was terrified of him. He had once made her watch while he beat two of his whores senseless for lying about money and then disfigured their faces with a cigarette. But at least he always had some H around.

Donna had twelve brothers and sisters, scions of Juan Pablo Alvarez, a hollow-eyed, dark-skinned man possessed only of limitless poverty and limited intellect who had perpetuated his clan with merciless tenacity by siring a new offspring every year. Thus could yet one more and one more and one more of his gaunt children sit shoeless and in tatters on the warped, splintery boards of the railless porch and stare vacantly with neither curiosity nor yearning at the wasted flatlands about them, fecund only with the rusted hulks of junked cars lying lifelessly about like they themselves, victims of the air and the sun and the rain. But at least the children could abandon their sordid nest like migratory birds, which most of them had already done. Donna's mother was a white woman who had met Juan Pablo in a bar in South Phoenix eighteen years ago and stayed drunk every succeeding day, until she finally became barren out of sheer self-defense and sober because the pills that the Indian Health Services nurse practitioner made her swallow caused her severe nausea every time she took a drink. Juan Pablo, apparently lacerated to the quick by the meaninglessness of his life, now that his wife neither drank nor proliferated unwelcome offspring from her tortured labia, expired softly in his sleep one night. They said it was a heart attack. But Donna knew that it was abyssal despair and not abysmal angina that had finally wreaked its ultimate toll on those flat, desolate black eyes.

Outside, it was still well over ninety degrees. The sliver of pallid moon was too anemic to illuminate the land, and the lusterless stars in the murky sky appeared equally enervated. The sky had no depth, the stars no glitter, like a picture made in a first-grade art class, a black sheet of construction paper as the background, a little yellow moon like a curled shaving cut from a hunk of cheese lying on the peak of

Mummy Mountain a few miles away in Paradise Valley, and a bunch of dull gray paper stars pasted along the top of the paper.

She walked on the rutted asphalt road to avoid the rocks and small cacti and garbage in the ditches by the sides of it. She was wearing a tight black elasticized miniskirt that came to just an inch below her bared pubic hair and a hot pink tube top in which her ample breasts jiggled as she walked. She had brushed back her long seal brown hair and rubber-banded it into a careless ponytail. She hadn't bothered to brush her teeth to sweeten her breath. It wasn't Big Gun's mouth that he'd want her to kiss.

She rapped on the wood slat door of the old shack. She could hear a radio playing low from somewhere inside, heavy metal, and dim light seeped out between the desiccated slats. The door opened an inch and someone peered out at her. The door opened wider and she walked into a small living room.

A lamp was on in the corner, and she recognized Anna Luhan sleeping on the threadbare couch. Anna had whored downtown Phoenix with Donna most weekends until Donna had graduated to the Scottsdale hotels. Big Gun Pete was sitting on the floor in front of the couch. His eyes were dilated, his mouth hanging open. A younger man sat next to him, staring hollowly at Donna. She had seen him several times before. He was originally from Whiteriver on the San Carlos Reservation up north and had the dark skin and meaty, thick face of the Apaches. Everybody called him Tony "Brown Horse" because he had been a heroin mule for the past couple of years between Sonora, Mexico— where the brown heroin came through the border— and Big Gun Pete on the Salt River Reservation.

Pete got up slowly and took her by the arm. He led her into the small bedroom and turned on the light switch. A bare bulb overhead weakly lit the room. He closed the door.

"Why you ain't down t' the civic center makin'

some money?" He stared harshly at her. His eyes were lambent anthracite beads, his black hair hung in matted dreadlocks to his shoulders, and his round, flat, emaciated face was pocked with acne scars. He was of medium height and heavily muscled with huge weight lifter's arms and shoulders. He stank of dried sweat and booze.

"I'll go work the hotels up on Scottsdale Road."

"You ain't gonna work them hotels lookin' like *that*."

"I'm sick, Pete. I need a hit."

"You got bread?"

She shook her head.

"How you gonna get a hit?"

She put her hand on his crotch and rubbed him through his Levi's.

"Jus' two nickels," he said. "Jus' so's you get straight enough to get back on the street tomorrow night and work the niggers for me."

She nodded and was suddenly seized by the worst cramps she had suffered tonight. She shuddered and gritted her teeth until the pain passed. "Give me a hit, Pete, please. I got to have it."

He studied her and nodded. He walked a few feet to a battered three-drawer dresser and lit a candle. He emptied a small cellophane container the size of a matchbook into the bowl of a spoon and held it over the flame until the powder congealed to a sticky brown liquid. Then he tore the sealed paper wrapper off a disposable syringe and aspirated the liquid into it. Donna tied a rubber tube around her left bicep and made a hard fist to distend the vein on the inside of her elbow. Pete injected her, and she pulled the rubber cincture off and sat down on the edge of the bed. Pete sat next to her.

In less than five minutes the claws were no longer grabbing her stomach, and the pain lines in her sixteen-year-old face had smoothed out. She smiled sweetly at Pete and licked her lubricious lips. He unbuttoned his Levi's, pushed them down, and kicked them off. He lay back on the bed, and Donna knelt on the floor between his legs and busied her mouth with feigned pleasure.

She wanted the second hit as soon as she finished Pete. He was never solicitous to her afterward, so she cooked her own heroin and injected herself behind her left knee. The hit this time was quicker, and it didn't feel good like the first one. She looked at Pete sitting listlessly on the side of the bed, drinking from a Jim Beam bottle, his lower body still nude, his "Big Gun" shrunken and lifeless, and suddenly she felt as though she were spinning like a dervish. Everything in the room became achromatic and began to billow with smoke. She saw Pete's face turn strange as he watched her, and then she fell to the floor in a heap.

Pete walked over to her and slapped her in the face. She didn't move. He hit her hard again. Nothing. He sat her up against the wall and shook her, but she slumped unconscious to the floor.

Big Gun Pete and Tony Brown Horse carried her out the back of the shack to Pete's 1995 raked and lowered candy-apple red Camaro and put her in the backseat. Showing no headlights, Pete drove west down Thomas Road out of the reservation and turned north on Hayden Road, deserted at two o'clock in the morning. He neared the baseball diamonds used by the big league baseball teams for spring training. He parked across the road from the ball fields, dragged Donna to an immense Aleppo pine by a small duck pond, and sat her up against the scaly trunk. She was still unconscious, barely breathing. He went to the Circle K convenience market a few blocks south and called nine-one-one.

"There's a chick OD'ed sittin' next to a tree in Indian Bend Wash across from where the Cubs and the Oakland A's play," he said and hung up.

*   *   *

Donna had been in detox once before, when she was arrested for prostitution two years ago. It was a dungeon run by juvi court in East Mesa, where all the Mormons lived, who thought that anything stronger than tomato juice would get you damned to eternal hellfire. It had been the old-style detox: a bare gray plaster room with a metal cot bolted to the floor, no mattress or bedding, no clothes, a sink and a toilet, and you just shit and pissed and vomited all over yourself for four days until you got the heroin cleaned out of your body. And then they hosed you and the room down, and some fat matron told you to go over to East Osborn Road to register for methadone therapy at the Indian Health Services Addiction Treatment Center. But the meth was a worse hit than heroin, a duller high but much longer lasting, and after three weeks she had gone back to hustling blowjobs in the black slum around the Civic Center in downtown Phoenix.

This detox was different. She woke up on clean white sheets in a shiny white-walled room in Scottsdale Memorial Hospital. She assumed that because of her brown hair and fair skin and light brown eyes, the ambulance attendants had taken her for a white girl and brought her here instead of to the Indian Health Clinic just a few miles away on the reservation. Officious nurses gave her shots of something or other that cleaned her up in a few days without once getting the cramps and the dry heaves and seeing the pink monster with the long green claws and breath like rotted fish. Then two nuns with short-cropped gray hair, wearing white shirts and what looked like men's black vests and pants, took her out of the hospital one morning and drove her to a big old house on Washington Street in Tempe. It had a chain-link fence all around it topped by razor wire and a sign on the driveway gate that read, "HOME OF THE GOOD SHEPHERD, DIOCESE OF PHOENIX."

*   *   *

"That guard'll cut yo' guts out wif that knife she carry," Marla Pickett said. She lay in the bunk bed next to Donna's. "I seen her a couple times, just never had her on my room. *Shee-it,* this place beat the hell outta that."

Donna listened closely to the girl's whispering. They were in a small bedroom in the Home of the Good Shepherd. It was just after lights out, nine o'clock, and one of the nuns would open the door a crack in a minute or two and make certain the girls were quiet and in bed. There were thirty girls in fifteen bedrooms in this place, and according to Marla, they were the lucky ones. If you got picked up for soliciting and got sent to the Black Canyon Detention Center, the juvenile prison about twenty-five miles north of Phoenix off the Black Canyon Freeway, you were lucky to come out alive, let alone all in one piece. If one of the other girls didn't stove your head in with a bucket full of floor wax, then one of the guards would be sure to put you in the infirmary at least twice during your sentence.

"I seen her kick the livin' shit out of a thirteen-year-old girl just for sayin' *damn.* That's all she say, *damn.* And then she—" Marla stopped abruptly in mid-sentence as a laser of light cut through the room from the doorway. The door then closed softly. They heard the click of the dead bolt from outside.

"This place is okay," Marla continued. "Just watch out you don't piss off Sister Veronica."

"She's the one who wears the big gold cross and chain?"

"Yeah, she's the one they calls 'mother superior,' somethin' like that, anyhow. Whatever they calls the top lesbo. If she don't want you here, you gets drug over to Black Canyon. Then yo' ass is grass."

Donna had been there for two days since leaving Scottsdale Memorial Hospital. She was in the Reception Pod with the other new arrival, Marla, and they would be released into the Home Center tomorrow.

Until then they were isolated from the rest of the girls, fed in their room, locked up twenty-four hours a day except for the six hours of psychological testing and the one hour physical exam and the one hour each afternoon that they were permitted to spend exercising or walking around outside in the high cinder-block-walled "recreation yard."

"Why'd they put you here?" Donna whispered.

"They found me downtown passed out. I got a bad hit on some crack and tequila, blew my mind pretty good. Juvi judge say he gimme a break this time, send me back to the nuns again."

"You ever been in Black Canyon?"

"Yeah, twice. First time I was fo'teen. My pimp rob a Texaco station over to Maryvale, and I holds the gun on the guy while Blackjack cleans out the cash register. Some cop drove by right when it was happenin'. And then the second time was last year, I was sixteen. Some john goes to shove a beer bottle up my snatch. I bangs him over the head wif it and tries to grab his wallet. We was in a alley over by the civic center, and he starts screamin' and a private security guy got me. I done eleven months in Black Canyon that time."

"This place doesn't seem so bad," Donna whispered. "That nun, Sister Danielle, seems real nice."

"None a them nuns give a shit about us fo' real," Marla said. " 'Servants a Jesus' they calls themselves. My black ass! They gets a ton a money from the fed'-ral gubmint for the drug program, so they acts as if it's us that matters, but it ain't. It's just the money."

"How long do they keep you?"

"Till the juvi judge cut you loose. Kept me the first time six months. I don't know this time."

"What's the trick getting out?"

"Get straight, look straight, look like you reads that Bible they gives you, smile young and sweet like you never heard them devil words, *Hey honey, hows 'bout suckin' me off fo' twenny?*" Marla snorted. "Then they'll hook you up wif some rich bitch who gets her kicks around here doin' volunteer work, and she'll sponsor yo' ass outta here into her own house."

"That what happened to you?"

"Naw, hell no. Nobody want a nigger who already gots two little babies. They just lets me out one day, gives me a hunnerd bucks, tells me to stay outta trouble. So here I is again. But you gonna be okay. You real pretty, look like somebody's kid sister. Somebody'll latch onto you. You gonna make out like a bandit."

• TWO •

"God damn him, Gwenny. I just want to kill him."

"Now, now, Mary Kate darlin'," Gwen McLemore said, "there's much nicer things t' be doin', like slicin' his wee tidbit off like that Bobbitt woman."

They sat in the rear pew of Saint Paul's Cathedral, whispering together after the eleven o'clock Sunday mass. Mary Kate grinned despite herself. Gwen had never lost her Irish accent, but when she lapsed into her musical farm girl brogue, it lent an air of charm to almost everything she said.

"Aye, Gwenny darlin', and then 'twould be me in trouble." Kate mimicked her.

"Ya don't think killin' 'im will get ya in trouble, darlin'?"

Mary Kate laughed. She and Gwen had been best friends since Mary Kate's senior year in high school, nine years ago. She had shared everything with the pretty, brown-haired Irish girl with the button nose and sparkling brown eyes—everything but boyfriends. Gwen was now studying for her doctorate in educational psychology at Boston College.

"He got thirty days in jail this time," Mary Kate said, serious again. "His lawyer did something slick, whatever it was, and they didn't charge him with possession of narcotics for sale. But he's doing thirty days, and he's got to go to some special drug-treatment center when he gets out."

"Good. Maybe it'll finally clean him up."

"I wish I believed that. This is the *fourth* time he's been arrested. Our marriage has gone to hell in the last couple of years."

"Well, wait and see if this thirty days and the drug treatment straightens him out."

Mary Kate shook her head grimly. "Nothing's going to straighten out our marriage. He told me he never really wanted to marry me, he only did it because our fathers are partners in business, and his parents expected us to get married. Can you believe that?" Her green eyes flashed with a mixture of anger and resentment. "And he says he thinks of me more like a sister than somebody he wants to make love to."

Gwen rolled her eyes. "Then he's a skunk for sayin' such a nasty thing, and that's all there is to it. And surely you know it's not true."

Mary Kate shrugged.

"I was with you both plenty of times back in the early days of your marriage," Gwen persisted, "and he loved you then, plain to see. It's just nasty, rotten talk he's doin' to you now."

"It's drug talk and booze talk," Mary Kate said. "He once had beautiful hazel eyes that changed colors in different light. Now his eyes are always bloodshot and they don't shine and they're all washed-out pale. And every time he picks Jennifer up from the day-care center after work, I'm terrified that he's going to stop off and have some whiskey and cocaine or angel dust, and then he'll drive that little Mercedes of his through a red light, and that'll be the end of Jennifer. It's getting so bad that I've been thinking about quitting my job so I can stay home with her."

"Quit teaching?"

Mary Kate nodded and grimaced.

"Then it's high time you do somethin' about him, Mary Kate," Gwen said gently.

Mary Kate's eyes were sad. "Well, I guess I have a

month to think about it while he's a guest of the state."

"Too bad. And Christmastime, too."

"Well, I'm not letting him ruin *my* Christmas and *Jennifer's*. Want to come with us to Scottsdale?"

"I thought Monsignor Burke assigned you to watch over the fifth and sixth grades at the high mass for the school?"

"No, Jenny McBain is doing it this year. I did it the last two Christmases."

"So you're goin' to Scottsdale even with Brian in jail?"

"I sure am. I've had this Christmas trip planned for four months. We couldn't go to San Francisco last summer because he was on probation from that last arrest. So there went our summer vacation. This time I'm not hanging around here again like it's *Jenn and me* who are in jail. You don't have any classes till after the Christmas break, right?"

"Aye."

"Want to come?"

"And get away from all this fine weather?" Gwen chuckled. Yesterday's thunderstorm had turned to snow overnight, and it was ten degrees outside. She studied her wristwatch. "Gi' me three minutes t' pack, Mary Kate darlin'."

When Mary Caitlin O'Dwyer was nineteen, she had gone over the Christmas school holiday with her parents to Scottsdale, Arizona. On Christmas day it had been seventy-three degrees, the sky was a delicate robin's egg blue, and speckled gray cactus wrens and brilliant red cardinals were chirping in the saguaro cacti right outside the window of their hotel bungalow. Purple and yellow and white and striped pansies were blooming everywhere as though it were spring.

She hoped that Scottsdale had not changed, or that her memory of it had not been a mirage.

They ascended from the frozen heaps of soot-tarnished snow lining the Logan International Airport runway, over the gelid slate gray waters of Boston harbor, into the bulbous black cumulus clouds hanging like pregnant killer whales over Massachusetts. But a mere four hours later they descended through the pellucid azure sky over the fertile crop fields around Phoenix Sky Harbor airport, warm with sunshine, and green and yellow and orange with ripening crops.

Mary Kate held Jennifer in her lap and pointed. "See, there's a field full of spinach and carrots and squash."

Jennifer wrinkled her nose. "Do I have to eat 'em?" she asked in her tiny voice.

Mary Kate laughed. "No, honey. We'll find a field full of ice cream for you."

Jennifer giggled.

"Make it chocolate for me," Gwen said.

"Do ice cream really grows on little bushes?" Jennifer asked, her face serious.

Mary Kate kissed her small, pouty lips and hugged her close. "No, honey. It gets made in factories."

"Can we get one of them?"

"Well, I'll ask Grandpa. Maybe he'll want to give up making computer chips and stuffy old junk like that and buy an ice cream factory."

Jennifer nodded avidly and smiled.

They took a cab to the Hilton Hotel on Scottsdale Road, and not only was the city as beautiful and clean as Mary Kate had remembered, but it was also attired everywhere in gay and colorful Christmas decorations. They checked into the two-bedroom suite that Kate had reserved. There was a small child's bed with short rails in Jennifer's room.

"You were goin' to sleep apart from poor Brian?" Gwen mused, surveying the two queen beds in the second bedroom.

Kate laughed. "No, I had a king-size reserved. I

changed it to two queens. I kick in my sleep. I didn't think you'd like that."

"I punch," Gwen said, rolling her hands into fists.

"Put up yer dukes!" Jennifer said, also making fists.

Gwen and Mary Kate burst out laughing. "Where'd you pick *that* up, honey?"

"Three Stooges," Jennifer said and giggled.

Mary Kate swept her up in her arms and kissed her on the cheek. "Either of you hungry?" she asked. It was almost four o'clock.

"Not me," Gwen said. "The one fine thing about first class on an airplane is that they give you edible food for lunch."

"Me neither." Jennifer shook her head. "Can we go swimmy?"

"Sure, honey. They have a heated pool."

"Oh, goody!" Jennifer said.

"Let's find your bathing suit," said Mary Kate. She walked into the other bedroom, where the bellman had put the small pink valise.

She came back without Jennifer a moment later. Gwen had her valise open on the bed and had already hung up her clothing in the closet. Mary Kate opened her suitcase and fished in it for her bikini. Both she and Gwen took off their clothes unself-consciously and put on their swimming suits. Mary Kate had been on the track team back in high school, and Gwen had been the coach. They had dressed and undressed in the same locker room for years.

"Wow!" Gwen said. "You'll be havin' to fight off the young men in *that* skimpy little thing. The bottom's only a couple of strings, and the top's just two little patches."

Mary Kate smiled. She was tall, long-legged, and buxom, with boyishly narrow hips and slender legs and arms. "And how about you, Gwenny darlin'?"

Gwen grinned. She looked down at the well-filled one-piece hot pink suit. "What am I supposed to do, find an old black cotton thing with a big flouncy peplum?"

Kate put her arm around Gwen and said confidentially, "No, darlin', just wear a terry cloth robe so you don't give all the lads wee lumps in their pants."

They both laughed. They walked into Jennifer's room, and Mary Kate helped her struggle into the bathing suit. She took the plastic "swimmies" out of Jennifer's valise, blew them up, and pulled them up on Jennifer's biceps. Then she picked her up in her arms, kissed her on the nose, and sat her in the crook of her arm. They took three big towels out of the bathroom and walked to the hotel patio.

Next to the huge swimming pool was a much smaller wading pool for children. Mary Kate put Jennifer into it, and Jennifer splashed away, giggling and laughing. Gwen and Mary Kate sat on the edge of the pool next to a dozen mothers, their feet dangling in the water. It was seventy-five degrees, and the ryegrass lawn was thick and emerald green, edged by beds of multicolored petunias and pansies. The lawn was cluttered with people on towels and chaise longues. It was just three days before Christmas, and the hotel was obviously full of sun-seeking tourists. Many had the white winter skin of easterners, including Mary Kate. Gwen's complexion was olive, and she looked as though she had been sunning on a beach in Bermuda all winter.

Jennifer splashed around for a few minutes and got into a little scuffle with another girl, perhaps a year older and five pounds heavier, over a foot-long inflated dolphin floating on the water. Jennifer lost the dolphin-tugging match and came over to her mother rubbing her eyes, her small mouth an inverted U.

"You can have it after a while, honey," Mary Kate soothed. She kissed her daughter's eyes. "Now, don't cry. Have fun."

"Okay," Jennifer said, her mourning quickly dispelled. She splashed back into the water and a moment later was playing with the abandoned dolphin.

Mary Kate and Gwen sat lazily on the Kool Deck and basked in the sunshine. Jennifer came up to her mother again.

"Can I have a ice cream?" She pointed at the stainless steel cart with the red-and-white-striped umbrella on top.

"Sure. Come on."

Mary Kate picked her up out of the water, stood her between her legs, and patted her dry with a towel. Then the three of them walked to the ice cream cart. Jennifer got a chocolate-coated bar, Gwen a sugar cone with a nut-encrusted chocolate top, but Mary Kate declined.

"Nothing for me," she said to Gwen. "I'll gain ten pounds."

"On you it would look good," Gwen said with a wry chuckle.

They walked over to two empty chaise longues, and Mary Kate sat Jennifer beside her.

A beautiful, well-muscled man walked up between the two chaises. He had curly hair literally glowing golden in the sun, his skin was bronze, and he looked like Robert Redford about twenty years ago. He was holding a large styrofoam cup.

"Can I buy you a beer?" he said, looking hungrily at Gwen.

"No, thank you," she answered. "I never drink till dark."

"I can wait."

She smiled at him. "I'm flattered, mighty flattered indeed. But I'm not available."

"That's a cute accent you have."

"Well, where I grew up it isn't considered cute. It's just kind of normal."

He laughed. He looked from side to side slowly, then turned around and hooded his eyes with his hands. He turned back to Gwen. "I don't see any husband."

She held up her left hand and pointed her ring finger with the thin gold band toward him.

"So what?" he said. "A little variety might do you a world of good." He gave her his best "I'm beautiful, and you'll be lucky to have me" look.

"Jesus," Gwen said.

"What?"

"I'm married to Jesus."

"What's a *jayzuz?*"

"Oh, I'm sorry. There's that wicked little accent again. I mean Jesus Christ." She articulated the words carefully.

He looked at her and wrinkled his brow. "What?"

"I'm a nun."

His eyes traveled her body. "Bullshit!"

"That's what I sometimes say, too." She smiled mildly at him.

He looked at her askance. "You're serious?"

"Aye," she said.

"Damn, what a waste," he muttered and walked away.

Mary Kate and Gwen smiled at each other.

"I guess I'll have to buy the thing with the peplum, after all."

Mary Kate rocked with laughter. She turned to Jennifer, who had finished her ice cream, and had some of the chocolate smeared around her mouth. Mary Kate took a tissue out of her purse, moistened it with her tongue, and wiped the chocolate off.

She lay back on the chaise and hugged Jennifer to her bosom. In minutes Jennifer was snoring softly.

All five days of the Scottsdale vacation followed the same pattern except for midnight mass at Our Lady of Perpetual Hope Church on Christmas Eve, with Jennifer in her new frilly pink dress curled up and asleep beside her mother. And Christmas Day high mass, with Jennifer in the playroom with dozens of other children.

During the silent devotional, when most of the con-

gregation sat staring around, fidgeting, bored, waiting
for the priest to get on with it, Gwen knelt on the
padded kneeler in front of them and wept quietly.
Mary Kate had never seen Gwen cry, not in all of the
years they had been best friends—except once every
year during the high mass silent devotional on Christmas Day. She would kneel and hold her rosary and
squint her eyes shut, trying to hold back the tears, but
they always came. And Mary Kate would feel her
pain. She blinked back her own tears and put her hand
softly on Gwen's trembling shoulder.

Suddenly she was back in parochial school, and
Gwen McLemore, a Sister of Mercy nun, was in front
of the class. She was very cute, young, almost too
pretty to be a nun. Just a self-effacing girl from a tiny
farming village in southern Ireland.

Gwen's favorite books of the Bible were Ecclesi-
astes and Job, because they taught the timeless truth
about man's fate in this world and why he must strive
for the next: *"The race is not to the swift, nor the battle
to the strong,"* she used to recite. *"Food comes not to
the wise, nor wealth to the intelligent, nor success to
the skillful. But time and chance govern all. No one
knows when his hour will come. Like a fish caught in
a net, a sparrow in a snare, so are people trapped when
misfortune suddenly befalls them."*

Mary Kate had been seventeen years old then, a
senior at St. Mary's School for Girls, and Gwen was
just twenty-four. They became very close friends.
Gwen was from a poor family, and she had gotten
pregnant at the age of fifteen. Her upbringing was so
intensely Catholic that she could never even imagine
an abortion, so she had simply begun wearing tight
belts and then loose dresses and had only been discovered in the seventh month by her mother's sharp eye.
She had given birth to the baby girl at the local
clinic—she had no money to run to another town for
anonymity—and it was the scandal of the town. By
the time she got home her new baby had already died.

"A fever," her mother had said, her eyes wet and tortured. But Gwen knew by the look in her father's eyes that he had killed the baby. There were already eleven mouths to feed, all of them wailing with hunger. No food for yet another, certainly not for a girl whom the priest had refused to baptize because a bastard was unfit to be admitted to the kingdom of God.

Gwen had looked Mary Kate in the eye. "Can you imagine such a thing, Mary Kate? Too devout to think of permittin' my tiny daughter to live, but somehow untroubled by suffocatin' her with a pillow?" She shook her head in disbelief.

"I expected good things, and evils are come upon me," Gwen would recite from Job. *"I waited for light and darkness broke out. My inner parts have boiled without any rest. . . . Let God weigh me on the scales of justice, and He will know that I am innocent!"*

She had gone to Dublin and worked as a cleaning girl in a hotel near the waterfront until she had earned enough money for passage to America. Then she had come on a tourist visa and gone to South Boston, where she had heard that all the Irish start in America. In a week she ran out of money to eat or find lodging and ended up at a Dominican convent where she was given food and a cot in the basement along with eight other girls. They all had similar stories to tell.

Gwen had left the cloistered nuns when she landed a job as a maid in a hotel. Then one day a guest had gotten drunk and tried to rape her. She had fought him off, but not before getting a broken nose and a broken eye socket. She had awakened in a Catholic hospital with her face swathed in bandages from the plastic surgery. A Sister of Mercy nun who worked as a social worker there had suggested that she go to the novitiate of the Sisters of Mercy.

"Believe on Him, Mary Kate," Gwen would always say. *"Believe on Him, and be damn sure you believe in yourself!"*

• THREE •

Mary Kate sat on the sofa in the living room of her home. Gwen McLemore sat next to her. Lightning crackled over Marblehead harbor outside the huge picture window, and rain corrugated the churning water. An explosion of thunder sent a tremor through the plate-glass window.

"I can't take any more," Mary Kate said, hoarse and teary. "He really scares me. And just five days after he gets out of jail, he gets arrested *again* last night. This time the judge won't let him out on bail, because he was still on probation for the last time, and they've already charged him with a felony for all the cocaine he had on him. His lawyer says he doesn't think he can work it down to a misdemeanor again."

"Maybe you'd best go see Father Seamus," Gwen said.

Mary Kate looked searchingly at her. "You really think I should?"

"Aye." Gwen was solemn. "You've tried hard enough. If Brian keeps it up, Jennifer'll get hurt, sure. You can't be lettin' that happen."

Mary Kate put her face in her hands and wept.

Archbishop Seamus Gerrity's office was in the enormous Gothic Cathedral of the Holy Cross in Boston's South End. What had once been among the most Irish enclaves in America had long since become a melting pot, but the Irish had left behind New England's largest Catholic church and the showplace of the archdiocese of Boston.

Stunning Renaissance tapestries hung from two walls of the archbishop's office, and Raphael's *The Finding of Moses* graced the third. It had been presented to Bernard Cardinal Law by Pope John Paul on the pontiff's 1979 visit to this cathedral. Gentileschi's magnificent painting of *Judith and Holofernes,* which had hung for years in the library of Mary Kate's parents' mansion in Manchester on the Sea, now hung above Archbishop Seamus Gerrity's rolltop oak desk. The painting had been a personal gift to Seamus, Brendan O'Dwyer's closest friend.

The archbishop was six feet tall and burly, with a full head of graying red hair and a ruddy, full-cheeked face. It always seemed to Mary Kate that he could be any one of the Irish longshoremen sitting at the bars in Boston harbor, relaxing with a pint of Guinness stout after a hard day's work, laughing at the other fellows' tall tales and hoping for a better day tomorrow.

"Have you prayed to the Holy Virgin about this, Mary Kate?"

"I have, Your Grace."

Seamus Gerrity studied her face with his intense blue eyes. "And your father? What does he say?"

She shrugged. "You know he's not happy about it, Father Seamus. But he knows Brian, he's seen him drunk and on drugs. He realizes that it's inevitable. Even Brian's parents aren't fooled anymore. One of these times Brian is just liable to wrap his car around a tree and really hurt Jennifer. Or kill her. I can't let that happen."

The archbishop nodded slowly, resigned. In a somber voice he recited one of the necessary formulas for an annulment. "And so Brian's told you, then, that he took his holy vows of marriage never intending to fulfill them, that he knew even before the wedding that the marriage wouldn't last?"

Mary Kate swallowed and nodded, avoiding the archbishop's eyes. He was one of the few people in the whole world whom she truly loved. He had been the pastor of St. Paul's Cathedral since before she was born, and he had baptized her twenty-six years ago, given her her first communion wafer eighteen years ago, heard her real and imagined sins every Sunday since she had begun going to confession thirteen years ago, officiated at her and Brian's marriage four years ago, and even after being consecrated as archbishop of the diocese and leaving St. Paul's, he had baptized Jennifer two years ago.

Being the daughter of Brendan and Catherine O'Dwyer meant private masses by Father Gerrity in the chapel in their home in Manchester by the Sea, private confessions, elaborate Sunday luncheons with Father Gerrity and other priests, bishops, archbishops, and princes of the church, who would always make it their business to pay tribute to one of the most dependable contributors to Catholic causes in all of Boston. It also meant that when the O'Dwyers' little girl needed an annulment, even after a four-year marriage and a daughter, nothing on earth would stand in her way. God's will be done.

Brian did not contest the annulment, and when Mary Kate's lawyer filed a petition in court for "sole custody and denial of visitation," together with a list of Brian's arrests and convictions for drunkenness and drug possession and the pending felony charge, Brian didn't even appear at the courthouse for the scheduled hearing.

Mary Kate needed to change her life. She didn't want to live here in Marblehead in a house just a few miles from her parents. Every piece of furniture reminded her of Brian. The scent of his aftershave was still in the bathroom and the bedroom, as though it had indelibly permeated the walls and curtains and sheets. Her mother and father came over almost every evening, believing that their daughter needed their comfort and concern, and she felt restless, uneasy, like a little girl again without a life of her own.

She thought of where she could go, not seriously at first, just fleeting daydreams. But the notion of leaving grew into a conviction that she must leave, and the snowstorm that piled three-foot drifts in her driveway one night a week later, in the middle of the particularly bitter winter, was the last straw.

She and Jennifer went to dinner at her parents' home in Manchester as usual on Saturday evening.

"I want to move to Scottsdale," Mary Kate said. She looked around tentatively at her parents, expecting to see shock in their eyes, but there was none. Her mother wiped her lips with her linen napkin and laid it on the dinner plate.

"We've seen how restless you've become, dear," Catherine said. She had grown a little heavy over the years, but Mary Kate's features and her five-foot-eight height were obviously from Catherine. If you placed their photographs side by side, you would instantly know that you were looking at mother and daughter. "Maybe it's the best thing for you."

"Of course, you'll leave Jennifer with us," Brendan said, smiling at his granddaughter.

"Oh sure, Daddy," Mary Kate said. "I'll just come visit now and then."

They laughed easily. Jennifer was intently eating Captain Crunchberries in her high chair by the twenty-foot-long and eight-foot-wide walnut dining table. The laughter made her look up and beam brightly, giggle for a moment, then return to the heady task of cornering a pink crunchberry in the big bowl.

"Scottsdale is a beautiful place," Catherine said. "Maybe your father and I will come with you for a few days and help you find a house. If you don't mind, that is."

"I'd love that," Mary Kate said, genuinely relieved and pleased. She had feared that her parents wouldn't want her to leave Boston. She was their only child because of serious complications during her mother's pregnancy, and she, and then she and Jennifer, had always been the center of her parents' lives.

"Thank you for understanding," Mary Kate said. She got up from the table, walked to the head of it, and kissed her father on the cheek, then walked around to his right and kissed her mother.

"We've seen this coming for a long time," Brendan said. "You've got your own life ahead of you, and I'm glad that this mess with Brian is over. The only thing we want for you is that you're happy."

"Come on," Catherine said. "We'll have our cake and ice cream in the den." She rang a little bell on the table beside her, and an elderly, liveried butler immediately came into the dining room, followed by a uniformed maid a third of his age.

"We'll take dessert in the den, Sean," Catherine said.

"Aye, mum."

"And bring that fine bottle of Courvoisier that I hid up in the cupboard," Brendan said. "We're having a little celebration." He eyed the butler. "I hope there's still some left."

Sean splayed his arms in innocence. "The whole bottle, m'lord." His untamed brogue was thick and comical.

They laughed.

The day after her parents left Scottsdale, Mary Kate called Gwen for the sixth time in the two weeks since she had left Boston.

"The house is just gorgeous, Gwen. You'll really love it."

"Just so long as the sun shines, I'll love it, darlin'. It was eleven degrees here today. I'm havin' trouble thawin' out."

Mary Kate laughed. "You can come here anytime you want and thaw out."

"So tell me what it looks like."

"It's perfect." She began to gush with pleasure. "The painters and paper hangers left an hour ago, and Jennifer's room is wallpapered in this really cute pink background with sheep in a huge meadow. You have to see it to see how pretty it is. And I got all matching pink and white fabrics for the curtains and the duvet cover and skirting for the bed. Jennifer loves it. And I did my bedroom in a really neat Ralph Lauren plaid, and the walls are painted deep blue. Mom went with me to a furniture store, and we got a lovely beige leather sofa for the living room and a matching recliner and a wing chair upholstered in a forest green background with a hunt scene, you know, a bunch of people fox hunting, wearing muted red coats and on rust-colored horses, and it's just perfect. Daddy's sending out that series of hunt prints to hang in the living room—you know, the English lithographs he's had in the library for years—"

"Those *Fore's National Sports* prints?"

"Right, right!"

"They'll be gorgeous there."

"And the kitchen window overlooks a patio full of orange trees, and the gate out the patio leads down to a duck cove in this beautiful little man-made lake. It's just like a seascape, prettier than I thought I'd be able to find here."

"Well, I can't wait to see it."

"Come out, any time, you know that."

"Thank you, darlin', but right now Professor Hurley, my dissertation professor, is puttin' me through hell, makin' me rewrite and rewrite till I'm blue in the face. I'd best not be strayin' too far from my desk for a while."

"Well, Jennifer and I both miss you."

"Have you found a teachin' position?"

"Yes, yesterday. Father Seamus recommended me

to the diocese of Phoenix, and the bishop called me yesterday and said they'd like to have me teach fifth grade at Saint Daniel's Academy. It's just fifteen minutes from here. I'm really excited."

"That's wonderful. I'm sure you'll soon be forgettin' all the mess that went on here with Brian."

"I already forgot," Mary Kate said and laughed.

· FOUR ·

Mary Caitlin O'Dwyer still felt like Columbus discovering the New World, even though she had been in Scottsdale for almost three months now. It was early April, and at six in the morning it was already sixty-five degrees. She had bought a specially made buggy carriage with three big, thin wheels, which was used by joggers to enable them to wheel their infants in front of them on their jogs.

"Mommy, I jogging, too!"

"No, honey. You ride. Mommy wants to run fast, and you wouldn't be able to keep up. You'll be real happy in the buggy. It'll be fun."

"Okay," she grumbled, pouting.

Kate picked Jennifer up and put her into the carriage, rested her hands on the push bar, and began to lope along the path around the lake at McCormick Ranch. Kate's hair glinted reddish in the sun, and her soft green eyes followed the antics of the mallard ducks swimming and splashing in the coves behind the houses.

The small man-made lake stretched for a mile north and a half mile south of her house and was bordered on the west, just below her patio, by an asphalt jogging and biking path. Her house was in a long curving row of light brown stuccoed Mediterranean-style houses overlooking the lake.

Here in Scottsdale no one called her Mary Kate.

She was simply Kate. She loved her half-hour jog along the lake, something that she did at six o'clock most mornings. It was light outside, and there weren't any muggers or bums around to menace or hassle her. Jogging had become an indulgence in self-pity and escape back in Boston, a way to get out of the house and be free of Brian for a few precious minutes. But she didn't have to worry about him any longer. Scottsdale was a new life, clean and fresh and safe, and the morning jog was Kate's own time just for herself, to think and dream and feel free as a gazelle. Even being a single mother hadn't significantly changed her life. She had really been on her own for years, since Brian had married himself to drugs.

Many of the residents of McCormick Ranch also jogged or rode bikes or walked early in the morning, and she had met several of her neighbors in this way. Edith Owens, who lived three houses down from Kate, had brought over cookies and cake for Jennifer several evenings. She had three grandchildren herself, but they lived in Minneapolis, so Jennifer was reaping the bounty of a lonely grandmother's affection. Edith and her husband were avid bicyclists who were out on the asphalt path every morning. They waved at her gaily as they passed.

"Hi, Jennifer," Edith called out and waved.

Suddenly Kate heard heavy footfalls behind her and looked around. A man about thirty years old, slightly balding, her height and stocky, jogged up beside her. He had reddened cheeks and was sweating profusely.

"Hi," he said.

"Hi."

"I'm your neighbor." He paused to gather his breath. "Just moved in across the street a couple of weeks ago." Puff, puff. "Victor Hodges."

"Hello, Victor, I'm Kate O'Dwyer," she said, smiling pleasantly. "I saw your wife and two sons moving some things in the other day."

"She wants me to get in shape," he panted. "I'm probably going to have a heart attack instead."

"Just keep a slow pace. You'll be fine."

He rolled his eyes. He jogged another fifty yards and then slowed. "That's all I can take," he gasped. "Don't tell my wife I didn't make it around the lake. She'll put me on a diet."

Kate laughed and waved back at him. She ran on steadily, absorbed in thought. Later this morning she would be going to juvenile court to be appointed the foster mother of a sixteen-year-old girl. She had met the girl just a few days after coming to Scottsdale. It was Gwen's doing. Gwen had given Kate the telephone number of Sister Veronica Demiro, a nun who ran a drug-abuse treatment center for teenage girls.

"There's a special need the soul has, you know," Gwen had said. "Not just goin' to work and comin' home each day and maybe now and then buyin' a new sofa or a Baccarat vase. The soul needs to be nurtured by doin' somethin' good for someone who really needs you, and you not seekin' any reward for it except the love that Jesus gives you for bein' a good Catholic."

The first week at the Home of the Good Shepherd had been unexpectedly difficult, almost scary. These girls weren't like the girls with whom Kate had spent her high school years: chattering, animated kids in ponytails and braces and stylish Ann Taylor and DKNY dresses and the latest fad in Guess shorts. Most of these girls had the haunted stares and hard faces of the prostitutes whom Kate often had seen by the train station in South Boston near where she had taught school, and the runaway girls she had seen with the derelicts by the entrance to the Cathedral of the Holy Cross, their palms upturned for nickels and dimes, sullied eyes, their faces dirt smeared, wearing filth-stiff clothes.

Donna Alvarez was strikingly different. Her smile was infectious, and her eyes were alive. They had actually sparkled when she shyly shook hands with Kate the first time they met.

"I'm very pleased to meet you, ma'am," Donna had said in a timid voice, obviously having been schooled by the nuns in how to act toward the "Volunteers." They were in Sister Veronica's office, the second week that Kate had been coming to the Home on Monday and Wednesday evenings. The Volunteers were women whose only task was to mingle with the girls, sit with them at supper and afterward in the television and game rooms, and by their examples to show the girls how to be young ladies, to speak without swearing, to act politely, so that they could be placed in foster homes and not be thrown out after a few days and be forced back on the streets.

"Donna's really a lovely girl, despite the trouble she's been in," Sister Veronica had told Kate after Donna left the office. "Considering the home she came from, she's lucky just to have survived without any apparent permanent scars. She's just a sweet sixteen-year-old kid who hasn't had a chance or a break."

The nun's words had proven true. Kate had spent more and more time at the Home, talking to Donna, getting to know her, developing the bond of a big sister and little sister separated by ten years. After a few weeks Kate had begun bringing Jennifer to the Home to observe her interaction with Donna. And when the two girls were together, playing dolls or house or jacks or just giggling, Donna was an uncomplicated, spunky teenager, like any sixteen-year-old girl should be, smiling and laughing and loving.

Donna couldn't stop beaming when Kate told her that she wanted her to come live with them in Scottsdale. "We'll be the O'Dwyer sisters," Kate said. They hugged each other.

"So are you goin' to adopt her?" Gwen had asked after Mary Kate had been a volunteer at the Home for almost two months.

"Well, I can't yet. First I get appointed as her temporary guardian for a two-month probationary period—you know, foster mother—and then if everything works out, I'll go to court to adopt her."

"Good. Open your heart to the girl, really give her hope of a new life. The Sisters of Mercy did that for me, just as Jesus did for Mary Magdalene. It's a wonderful thing you're doin'."

The principal of Saint Daniel's Academy, Monsignor Reilly, had given Kate the day off so that she could go to the Juvenile Court Annex located way out in west Phoenix. Donna Alvarez would be waiting there with Sister Veronica.

Kate parked among fifteen other cars at Merry Moppets and walked hand in hand with Jennifer into the big playroom. Other mothers and two fathers milled around the table that was always set up in the morning with donuts and milk and coffee. Jennifer skipped away when she spotted her friend Suzy. Kate had plenty of time before she had to be in west Phoenix, so she walked up to the table and eyed the jelly donuts.

"I'd kill for one of them," the woman next to her said. She was the day-care center supervisor.

"Hi, Jackie," Kate said. "Five years ago I could have eaten the whole tray. Now just one of them goes straight to my behind."

Jackie nodded and frowned.

"How's Jennifer doing?"

"Terrific, really terrific. The other kids all love her, and she has two real close friends."

"Good, that's great."

One of the fathers came over to them. He was attractive, in his late thirties, a society-type gynecologist whose wife had run off a year ago with another woman. The word among the Merry Moppets mothers was that he was a jerk, and the three times that he had sidled up to Kate here, at the donut table, he had leered at her and reeked of some horribly sweet aftershave. And he always said the same thing.

"When you going to come in for a pap smear?" he said, smiling at Kate.

She turned to him, not returning his smile. She glanced at her watch. "Shouldn't you be at the hospital peeking between women's legs?"

He chuckled. "My day off."

"Lucky women," Kate said.

His smile faded. "Well, got to get to the golf course."

Kate and Jackie watched him leave.

"Real charmer," Kate said.

Jackie rolled her eyes. "Can you imagine being married to *him?*"

"Actually, I can't imagine being married to anyone right now."

"Ain't that the truth."

• FIVE •

An ornamental ceiling fan, slightly out of sync, jiggled overhead with a monotonous click, click, click, but it had no noticeable effect on the heat in the high-ceilinged courtroom. April in Phoenix was supposed to be perfect weather, so the air conditioning hadn't been turned on yet in the courthouse.

Michael Fallon walked into the courtroom and sat down next to Harvey Stidham in the rear of the spectators' section of Judge Richard Coppler's courtroom. Stidham was a deputy county attorney for Maricopa County, which encompassed Phoenix, Scottsdale, Mesa, Tempe, Glendale, and a dozen smaller communities.

"How's it going?" Fallon said quietly.

Stidham shook his head and frowned. "*You* spend fifteen minutes with the boy's parents and tell *me*," he said under his breath.

"I can imagine," Fallon whispered. He was broad through the shoulders and tall, with a square jaw and deep-set eyes. His eyes were gray and gentle under heavy brows, and his forehead rose to a widow's peak. His sandy hair was straight and limp in the humid heat and fell carelessly to just above his eyebrows. He was thirty years old and had the look of a scholarly, serious man. He squinted just a bit as he studied the latest police reports in the open file on his lap.

At the front of the courtroom, a couple of lawyers

were arguing to the judge about something. The room was crowded with silent spectators, waiting for the Carpenter case to be called. The murdered boy's mother sat in the second row, sobbing into a wad of soiled tissues. She wore a long, drab gray dress to her ankles, black stockings, and black laced shoes. Her hair was obviously a cheap wig that was a little twisted on her head. The boy's father sat stonily erect beside her, unbudging, his jaws clenched so tightly that his cheeks popped out like peach pits. He wore a black suit coat and black trousers and a starched white shirt with a thin black wool tie. His face was narrow, almost gaunt, as though he had long ago given up eating.

Stidham had just spent a severely depressing fifteen minutes with the boy's parents in his office, trying to steady them, to reassure them that everything would go smoothly, that their little boy's killer would not get off.

"*State* versus *Carpenter,*" Judge Coppler called out from the bench, looking around the crowded courtroom.

Harvey walked to the prosecution table. "Harvey Stidham for the State, Your Honor." He was short and thin in his early forties with a round, heavy face and iron gray hair.

"Michael Fallon for the defendant, Henry Carpenter, who is present in the jury box, Your Honor. The public defender had a conflict on this case, so I was appointed by Judge Hill." He sat down at the defense table. This was a terrible case, and he would have liked to turn down the appointment. But he couldn't, he needed the money. Defending men like Carpenter was necessary, but it certainly wasn't heartwarming.

The accused was a short, slight, middle-aged white man with thick gray hair, a craggy, pale face, as though he shunned the sun, and a crooked, punched-over nose. He looked nervously at Stidham and the judge.

"Your motion to suppress, Mr. Fallon," the judge said.

"Yes, Your Honor." Michael stood up at the table. "May it please the court, I'd like to make a short opening statement to review the facts leading up to the arrest. It will make the hearing a lot shorter, and these particular facts are not in dispute."

"Very well."

"On January 13, ten-year-old Jimmy Dixon was seen by Sylvia Graber, the playground supervisor at Goldwater Elementary School, getting into a battered yellow Ford sedan near the playground." He read from his notes on a yellow pad. "The boy's actions appeared voluntary, so Mrs. Graber didn't pay any particular attention, except that she says the driver had gray hair and appeared to be forty to fifty years old."

Carpenter swallowed and looked down, as if to hide his features from the appraising stares.

"An hour and a half later, Jimmy's mother went to the playground to look for him, since he was late getting home. She and Mrs. Graber immediately called the police. Mrs. Graber has lived in central Phoenix all of her life and knew this neighborhood very well, and she thought she had seen a battered yellow Ford parked several blocks away. She remembered seeing it four or five times. When the police car responded to the playground, she went with Officer Roy Carmen. They drove around the neighborhood, and she pointed out what she believed was the car, but she wasn't certain. It was parked in front of a small house on Heatherbrae near Nineteenth Avenue. The officer circled the block, and Mrs. Graber saw another parked car that she also thought might be the one. Officer Carmen didn't know what to do, so he kept on driving, and as they neared the first car again, a gray-haired man who appeared to be in his forties came out of a house on Heatherbrae and got into it. Mrs. Graber couldn't identify him at all. Officer Carmen pulled up alongside the car and parked, blocking it from being moved.

"At this point, the subsequent events become critical to the motion, and the defense calls Officer Roy Carmen."

Carmen was short and stocky. He wore the Phoenix police summer uniform, a white short-sleeved shirt, dark blue trousers, and spit-shined plain-toed black shoes. His hair was black and wavy. He walked forward, was sworn by the clerk, and took the seat in the witness box.

Michael Fallon nodded to him and smiled. "Please state your name and occupation."

"Roy Carmen, patrolman with the Phoenix Police Department."

"Officer Carmen, you're the one who placed the defendant under arrest on January 13. Is that correct?"

"Yes, sir."

"Tell the court the circumstances."

"Well, I pulled up beside the guy, and I got out and asked him to get out of the car. He was cooperative, and he got out. He gave me his driver's license, and I went back to my car, got on the radio, called in the name 'Henry Carpenter' on the license and also the plate number of the car for a registration check. It comes back to Henry Carpenter. I call the Phoenix Police Department for NCIC—that's the records from the National Crime Information Computer—and there's a Henry Carpenter listed as on parole from Arizona State Prison for burglary. By then the defendant is yelling at me that he's got to leave and wants his license back.

"I go back over to him and tell him I'm investigating the disappearance of a ten-year-old boy from Goldwater Elementary, and he says he doesn't know anything about it. I look in the car, but there's nothing in plain view, no blood, weapons, clothes, nothing. I ask him if he'll come downtown to the police department with me, and he says no. Well, I didn't know exactly what to do, and I didn't want the guy driving off on me, so I remained parked beside his car."

"Did you place him under arrest?"

"No, sir. I didn't think I had probable cause at that point."

"All right, go ahead, Officer Carmen."

"Well, the defendant says I have to move my car, since he wants to leave. I tell him I'm just going to call for some more information, that I'll leave in a minute. He calls me an asshole and then goes back and sits in his car. I call for my supervisor, and about ten minutes later Detective Lieutenant Paul Barnes drives up. By then the body of a young boy had been found by a city sanitation worker in a garbage dumpster in Washington Park, up near the Black Canyon Freeway and Bethany Home Road. The boy had been stabbed multiple times and was nude. His penis and testicles had been removed."

The courtroom was morbidly silent. The spectators wore grim expressions. Carpenter blandly stared unblinkingly at the officer.

"Barnes gets a radio call and advises me that the boy's mother has just identified the body. I tell him what we have on Carpenter, and he instructs me to search the automobile. He says that since this Carpenter is on parole, we have the right to search his vehicle. He says to try to get a hold of his parole officer to come over to do a search. I call the parole office, but he isn't there, and they don't know when he's coming back. So I tell Barnes, and he says to go on over and search the car. I go over to the car and ask Carpenter for the key to the trunk, and he tells me no in not such a nice way.

"I got a short crowbar out of my car and pried the trunk open. There was an old suitcase in it. It was locked, so I pried it open, and inside it was a man's plaid shirt that had large, dark stains, still a little moist, that looked like blood, and a big kitchen knife, like one of those French chef knives, that looked like it had some blood smears on it." He coughed a couple of times and cleared his throat. "There was also a little plastic baggie, and there was what looked like a penis and testicles in it."

A loud murmur erupted among the spectators. Judge Coppler rapped his gavel several times and stared menacingly around the courtroom.

"That was it," Carmen continued. "Barnes placed the subject under arrest. The crime lab subsequently reported the blood on the shirt and the knife to match the murdered boy's blood. Also the body parts in the baggie were the boy's."

"No further questions," Fallon said, taking his seat at the defense table.

"No questions," Harvey said.

"Argument?" the judge asked. "Mr. Fallon?"

"Your Honor," Mike Fallon said, rising at the defense table. "At the first point at which the police officer refused to permit Henry Carpenter to drive away in his car, Mr. Carpenter was technically under arrest, since arrest is defined as any involuntary restriction on free movement. But even the officer admits that he lacked probable cause to make a legal arrest at that time. Therefore, everything that occurred subsequently was the unconstitutional fruit of the poisoned tree under the United States Supreme Court's decision in *Wong Sun* and further unconstitutional under *Chapman* versus *New Hampshire,* and all evidence seized in the search of the car must be suppressed." He sat down.

Judge Coppler's face was drawn. His eyes narrowed and twitched, and he looked almost apologetically at Harvey. "Mr. Stidham, what evidence does the State have on this?"

"The parole agreement, Your Honor," Harvey said, rising from his chair and handing a document to the bailiff, who brought it to the judge.

"May I be heard, Your Honor?" Harvey said.

"Yes, sure."

"Paragraph 8c of the parole agreement, signed by the defendant when he was released from Arizona State Prison seven months ago, explicitly waives his search and seizure rights. It's a standard condition of release and has been approved by the courts."

"I'm well aware of that, Mr. Stidham. But we're both aware that the waiver applies to the defendant's parole officer only and not to all police officers in general. Do you have any evidence to present that the parole officer was involved in this search?"

Harvey's voice was just a bit muffled, his face dour. "No, Your Honor." He sat down.

Judge Coppler shook his head and rubbed his forehead hard with his left hand. "Any more argument, gentlemen?"

"May it please the court," Mike said, standing at the defense table. "This is a terrible case. But no matter how heinous the crime, no matter how reprehensible the criminal, the State may not resort to the commission of lawless acts in its war against crime. All war has rules which no party may violate with impunity, and the punishment for the violation of these particular rules is the suppression of the illegally seized evidence."

He sat down and breathed deeply.

The judge drummed his fingers stolidly on the file in front of him. "Mr. Stidham?"

Harvey stood up at the prosecution table. He looked at Michael Fallon, Henry Carpenter, and then the judge. "Your Honor, I confess that I don't quite get what we're after here anymore. Mr. Fallon says that the State must fight its war against crime by the rules, but what he really means is that only the State has to play by the rules, as though this were a football game or tennis match. So this man rapes and murders a little boy, and when a Phoenix police officer makes a technical search and seizure error, we blow a whistle and stop the game and penalize the innocent people of our state by letting the killer go free." Harvey stopped speaking and stared balefully at the murderer sitting in the jury box.

"I once thought that crime called for punishment. But then I went to law school, and now I've been prosecuting for fifteen years, and I know that punishment has nothing to do with crime. And this case is the perfect example of it.

"Mr. Fallon mouths flowery words about justice, and he says we have to let this trash go free because we have done him wrong. But that's absolute hogwash, and we all know it. That can't be justice. Justice means that the guilty must be punished. Justice means that innocent potential future victims must be protected. Justice means that where there is independent evidence to prove the crime, we must permit the police the latitude to make innocent search and seizure mistakes when it is perfectly clear that all they are trying to do is to protect all of us from the bloodthirsty predations of the Henry Carpenters."

Harvey sat down slowly and folded his hands on the table. He swallowed hard and stared straight ahead at nothing.

Judge Coppler hunched his shoulders over the bench and spoke in a low voice. "The shirt and the knife and the baggie are ordered suppressed. Do you have sufficient additional evidence to maintain your indictment against the defendant, Mr. Stidham?"

"Yes, we do, Your Honor. The identification by Sylvia Graber is solid, both of the car and the defendant, and the State will proceed with the prosecution." But even as Harvey said it, he knew better. The identification wasn't at all solid, and Carpenter would ultimately probably be a free man. But at least he'd stay in jail pending his trial, which might not be for six months, nine months, even a year. And if God was really good, maybe there would be a jailhouse brawl, and some mind-blown crack or angel dust freak would spill Carpenter's brains all over the cell floor. You could always hope for the best.

"All right. Defendant Henry Carpenter will remain in custody pending trial." The judge banged his gavel and walked off the bench to his chambers.

The bailiff led Henry Carpenter from the jury box to the defense table. He was handcuffed, and he grabbed Mike Fallon's right hand in both of his and started pumping it up and down excitedly.

"Oh, thank you, Mr. Fallon! You sure kicked that prosecutor's ass!"

Mike pulled his hand away abruptly and stepped back from Carpenter. The bailiff led the killer away. Mike's mouth twisted as though he'd bitten into an unripe persimmon.

Stidham gave Fallon a withering glance and walked out of the courtroom, the dead boy's weeping parents close behind him.

Mike walked out of the courthouse feeling guilty, as though he himself had committed a criminal act. He crossed the street to the parking complex and drove quickly out of downtown Phoenix. Some days are worse than others, he thought as he drove to the Westside Juvenile Annex, and this is one of the worst. And it isn't even nine-thirty in the morning yet!

You get appointed to defend a piece of shit who is masquerading as a human being, and you end up beating the rap for him. Mike hardly felt as though his representation of Henry Carpenter had been a victory for justice.

The rest of the morning promised to be much more pleasant, however. He had been appointed by a juvenile court judge to represent a sixteen-year-old adjudicated delinquent named Donna Alvarez. Donna had gotten off the streets, beaten a junk habit, and was on the verge of getting a new start in life. Thank God for a few happy occasions interspersed among the crap that he had to do taking criminal appointments.

But money was money, and a guy had to eat. And unless you graduated at the very top of your class or your father was somehow influential or rich, you didn't get a job with one of the big Phoenix firms. The law business in Phoenix had shrunk considerably in the wake of the RTC's destruction of the savings and loan industry and the resultant real estate collapse, and there just weren't many legal jobs around, even for an honors graduate of ASU. So when Mike had passed the bar exam sixteen months ago, he had rented a small office in the Phipps Tower in downtown Phoenix and was taking all the appointed criminal cases he could get.

He walked into the small juvenile hearing room and sat down at the empty table in front of the judge's bench. At the other table was Donna Alvarez, a cute kid with freckles on her nose, long brown hair in a ponytail, and light brown eyes. She sat beside an elderly nun in a charcoal gray business suit and a little white hatlet with short cropped gray hair and a sallow, blunt-nosed face with the aggressive appearance of a hammer in search of a nail.

Mike watched Donna's eyes light up and her face break into a wide smile when a tall, shapely woman with long strawberry blond hair walked into the small juvenile court hearing room. She sat down next to Donna, hugged her, and kissed her on the cheek. Donna's smile became even broader.

Mike Fallon found himself staring at the woman who was there to be awarded temporary custody of the girl. She was a knockout. He opened his manila file and scanned the top sheet. Mary Caitlin O'Dwyer was her name, the temporary-custody form said. He flipped through the pages of the file, scanned the vice reports on Donna Alvarez, starting when she was just fourteen: arrests for soliciting and possession of heroin, detox at Mesa's Children's Protective Services, methadone therapy at Indian Health Services on the Pima-Maricopa Indian Reservation, three more soliciting arrests but no convictions, then the referral to the juvenile court by Scottsdale Memorial Hospital

Controlled-Substances Abuse Center and her place-
ment at the Home of the Good Shepherd. Most of
the rest of the file were progress reports by Mother
Superior Veronica Demiro and Sister Danielle Salter.
The last three documents in the file were a background report on Mary Caitlin O'Dwyer, which Mike
read closely, and letters of recommendation from
Monsignor Terrance Reilly at Saint Daniel's Academy
and Seamus Cardinal Gerrity of Boston.

A cardinal? Mike looked over at the woman with a
new sense of respect. Her family obviously had real
juice. She was staring at him. Both of them looked
away self-consciously. He looked at her again, and
again she was looking back at him. And neither of
them turned away.

Maybe I ought to do my job, he thought to himself,
instead of sitting here like a boob. He stood up and
walked over to the front of the table.

"Donna, I'm Michael Fallon. I'll be representing
you at this hearing."

The girl looked at him with suddenly frightened
eyes. She was clutching a big black Bible tightly in
both hands.

"Don't be afraid," he said as gently as he could.
"I'm on your side."

She looked at Kate O'Dwyer and received an encouraging nod.

"Is there anything you'd like to say to me?" he
asked.

Donna shook her head slowly.

"All right. If at any time during the hearing you
don't understand something and want to speak to me,
just say so. The judge will call a recess and we'll be
able to talk as long as you want. Okay?"

She nodded, her face serious but no longer afraid.

"May I speak with you a moment privately, Miss
O'Dwyer?" This wasn't an essential element of his
job, but he had the right to question her, to determine

her fitness to be the girl's guardian. And on what other pretext was he going to talk to her?

"Yes, of course," she said. She wore hardly any makeup, just a little brown mascara on her long eyelashes, a bit of eyeliner, and a soft, understated red shade of lipstick.

He watched her get up from the table, and she was really beautiful, graceful. She had slim arms and legs, and her large breasts pressed against the front of her light rust-colored sleeveless silk shirtdress, which buttoned from a scooped neckline down to the hem just above her knees. He watched her walk away from him down the aisle to the rear of the courtroom, and he swallowed.

She turned around at the double wooden doors and waited for him.

"Why don't we go out in the hallway?" he said. "We can sit down for a couple of minutes. There are some questions I'm required to ask." He shrugged offhandedly and smiled, feeling oddly embarrassed.

Her green eyes studied him steadily, gently. She walked into the hall and he followed. She sat down on a four-foot-wide wooden bench against the far wall, and he sat next to her. She smelled delicious.

"So," he said, opening the file to her application form, "you're recently here from Boston?"

"Yes. Actually, I lived in Marblehead. That's just a little north of Boston. I grew up in Manchester by the Sea, north of Marblehead."

Her voice was businesslike, strong, and self-assured.

"Yes, I know," Mike said. "My family's originally from Boston." Actually, they had lived in *South* Boston, where the *poor* Micks lived. Only the richest Irish, called "Lace Curtains" by everyone, could afford to live in Marblehead or Manchester.

She regarded him with what he hoped was interest, her head tilted a bit to one side.

"You're divorced, one child—"

"No, actually, it was annulled."

He nodded. "Yes, I'm sorry. I apologize that I didn't have much time to study the file." He smiled at her, and she nodded in understanding.

"And you have a three-year-old daughter, Jennifer?"

"Yes, it's all there in my application," she said, pointing at the file. Her smile was becoming one of amusement. She seemed to find his nervousness charming. The palpable attraction between them made them both stare at each other.

"You live at McCormick Ranch in Scottsdale," he said, glancing back at the file, "but your only income is from teaching fifth grade at Saint Daniel's?"

"My parents are well-to-do, and they bought the house for me."

"You're a lucky girl."

Kate nodded and smiled. "I agree. My parents and I have always been very close. My father still thinks of me as his little girl."

"I hope he ain't real big," Mike said with a trace of a Texas drawl.

She laughed. "He's as tall as you are and fifty pounds heavier, and he's very protective of me."

Mike chuckled, happy that the stiffness was dissipating between them. "Cain't blame 'im," he drawled again.

"You may be from Boston, but it doesn't sound like you grew up there," she said.

"No. Fort Stockton, Texas."

The door opened and the bailiff looked out at them. "Judge Collins is on the bench."

"Okay," Mike said. He followed Kate into the courtroom. She sat down next to Donna. He walked up behind the other table and remained standing while the judge leafed through the file before him.

Judge Harlan Collins was a big, heavy black man in his late forties. Mike had been in his courtroom and his chambers several times on other juvenile court hearings, and he liked Collins. He was gruff-speaking and down-to-earth, and he loved to recount stories—genuine or apocryphal, who could say?—of his exploits as one of the first black football stars at the University of Alabama in the late 1960s. "Those little white girls hadn't ever been close to a black person before, 'cept maybe their mammies and their gardeners, but 'stead a bein' scared by us boys, they were downright curious." He would wink and slap his knee and chortle merrily.

"All right," Judge Collins said, "this is the hearing in the matter of the temporary guardianship of Donna Alvarez. Good afternoon, Mr. Fallon." He glanced briskly at Mike. "Sister Veronica, nice to see you again."

She nodded at him, her face as immobile as granite.

"Make it happen, Mr. Fallon," the judge said, settling back in his big brown leather swivel chair.

"May it please the court, I'm representing Donna Alvarez, age sixteen, here seated between Sister Veronica and Miss Mary Caitlin O'Dwyer. Miss O'Dwyer's application to be appointed foster mother has been verified by the juvenile court staff investigator, and the senior referral officer has recommended approval. I have spoken to Donna and Miss O'Dwyer, and there are no changes in the status of the application or the ward's desire to live with Miss O'Dwyer. It is my judgment that the best interests of the child will be served by approving the foster-parent relationship." He sat down.

"Very well," said the judge. "Sister Veronica?"

The nun stood up at the table, addressing the judge in a husky smoker's voice. "Donna Alvarez has successfully completed the adjustment program at the Home of the Good Shepherd, Your Honor. We have no indications that she poses a threat to herself or the community if she is released from custody and placed with Miss O'Dwyer. I have known Miss O'Dwyer for almost three months, and I strongly attest to her fitness to be the girl's foster mother." Sister Veronica sat down.

Judge Collins opened the file on the bench. He hunched forward over it and signed a document that he then handed to the court clerk, sitting to his right on a lower section of the bench. She stamped it and held it up toward Mike Fallon. He walked up to the clerk, took the sheet of paper, and scanned it.

"You take care of getting it copied and distributed, Mr. Fallon," the judge said. He looked sternly at Donna. "You're getting a chance to do something good with your life, young lady. The only reason I ever want to see you here again is to make this custody arrangement permanent. Otherwise, I may have no option but to place you in the loving care of the State Department of Juvenile Corrections. Do you understand?"

Donna gulped, too afraid to look at him. "Yes, sir," she said.

"All right. Madam clerk, set a review hearing for two months and notify all parties," Judge Collins said. He rapped his gavel and left the bench.

Kate O'Dwyer leaned over and kissed Donna on the cheek. They stood up and walked hand in hand out of the courtroom, following the nun.

Mike wanted to talk to Mary Caitlin O'Dwyer, to ask her out to dinner, a movie, anything. But he didn't know how, the situation was too awkward. He couldn't run after her now and make a fool out of himself. And what if she said no, she wasn't interested, or she had a boyfriend? He watched the door close behind her.

· SIX ·

"She's a bitch, man," Big Gun Pete said.

"Hey, I hear ya," said Tony Brown Horse. "How'd ya find 'er?"

"Her sister Louise. She came over this mornin' all strung out. I traded her a nickel baggie for Donna's address and phone number."

They were sitting in Pete's shack smoking crack cocaine and taking turns drinking from a quart bottle of Four Roses.

"I called her this mornin', the little bitch. She tol' me she won't do the hotels for me, she got a good gig goin' with a rich white broad, don' wanna blow it."

Tony snickered. "She can blow me anytime, man. She got a tongue like a mongoose."

"Shit, I ain't got no pussy can work the Hilton and the Safari like she usta, man." Pete held a lighter over the top of the crack pipe, took a long pull, and coughed.

"Ya gotta get her to work," Tony said. "She can make ya real bucks."

"Damn straight, man. Them sluts I got right now ain't makin' me a dime. If ya lined 'em up naked in the window of a pussy boutique, nobody'd even stop to window shop."

"Yeah, them bitches got so many purple snakes all over 'em from shootin' H, they look like zebras." Tony laughed. "Ya gotta go talk to Donna, man, punch a little respect into 'er. She got fried brains from all that heroin."

"Yeah, she don't think right. But now that she's off the shit again, them fat white guys up at the hotels'll pay a hunnerd, two hunnerd a pop. She looks real high class when she's clean, man, like a high school cheerleader. Shit, I know two weirdass white dudes who'll give me maybe five hunnerd bucks if she'll go three ways. Coupla weirdass switchers. Pecker or pussy, it don' matter to 'em as long as it's real young."

Tony nodded. "They're the best payers, man. What're ya gonna do?"

"I dunno. I'm gonna go see 'er tomorrow. Louise says the rich broad teaches school, ain't home all day."

"Pop 'er one, man, that's what she needs. Ya gotta pop the bitch a good one." Tony smacked his right fist into his open left palm. "Put the fear a God in 'er."

Michael Fallon lived in an apartment in Phoenix on Camelback Avenue near Fortieth Street, thirteen miles and at least a half million dollars from Scottsdale's opulent McCormick Ranch. He sat on the sofa in his small living room, the television playing unheard and unwatched, and stared at the small slip of paper on the cocktail table in front of him. He had waited two days, long enough that she wouldn't think he was too anxious. He had jotted down Miss O'Dwyer's telephone number before turning the file back to the juvenile court records clerk. It was probably unethical for him to have done it, he thought, to get personal information from the confidential file of someone he met in court in the course of his duties. But what would they do to him, shoot him? Probably not.

Anyway, her phone number might be in the telephone book or information. If so, it was public and he'd have done nothing questionable. He reached for the telephone, called information, and she did indeed have her number listed. Good. It helped him overcome his uneasiness at calling her. Maybe she didn't mind getting calls. He dialed her number.

"Hello," she said. He immediately recognized her voice.

"Hi. This is Michael Fallon. I'm the guy from court two days ago."

"I remember." Pause.

He suddenly didn't feel very glib.

"Do you have some more questions for me?"

He frowned, feeling like an errant schoolboy. "No, not official ones, anyway. I called because I would like to go out with you. Unofficial." His voice was suddenly a bit hoarse. He cleared his throat.

Pause. "Well, that's nice of you, but for a couple of weeks I'm going to stay here at the house in the evenings, just until Donna really settles in."

"Oh, yeah, sure," he said, his voice too small, betraying much more disappointment than he wanted it to. He'd never been good at asking for a date. Most guys were like him in that regard, he had come to realize, despite the bravado with which they bragged to their friends. Getting turned down was painful.

"But I hope you'll call me and ask me then."

His face and voice brightened. "I will, I certainly will."

Kate had felt a little concerned the first few days when she left in the mornings for Saint Daniel's Academy. She felt that she knew Donna quite well, having spent three evenings a week and all day on Saturdays with her for two months. And Jennifer had always come along in the past six weeks, so Kate had seen the two girls develop a relationship as close as even sisters could be. But taking Jennifer out of Merry Moppets for all but two days a week and leaving her alone with Donna simply made her anxious. The first day was especially difficult. Kate had so much trouble concentrating on the geography lesson that during recess two of her ten-year-old students came up to her looking worried.

"Are you sick, Miss O'Dwyer?" Carole Downey asked.

"No, honey, I'm fine," Kate said.

"You look like you're sick," Millicent Gregg said.

"Well, I'm sorry I look so sick." Kate smiled at the girls. "I promise you I'm okay."

"My daddy can help you, 'cause he's a doctor," Carole said.

"I know, dear. Thank you. If I need to, I'll call him."

"Okay," she said, and the two girls joined hands and ran toward the merry-go-round.

Kate had made a special effort after that to appear her normal cheerful and pleasant self. It had been hard that first day, but each day it became easier, and after three days the anxiety was completely erased by Jennifer's own reaction to the sudden change in her life. She liked staying home with a big sister better than being at the day-care center all day. Donna played dolls with her, and they went down to the lake and fed the ducks, and they walked over to the park a few blocks away and played for hours on the swings and merry-go-round and monkey bars. Donna was terrific. Jennifer loved her like a big sister, and that was exactly what Kate had hoped.

Kate hadn't really known what to expect of Donna's living habits. After all, at the Home of the Good Shepherd the girls were compelled to make their beds and clean their rooms and take showers. But that concern, too, had immediately evaporated.

Donna was immaculate. Kate had taken her straight from the juvenile court hearing to Bullock's Department Store to buy her some clothes, since the only things she had were the black mini-skirt and the pink tube top she was wearing the night that she had OD'd and been brought to Scottsdale Memorial Hospital. At Bullock's, Donna had picked out two pairs of faded

Levi's, three T-shirts, and several blouses and skirts. They were always neatly washed, ironed, and folded in her dresser or hung in her closet. She made the bed every day, and her room was spotless.

One evening Kate passed Donna's room and saw her sitting cross-legged on her bed, her face cupped in her hands, her elbows propped on her knees, the Bible open in her lap. Kate knocked on the doorjamb.

"Hi," Donna said, looking up from the Bible.

Kate walked into the room and sat down on the edge of the bed. "I hope you know that you don't have to read the Bible to impress me," she said.

"Oh, yeah, yeah sure, I know that." She blushed, embarrassed.

Kate felt guilty. "What do you read in there?"

"Oh, I always just read the Canticle of Canticles."

Kate smiled. The sisters at the Home had given Donna an old Douay-Rheims Bible. In the new Confraternity Bible that the Church was now using, it was called the Song of Songs. "Yes, it's beautiful," Kate said.

"Yeah, really." Donna pointed at a line. "It says here that it's all about the 'happy union of Christ and his spouse,' and that 'the spouse of Christ is the Church.' But it looks to me like just plain love poems."

Kate turned the Bible around and read where Donna was pointing. "That's what the official church interpretation is, I guess, but I have a real close friend who's a nun, and she thinks just like you."

Donna lifted the Bible and read: " 'Let him kiss me with the kiss of his mouth: for thy breasts are better than wine.' " She looked at Kate and smiled. "That doesn't sound like church talk."

Kate laughed.

"And this, listen how beautiful it is. 'Thy two breasts like two young roes that are twins, which feed among the lilies.' " She looked at Kate. "What are *roes?*"

"They're female deer. Today we call them *does.*"

Donna smiled mischievously. "You mean like Sears and Doebuck?"

Kate laughed again, charmed by the girl's innocence and intelligence.

"Listen to this," Donna said. " 'I am a rose of Sharon, a lily of the valley. . . . Behold, my beloved speaketh to me: Arise, make haste, my love, my dove, my beautiful one, and come.' " She looked up at Kate again. "God, that's beautiful. Nobody ever loved me like that. They just wanted me for ten minutes, to hurt me." Her lips trembled.

Kate looked into Donna's mournful eyes and said, "Someday somebody will love you just like that, some very lucky man." She slid close to her on the bed and hugged her.

On Sunday, Kate took her to early mass at Our Lady of Perpetual Hope Church. Donna tried very conscientiously to mimic everything that Kate did. Afterward, Kate introduced her to Father Francis Baedecker, a rather forbidding gray-haired old man, and she was as sweet and polite and shy as any other sixteen-year-old girl would have been. Whatever trouble she had been in didn't appear to have afflicted her soul.

Jennifer had spent the mass in the youth center with the other kids, and she was cranky when they got home. Donna put her in bed and sat with her, and she dozed off immediately. Donna tiptoed out of the bedroom and closed the door gently. Kate was in the kitchen, staring into the refrigerator.

"We don't have anything to eat," she said. "I better go shopping later."

"There's plenty of eggs," Donna said, sitting down at the table.

"Yeah, but that's too much cholesterol. They'll clog up our hearts if we eat too many."

"Nothing could clog up my heart being here," Donna said.

Kate closed the refrigerator and turned around. There were tears in Donna's eyes. Kate walked up to her and hugged her face to her breast.

"I never knew there were people like you," Donna said.

Kate bent and kissed her on the forehead. "I love you, honey. I'm so glad we found each other, and Jennifer loves you, too."

Donna's lips quivered and tears rolled down her cheeks. Kate sat down across from her.

"My sister Louise sold me to an old man when I was twelve," Donna whispered. "He was about forty, and he lived in a big house on the reservation, and she got enough money for me to buy two papers of heroin."

Kate swallowed. "You don't have to tell me any of these things, Donna."

"I know," she whispered. "But I need to."

Tears began to well in Kate's eyes.

"He made me do all kinds of things, and when he fell asleep, drunk, I ran away. I felt so filthy that I thought I was going to die. We didn't have a shower at home, so I ran to an irrigation ditch, and there was water in it, and I jumped in, but it was all mud underneath and I got covered with it. I went home and my mother was sitting on the porch like always, and I told her what happened, and you know what she did?"

Kate shook her head, her face grim.

"She went into the house calling, 'Louise, Louise,' and asked her if she had any of the money left 'cause she wanted to buy some wine."

Kate couldn't keep the tears back.

"I never thought I'd ever get to be in a place like this," Donna murmured, "with people like you. I never did."

"You never have to be anywhere else again," Kate said. She dried her cheeks with her hands and smiled at Donna. "Let's get crazy and call out for a pizza."

Donna nodded. "Yeah, that'd be great. I love pizza."

Mike Fallon waited exactly two weeks and called, not wishing to appear overly anxious. He hoped that she had not forgotten him.

"Hi, this is Michael Fallon. Remember me?"

"Of course. I'm glad you called."

That made him feel good. "Would you like to go out to dinner tonight?"

"I just ate. But I made much too much lasagna for just me and Donna and Jennifer. You're welcome to a piece if you're brave enough."

He sat up straight on the sofa and smiled. "I'll bring my AlkaSeltzer."

"Do you also happen to remember my address?" She chuckled lightly.

He was embarrassed. "No, I swear I didn't write it down," he lied.

"One-two-one-oh-nine-seven North Via de Frontera. The houses all look pretty much alike from the front. It's the one with the big clay pot of yellow cana lilies by the front door."

"I'll be over in a bit."

It took him forty-five minutes to find her house, because he got lost three times in the maze of streets by the McCormick Ranch lakes, even though he had a supposedly detailed map of Scottsdale with him. By the time he finally found Via de Frontera, it was too dark to tell the colors of the cana lilies in the pots in front of many of the almost identical houses, and the numbers on the mailboxes were small and almost useless in the dark.

She answered the door and smiled at him with unmistakable pleasure. Her long hair was in a loose ponytail, and she was wearing red cotton short shorts and a simple white cotton V-neck T-shirt. She had no makeup on and was barefoot and looked gorgeous.

"How nice to see you again, Mr. Fallon," she said.

He walked inside the house and said, "Mike."

"Mike. Call me Kate."

Donna Alvarez was in the middle of the living room floor, between the cocktail table and the blaring TV set, playing with Jennifer. They had a miniature baby stroller and a half dozen assorted dolls.

"Hello, Mr. Fallon," Donna said, the fear of two weeks ago completely gone from her face.

"Hi, Donna. How are you getting along?"

"I've never been so happy, Mr. Fallon."

Her face showed it. Mike smiled at her and nodded. "Good. I'm very pleased for you."

She got up from the floor, ran to him, threw her arms around his neck, stood on tiptoes, and kissed him on the cheek. He felt a surge of joyful exuberance for her and hugged her. She took his hand and brought him to Jennifer.

"This is Mr. Fallon, Jenny. He's our friend."

The little platinum-blond-haired girl was too absorbed tucking her dolly into the stroller to pay any attention to Mike.

"Hello," she said in her tiny voice, not looking up from her more important task.

"She's busy right now with Cynthia," Donna said. She squeezed Mike's hand, then flopped to the floor next to Jennifer to rejoin the play.

Mike walked back to Kate. She gave him a wonderfully sweet smile and walked into the kitchen.

"You're a nice guy," she said, her voice soft and serious.

"Bet your ass," he said, pleased and emboldened by his reception and the look on her face.

She burst out laughing.

The kitchen smelled enticingly of garlic and oregano and Parmesan cheese.

"You're about to discover why my husband fled from me," she said, taking a half pan of lasagna out of the oven.

"I can't believe that any sane man would ever flee from you."

She glanced at him, smiled, and put the pan on the counter. "You really don't have to eat this, you know. I can call out for a pizza."

"It can't be that bad. It looks great."

"Looks can be deceiving. I went to school at Wellesley, and I never had to cook in my life until I married Brian. And we used to eat out most of the time, so I didn't learn very much."

"Quit trying to scare the hell out of me and let me try a piece. I'm starving."

She cut a square, put it on a dish, placed a fork on top of it, and handed it to him. He cut off a corner, held it up on the fork and examined it, put it in his mouth, chewed carefully and slowly and tilted his head from side to side in gourmandish contemplation, his eyes squinted shut.

"What's the number of the pizza joint?" he said.

She laughed. "I told you."

"I'm kidding." He went to the table and sat down, forked another mouthful. "Never had anything so good in my life."

"I love first dates," she said. "Everyone's always so careful and polite. Just wait until you've known me awhile."

He looked at her soberly. "I can't wait." He suddenly had goose bumps on his arms and felt silly. He took another mouthful of the overcooked, rubbery lasagna, with much too much oregano, and chewed heartily.

"Have you ever been married?" she asked, bringing a bottle of Valpolicella and two glasses to the table. "Or maybe I ought to ask if you *are* married." She sat down and poured the wine.

"Nope and nope," he said.

"A guy who looks like you? A lawyer? How come?"

He regarded her blandly. "I'm gay."

"I'm serious."

He studied her face. "Is this true confession time?"

"If that's what it takes."

"My mother and father both came over from Dublin as soon as they got married. They couldn't even find jobs over there, and my mother's oldest sister was living in South Boston and said there were plenty of jobs. Ten years later, my dad and my younger brother, Terry, were killed in a car accident when I was seven. We were on our way to live in Phoenix, where he had a job waiting, and the accident happened just outside of Fort Stockton, Texas, which is about two hundred miles from El Paso and a mile from nowhere. My mom figured it was an omen from God and God's will that we stay near my father and brother, so she got a job as bunkhouse cook for a cattle ranch, and I grew up there. I joined the army as soon as I turned eighteen so I could get the G.I. Bill, and I came to Phoenix when I got out. I had to work all kinds of jobs to get through ASU, and I've never had two ten-dollar bills in my pocket at the same time." He shrugged. "My apartment is about the size of this kitchen." He looked around, measuring it. "Well, maybe a little smaller. I drive an '89 Chevy pickup truck, I have two suits, and I do court appointments for paltry fees that would be illegal if I belonged to the pipe fitters' union."

She was staring askance at him.

"You said true confession."

She nodded. "But I was only joking."

They both chuckled.

"How about you?" he asked.

"Well, since you already read all about me in my custody application, I'll tell you at least half the truth."

He smiled.

"My parents are richer than Rockefeller. I'm a good

Catholic. I believe in God. My father just got his closest friend elevated to cardinal, and Cardinal Gerrity will undoubtedly vote for my father the next time there's an election for pope." She laughed. "I drive a '94 Chrysler convertible, I have a three-year-old daughter who I love more than myself, and I have a savings account and a trust fund."

Mike raised his eyebrows and pursed his lips. "You sound like a hell of a catch to me."

She shook a schoolmarmish finger at him. "My father always told me that when you marry for money, you have to earn it, and it isn't so easy, and it isn't very honorable."

"I promise I won't marry you for your money."

"I'll hold you to that. And anyway, it's my parents' money, not mine."

"I do solemnly swear to be an honorable suitor who treats you with respect and never asks you for a loan or tells you any lies." He looked down at the plate. "Unless I have to eat any more of this."

She shook her head in mock disappointment. "So much for first-date politeness."

"I never like to be hospitalized on my first date."

She burst out laughing. "Don't ever say I didn't warn you." She got up and looked in the refrigerator. "I've got some hamburger, couple of hot dogs, some cold chicken."

"Actually, I ate before I called."

She smiled at him. "Take your wine. Let's go out back and watch the ducks."

They walked onto the patio through the kitchen door. Lamps along the jogging path below lit the placid lake with soft yellow glows, and a citron moon brightened the aubergine sky. They sat under an orange tree on a small aluminum-frame lawn settee. Kate poured more wine into both of their glasses and then balanced the bottle precariously between them on the thick seat pad.

"Is this like with the medieval knights?" Mike said.

"The maiden would sleep next to him with a broad-sword between them."

"You got it, buster."

He laughed and sipped the wine.

"It's wonderful here in the evenings," she said. "There are never any big storms, the sky is usually clear, and the weather is terrific."

"Wait till June. You won't think it's so terrific. It won't go below ninety degrees until at least midnight. And out here it's pretty humid because of the water."

"Yeah, I know. I've heard all about it from every-body. But the heat doesn't bother me nearly as much as the cold did in Boston."

"What made you come?"

She shrugged. "Just a change, really. Nothing earth-shattering. I'd been out here once for a winter vaca-tion with my parents and then again this last Christ-mas, and I just loved it. It's everything that Boston isn't."

"Is your ex-husband still back there?"

"Yes. He's the son of my father's business partner. We grew up together, always lived a mile apart, went to the same elementary and junior high schools. We should never have gotten married. But I have no hard feelings, I wish him well."

"That's a good attitude."

"It sure is," she said, looking kittenish. "Of course, I'm lying. I hope the rotten bastard develops pancre-atic cancer and dies slowly in unbearable pain."

Mike laughed.

Kate poured some more wine into their glasses and put the bottle on the ground by her side. Several duck-lings splashed into the little cove past the jogging path and caused a dozen other ducks and ducklings on the bank to squawk raucously for two minutes.

"Donna really looks happy," he said, sipping the wine.

"Yes, she's terrific. She's a good kid who's had a hell of a life, just unbelievable. I can't even think about what she's been through, and she's only sixteen, for God's sake. But she's going to be fine. I'll register her at St. Mary's for summer school in June, so she can do some catching up, and she'll be able to go into the eleventh grade in September."

"She's a lucky girl."

"So are Jennifer and I. She fits in here just like a member of our family."

They sat silently for minutes, basking in the pleasure of being together.

The kitchen door opened, and Donna called out, "Kate, Jennifer has to go to the bathroom. She wants you."

"Okay, honey," Kate called back. "I'll be there in a minute." The kitchen door closed.

She turned to Mike. "It's about time to get Jennifer to bed. She might get a little cranky if I don't sit with her for a while. I'm glad you came over."

"So am I," he said. "Very glad."

She got up from the settee, and he followed her into the house. They put their wineglasses on the kitchen table and walked into the living room. Kate opened the front door for him.

"I'd love to have some more of that lasagna," he said.

She laughed. "Well, I can certainly save it for you, since everyone around here refuses to eat it."

He smiled. "How about tomorrow night?"

"I can't," she said. "I promised to take Donna and Jennifer to the Phoenix Zoo and then Fantasy Island over at Encanto Park. But how about Friday night? You can buy me a hamburger at Houston's Restaurant, and maybe we can go to the movies."

He nodded. "Six?"

"I'll be ready."

He waved at Donna as he left the house, and she waved back.

"He's a doll," Donna said to Kate.

"I noticed," Kate said and smiled.

· SEVEN ·

Big Gun Pete's mama didn't raise no fool. He knew that if a Pima-Maricopa Indian with dreadlocks drove a raked and lowered Camaro into McCormick Ranch and parked and got out and walked into one of the houses by the lake, there would be eighteen little old ladies peeking out of their windows bug-eyed and then scurrying to their telephones to call the police. So he tied a red workman's bandana around his head, put on an old straw hat, a frayed blue chambray shirt and a faded pair of denim overalls, and drove one of his heroin mule trucks to Via de Frontera. It was a nondescript off-white and slightly battered Ford F-150 pickup outfitted with lawn tools and an electric mower to look like a gardener's truck. It even had a poorly painted sign on the driver's door that read YAZZIE LAWN SERVICE, and under it three digits of the telephone number had conveniently worn off.

It was one o'clock Thursday afternoon, and there were other gardeners in the neighborhood along with a plumbing truck parked a block away and a U.S. West telephone repair truck just down the street. Pete parked the truck in the driveway in front of the garage door. He got out of the truck, looked around carefully to make sure that he wasn't attracting any attention, walked to the front door, and rang the bell.

A moment later Donna Alvarez opened the door. She looked at him with wide eyes, her mouth open in shock, and immediately tried to close the door. He pushed it open and closed it behind him. She backed up from him.

"You can't be here," she said in a harsh whisper.

"You alone?"

"The baby's taking a nap. She can't see you here. She'll tell her mother."

He stepped to her and slapped her hard in the face.

"Don't hurt me, please don't hurt me." She bent away from him.

"I ain't gonna hurt ya." He kept his voice low. "Just shut your goddam mouth."

She slowly stood up straight.

"I need ya to work for me. I got a couple white guys wanna do a train. It's two hundred fifty bucks for ya for an hour."

She shook her head. "I can't leave here. I have to stay with the baby."

"Ya don' have to leave. I'll bring 'em here."

"You can't do that. They'll put me in Black Canyon."

"Nobody gonna know. We'll come at night when the bitch is out and the kid is sleepin'."

"No, no," she said.

"Hey, come on, Donna," he said soothingly. "I ain't gonna get ya in trouble. It's me, baby. Ain't I always done right by ya?" He stepped up to her and hugged her, enveloping her in his powerful arms.

She was afraid to shrink from his grasp, fearful of what he might do to her.

"Come on, baby. I got a present for ya," he said. He pulled her by the hand into the kitchen and pushed her into a chair by the table. "I got some a the best shit you ever had, baby, China white, special for *you*." He took a wrapped disposable syringe out of his overalls pocket, fished in his hip pocket, and pulled out a small square of wax paper.

"No, Pete, please. I don't want it anymore. I'm doing good here, Pete. Please." She began weeping loudly, and Pete backhanded her hard across her cheek. She almost fell off the chair and righted herself with difficulty. She stared at him mutely, terrified, as he took a spoon out of the drawer, cooked the heroin over a stove burner, and drew it into the syringe.

"Come on, baby, you be in heaven in five minutes." He grabbed her ponytail and pulled her to her feet. "Pull 'em down."

She was too frightened not to obey. She unbuttoned her Levi's, pushed them and her underpants down around her ankles, and stepped out of them. She covered herself with both hands like Botticelli's Venus.

He grabbed her arm and turned her around roughly, pushing her upper body over the kitchen table. He knelt behind her and injected the blood vessel behind her knee.

She flinched with the prick of the needle, and hugged the tabletop, afraid to move. He injected what was left in the syringe into his arm and slowly undressed, waiting for the hit.

After a few minutes, she no longer felt tension in her body. Her tears stopped and her breathing became soft and easy.

She felt his fingers probing her, massaging her, and then he spread her lips with his fingers and pushed himself into her and he was big and it felt good. She responded to him, wet and swollen, and he rocked and rocked, faster and faster, groaning, exploding, and her body was no longer her own but a foreign being distant from herself, floating somewhere way above pain and torment.

"When's the bitch gonna be gone, baby?" she thought she heard him ask over and over, and she heard that other being mumble something, but she couldn't understand what.

She woke up suddenly, feeling a tug on her arm.

"Go feed the duckies?" Jennifer asked, her bright blue eyes peering intently into Donna's.

Donna sat up, trying to remember what had happened, but it was all fuzzy and unfocused. Pete. Heroin. She looked down at herself, and she was fully clothed, her Levi's buttoned. A wave of nausea overwhelmed her and she leapt up from the chair, rushed to the sink, and vomited violently several times. She steadied herself over the sink, and the dizziness gradually subsided. She felt better and looked around the counter. Pete had cleaned up, washed the spoon. There was nothing left of him here except the wetness between her legs. She couldn't remember exactly what had happened, but she knew. She ran the water to clean the sink.

"Donna, you sick?" Jennifer said behind her.

Donna turned around and forced a smile. "No, honey, I'm fine. Let's go feed the duckies."

She opened the pantry, took out the loaf of bread that they used for the ducks, held Jennifer by the hand, and they walked out the kitchen door. They went through the wrought iron swinging gate that opened onto a half dozen stone steps leading down to the asphalt jogging and bicycling path. A few elderly people were strolling. They crossed the asphalt path and walked down the ryegrass slope to the bank of the cove, where at least fifty ducks were pecking in the grass. Many were just toddlers, small and chirping. A few were large, quacking loudly. They all recognized the look of a little girl with a big bag of food, and they waddled toward her.

Jennifer opened the bag and began throwing pieces of bread around her. The squawking ceased and squabbling broke out everywhere among the ducks. But there were enough treats for all of them, and soon they were quietly gobbling down the bread.

Donna sat down on the bank and watched, but she saw nothing. She didn't know what to do. She knew what Pete had done to her with the heroin. One hit was all it took to put a junkie back on the habit. But she couldn't let it happen, she wouldn't. But how could she stop him? She was terrified of him. He would kill her.

Can I call the police, she thought, tell them what had happened? No, that won't work. With my record they'll take me back to juvi, probably send me to Black Canyon. And I can't tell Kate. She wouldn't ever want me to be near Jennifer again. Oh God, oh God, what can I do?

She felt destitute, abandoned, hollow-chested, as though Pete had cut her heart out and left a gaping hole.

"I . . . I can't say anything. Please, please don't let Kate ever find out," she whispered to herself.

The moldy odor of the matted, rotting leaves and grass by the water's edge began to assault her, and instead of hearing joyful cooing of a couple of woodpeckers between rat-tat-tats on the big Chinese elm nearby, she heard it as mournful wails. What was that song her mother always liked? She had a cassette of Hank Williams, some old guy who sang sad songs and drunk himself to death a long time ago, and her mother would sit on the porch like a great smelly lump of decaying meat for hour after hour and listen to it:

> *"Ya ever see a robin weep,*
> *when leaves begin to die?*
> *Like me he's lost the will to live,*
> *I'm so lonesome I could cry."*

And her mother would sing along with it and change the last word every time: *I'm so lonesome I could die.*

I'm so lonesome I could die, Donna thought. But I don't want to die. I don't want to die. Oh God, oh God, oh God, I don't want to die. I don't want to go back on heroin. I don't want to be anywhere but here.

There was a Catholic priest who used to come around the reservation years ago. He'd come to the shacks of the poorest Indians and tell them to have faith and believe in the salvation of Jesus Christ.

Donna had been nine or ten then, and she and Louise would go to the church on Longmore Road on Sunday mornings, because after mass there would be cookies and cakes baked by some of the white ladies who lived nearby. The priest had come by one Friday afternoon, and her father had been mean drunk, the way he sometimes got when even a quart of muscatel and a can of hair spray couldn't mask his realization that he was a gutter bum without hope or a future or even a past that had more significance than a puff of wind. The priest had berated him for being drunk around his children, so he had punched the priest a vicious blow to his thin stomach and thrown him off the porch. The man had gotten up slowly, dusted off his threadbare black coat, and limped away to his car.

Donna had wanted to keep going to church. She liked to hear how baby Jesus had been born as poor as she was and how if you believed in him everything would be fine and you'd be happy someday. And she wanted the cookies and cake. But she couldn't ever go again. Her father said he'd beat her if she did. These past two Sundays, going to church with Kate, had been wonderful. She hadn't forgotten—

Jennifer ran up to Donna, breaking into her reverie. She was holding a baby duck in her hands, close to her chest. "Can we take her home" she said.

"No, I don't think that would be nice. I think she's too young, and she needs to be with her mommy just like you do."

"Okay," Jennifer said, her voice sad. She squatted and put it on the ground and watched it waddle away. "Bye-bye, baby ducky," she called out.

"Come on, honey, let's go inside and have a snack, okay? Then we can go over to the park and go on the merry-go-round."

"Oh, goody." Jennifer got up and hopped up the stone steps with both feet, then skipped through the patio into the house.

Donna followed closely. She had to wash, to get rid

of the filth and the stink of Big Gun Pete. And she had to think of how to keep him from ever coming near her again.

"Hey, bro, when I tell ya I got it all set up, it's all set up," Big Gun Pete said.

Philip Wilkott pressed the telephone receiver as closely as he could to his ear, as though he didn't want any of the words to escape into the atmosphere around him. He was sitting in his private office talking on his private phone, but talking about these things on the telephone always made him feel as though his mother were listening in on the extension, as she used to do when he was in high school.

"She's the best, man, I'm tellin' ya. Just what ya like."

"How old is she?"

"Fourteen, fifteen, I dunno," Pete lied.

"She a pro?"

"Hell no, man. She's a high school kid, got a hot little box, just loves sex, man."

"Is she going to care what Grant's doing?"

"She ain't gonna care what anybody's doin', man. Just bring your dick along and she'll be happy."

"How much?"

"Five hunnerd."

"You're nuts."

"Not for this little honey, man. She's worth even more."

Phil paused, biting his lip. "Okay, but I see her first. If she isn't what you say, we split and no dough."

"Hey, man, no sweat. I ever cheat ya? But before ya touch her, ya pay."

"All right," Phil said.

"I'll be in the parking lot behind the Hilton, across from the Borgata. Nine o'clock tomorrow night."

"Okay. But if I'm not there by nine-thirty, I couldn't come."

"Hey, man, if you miss out on this, you'll never forgive yourself. I ain't talkin' no bull."

Pete put the cellular telephone down on the passenger seat of his Camaro and whooped. "Big time, baby! Big time!"

He started the engine and left the parking lot in front of the park at the corner of Scottsdale Road and Indian Bend, just five minutes from where Donna was living. He knew that it was Donna's first hit in over six months. She'd wake up and remember practically nothing. But she'd damn well remember the junk and the high, and by tomorrow night she'd need another hit so bad that she'd suck off the whole Mormon Tabernacle Choir for a nickel bag. That's one thing Pete could always count on: once a junkie, always a junkie. A hype can be off the shit for a month, a year, three years, but just one hit and she's hooked again.

Big Gun Pete felt good. He drummed on the steering wheel and mouthed the words to the Ice-T rap song playing loudly on the radio. Donna would be good for twenty or thirty times before she got so burned out on H again that she wasn't good for anything but the niggers. Let's see, thirty times five hundred is fifteen thousand dollars. Damn! That's real money. He had always been good at making money. His mama didn't raise no fool.

"You haven't forgotten about the luncheon?" Philip Wilkott's secretary spoke through the office door, which she had opened just a crack. Her name was Sherry something or other, and she was twenty-three years old, divorced, reasonably attractive, tall and shapely and eager to please—very eager—but totally incapable of getting the hang of Word Perfect 6.0 for Windows. She had worked for him for less than two months, and the letters that she typed had to be redone by the pool computer operators who came in at night.

The hiring interview had been a bit awkward, unanticipated, her brushing her breasts against his shoulder when she bent over beside him to point at something on the typing test she had just taken. He had looked up at her, handsome and boyish, a little sheepish, and she had pressed her crotch against his forearm resting on the arm of his chair. He had moved his hand tentatively to the cleft of her legs and rubbed, feeling her hair through the thin silk skirt. No panties. Her eyes were dreamy. He had turned his face into her and smelled her lust, and she had quickly knelt by his chair, unzipped his pants, and attacked him like a 4-H champion milkmaid. He didn't even care that the door was unlocked. A moment like this was worth a little risk. But in the ensuing weeks he had been more careful and had always made sure that the door was locked. After all, it wouldn't be very rewarding if his father found out.

"You only have twenty minutes, Phil," she said, walking up to the front of his desk and smiling her thirsty smile at him, licking her lips slowly with the tip of her tongue. But he had no time.

She had grown rather presumptuous over the weeks, calling him Phil several times lately, even in front of some of the other lawyers in the firm. You stick your dick between a bitch's lips, and suddenly she thinks she owns you. Well, time to get a new secretary, maybe one who can type this time. Sherry was still a probationary employee—all the secretaries were for the first six months. He'd get the old hag who ran personnel to review her work and fire her for incompetence and give her a couple of thousand bucks' severance pay to ease the pain. He'd take care of it when he returned this afternoon. Right now he had to hurry. His father was always pissed off at him when he came late to the monthly partners' luncheons in the private dining room at the Phoenix Country Club.

Everyone called his father "Tom Terrific." Thomas Osborne Wilkott was the sixty-two-year-old son of Herbert Wilkott, the founder seventy years ago of the

Western Commerce Bank, which had merged and merged and merged again and was now part of the Bank of America. Herbert's wife was the daughter of the then governor of Arizona. It had been a lucrative and fortunate union. They'd had three children, Tom the youngest, and had taught them hard work, the manipulation of power, the abuse of privilege, and the use of money. What power and privilege couldn't win, money could buy. Tom Terrific was the managing partner of the second largest law firm in Arizona.

The real problem with being Tom Terrific's only begotten son was that nobody thought that Phil was terrific at all. He knew that the only thing they thought about him was that he was the son of the Republican "king maker" of Arizona, and that was all that made him someone to notice. Here in front of his father they would slap him on the back, include him in their joke telling and conversations, and make a grand show of camaraderie. But it would end when he walked out the door in two hours, and he could always imagine their malicious whispering behind his back.

Shit! The meeting was already starting. Phil walked as silently as he could to his place at the head table, where the division supervisors sat. He was the supervising partner of the Scottsdale branch office, and his place was right next to his father's, who was now standing, tapping his water goblet with a spoon to command attention and quiet. His father was pointedly ignoring him. Phil could feel his head bow slightly and his shoulders slump as he subconsciously tried to make himself unobtrusive, unnoticeable. It was an uncontrollable reflex, a "smalling" of his body that had happened to him in front of his father for years. But it was hard for Phil to hide. He was about six feet tall and athletic. He had wavy blond hair and a Ken doll face that women always fell for. He was wearing a custom-tailored gray Brioni suit, a heliotrope shirt, black silk tie, suede Gucci loafers, and a diamond-studded Patek Philippe "perpetual" wristwatch that had cost almost two hundred thousand dollars.

He walked to his chair and sat down in front of the firm's senior partner, one hundred and seven men, and two women. The two oldest cunts in the firm had been elevated to seniority after the chairman of the Arizona governor's Equal Opportunity Commission recommended to Tom Terrific that the best way to keep the U.S. Justice Department from filing a discrimination complaint was to "show nigger" just like all the other law firms were doing. Well, showing nigger around this place would have been unforgivably uncomfortable for everyone, so Tom Terrific had done the less distasteful thing: he showed cunt.

Phil blocked out his father's voice and stared in a near trance at the wineglass in front of him. Phil had had to show a little cunt in his own way: he had married one of the richest society girls in America, Amanda Cassidy. Mindy had the kind of face and body that made it essential that her father be very wealthy indeed if she had dreams of marrying a handsome man from the right family. Well, maybe not that ugly, Phil thought, but without the $328,000-a-year trust fund, she would have had to marry some poor sucker who had lost his contact lenses. Her father, whom everyone naturally called "Hopalong," was a commodities plunger in Chicago. When the price of gold had been unfixed by the government back in the mid-1970s, it had gone from something like thirty-three dollars a fine troy ounce to well over six hundred dollars. He had become fabulously rich by scraping, borrowing, and stealing enough money to pick up a few hundred thousand ounces in 1973, on an inside tip from his roommate from University of Virginia days who had become an undersecretary of the Treasury.

Mindy had gone to all the right schools, spoke French, and wore genuine emeralds, so people quickly forgot how homely she was. And at the birth of each of their sons, Mindy's father had put five million dollars into a Clifford trust for them. At least that was some consolation to Phil for having to act the happily married family man.

But she might as well have sewn up her pussy for all she wanted to use it. She hadn't spread her legs for him in months. Tonight would be better. Phil saw the fourteen- or fifteen-year-old cheerleader in his mind's eye, lying on a crisp white sheet, her legs apart, pushing her luscious pink tulip toward his face. And Grant would be there too, his lips wet and inviting, his erection as stalwart as a centurion's spear. Well, thank God there was something to look forward to. The last three years had been pretty fucking miserable.

"Where are my girls?" Kate called as she walked into the living room after school.

"Here, Mommy!" Jennifer squealed, running down the hallway from her bedroom.

Donna followed Jennifer into the living room. She was coughing and sniffling, wiping her nose with a tissue. Her eyes were a little bloodshot.

"I guess you caught a cold, huh?" Kate said.

Donna blew her nose. "Yeah, I don't know where I got it. I went swimming in the cove down there yesterday afternoon. Maybe the water was too cold."

"Maybe you'd better stay home and go to bed."

"Gee, I really hate to. I've never been to a zoo."

"There'll be a million more opportunities. I think you better nurse that cold so it doesn't get worse."

Donna looked disappointed and nodded. Kate and Jennifer left. Donna listened for the car to drive away, then sat down on the sofa. She was beginning to feel sick already, and she didn't want Kate to see her like this. She might get suspicious.

The Phoenix zoo was quite small, and Kate and Jennifer covered it from beginning to end in an hour.

They had come here before dinner because of the marvelous junk foods that were sinful not to eat at the Encanto Park carnival in downtown Phoenix. So when Jennifer finally tore herself away from the monkeys and chimpanzees and waved good-bye, they left the zoo and drove to the little carnival in Encanto Park, where the junk-food mecca lined the short midway.

Over half of the snow cone bit the dust when Jennifer forgot to hold it upright. She cried for a few seconds, then decided that cotton candy would fill the void. She ate most of it and half a box of Cracker Jacks, and Kate held her over a water fountain while Jennifer washed her face and sticky fingers. Kate dried her off with a handkerchief.

Jennifer rode the railroad train, and then she and Kate pedaled a small boat on the man-made creek around "Fantasy Island." They got out at the boat dock and started walking to the parking lot.

"Mommy, can I go on the horsies?" Jennifer asked.

They were beside the carousel, twenty feet away behind a low fence. Kate watched it going around and glanced at her watch. It was almost seven-thirty.

"It's getting kind of late, honey."

"Mommy, please," Jennifer pleaded.

Something caught Kate's eye. Among the little girls and boys on the perpetually leaping horses was a big man wearing a cowboy hat and cowboy boots, his boots touching the floor each time the palomino made a low dip. He touched his fingertips to his hat as he passed them.

"Howdy, ma'am," he called out.

She smiled at him.

"Who's that, Mommy?"

"He's a friend of mine, honey."

"How comes he's here?"

"Well, I don't know," Kate said.

The calliope music slowed and the carousel stopped. Children ran off, others began running to the horses of their choice. Kate paid a dollar to the man in the small booth and brought Jennifer to a black horse a few feet in front and to the side of the palomino. She put Jennifer on the horse and looked back coyly at Michael Fallon.

"Isn't this a far cry from a ranch in Fort Stockton, Texas, Mr. Fallon?"

"Why, heck no, ma'am," he drawled. "I come here t' take my stallion out for a ride most ever' evenin' 'bout this time."

She chuckled. "Have you been riding that bronco long?"

"Almost two hours." He winced. "My butt's killing me."

She laughed. The calliope sprang into full voice and the carousel began turning. Kate held Jennifer tightly and looked over at Mike from time to time. You are a really good-looking guy, she thought, very handsome. Or am I just seeing things, romanticizing? I've been very lonely for several months, maybe for several years. Am I seeing more in you than there really is? No, I don't think so. But, of course, it's too soon to tell. But it certainly is flattering that you would ride a carousel horse for two hours on the off chance that we'd run into you. That's a very charming thing to do, Michael Fallon.

The carousel slowed, and the "Entry of the Gladiators" stopped playing on the big speakers. Kate took Jennifer off the horse, and Mike dismounted behind them. They walked away from the carousel, and Kate stopped in the middle of the midway and turned around.

"This was very sweet of you," she said. "I'm flattered."

He shrugged, looking a bit embarrassed. "I wanted to see you again right away, make sure you weren't just my imagination."

"And?"

"And you weren't just my imagination."

She studied his face, and he was not merely a good-looking guy who knew it, hitting on her. There was unmistakable sincerity in his eyes. Wow! This is happening fast. Too fast? I don't know. But I really like this Michael Fallon. I like him a lot.

"Mommy, Mommy, we going?" Jennifer whined, pulling Kate's hand.

"Well, I reckon I'll mosey on home 'n take me a bath in some liniment," Mike said, patting his back pocket. "It's tough ridin' herd all evenin'." He smiled at Kate.

She laughed. "See you tomorrow night, cowpoke."

"Wouldn't miss it for the world, ma'am."

• EIGHT •

Donna woke up at three o'clock in the morning, and the claws had already begun to lacerate her belly. She knew the feeling well. She needed a hit, but she wouldn't. She was going to beat this. She wasn't going to lose everything.

Her bedroom was next to Jennifer's in the south part of the house. Kate's bedroom was on the north side. They were separated by the kitchen, dining room, a small guest bedroom, and living room, so Kate could hear only loud sounds from this side of the house. Donna got out of bed and stumbled into her private little bathroom. She switched the light on, propped herself straight up in front of the medicine cabinet mirror, and grimaced at what she saw. Her eyes were bloodshot, and her pupils were abnormally dilated. There was a large, livid bruise on her right cheekbone. Damn! It had only been a little red mark yesterday.

Marla, her roommate back at the Home of the Good Shepherd, had told her that you could sometimes beat off withdrawal with whiskey, at least diminish the pain and lessen its visual affects. You'd look kind of normal, but you'd be drunk, and being drunk was more normal than being strung out. She pulled out every drawer looking for makeup, but there wasn't any. All she had was the mascara and eyeshadow and lipstick that Kate had bought her last weekend at Neiman Marcus. Kate must have all of her stuff in her own bathroom.

She turned off the light, waited for her eyes to adjust to the darkness as much as they could, and tiptoed through the house to Kate's bathroom at the far end of the hallway from her bedroom door. There was also a door in the bathroom leading directly into Kate's bedroom. She crept inside and closed Kate's door. Then she realized that she couldn't risk turning the light on. She tiptoed back to the kitchen and fished under the sink for the flashlight. Back again in the bathroom she switched it on.

There were all kinds of little makeup jars on the counter, despite the fact that Kate never wore very much. Donna studied them and picked up one that was as close as she could find to her own coloring. She took it, opened Kate's door as it had been, and left the bathroom. In her own bathroom, she rubbed the makeup over the bruise on her cheek and was satisfied with the result. She tiptoed back into the living room and studied the liquor bottles on the small bar at the end of the wall unit. When her father had any money, he used to drink Four Roses. But there wasn't any here. There were several bottles, one with a label that said it was "Single Malt Scotch Whiskey."

She switched the flashlight off and waited for her eyes to adjust again. The bottle was almost full. She drank from it in three long gulps, almost vomited, steadied herself, and drank three more. The bottle was still a quarter full, and she replaced it on the bar. She tiptoed back to her bedroom, got into bed, and passed out after a few minutes.

When she awoke, her stomach burned and she had a throbbing headache. Sunshine was lemon yellow through the partially opened wood-slat venetian blinds on the window. She sat up, but pain in her head and eyes made her lie back again. She waited for several minutes until she thought that she could balance herself and stood and walked gingerly to her bathroom. She studied her face in the mirror. Not so bad, really. The bruise was well hidden. Her eyes were bloodshot, but the pupils looked normal enough. She appeared as though she had a cold or the flu, but that was all right.

She brushed her teeth, keeping her head as still as possible to keep it from throbbing. She combed her hair back into a ponytail and banded it. Then she scrutinized herself closely again and hoped that she could pull it off. She went into the bedroom and dressed in her usual Levi's and T-shirt. She opened the adjoining door to Jennifer's room, and Jennifer was snoring softly. She closed the door quietly and went into the kitchen. The little clock on the coffee pot blinked 7:26 in red LCD numbers. Good. Kate always left at 7:30. The coffee was almost gone. This was the first time that Donna had slept so late, and she had a bad cold to use as an excuse. She poured orange juice from the container in the refrigerator into a large tumbler. Kate came rushing in behind her.

"Can't be late today," she said. "Teachers' meeting. Where'd I put my keys? Oh, there they are." She took her purse and keys off the kitchen table.

Donna turned around and drank from the glass, not wanting the orange juice, but using the glass to shield her face.

Kate was already out of the kitchen. "See you at five or five-thirty," she called back. The door to the garage slammed shut a moment later. Donna spun around and vomited the orange juice into the sink. She cleaned it, then walked into Kate's bathroom. It was too fancy to have a medicine cabinet on the wall, just a big mirror covering the entire wall behind the two-sink counter.

She pulled open the drawers, and one of them was filled with drugs. One thing Donna knew about was drugs. She studied the labels and found one that read "Valium 5mg." That might do it. They just might take the headache and nausea away. Maybe she could really get through this mess. There were plenty of pills. Kate wouldn't miss a few. She took six.

In the kitchen she swallowed down two of them with a sip of orange juice, hoping that she wouldn't vomit it all up. She leaned against the sink, shuddering with the hopelessness of what she was doing. She began to weep and could not stop. Oh, baby Jesus, please help me, please help me.

When she felt sure that she wouldn't vomit again, she walked quietly into Jennifer's room. Still sleeping. She tiptoed into her own room, closed the door quietly, undressed, and took a long, cold shower. The Valium was taking hold now. She toweled off and studied her face in the mirror. Much better. Much, much better. She reapplied the makeup to her cheek, dressed, replaced the makeup in Kate's bathroom, sat down at the kitchen table, and waited for Jennifer to awaken.

By five o'clock, Donna felt as though she would die any minute. The heroin, the scotch, the Valium. She had looked at herself in the mirror every twenty minutes all afternoon, and the sight was scary. She would have to cough and blow her nose constantly, complaining of a cold, or she'd never pull it off. Luckily, Kate was going out with Mr. Fallon. She'd be home only long enough to fix herself up and change clothes.

Donna had managed to get through the day alive, despite the incredible energy and constant motion of a three-year-old girl. Donna couldn't even remember ever being as young as Jennifer, and she certainly couldn't recall being so happy.

Kate came home at twenty minutes to six and came into the kitchen, where Donna and Jennifer were eating hot dogs.

"Everything okay?" Kate asked.

Donna nodded and smiled.

"Hi, Mommy," Jennifer said gaily.

"Oooh, look at your face and hands," Kate said. "You look like you fell in a big barrel of ketchup."

Jennifer giggled. "I like ketchup."

"Okay, girls, I have to run, I'm real late."

"Bye, Mommy."

Kate hurried through the house to her bathroom. When the doorbell rang at a few minutes past six, Donna remained in the kitchen with Jennifer. They were both eating ice cream. On the third ring, Kate opened the door, Donna heard muffled sounds of greeting, Kate called out, "Be back around midnight," and the front door closed. Silence.

Thank you, baby Jesus, Donna thought. Thank you.

Kate and Mike ate hamburgers at Houston's on Scottsdale Road near Lincoln Drive and stared at each other self-consciously from time to time. They chatted idly and easily. They were both old enough and experienced enough to distinguish infatuation or puppy love from the kind of thing that was happening between them. It was happening quickly, but that's how it was sometimes.

"Was that you I read about a couple of weeks ago in the morning newspaper, about you defending that guy who raped and murdered a little boy?" Kate asked. "Or are there two Michael Fallons practicing law in Phoenix?"

"I plead guilty."

"You should."

He nodded. "I realize that it's pretty hard to understand that democracy is predicated on the core concept of curbing the government's power over its citizens, and the only way to do that is to punish it if it abuses that power."

"Yes, I do understand that. But throwing out evidence so that an animal like Henry Carpenter will probably go free because of some legal technicality isn't punishing the government, it's punishing us."

Mike shrugged. "Well, I'm a lawyer, but I'm not the

one who created that rule of law. The United States Supreme Court imposed it on the federal government about eighty years ago and then on the states almost thirty years ago. It's stood the test of time."

"Maybe the time has come to change it?"

"Lots of people think so. But I'm not sure what we could substitute in its place that would be quite as effective."

She thought for a moment, then regarded him with a wry grin. "I have it. We suppress the evidence, but if it's really strong evidence anyway, we take the guy out and shoot him."

Mike laughed. "Now, there's a real practical solution."

She nodded. "Uphold the rule of law, but make sure that the animals don't prey on any of the rest of us."

"I'll be happy to suggest it to my old constitutional law professor at ASU. Maybe he hasn't thought of it."

She smiled, absently ate a couple of French fries, then looked intently at him. "There was a time when people thought that it was their *religious duty* to punish criminals. Criminals were sinners, sinners had transgressed the moral law, and the sinner had to be flogged or imprisoned or executed if his crime was serious enough. Now it seems like we've become so . . ." she paused, "I don't even know what the right word is, theoretical? philosophical? squeamish? that we can't deal with the *criminal*. All of a sudden we're crippled up dealing with the *concept* of democracy and the *concept* of state power and the *concept* of whatever. It's like we don't believe at all that there's any God or moral law or higher truth that we have to follow."

He leaned over the small table toward her. "Why are we suddenly having a discussion about legal theory and religion? Don't you think we ought to just discuss the weather and the Academy Awards like any other normal couple?"

"No, I want to get to know you." She put her hand on his on top of the table.

He looked into her eyes and nodded. "Okay, fair enough." He paused. "I don't know about God. I went to mass every Sunday morning until I left home. Then I kind of just faded away from the church."

"I'm not talking about the church as an institution," she persisted. "I'm talking about God. I'm talking about morality. We don't seem to be guided by anything like that anymore. What happened to the central belief of everyone's lives for the last two thousand years that if we sinned against the laws of God we would be punished? It was once as simple as that, wasn't it?"

He pursed his lips and thought for a moment. "Henry Carpenter kidnapped a ten-year-old boy. The boy was cute and cheery and came from a family that loved him and cared for him. Carpenter sodomized him, cut off his genitals, and then murdered him. The medical examiner's report indicates that the cutting off happened while the boy was still alive. Where was God when He was supposed to be protecting Jimmy Dixon?"

She pulled back from him and swallowed. "Why are you a lawyer? Why do you defend garbage like that?"

"I don't know. Maybe because I can't make cabinets, I don't know how to repair engines, I start sneezing when I mow a lawn. I don't have the ability to write novels or poetry or to teach English to high school students. But let's get back to God. We all look for evidence that we ought to believe, and maybe that evidence is harder and harder to find."

"I think that God doesn't intervene in our everyday affairs," Kate said. "His spirit is always with us, and our lives and souls are in his keeping. But in everyday things God isn't involved."

Mike shook his head. "The murder of Jimmy Dixon wasn't an everyday thing, at least not for Jimmy and his parents. If God really is the source of morality

and the all-loving and all-caring protector that Father
Fitzgerald back in Fort Stockton always described in
his sermons, He should have done something for
Jimmy."

She looked at him soberly. "There's a lot more to
you than I expected."

"I've thought plenty about these things. I just have
no answers."

She smiled at him. "I do."

"Really?"

"Yes. When you walked into the courtroom on that
Monday morning, I knew that God was watching
over me."

He sat stiffly, disarmed, and studied her eyes. She
was not being flippant. She looked away, her face a
little sheepish. "Pretty hokey, huh?"

"No," he said quietly. "That's the nicest thing anybody ever said to me."

She looked back at him, her cheeks and the tip of
her nose pinkened with a blush. "I just embarrassed
myself."

"Do it again," he said.

They both laughed, softly at first, then louder, attracting the glances of several persons at nearby
tables.

"Maybe we'd better let these people eat their onion
rings in peace," she said quietly.

They walked outside and stood beside the passenger
door of his truck.

"Want to go to a movie?" she asked.

"No."

"What do you want to do?"

"Take you to my apartment."

"What would we do there, watch television?"

"We could."

"You think we would?"

"I hope not."

"You know, buster, just because I said a nice thing
to you a couple of minutes ago doesn't mean that I'll

let you ravish my body and go running off into the night. I'm way past games."

He shook his head slowly. "I won't go running off."

She stood on tiptoes and gave him a quick kiss on his lips. He pulled her to him and they kissed longer, and their breath came quick and warm.

"Hey, bro, wanna do a line?" Big Gun Pete asked.

"You got some good stuff?" said Phil Wilkott.

"Yeah, let's see what you got," Grant Felsen said from the backseat. He was short and slight with shiny brown hair, soft blue eyes, long eyelashes, and a delicate-boned face.

They were sitting in Phil's 1995 Cadillac Seville, parked behind the Hilton Hotel. Pete took a glass test tube filled with white powder out of his pocket and removed the small cork. He took out a smaller glass tube and handed them to Wilkott. Wilkott inhaled cocaine into each of his nostrils through the small tube. He passed them to Felsen in the backseat. Felsen snorted, then handed them back to Pete.

"Okay, man," said Wilkott, snapping his fingers. "Let's get it on."

He switched on the engine, and Pete directed him to Via de Frontera. It was nine-fifteen, quite dark, and the small curl of moon was insufficient to brighten the earth. The only lamps were along the path behind the homes, and the weak light didn't help very much to find the house. Pete recognized the twisted juniper planted by the front of the driveway. They parked on the street a few homes away.

"Wait here," Pete said.

He got out of the car and closed the door softly. He walked to the front of the house and peeked through the crack in the curtains drawn over the picture window in the living room. A light was on inside and he could hear the television playing, but he couldn't see anyone.

He had anticipated everything. His mama didn't

raise no fool. Yesterday he had studied the lock on the rear door into the kitchen. He had looked through the house and knew where and what the rooms were. He walked around back to the patio, climbed the four-foot stuccoed masonry wall, and walked carefully to the kitchen door. It was a standard doorknob with no safety rod, and he opened it in three seconds with his hard plastic-laminated driver's license. He put the license back in his pocket and pushed the door open. It creaked slightly, and he froze for a moment and held his breath. Nothing happened. He went inside the dark kitchen and left the door open so it wouldn't make any noise again.

He was wearing tennis shoes, and the floor was tiled cement. His footsteps made no sound. He walked toward the doorway into the living room and looked slowly around the doorjamb. Donna was sitting on the couch. Both table lamps were on as well as the television. Donna was hugging a pillow to her stomach and rocking back and forth, her face twisted in a look of agony. Pete walked up in front of her and touched her forehead.

She opened her eyes, startled, and tried to focus on him. Then she stopped rocking and her mouth fell open in shock. He covered her mouth with his hand and sat down on top of her legs, straddling her.

"Shut up!" he growled, keeping his voice low.

She nodded her head, and he slowly took his hand away.

"Anybody else home?"

"The baby," she whimpered.

"I got some more China white for ya. Straighten ya out in two minutes."

She was dizzy and nauseated and had had the sweats ten times during the afternoon and evening and three more times just since Jennifer went to bed an hour ago. She craved the heroin more powerfully than anything else in the entire world at that moment. The immediate availability of the ethereal relief that she knew would be the precious gift that the narcotic promised her was irresistible. She had lost all will to resist.

"This shit gonna set ya free," he said softly.

"No," she moaned.

He had prepared the heroin syringe an hour ago and took it out of his pocket, unwrapped it, got off the sofa, knelt at her bare feet, and injected it between two of the toes of her left foot. She stiffened and gasped a little at the pain, then became limp again. He sat down beside her and waited. Two minutes, three, eight.

"You okay now?" he asked.

"Yeah, real good," she said, her voice dreamy and distant.

He stood her up, and they walked into her bedroom.

"Undress," he ordered.

She did.

"Brush your teeth and put on some perfume."

She did.

"Get in bed. I'll be right back."

He shut the kitchen door and turned out the living room lights, leaving the television on to provide minimal illumination. He went to the Cadillac and opened the driver's door.

"Quiet," he said.

The three men walked into the house. Big Gun Pete led them into Donna's bedroom and switched on the light. Donna was lying in bed on her back, nude, her legs spread, her arms folded behind her head. She was lovely, smiling, looking dreamily at them, a freckle-faced girl with heavy breasts and a teenager's slender body.

"Pay me," Big Gun Pete said, holding out his hand.

Phil Wilkott reached into his front pocket and pulled out a folded packet of bills. "For both of us," he said, handing it to Pete.

Pete counted the money. "Fifty more for the coke."

Wilkott looked at him and frowned, then back at Donna. He reached in his back pocket, pulled out his wallet, withdrew fifty dollars, and handed it to Pete.

"She's all yours," Pete said. "Just keep it quiet. There's a baby in the next room." He pointed at the adjoining door. He left the bedroom, closed the door behind him, keeping it open just a crack, and watched.

Wilkott and Felsen both undressed, folding their clothes neatly on the upholstered chair. They turned to each other and embraced, kissing, probing each other's mouth with their tongues, and stroking each other's penis.

Wilkott got to his knees and hungrily sucked on the smaller man's huge penis.

"Come on," Felsen groaned, "come on, come on."

Wilkott stroked and sucked, moving his head around and around, and Felsen erupted in his mouth. They remained that way, rocking together rhythmically, savoring the orgasm for several minutes.

Felsen remained erect. He climbed between Donna's legs and buried his face in her vulva, sucking on her. She was motionless, so high on heroin that she had no consciousness of what was happening. Wilkott took a small tube of petroleum jelly out of his pants pocket and rubbed a glob of it around the end of his penis.

Felsen raised up to a kneeling position, turned Donna over onto her stomach, and lifted her hips until she too was kneeling, the back of her thighs braced against the front of his, and he entered her. Wilkott got on the bed behind them. Felsen groaned and straightened up with the entry.

"Oh yeah, oh yeah." Felsen began to gasp. He rocked with the thrusts. At the same time he plunged deeply in Donna. Suddenly she twisted her body and pulled away from him, flopping to the bed, writhing and trying to turn over on her back. He bashed her in the temple with his balled fist, and she stopped moving, her eyes closed. He lifted her to him again.

Big Gun Pete closed the door quietly. He felt queasy. Damn, what a couple of perverts! He walked into the living room to watch TV.

Mike sat languidly at the intersection of Camelback and Scottsdale roads, waiting for the light to change.

"That was terrific," she said dreamily, looking over at him. "The earth moved."

He laughed. "It'll even be better when we get synchronized."

"Yes. You were just a trifle quick."

"You know what Woody Allen says about that," Mike said. "He never has a premature ejaculation. They're all right on time."

They laughed.

He pulled his truck into the driveway. The house was dark.

"Good, Donna's asleep. Come on in, let's have a drink," she said.

They got out of the truck, and she unlocked the front door. She switched on the lamp beside the sofa. "I'll just check on Jennifer."

She went down the hallway, opened the bedroom door, and walked up to the small bed. Jennifer was on top of it naked. The covers were on the floor.

"What in the world?" Kate murmured, gently pushing a tangle of curls off her daughter's forehead. Jennifer moaned. Kate ran to the door, switched on the light, and ran back to the bed.

A fresh bloody bruise oozed on her forehead. She seemed to be unconscious, her breathing labored. Blood streaked her tummy and her legs and was splattered all over the sheet.

"Mike! Mike!" Kate screamed.

"Jesus," he gasped, rushing up beside her. "Oh, my God." He touched Jennifer's cheek tenderly. She let out a gurgled groan.

"Hospital, got to get her to a hospital." He turned

to Kate. She was standing lifelessly, paralyzed, her hands pressed over her open mouth.

He shook her gently by the shoulders. "Kate, Kate."

She looked at him and slowly dropped her arms.

"Kate, are you okay?"

She coughed and gasped. "Yes."

"Take her to the truck. Where's Donna? I have to see if Donna's all right."

Kate pointed at the two-way door. He waited until Kate picked up a blanket, wrapped Jennifer in it, and carried her out of the room. Then he rushed into Donna's room and switched on the light. She was sleeping under a blanket. He touched her forehead and she didn't move. She had a purplish bruise on her cheek, mostly hidden by pancake makeup, and a larger red one on her temple. He pulled the blanket back, and there was no blood, no obvious injuries. He covered her and shook her.

"Donna! Donna!"

The girl opened her eyes, blinking rapidly. Mike pulled her to a sitting position. She opened her eyes wider, trying to focus on him. They were bloodshot, weirdly dilated.

"I don' wanna," she said in an angry voice. "I gotta sleep. I don' wanna."

She fell back on the pillow and rolled on her side and passed out. Mike had no idea what was wrong with her. She must be badly hurt. Some animal had broken in and raped a three-year-old and a sixteen-year-old. Oh, my God, my God.

He wrapped her in the thin cotton blanket and brought her out to the pickup. He put her on the driver's seat and got in, pushing her to the middle. Her head lolled back on the top of the seat.

Kate was sobbing hysterically, her face buried in Jennifer's blanket. Mike backed the truck out of the driveway, screeching the tires, gunning it. His mind was reeling in shock and confusion, and he breathed deeply to calm himself. He knew that Scottsdale Memorial Hospital was only about ten minutes away at this time of night, and he couldn't think of any other hospital that was closer. He sped down Scottsdale Road at sixty, seventy, eighty miles an hour, slowed enough at two lighted intersections to make sure there wasn't any cross traffic as he ran the red lights, then slowed to fifty as he neared Camelback Road. There was a lot of Friday late-night traffic, since the bars had just closed at one a.m. He had to come to a stop. He looked over at Kate, and she was sitting up now, her face contorted, tears still pouring in rivulets from her chin. Jennifer and Donna were both motionless.

The light changed and he gunned the pickup once more, slowing again at Indian School Road for a red light, and running it after two cars had crossed in front of him. He was in the heart of downtown Scottsdale and turned onto Civic Center Drive with squealing, skidding tires. Blue and red blinking lights on a police car were suddenly close behind him. He floored the gas pedal and turned into the entrance to the hospital. A large neon sign said EMERGENCY, and he pulled up next to an ambulance in front of two swinging doors. He threw open his door, put his arms under Donna, pulled her with him as he backed off the seat, and lifted her out of the cab of the truck.

"Hey, buddy!" a voice boomed behind him. "What the hell kinda drivin' is that?" Mike turned to him, and the police officer's sneer immediately turned to concern. He glanced into the truck and saw Kate, sitting stock still holding Jennifer.

"Help her!" Mike said.

The policeman ran around the front of the truck. He opened the door and called out, "Ma'am! Ma'am, you need help?"

Kate shook her head vigorously, got out of the truck, and walked toward the swinging doors. The policeman ran ahead and pushed one open, holding it as Mike followed Kate inside.

The young woman sitting behind the counter had

seen too many emergencies to be stirred by this one. She was drinking coffee from a styrofoam cup and turning the pages of *Star* magazine. The door into the treatment area was controlled by a buzzer on her desk.

The policeman banged on the door. She looked at him blandly.

"There's no doctor available right now," she said. "They're all working on the accident that just came in."

The policeman was in his early forties, mostly bald with a fringe of graying black hair, stocky and medium height with a heavily jowled face and the scarred, thick eyebrows of a fighter. He leaned over the counter in front of the woman.

"You open that door!" he barked.

She practically leapt out of her chair. She held the buzzer down, and the policeman held the door open for Kate and Mike. They walked into the large room. A half dozen nurses were sitting on stools around a high counter writing in charts. Two women sat at another low counter punching away at computer keyboards. Two men in green gowns, doctors or hospital residents, were talking on telephones.

One of the nurses looked up and jumped off the stool.

"What's up, Larry?" she said to the policeman.

"You tell her," he said, turning to Mike.

"They've been beaten and raped. This one's sixteen," he said, looking down at Donna in his arms. "The baby is three." He looked over at Jennifer.

"Come with me," the nurse said in a calm voice.

She took Kate gently by the arm and walked her down a hallway into a large, empty treatment room. Mike followed. There were four beds inside. Mike laid Donna on one of them.

"Can I take her?" the nurse said to Kate, looking into her eyes.

Kate stood still, blinking her eyes rapidly. Then she nodded and handed Jennifer to the nurse. The nurse laid her on a bed. She unfolded the small blanket, stared at Jennifer, and gasped. She covered Jennifer, steadied herself, recaptured the calm look that she had to maintain to act reassuring, and turned back to Kate.

"Are you going to be all right?" she asked, peering into Kate's eyes.

Kate nodded slowly. She had stopped crying. Her face was calm, and she showed no emotion.

The nurse went to a small armchair, brought it behind Kate, went around to face her, and again stared into her eyes.

"I want you to sit down. Can you understand me?"

"Yes," Kate whispered. She backed up slowly, felt the chair seat on the back of her legs, and sat down.

The nurse walked close to Mike. "She's in bad shape," she said to him. "We've got a team that handles this kind of thing, but it'll take probably an hour for them all to get here. I'm going to get our duty gynecologist right now. Do you have any physician that you want me to call?"

Mike thought for a moment and shook his head. "I really don't know," he said quietly. "Just a minute."

"Okay, I'll be right back." The nurse left the room.

Mike knelt in front of Kate. "The doctors are coming right away. Is there a particular doctor you want them to call?"

She nodded, thought for a moment, then shook her head, her eyes glazed. "I can't remember," she gasped, her voice choked.

Mike stood up. The policeman walked up to him.

"Can you talk to me for a minute?"

Mike nodded. They walked to the far end of the room.

"What happened?" he said quietly.

"We don't know," Mike answered. "I've known her for a few weeks. We were out on a date, came home at one o'clock, found them like that. We don't know how it happened or who or anything."

"Okay, I've got to go out and call the detectives. You going to be all right?"

"Yes."

The policeman left the room, and Mike walked up beside Kate. A moment later the first nurse came into the room with another. They began taking the girls' vital signs, recording them on a clipboard. A young man walked in. He was wearing wrinkled green pajamas, a stethoscope, and a harried look. He didn't look at Mike or Kate and walked directly to Jennifer's bedside.

"How's she doing?" he asked.

"Eighty over fifty-eight, ninety-eight point six, sixty-three pulse."

"Good, good," he said. He carefully pulled away the blanket. He looked at the nurse, his face grim. "Why don't you see if they'll wait outside?"

The nurse turned around and faced Kate. "Dr. Wool is going to take care of her. She's not in any critical danger. Do you understand me?" she asked gently.

Kate nodded. Everything was in slow motion to her, as though it were happening under water. She was having difficulty catching her breath; each gasp felt thick with mucus and hurt her lungs. She heard people talking to her and heard responses and knew that they were made from her own voice only because she could feel the vibration of her vocal cords, as though someone were strumming a big bass violin up against her neck. But she understood neither the content of the questions nor her responses. Until now. Until the nurse's light blue eyes and soothing voice finally reached into Kate's heart and squeezed it and made it start pulsing regularly again.

"This is not life-threatening," the nurse said. "Do you understand me?"

Kate nodded. "Yes," she whispered.

"Perhaps it would be better if you waited outside."

Kate shook her head.

The nurse patted her hand on the chair arm. "Okay." She turned around.

The doctor leaned over Jennifer, examining her for several minutes, his body and the nurse's shielding her from Kate's and Mike's view.

"Get me a kit," he said. "I've got to take some smears. Is Murray Robertson on call?"

"Yes, I got him."

"Good. The repair can wait till he gets here. Let's get a complete blood. And while we're waiting for Robertson, let's get a cranial series. I think she's got a concussion but nothing worse."

The nurse got a small tray out of a wall cabinet and handed it to the doctor. He laid it on the bed next to Jennifer and bent over her again.

The other nurse, who had been examining Donna, walked up to the side of Jennifer's bed and faced the doctor.

"Pinpoint, non-reactive pupils, hypotensive, with a pressure of eighty-four over twenty and bradycardia."

The doctor nodded, handed the tray to the nurse beside him, and turned around.

"Are you the parents?"

"She's the little girl's mother," Mike said, "and the other girl's foster mother."

"Does the older girl have a history of drug abuse?"

Kate's head snapped up.

"Yes," Mike said. "She was a heroin addict."

The doctor walked over to Donna's bed with the other nurse and began to examine her.

Various people began moving in and out of the room. A lab technician came in carrying a large tray of syringes and test tubes. First he went to Jennifer's bedside, then to Donna's. A man came in wheeling a tall oxygen tank and put a clear mask over Donna's nose and lips and turned a valve on the tank.

A young man in a starched white uniform came in and walked up to Jennifer's bed. The nurse turned to

Kate and said, "He's taking her to X-ray now. You can go along if you want to."

Kate nodded. She and Mike followed behind the bed as Jennifer was wheeled into the radiology lab. An elderly woman with gray hair in a bun and hatchet face very gently placed Jennifer on the table and posed her in various positions while X-rays were taken. It took only a few minutes, and the young man wheeled Jennifer back to the emergency room.

Kate didn't say a word or show emotion, and Mike glanced at her fearfully from time to time.

A pleasant-looking man in his fifties, dressed in gray slacks and a muted dark and light blue plaid shirt, walked up to Jennifer's bed.

"Hi, Jane," he said to the nurse and smiled.

"Hello, Dr. Robertson." She handed him the clipboard on which she had been writing for the past hour. He studied it, nodded, and handed it back to her. He bent over Jennifer and removed the blanket.

He covered her after a moment and turned around. "I'm going to have to put a few stitches in her. She has a small tear, but it's not serious, something like the episiotomy that you may have had when she was born. Can you sign a release for me?"

Kate nodded. She was hugely relieved and burst into tears with a surge of release of the emotions that had been capped until now. She wept into her hands for a few moments, then took a tissue that Mike handed her and wiped her eyes.

She looked up at the doctor and nodded. "Yes," she said, her voice weak and low.

The nurse handed her the clipboard. Kate read the form, filled in two blanks, and signed her name.

"Okay," Dr. Robertson said. "I looked at the skull series before coming in. There's no fracture, no appearance that I can see of blood clotting at this point. She's probably only suffered a mild concussion, but that will need some follow-up testing to make sure there's no hemorrhaging and hematoma formation. I think that your daughter's going to be just fine."

Kate nodded and was able to force a small smile.

"I'm going to have a look at the other girl while they prepare Jennifer for surgery. Jane will take you over to the surgery waiting room. I'll be back to talk to you in about an hour."

"Thank you, Doctor," Kate said hoarsely. She stood up and walked slowly out of the room with Mike by her side. In the hallway she stopped and shuddered as a wave of nausea radiated through her. Mike wrapped her in his arms and hugged her until her trembling ceased. She felt weak-kneed and unsteady for a moment, then breathed deeply.

"I'm glad you're here," she said. "I couldn't have done this alone."

"Everything's going to be okay," he said. He kissed her cheek and wrapped his arm around her shoulders. They walked behind the nurse to the surgery waiting room. The nurse left, and they sat down on a cracked green naugahyde couch. They slumped, still and silent, drained of energy. Fifteen minutes, twenty minutes.

A man and woman came into the waiting room. The man was a little shorter than Mike and heavier, his paunch pressing against the white dress shirt he wore under a shiny blue polyester suit. He had blond hair, thinning and turning to gray around his ears. He appeared to be in his early fifties. The woman was tall and slender, dressed in a light gray wool suit buttoned high to her neck. She had auburn hair cut very short and was quite attractive, about Kate's age. She smiled pleasantly at Kate as they approached.

"I'm Detective John Steigman with the Scottsdale Police Department," the man said, extending his hand toward Mike. His voice was thick and gravelly. "I'm the head of the juvenile sex crimes detail. This is Janice Cooling, she's our rape crisis counsellor."

Mike stood up and shook hands with the detective.

"This is Mary Caitlin O'Dwyer. She's the little girl's mother, the older girl's guardian."

"Hello, Mrs. O'Dwyer," the detective said. "We're very sorry about what's happened. I'm delighted that the doctor says they'll both be fine."

Kate nodded.

"We need to have some information from you. Are you up to it now, Mrs. O'Dwyer?"

Kate cleared her throat. "Yes, I think so."

"The more information we have and the sooner we get it, the more chance we have to find the animal who did this."

"I understand," Kate said.

Detective Steigman pulled an armchair around and sat down facing Kate and Mike. Janice Cooling sat on the sofa next to Kate. Mike told him what had happened when they returned to Kate's house. Kate answered the detective's numerous questions about Donna Alvarez, but she knew very little.

"She almost overdosed on heroin tonight," Detective Steigman said. "Has she been back to the Salt River Reservation since she left the Home of the Good Shepherd?"

"Not that I'm aware of," Kate said. "I don't know how she'd get there. She doesn't have a car. It's too far to walk."

"Well, it's only about six miles from McCormick Ranch to the reservation. She could take a bus down Scottsdale Road and be there in twenty minutes."

Kate shrugged. "I guess so. But Jennifer hasn't ever mentioned to me, in the almost three weeks that Donna's been with us, that Donna left her during the day or that she went anywhere out of the house with Donna, except down to the lake and over to the park a few blocks from us."

"She could have met somebody. She could have taken a bus to the reservation and back while Jennifer was having a nap. Somebody could have visited her at your house."

Again Kate shrugged. "Sure, it's all *possible*. But I don't think so. I've known Donna for three months. I'd be very surprised if she did that. I think that whoever raped her must have injected her with heroin."

The detective shook his head. "I don't think so, Mrs. O'Dwyer. The injection she got today was between her toes. There's a little bruise there but no track. It's fresh. But she also has a heroin track behind her left knee that has to be at least a day old."

Kate shook her head and looked sadly at Mike. "Dear God," she murmured.

"Would you object to giving me a key to your house so I can get an ID unit out there right away, before anybody goes back and possibly contaminates the evidence? The forensics techs will be out of there in two or three hours."

"No, of course not," she said. "I want you to." She took her keys out of her purse and handed them to him.

"Good, good. They'll have to roll both of your prints for elimination. They can do that in a day or two." Steigman looked from Kate to Mike, and they both nodded.

Dr. Robertson came into the waiting room and looked toward Janice Cooling. She got up and walked across the room to him. They stood talking for a moment, their faces grave and taut. Then they came up to the sofa, and the woman sat down again next to Kate.

Kate stared at the doctor, suddenly frightened again. She felt the woman put her arm around her shoulders.

"I don't know how to say this any way other than to just say it," Dr. Robertson said. His voice was hesitant and lacked its earlier soothing steadiness. "Your daughter is fine. Her injury will heal completely with no complications. But I sent the semen that was taken from her and the other girl over to St. Luke's pathology lab for testing, and the pathologist"—he paused and cleared his throat, appearing reluctant to continue—"the pathologist is sending them on to UCLA Medical Center."

"I don't understand," Kate said.

Dr. Robertson breathed deeply. "The semen has to be tested for the presence of HIV antibodies."

Kate wrinkled her brow, looked at Mike and then back at the doctor. "Are you talking about AIDS?"

"Not exactly, Ms. O'Dwyer. If there actually are antibodies present, it means that the rapist is infected with the HIV virus but may not yet have contracted AIDS, and maybe never will."

"And the girls?" She had to choke out the question.

He paused, reluctant. "There would be a statistically high likelihood that they've been infected by HIV and could contract AIDS. We don't have the facilities here in Phoenix for a reasonably definitive test so soon after contact. I'll have a better idea this afternoon."

Kate felt as though someone had crushed her body with a sledgehammer. And then she felt nothing.

· NINE ·

Michael Fallon had no idea what to do to help Mary Caitlin O'Dwyer. Probably there was nothing that he could do but be there for her when she woke up. It sickened him to watch two orderlies lift her into the hospital bed in the neuropsychiatric ward of the hospital and immobilize her ankles and wrists tightly to the bed frame with leather restraints. Just precautionary, they had told him, so that she wouldn't hurt herself. But it nonetheless brought back visions of old movies in which the maniacs or alcoholics or innocent victims were trussed up in straitjackets.

Mike went down the elevator to the all-night cafeteria and changed several dollars for quarters. He went to the bank of pay phones in the hospital lobby, called Boston, and got the telephone number for Brendan O'Dwyer in Manchester by the Sea. He glanced at his watch: two-thirty. Just four-thirty or five-thirty back East. Was it daylight savings yet? He hesitated. What a hell of a wakeup call. Well, they have to know.

"Yeah?" a very tired voice said.

"I'm trying to reach Brendan O'Dwyer."

"Not at this time o' the mornin'." A thick brogue.

"Are you Mr. O'Dwyer?"

"I'm the houseman. I can't wake himself up at this time o' the mornin' and not get meself skewered."

"I'm calling from Phoenix. His daughter and granddaughter are both in the hospital."

A gasp. "Oh, me God. Are they bad?"

"No, no. They'll both be okay. But I think I'd better talk with Mr. O'Dwyer."

"I'll get him, sure."

Mike stood waiting for what seemed like forever. The operator asked him to deposit two more dollars, and he did.

"Who is this?" The voice was thick and fearful.

"Mr. O'Dwyer?"

"Yes."

"My name is Michael Fallon. I'm a good friend of your daughter's. There's been a—a—ah—" he stuttered, not knowing exactly what to say, the truth seeming much too much for a telephone call at four-thirty or five-thirty in the morning—"she's been in an accident. She's going to be fine. Both Kate and Jennifer are in the hospital here." Pause. He swallowed. "Jennifer's a little worse than Kate."

There was silence for a moment, then muffled sounds of him speaking with someone.

"What's 'a little worse' mean?"

Mike breathed deeply. "Well, I'm no doctor, Mr. O'Dwyer. But they are going to be okay."

"How long will they be hospitalized?"

"I think more than a couple of days."

"All right. My wife and I will be there on the first plane. What hospital are they in?"

"I'll be happy to pick you up at the airport."

"That's not necessary."

"Well, I think I *should*. We can talk a little more about the accident before you see her."

Pause. "Are they disfigured? Was there a fire or something? Were you involved?"

"No, no, Mr. O'Dwyer. I'm trying *not* to frighten you, but I'm doing a terrible job of it."

"Just tell me what happened, God damn you!" The bellow through the telephone receiver hurt Mike's ear. He knew that the father was right. He had a right to know.

"Mr. O'Dwyer, Jennifer was raped by someone. We don't know who. Kate is being treated with some anti-depression medicine, and it may take a little while for both of them to come out of it."

There was a long silence. Murmurs, a thin scream, muffled conversation.

"My houseman is making us reservations right now." His voice was very small and weak. "Give me your phone number. I'll call you right back."

Mike leaned against the wall and waited for the phone to ring. He stuffed his hands deep in the pockets of his Levi's and stiffened his body. Exhaustion had suddenly enveloped him like a hard, high wave on a beach that knocks you down and throws you around, and you can't fight against it.

The phone rang, and he jerked up straight and picked up the receiver.

"We're arriving on TWA at twelve-seventeen. How will we recognize you?"

He thought for a moment. "I'll hold up a sheet of paper in front of me with Mike on it."

"Okay. I appreciate what you're doing, Mike." He hung up.

Mike left a note on the swing-arm tray in Kate's room, telling her that he would be back at about one o'clock Saturday with her parents. He drove home. He twisted and turned on the bed for two hours and finally fell into troubled, restless sleep.

Brendan O'Dwyer was huge, six foot three or four and probably two hundred seventy-five pounds. He was dressed in black wool slacks and a white dress shirt, carrying a camelhair overcoat over his shoulder. He had ruddy cheeks and Kate's green eyes and thinning gray-sandy hair cut short. Catherine O'Dwyer was tall and a bit heavy around the middle. She was wearing a navy blue wool skirt and a baby blue cashmere sweater. Her hair was Kate's, thick and strawberry blond, and Jennifer's blue eyes came from her.

"This is Gwen McLemore," Brendan O'Dwyer said, introducing the young woman who was with them. "She's been Kate's best friend since high school."

She held out her hand to Mike and shook his hand firmly. "Nice to meet you, Michael," she said in a pronounced Irish accent.

Gwen was pretty, even wearing no makeup, and wore a navy blue wool business suit and black flats.

"I'm very sorry," Mike said, looking at Brendan, "but I only have a pickup truck, and I don't think we'll all fit. I didn't realize there'd be three of you."

"Is it a big pickup?" Gwen asked.

Mike nodded.

"Well, we'll all squeeze in, don't you worry," she said.

As soon as they got into the truck, Mike told them the truth about Jennifer, that there was a possibility of HIV infection. They were all morbidly silent for the entire twenty minutes it took to drive from Phoenix Sky Harbor Airport to Scottsdale Memorial Hospital.

He had called the hospital when he woke up at eleven o'clock, and the operator had told him that Mary Caitlin O'Dwyer had been released earlier. Mike knew where she would be.

When Kate saw her parents and Gwen McLemore, she leapt up from the chair, and all four of them hugged and burst into tears. They cried themselves out, not speaking a word, and walked up to Jennifer's bedside.

"They gave her some painkillers," Kate said. "She's okay. She talked to me an hour ago. She really can't remember anything about what happened. The guy must have hit her on the head and then did what he did. She's hurting from the stitches the doctor put in her, but that's all."

"Thank God she can't remember," Catherine O'Dwyer said.

They stood silently, watching Jennifer sleep peacefully. Mike stayed near the door, not wanting to intrude on the family.

"Without him," Kate said, looking over at Mike, "I don't know what I would have done. Probably dropped dead on the spot."

Her father and mother turned toward him, and their faces were much softer than before. Mike felt himself blushing, his skin tingling. This was a terrible place and a miserable way to meet a girl's parents.

"Is there someplace here to get something to eat, Mary Kate?" her mother asked. "Your father's diabetes, you know. He hasn't had a bite all day."

"I'm all right, Catherine."

"No, you're not, Brendan. I don't want you getting sick, too."

He frowned.

"I don't know," Kate said.

"There's a cafeteria downstairs," Mike said.

"I'm going to stay here with Jennifer," Kate said. "I couldn't eat anything, anyway."

"I'll stay with you, darlin'," Gwen said.

"We'll be right back," said her mother. She took her husband's hand, and they walked to the door.

"I'll stay, too, if you don't mind," Mike said.

Catherine O'Dwyer smiled gently at him and nodded. They left the room.

Mike walked up beside Kate. "You okay?"

She looked at him and tears filled her eyes. She shook her head. He took her in his arms and hugged her, and she wept softly.

"What about Donna?" Mike asked.

Kate wiped her eyes with a handkerchief. "Police came and got her. Violation of the conditions of her release. They took her to Black Canyon."

"Jesus Christ."

"There wasn't anything I could do," Kate said and shrugged. "And there wasn't anything I wanted to do."

Mike nodded. "But she's the only one who can tell

us who did this. If she's stuck in there, she may not be willing to talk."

Kate gave him a fierce look. "I'm certainly not bringing her back into my home."

"Listen, Kate," he said as soothingly as he could, "we don't even know what happened, what role Donna had in it. I want the police to get the animal who did this, and she's the only way."

Kate was quiet for a moment. Then, "The semen they took from Donna wasn't from the same man as what they took from Jennifer."

"What?"

"Yes. The doctor told me. And there were no signs of forced entry at the house, Detective Steigman said. That means that there were at least two men, and Donna must have let them in."

Mike rubbed his chin and mouth hard to press back a feeling of nausea.

"Detective Steigman is coming back at four o'clock," she said. "He was with the officers who arrested Donna, and he came up here to bring my keys back. He said they'd interrogate Donna and try to get her to talk."

"She's going to be withdrawing from heroin. She isn't going to talk to anybody."

Kate nodded. Her shoulders slumped. "I know. But maybe after a few days."

The three of them stood watching Jennifer gently sleep.

"Why?" Kate gasped. "Why Jennifer?"

Gwen turned to her and took both of her hands. "Remember what I always used to quote to you: 'I expected good things, and evils are come upon me,'" she recited in a soft voice. "'I waited for light, and darkness broke out. My inner parts have boiled without any rest.'"

"I never knew how true those words were."

Gwen held her at arm's length and looked hard into

her eyes. "It is now you must seek Him, Mary Kate. Don't shut Him away at this hard time."

"How could He let anyone do this?" Kate said. Tears fell on her cheeks.

" 'Who is on my side against the wicked?' " Gwen recited. " 'Who will stand up for me against the evildoers? . . . My God is my rock and refuge. He will repay the wicked for their injustice; the Lord our God will destroy them for their misdeeds.' "

Kate wiped her eyes and looked at Gwen. "Will He?"

"Believe that He will, Mary Kate. Believe on Him."

Mike was a little puzzled by the intensity of the religiousness, but he assumed that Gwen McLemore must belong to some religious order: the very short hair, no makeup, a business suit that did nothing to show off an obviously very nice figure, simple flat black slip-on shoes. And anyway, why should he be surprised by it? The first time that he and Kate had been out together, she had talked about God.

He pulled up the two blue naugahyde chairs that were in the room, and Kate and Gwen sat down on them. He got the small metal stool from the other side of the bed, brought it next to Kate, and perched on it. They were subdued, silently watching Jennifer sleep, adrift on their own thoughts.

I could easily become catatonic, Kate thought, just slip out of this horrible reality into a self-imposed netherworld. Gwen and I could go there together to find peace. Maybe Mike would come, too. She sighed deeply and pressed her eyes tightly shut. I can't take any more of this, God. I can't stand any more. Please protect Jennifer. Please make Jennifer well.

Detective Steigman came into the hospital room at a few minutes after four. He was obviously exhausted, his face creased and jowly, sagging like his shoulders, his hazel eyes the only thing about him that had any shine.

"This is Detective John Steigman, Dad," Kate said. "He's the chief policeman on this."

Her father shook his hand, studying him. Their eyes met, and O'Dwyer nodded, his clenched jaw relaxing.

"Looks like you've had a hell of a day," Brendan O'Dwyer said.

"Nothing like yours, sir," said Steigman. "I'm truly sorry."

O'Dwyer nodded. "This is my wife, Catherine, and this is our very good friend Sister Gwen McLemore."

Gwen nodded at him and smiled briefly. Catherine walked up to him, shook his hand, and smiled as best she could.

"I'm sorry, ma'am."

She nodded. "I know."

Jennifer was awake, feeling very little pain, playing with two dolls that Mike had gone to the house to pick up.

"Let's talk out in the hall," the detective said.

"I'll stay here with Jennifer," Catherine said.

Kate and Mike and Brendan O'Dwyer and Gwen followed him out of the room.

"The girl isn't talking," Steigman said. "She's in the detoxification unit over at the Juvenile Detention Center and says the only way she'll talk is if we give her a fix. We can't do that."

"How about other drugs?" Kate asked.

"She'll get them, but we can't question her while she's drugged. It's an illegal interrogation."

"So what?" Brendan O'Dwyer said. "At least you'd find out who did it."

"And then what would we do, sir? We couldn't arrest him or charge him with a crime. Any judge would throw the case out as the result of an unconstitutional interrogation."

Kate's father frowned and gritted his teeth.

"Do you have any ideas?" Mike asked.

Steigman nodded. "After the girl cleans up, I think Mrs. O'Dwyer should go to visit her, see if she'll talk."

Kate shook her head. "I don't ever want to go near her again."

"I can't blame you, Mrs. O'Dwyer. But whoever did this is out there probably going to do it again. This kind of child rapist is the most dangerous of all criminals. They have a compulsion that they can't overcome."

Kate breathed deeply and shook her head. "How long before she is going to be off the addiction again?"

"Usually four days."

Kate chewed on her lip, then nodded. "All right, I'll try. I don't promise I can go look her in the eye, but I'll try."

"Thank you, Mrs. O'Dwyer. It's the right thing to do, believe me."

Dr. Robertson came into the room an hour later to check on Jennifer. Mike, Brendan and Catherine left and waited in the hallway. Only Kate and Gwen remained. After a few minutes the doctor opened the door and came out to them. Kate was inside by the window, staring out, crying. Gwen's arm was wrapped around her shoulders.

"The pathologist at St. Luke's sent the semen from both Jennifer and Donna and specimens of both of their blood to the UCLA Medical Center for testing early this morning," Robertson said. "There's a very new test for detecting the HIV virus that's still experimental, administered only in a few highly specialized labs throughout the country, but we believe that it's dependable. And it gives us immediate results that the PCR test can't. I just got a call from the senior pathologist at UCLA. He says that Donna is okay, but Jennifer's blood tested positive."

Mike stood paralyzed. Brendan O'Dwyer let out an explosive breath and began to cough. Catherine walked to her daughter and Gwen and stood beside them at the window. She put her face in her hands and wept.

"Is it a certainty?" Mike asked, regaining his equilibrium.

The doctor shook his head slowly. "No. The only thing certain is the presence of HIV in the semen taken from Jennifer and not in the semen from Donna. But it's very difficult to diagnose HIV in the earliest stages, especially with infants, and we haven't used this particular test long enough to have statistics on it, particularly for a three-year-old like Jennifer. We'll only know for certain in six months. We'll test her with the ELISA test and confirm it with the Western Blot. They're conventional and conclusive. Then we'll know for sure."

"And if she *is* positive?" Mike asked.

"Then she has at least an eighty percent probability of contracting AIDS within the next few years." Murray Robertson gritted his teeth and his voice lowered. "Maybe as high as a hundred percent."

Kate's parents rented two suites at the Phoenician Resort, one for Kate and Gwen. They spent the days and evenings in the hospital room with Jennifer until she was released three days later. Mike spent the evenings at the hospital as well.

When Kate brought her home and put her in her own bed, she had a sudden feeling that neither of them would ever be safe in this house, even though at Detective Steigman's suggestion she had had dead bolts installed on all three doors and heavy steel locks on the sliding windows. She tried to fight back the fear as irrational, but she couldn't.

"I'd better keep her in bed with me tonight," she whispered to Mike.

"I know how you feel, like you never want to let her out of your sight again," Mike whispered. "But remember what the doctor said. She's barely three years old, she's never going to have any memory of

what happened, and she was almost certainly unconscious anyway. He said that it's best for her to wake
up in her own room with her own dolls and toys all
around."

Kate sighed and nodded. She put Cynthia and Harriet and Raggedy Ann on the pillow around Jennifer's
face. She and Mike quietly left the bedroom, leaving
the door open.

When Mike left the house that evening, Brendan
O'Dwyer walked out the front door with him. They
shook hands, and Kate's father's eyes became wet
with tears.

"You take care of them," he said. "We all have to
leave tomorrow. We're counting on you."

Mike nodded. "I'll take care of them."

Kate's father kissed him on the cheek and walked
back into the house.

The O'Dwyers went back to the Phoenician for
their last night in Scottsdale. Gwen had brought her
suitcase from the hotel to the house earlier in the
afternoon so that she could stay in the guest room this
night. Kate needed her, and Brendan and Catherine
didn't want Kate to be alone in the house.

Coming back to the place where her daughter had
been attacked had affected Kate visibly all evening.
She fidgeted and jumped at every sound. She sat on
the sofa with Gwen, trying to get her mind off Jennifer, talking about Boston, "the good old days" back
at Saint Mary's.

Gwen got the bottle of scotch from the bar and
two glasses.

"Here, it'll calm you down, Mary Kate." She poured
two fingers in a tumbler and handed it to her, then
poured some for herself.

"How did you do it, Gwen? How did you live
through it?" Kate asked, looking mournfully at her
closest friend.

Gwen shrugged. "I don't know. I just did. That's all

you can do when somethin' horrible happens, just live through it day by day. I don't have any special secret. No one does."

"Where is God, Gwen? Where was God when this happened?" She began to cry.

Gwen shook her head. "I can't answer you. I just know that as I get older, I become even more certain that there is a lovin' God and our lives are in His hands. But that's a matter of faith, Mary Kate. I guess that I *need* to believe and *want* to believe. But if you're lookin' to me for *evidence*"—she shook her head—"I haven't got it. I just haven't got it."

Kate dried her eyes and gulped what was left in her glass. She poured it half full with scotch and took another gulp.

"She's going to get AIDS, Gwen," she whispered, as though just saying the word brought on a terrible curse. "My three-year-old baby will die of AIDS." She looked at the nun, wanting desperately to be contradicted, consoled, anything. Tears once again fell on her cheeks.

Gwen could offer nothing but her own tears. She hugged Kate and they wept.

• TEN •

Today Kate saw Scottsdale as a hostile place. It was flat and arid, colored by trees and flowers made possible only by copious irrigation. Without herculean manmade efforts to pastel the sere brown landscape, it would be as blanched as other infamous desert places, Death Valley, or the sand dunes that stretch for mile after mile west of Yuma, Arizona. But billions of dollars and the stubborn will of some of the wealthiest people in America had metamorphosed Scottsdale into a lush oasis of rich homes and expensive shops.

She left Scottsdale and entered Phoenix, and the opulence petered out as she drove from east to west. Then she turned north on Interstate 17, the Black Canyon Freeway, and she entered an ugly, sun-scorched land of piled rocks and desolate hills where irrigation was obviously unknown and the scant rains of summer provided only enough nurture for a few scraggly weeds.

This is the right place for a juvenile corrections center, she thought, a prison for the desolate children who are society's weeds, whose lives are as fallow and fruitless as the land. Forsaken by their parents, abandoned by society for their miscreant conduct, this is their final step until they reach adulthood, if they are so lucky—or unlucky.

She parked in the lot outside the administration building. She had not wanted to come visit Donna

Alvarez, but Detective Steigman had called her four times in the past week asking her to make the trip. Mike had also urged her to go. It was the only way, he had said. And she knew that it was.

Steigman had called the director of the facility and told him the purpose of the visit. The detective requested that she be permitted to meet with the girl in a private room, not in the noisy, crowded visiting room. It wouldn't be conducive to the purpose of this visit. Kate was shown to an interview room reserved for attorneys, and moments later a matron escorted Donna into the room and left her alone with Kate.

Donna's fair complexion was almost gray. Her cheeks were hollow, and the skin under her eyes puffy and swollen with the ravages of heroin withdrawal. She stood, averting her eyes, in front of the small wooden table at which Kate was sitting.

"Please sit down, Donna," Kate said, forcing her voice to be strong and steady.

Donna sat down without looking at Kate.

"I want to talk to you about what happened."

Donna pulled her thighs up to her chest and braced them up with her heels on the edge of the chair. She hugged her legs and laid her face against them, looking to the side.

"Donna, you need to tell me what happened."

"The cops already asked me."

"You wouldn't tell them."

"Why should I? What'd they do for me?"

"I'm not the cops. And I did a lot for you."

Donna sighed and turned her face to Kate's. "I'm sorry what happened. I never loved anybody like I love you and Jennifer, and nobody ever loved me like you."

Kate had a lump in her throat that made her unable to speak.

"It wasn't my fault he did that. I didn't let him in. He must have picked the lock on the back door. Then he shot me up with heroin."

"There was more than one," Kate said.

Donna stared at her. "No, uh-uh. One guy."

"And that wasn't the first time you'd taken heroin in my house. You had at least one fix a day or so before."

"He forced me. He would've hurt me. I've seen what he did to other girls."

"Who?"

Donna looked at her and shook her head. Her voice became sullen. "When I get out of here, I don't go back to your house and be nice and clean. You don't want me anymore. I go back to the reservation, and I have to live. I have to survive somehow. How do I live a day if I snitch him off? He's a big man. He's a mean man. He'll burn holes in my face, and I'll end up in an irrigation ditch."

"They'll put him in prison, and he won't be able to hurt you or anyone."

She frowned. "No, they won't. He'll get out of it. He'll say I'm just one of his whore junkies, and it's true. Who'd believe me? You don't even believe me."

"But it's not only you. It's Jennifer."

She looked oddly at Kate. "Jennifer?"

"Yes. They took the semen from Jennifer, and the doctors say they can prove exactly who the man is by special tests they use."

"What?"

Kate studied the girl's face. She had known her long enough to know that she was genuinely bewildered.

"You don't know about Jennifer?"

"No."

"The police didn't tell you about her?"

Donna shook her head.

"She was raped that night."

Donna's mouth fell open. "Oh, God. Oh no, oh no, oh no." She began to cry. "I didn't know. I swear I didn't know. All I remember is getting the shot. He loaded me up so high, I can't remember anything."

"There were at least two men. The semen in you

wasn't the same as the semen in Jennifer." She
paused. "And the man who raped Jennifer has
AIDS."

"Oh, God, no." Donna wept for several minutes.
Then she put her feet on the floor and leaned slightly
toward Kate. "And me?"

Kate shook her head. "You're okay."

"Oh, God, I'm sorry, I'm sorry." Donna put her
elbows on the table and hid her face in her hands.

"You must tell me who the man is who gave you
the heroin."

Donna swallowed. "I can't, I can't. He'll kill me.
And whoever else it was, I don't even know. They'll
kill me."

"Please tell me, Donna. Please."

Donna shook her head. "I have to live. I have to
live when I get out of here." She pressed her lips
together in a hard line and stared down at her arms
folded on the table.

Kate's anger and frustration and agony over the
past week suddenly roiled together, and she felt as
though the top of her head were about to explode.
She couldn't hold anything back anymore. She swung
her open hand as hard as she could across Donna's
face. She grabbed Donna's hair and pulled her face
down to the table.

"God damn you! God damn you. All you do is
worry about yourself, and you killed my daughter."

"Stop, stop," Donna pleaded.

"Tell me, God damn you! Tell me!"

"Okay. Please don't hurt me."

Kate relaxed her hold on Donna's hair.

"Big Gun Pete on the reservation. That's all I know.
That's all I ever called him."

The door swung open, and the matron came into
the room. "What's the ruckus in here?" She looked
at Donna and then angrily at Kate.

Kate let go of Donna, got up abruptly, and walked
out of the room.

*   *   *

Kate had taken a week's leave from teaching at Saint Daniel's Academy. It was Friday afternoon, Jennifer was at Merry Moppets, and Kate was too agitated to go home and sit. She got off the Black Canyon Freeway at McDowell Road. She drove several blocks and parked in the structure next to the Phipps Tower, across the street from the Maricopa County Courthouse in the heart of downtown Phoenix.

She found Michael Fallon on the directory on the wall in the lobby and took the elevator to the third floor. The hallway was brown linoleum curling up along the baseboards. Dull fluorescent lighting overhead did little to diffuse the dingy darkness. The air was polluted with the odor of floor wax and stale cigarette smoke. The doors had smoked glass with a name in plain black letters and an opened skylight, like entrances into shabby rooms where Sam Spade and Jake Giddes or far sleazier types developed photos taken through the cracks of windows of wives cheating on husbands or husbands on wives.

Near the end of the hallway a door was open, flooding that piece of the corridor with light filled with floating dust motes. She looked tentatively inside. Mike was sitting in a secretarial chair at a small metal table, tapping away at a computer keyboard and staring at the screen.

"Hi," Kate said, walking into the small office.

"Hi," he said, swiveling his chair around. "What're you doing downtown?"

She sat down on the metal folding chair in front of his small oak desk strewn with papers.

"I've decided to sell the house," she said. "I just don't feel safe anymore. Those animals could come back."

Mike nodded. "Well, I don't think so, and the dead bolts should keep anyone out. But I can sure understand how you feel."

"I talked to a realtor yesterday. She said the market was real weak right now. I told her to try anyway. She's coming over tomorrow afternoon with the listing papers, and they'll put a sign up."

Mike nodded.

"I was just out to see Donna."

That brought him out of the chair. "Are you okay?"

She shrugged. "I feel really guilty about her. She says some guy picked the rear door lock and forced her to take the heroin. Maybe it's true. Is there any way we can ever know?"

"Possibly, if he picked it with something metal, a knife or screwdriver, there should be fresh marks. The police said there weren't any. If he used a credit card or plastic something or other, there may be tiny bits of it that could be recovered. Do you want me to ask Steigman to have their ID people go over it again?"

She thought for a moment and nodded.

"Did she talk?"

"Yes. His name is Big Gun Pete, and she says that he's the only one she knows was there. He lives on the Salt River Reservation."

"Great!" Mike sat down at his desk and punched numbers on the telephone. "Detective Steigman, please. This is Michael Fallon." He waited.

"John?"

"Yeah, how're you doing, Mike?"

"Okay. Listen, Kate was just out to juvenile corrections and talked to Donna Alvarez. She says the only one she remembers is Big Gun Pete. He lives on the reservation."

"Nobody else?"

"No."

"Okay. He should be easy enough to identify. I'll call the Indian police."

"Kate would also like you to send forensics back out to her place."

"What's up?"

"Donna swears the guy picked the lock on the kitchen door, she didn't let him in voluntarily."

"That's possible, I guess. It wasn't a safety tongue. Someone who knew what he was doing could open it in ten seconds with a credit card."

"Maybe there's some residue that they can recover, test against this Pete's cards if he has any, or something laminated. You can add burglary to the rape, stack him."

"Okay, good. I'll have ID call her. Tell her not to use the kitchen door until they've been out there again. And tell her thanks about Donna."

Mike replaced the receiver. "The forensics people will be calling you."

She nodded. "You coming over tonight?"

"Of course I'm coming over."

"I need one of your guns." She looked steadily at him.

He wrinkled his brow and studied her. "Who are you going to shoot?"

"Anybody who ever comes into my house again without my permission."

He nodded. "Fair enough. Ever shoot a gun?"

She shook her head. "But I heard that it's legal to have one here."

"Yes, and you can also get licensed to carry it concealed by going to a sixteen-hour training course."

"I don't need that. I'm not going to carry it around in my purse or my corset. I just want to have it at home in case I need it."

He nodded slowly. "Which one do you want?"

"The small one. I don't even know if I could shoot the big one."

"Okay, we'll go out this weekend to one of the shooting ranges, and I'll teach you. It's really very easy."

"Thanks." She got up from the chair and glanced at her watch. "Maybe you'd like to come over now? I don't have to pick Jennifer up until five."

He studied her. "You feeling better?"

"Not much, but I really need you," she said softly.

"Thank God," he said. He looked reluctantly at the computer monitor. "But I'm in the middle of a motion to reduce somebody's bond. I've got to get it filed this afternoon."

"What's he in jail for?"

"Burglary. He's a heroin addict. Broke into six poor people's houses out in Guadalupe. Two prior convictions. Judge slapped a twenty-two-thousand-dollar bond on him."

"How much could he actually post?"

Mike shrugged. "Probably nothing. I'm trying to get him released no bond."

"Will the judge do it?"

"No, but it's my job to try."

"Under these circumstances, can't it wait until Monday?"

He looked at her, and the suffocating grief that had enshrouded her for a week had begun to fall away. She was obviously coming to grips with what had happened and realizing that she either had to live *with* it or die *from* it. Her light green eyes had some of their luster back; her alabaster skin had a pinkish glow instead of an ashen pall. She had shed the Levi's and floppy shirts and sandals that she had worn all week and was dressed in a kelly green tight wool skirt and a mint green silk blouse that contoured her breasts.

"Yeah, I think Skeeter Morales can wait until Monday," Mike said.

John Steigman called the Salt River Pima-Maricopa Reservation Police Department. He had dealt with the chief, Henry Manuelito, a dozen times over the years. Felonies committed on the reservation were under the jurisdiction of the federal government, the business of the FBI, not the various city police departments around Maricopa County or the county sheriff. But when an Indian committed any crime off the reservation, it did fall into the jurisdiction of the sheriff or the police. In those cases, whether from legal necessity or reciprocity or just etiquette, no cop went on the reservation to arrest anybody without being accompanied by Henry Manuelito or one of his officers.

"How they hangin', John?" Henry asked.

"Down to my knees."

"Yeah, I heard. All the whores down at the Pussy Bar and Grill say you're the best-hung cop in Scottsdale."

Both men cackled maliciously. The ceremonial preliminaries over, Steigman turned to business.

"I'm about to get a warrant on a Big Gun Pete, lives out in your neck of the woods. You know him?"

Chief Manuelito snorted. "We all know him. If it's bad, he owns a percentage of it. What's the beef?"

"Right now it's rape. Maybe burglary. Maybe attempted murder, if his semen makes a match."

"Who's the victim?"

"Donna Alvarez. She was living with a nice family up at McCormick Ranch. Knew the guy from before."

"Yeah, Donna's a hype, been hustling for a couple of years to support the habit. I never busted her for it. I figured it was better for her to suck a few dicks than break into houses and go to prison for burglary. Anyway, I always felt sorry for her. She comes from pure shit. I had her old man in my pen here four hundred times. But Donna's not a bad kid, real pretty." He paused. "But from what she came out of, she never had a chance."

"What's her connection to this Pete?"

"He runs a few whores, sells dope. Where she lived is only a half mile from his place."

"You got an address?"

"No, there aren't any addresses over there on Thomas Road."

"How about a last name for my warrant?"

Manuelito thought for a minute. "I think it's Supremas, S-U-P-R-E-M-A-S. Nobody knows for sure, he may not even know, but that was his father's name, or the guy who thought he was his father. I'll give you a description for your warrant so it won't matter what his name is. Twenty-five to twenty-seven, five foot nine, two-ten or two-fifteen, acne scars, black and black, hair in braids, you know, like those Jamaican singers."

"Dreadlocks."

"Yeah, yeah, right."

"Any priors?"

"I don't think the guy's ever been nailed hard. The feds picked him up on possession for sale a couple of years ago, maybe three, but he beat it on a bad search. He's been popped for drunk driving once that I know of. Couple busts for receiving the earnings of a prostitute. That's about it."

"All right. I'm going over to file a complaint and get the arrest warrant now. You planning to be around in about an hour?"

Henry looked at the clock on his desk. "Yeah, can you make it by four?"

"I'll try. Depends on the judge, if I can get right in."

"Okay. I'll have some more boys here to help. This is a tough guy. It may not go down easy."

The shack was about forty feet square, made of corrugated tin and tarpaper for the flat roof, rock for a foundation, and clapboard and cinder block for walls. The front door was slatted wood with a peephole in the center. Behind it was a small outhouse. Next to that was a 1995 red Camaro and a much older once white Ford F-150 pickup truck outfitted with gardener's tools.

The shack had a small window on the west side, none on the east. Henry Manuelito drove the Indian police Ford Bronco slowly west down Thomas Road, crossed the irrigation ditch where it was shallow about fifty yards from the shack, drove on the rocky dirt, and parked about fifteen yards away from the solid east wall. He and three other Indian policemen got out of the Bronco and waited. Henry had an automatic pistol in his hand by his side. The other men carried pump riot guns, short-barreled, loaded with double-ought buckshot.

John Steigman pulled his unmarked tan Chevrolet behind the Bronco and parked. He got out and waited for the Phoenix police vehicle to park behind his car. The two uniformed officers exited the car carrying riot guns.

John walked up to the chief.

"Let's go," Henry said.

They spread out in a line and walked toward the shack. Suddenly the door of the outhouse opened, and a man came out buttoning his Levi's. He glanced to his right, saw the line of armed men twenty yards away, and ran toward the pickup truck.

Two of the Indian police ran behind the shack, leveling their shotguns at him. He slowly stopped and stood still, facing them.

"Now it's against the law to take a dump?" the man said.

One of the policemen covered him with the shotgun. The other patted him down and handcuffed him.

"Who is he?" Steigman asked. They stopped five yards from the side of the shack.

"I don't know," Chief Manuelito said, "but he isn't Big Gun Pete."

The two officers pushed the man up to the chief.

"Is Big Gun Pete in there?" Henry asked.

"I don't know who's in there. I was in the outhouse, stopped to take a shit. That illegal?"

One of the officers flicked the barrel of the riot gun into the man's crotch. He doubled over with a grunt, then straightened up slowly, gasping, his face twisted with pain. "Kiss my ass."

The gun barrel connected again. The man fell to his knees, bent forward, and vomited. "He's in there," he choked out.

"Anybody else?"

He shook his head.

The Indian behind him pulled him up by the hand-cuff chain and pushed him to the Bronco. Two of the Indian policemen and one of the Phoenix policemen walked around behind the shack.

Steigman and Manuelito went to the door and stood on either side of it, and a uniformed Phoenix police-man stood behind the detective.

The chief knocked on the door. "Hey, Pete, you in there?"

There was silence. The chief banged on the door with the side of his fist. Silence. Steigman pulled the automatic out of his shoulder holster and nodded at the chief.

Henry Manuelito threw his two-hundred-sixty-pound body broadside into the splintery wood slat door. The door shattered like an orange crate, and Henry crouched five feet into the shack, holding his 9mm Sig Sauer in front of him with both hands.

Big Gun Pete sat on the threadbare black sofa against the back wall. He slowly raised his arms in surrender.

"How ya doin,' Henry?" Pete said. "What's up?"

Henry stood up and walked toward him. "You're going away, son, you're going bye-bye."

Phil Wilkott sat watching television in the family room of his two-million-dollar home in Paradise Val-ley. His two sons, four and seven years old, were with their nanny in the playroom. His wife wasn't home. She was at a charity dinner with other rich women from Paradise Valley and Scottsdale, where they could show off their latest jewelry and say tacky things about anyone not in earshot and congratulate each other for their generosity in donating money for a dog ceme-tery. Yeah, a goddamn dog cemetery. The whole world was coming apart at the seams, and these broads spend two hundred grand on a goddamn dog cemetery.

He reached for the telephone. "Hello."

"This is Pete. I been arrested for rape. Two minors in Scottsdale last week."

Wilkott bolted up straight on the sofa. His chest hurt, and he felt disoriented.

"Hey, sombitch, you listenin'?" Big Gun Pete stood at the wall telephone in the booking room at the Maricopa County Jail. It was almost seven o'clock, and he was being afforded the one phone call to which he was entitled. Three jail guards waited for him.

"Ya gotta help me, man." Pete toned down his voice, trying not to be overheard by the guards.

"How the hell did it happen?"

"The little bitch musta snitched me off."

"Jesus."

"Jesus ain't gonna help, man. I don' wanna be stuck in here all damn weekend. You make my bond. It wasn't me done any a that weird shit, man. It was you 'n that fag you run with."

"I'm calling a lawyer right now. He's the best there is. He'll get you out as soon as he can. I'll give him the money to post your bond. Just keep your mouth shut. I'll take care of you."

"Ya better, man," Pete growled. He hung up.

Phil Wilkott gulped several deep breaths. He telephoned Richard Haywood and got his answering machine. He left an urgent message to call him back as soon as he got in. He paced the family room for over two hours, sweat soaking his shirt.

The telephone rang. He ran to it.

"Yeah, Rich, thanks for calling." Phil was breathless, his voice weak. "I got a problem. A guy's in jail that I got to get out."

"What's he in on?"

"Rape. One of them was three years old."

Pause. "You mean what happened last week over at McCormick Ranch?"

"Yeah. It's bad. This guy's getting real antsy. He just got arrested, and he's making all kinds of threats."

"What kind of threats can he make against *you?*"

"Listen, just go down there and get him out. I'll post whatever the bond is."

"It's not that easy. I can't go see him at night. The jail is closed to visitors. And if he just got arrested, there won't even be any bond set until the duty judge holds initial appearances tomorrow at one o'clock."

"Shit!"

"Who is this guy, your brother, your uncle? What's the big deal?"

"He's an Indian from the Salt River Reservation. Big Gun Pete is all I know. I don't know his last name. He sells me some stuff now and then."

"Sounds real nice. He's going to have to stay in till tomorrow afternoon."

"How come you get *me* out in two hours?"

"Because for you I call Jimmy Friedl. I did a favor for him once, and he owes me big time. He gives me a handwritten release order and sets an O.R. bond and I go get you. But he isn't going to do it for some Indian arrested for raping two kids."

"Get him to do it. That's what I pay you for."

"Come on, Phil. Get your head on straight. Jimmy Friedl lets you out on drunk charges and getting your ashes hauled in an alley, that kind of penny-ante stuff. He's not setting a bond in the middle of the night for the worst sex crime around here in years. The guy's going to have to wait till tomorrow."

"Shit! I hope he doesn't get crazy and spill his guts."

"What the hell can he do to *you*?"

"I can't talk on the phone. I'll meet you in the bar at the country club in twenty minutes."

Jennifer was fully recovered physically and seemed to have no memory at all of what had happened. She had turned three years old just six weeks ago, and Janice Joslin, a rape crisis counsellor with a doctorate in psychology, assured Kate that Jennifer would never have a memory of it. Dr. Joslin had counseled Kate a dozen times since the rape and had given her several articles to read from psychological and psychiatric journals as well as from the leading journal of forensic criminology. There had never been a case of a girl so young having later memories of such an event, not even in all of the repressed-memory cases that were becoming so fashionable. The earliest such memories in thousands of cases were those of a five-year-old. And coupled with Jennifer's age was the mild concussion that she had suffered, almost certainly prior to the rape, which also would act to preclude memory. Kate was satisfied that Jennifer's mind had not been injured by the rape.

The other matter was far more devastating. A PCR test, Polymerase Chain Reaction, was being performed at the UCLA Medical Center on the semen collected from both Jennifer and Donna. It could take as long as three more weeks for the viral cultures to mature so that the pathologist could confirm or reject the initial findings of HIV infection present in the man who had raped Jennifer and none in the other. But even the PCR test would ultimately be inconclusive in a girl of Jennifer's age. There was the remote possibility of a false positive, and the final answer, the ELISA and Western Blot tests, would take six months.

Every time that Kate and Mike looked at Jennifer, playing with Cynthia and Harriet and Raggedy Ann and her doll carriage, it was difficult for them not to relive and relive and relive the tragedy that had happened and to be haunted by the far more pernicious possibility that threatened to poison the future. But they could not display their own unremitting emotional distress to Jennifer. She was as cheerful and carefree as any little girl, and she was sensitive to her mother's moods.

She had asked numerous times when Donna was coming home, and Kate had told her that they just didn't know, because Donna's own mommy was sick, and she had gone back home to be with her like a good girl. As the days passed, Jennifer asked about Donna less frequently.

The telephone rang at a few minutes past six. Kate was in the kitchen, so Mike answered it.

"We got him," John Steigman said.

"Fantastic!" Mike said. "What next?"

"I called Harvey Stidham at the County Attorney's Office. You know, he heads juvenile sex."

"Right, I know him," Mike said.

"He'll file a Rule 15.2 request on Monday morning and ask for an accelerated hearing on Tuesday. We'll get a preliminary read at the hospital."

"Good! I'll find it on the calendar and see you at the hearing Tuesday. Thanks."

"Thank Kate. She did it."

Mike walked into the kitchen and embraced Kate from behind. She was watching pork chops sizzle in a skillet. He caressed her breasts and kissed her on the back of the neck.

"You didn't have enough?" she said.

"I'll never have enough."

"We'll be eating in five minutes."

"I've been eating all afternoon."

"You have a naughty mouth." She laughed gutturally. "Who was that on the phone?"

Mike stepped around to her side. "Steigman. They picked up Big Gun Pete."

"That's great! What about testing him?"

"The deputy county attorney in charge of the sex crimes against kids unit is going to file a request with a judge on Monday asking for a blood sample."

"Will the judge do it?"

"Yeah, sure. It's one of the court rules for criminal cases where blood ID is essential."

"When?"

"The hearing will probably be on Tuesday morning, and they'll take him straight over to the Maricopa

County Medical Center. It'll take maybe an hour to draw his blood and type it."

"Will they be able to tell if he's got HIV?"

"Not immediately. But a man's blood type is the same as his semen type. The man who raped Donna was type A, and Jennifer's rapist was type O. If this guy is also A or O, then they'll send the blood to UCLA Medical Center for a DNA match."

"You mean the same kind of tests they used in the O. J. Simpson case?"

"Right."

"But Simpson's lawyers kept telling the jury and everybody that the tests were contaminated and full of inaccuracies."

"Yeah, well, that's what they pull to try to confuse the jury, and they hire experts for a ton of money who confuse the jury even more. But it's not true. Body samples collected—you know, blood, semen, whatever—can be old and contaminated, and it doesn't affect the DNA at all. The only contamination that actually could affect the DNA reading would have to happen during the laboratory testing, if the technician does it wrong. And then what happens is *not* that they may end up identifying the wrong person, but that the test is inconclusive and they can't identify *anybody*."

"So let's say they get a DNA match on this Big Gun Pete. Is it absolute proof of identification?"

"Yeah, sure, within the realm of reason anyway. Everyone except identical twins has unique genes. That's why we all look different. The DNA is the material in our genes that carries the different traits. The doctors who study this stuff say that the chance that there would be two people who weren't identical twins but had identical DNA is astronomical, like one in hundreds of millions or a billion. In other words, pretty damn unlikely. Way beyond a reasonable doubt."

"Mommy, we gonna eat soon?" Jennifer said, skipping into the kitchen.

"Sure, honey. Mommy's putting it on the plates right now."

Two hours with Phil Wilkott at the club had been a very unpleasant way to spend a Friday evening. But it was a living, and whoever said it would be all gravy? Richard Haywood folded the check for fifty thousand dollars and put it in his shirt pocket. Well, some guys cut open people's assholes for a living. Shit is shit, and it can make you money. I'm a goddamn alchemist, he said to himself. I turn shit into gold.

He went to the jail at eight o'clock in the morning to visit Pete. The only Pete arrested last night was named Supremas. Haywood filled out the attorney's questionnaire, flashed his bar card, and waited in the interview room.

Haywood was a short man and stocky, balding, brown hair and eyes, fifty-one years old. He had been practicing law for twenty-four years and was widely considered to be the best orator who had ever walked into a Phoenix courtroom. He might not have been the best questioner or cross-examiner of witnesses, but he had something even more important: he was magic with a jury. His voice was deep and sonorous, his eyes steady and honest, and he made jurors laugh and cry and love him. That same endearing quality, whatever it was—call it charisma or personality or presence— also helped him easily win the confidence of clients.

He spent forty-five minutes with Big Gun Pete, confirmed the story that he had heard last night, and told him he'd be back for the initial appearance. He left the interview room and washed his hands thoroughly in the visitors' rest room.

Initial appearances of arrestees were conducted each afternoon beginning at one o'clock. The prisoners were in the hearing room at the jail, and the duty judge, deputy county attorney, and defense lawyers sat in a courtroom in the county courthouse and took part in the proceedings on closed-circuit TV.

It took about a minute for Judge Rothstein to set Pete's bond. "Let's see. Rape of a sixteen-year-old, rape of a three-year-old. Very, very nice. Do you have counsel, Mr. Supremas?"

"Yeah, Hayward, somethin' like that," Pete said.

"I'm his attorney, Your Honor," Richard Haywood said, walking up to the bench.

"And a lucky boy you are, Richie my lad. Bond is set at five hundred thousand dollars."

"May I be heard on a bond reduction at this time, Your Honor?"

"No, file it Monday," the judge said, his usually pleasant demeanor fading. "If I let this gentleman out, I'll be drawn and quartered."

Haywood drove to the jail immediately. Pete would be furious. That wasn't good.

"You said you was gettin' me out, man," Pete said sullenly. "A half a million bucks, man. What kinda shit's that?"

"Even your friend can't post that kind of a bond."

Pete stared at him, his face malevolent.

"Don't worry, I'll take care of it first thing Monday. I'll make a motion for a blood exam, if the county attorney doesn't beat me to it. If what you told me is true, you're going to be out of here by Tuesday or Wednesday, guaranteed. Take it easy. You're making an important friend. I'm sure he's going to be very happy about you helping him. Don't get crazy in here. Just hold tight."

"I'm gonna need some bread, man. This ain't for free."

"Look, that isn't up to me. I'm just the lawyer here. But I have a feeling that he'll be happy to make you happy. Just hold tight."

Pete nodded. "Jus' don' screw with me, man. Nobody screws with me."

• ELEVEN •

Judge Friedl's courtroom was uncrowded on Tuesday morning. There were the usual sets of lawyers arguing with each other. Several elderly retired men sat in the spectators' pews, deriving greater satisfaction from watching the spectacle of real-life drama than the show-biz version on the talk shows and soap operas. There were a dozen other people as well, perhaps litigants, friends, family.

Mike Fallon sat down in the rear pew of the courtroom. Harvey Stidham came through the swinging entry door and walked to the long wooden table closest to the jury box.

Some genius had finally discovered that the weather outside was beginning to climb toward the nineties, and the air conditioning had been turned on. It was comfortable in the courtroom.

A sheriff's deputy came through a side door into the courtroom leading three men, chained together hand and foot, wearing dark blue jumpsuits. Another deputy followed. The prisoners sat down in the jury box, their chains jangling. Two of them were white men. The Indian with dreadlocks had to be Pete. To describe him as fearsome and ugly would be to understate the obvious. Mike shuddered at the thought of this man leaning over Jennifer or Donna. It made his skin crawl.

The bailiff came into the courtroom, walked to his small desk, and rapped a gavel slowly three times.

"All rise."

Everyone stood up, and the judge came into the courtroom and sat down on a brown leather swivel armchair at the elevated bench. James Friedl was doing a year stint, along with four other judges, in the sex crimes division of the Maricopa County courts. He had been assigned to this case by the court administrator's office, as all judges were assigned in rotating order as cases were filed. He was in his late thirties, short and heavy with thinning brown hair. He had been the president of the Young Republicans in law school fifteen years ago, and upon graduation he had been hired by an archconservative firm in Mesa. Its senior partner edited a monthly hate sheet that blamed virtually all of the ills of society on Jews and Negroes. The seven other members of the firm, including Friedl, had somewhat less distorted mind-sets, but they kept their views to themselves. In Mesa it was far from an impediment to one's career to be a racist or an anti-Semite.

Two years ago, when Arizona's conservative Republican governor had run for reelection, he had won the hearts and minds and votes of Mesa's right wing, which was the majority in Mesa, by appointing Friedl to a judgeship. For most defense attorneys and prosecutors alike, Friedl had not been a praiseworthy addition to the bench.

John Steigman and a uniformed police officer entered the courtroom and sat down beside Mike.

"This judge is a real asshole," Mike whispered.

Steigman nodded and frowned. "How the hell can Big Gun Pete afford Rich Haywood?"

Mike shrugged. "I guess the drug business is pretty good."

"What do you have, Mr. Stidham?" asked the judge.

"State versus Supremas, Your Honor. State's disclosure motion."

"Who's Supremas?" asked the judge.

"He's the one on the right, Your Honor," said Richard Haywood, standing at the defense table.

The judge looked over at him. "Good morning, Mr. Supremas."

Big Gun Pete nodded, his face surly.

The judge opened the file on the bench and read the top two sheets. "You have anything to say, Mr. Haywood?"

"No objection, Your Honor."

"So ordered," the judge said, signing the document in the file.

Stidham walked toward him holding a release order.

"Do not approach the bench without permission, Mr. Stidham."

"May I approach the bench, Your Honor?"

"No. Give that to the bailiff."

"Thank you, Your Honor."

The bailiff took the order from him and handed it to Judge Friedl. Harvey Stidham turned around and walked back to the prosecution table. He rolled his eyes at John Steigman. The bailiff brought the signed release order to him.

"Who's next?" the judge asked.

Stidham strode down the aisle and left the courtroom. The uniformed officer, Steigman, and Mike Fallon joined him in the corridor.

"The guy loves you," Steigman said.

"Yeah, no shit. About three years ago, before he became a judge, I kicked the little prick's ass in a big murder case. He defended a real prince among men, white guy who sodomized and murdered two black junior high school girls. The guy was from Mesa, and the girls were from South Phoenix, so naturally the defense was that they were both prostitutes, high on crack, and had picked him up and tried to rob and kill him. Only problem was, the girls didn't test positive for drugs, and the pathologist testified they were both virgins. Judge Wofford dropped the pill on him. Since then me and Friedl haven't been great pals."

He looked past Steigman and appeared to notice Mike for the first time. "What are you doing here? You going to bring a motion to suppress for that maggot?"

Mike shook his head. "No. One of the victims is the daughter of a very close friend of mine."

Stidham nodded. "Shoe is on the other foot, huh?"

Mike clenched his jaw and said nothing.

"Come on, Harvey, cool it," Steigman cajoled. "This is a bad one."

"They're all bad ones." The prosecutor handed him the release order. "Call me as soon as you get the results." He turned around and walked down the hall to the elevators.

"Where you going to be?" Steigman asked, turning to Mike.

"At my office. I'll wait there."

"Okay." Steigman looked at his watch. "I'll call you. Probably around ten."

"Thanks."

It was shortly after ten when John Steigman called. "No go," he said.

Mike stiffened in his chair. "Are you sure?"

"Yeah, he's type AB. The rapists were O and A."

"Damn," Mike muttered. He thought for a moment. "How about the burglary? Your ID guys found some plastic fibers on the tongue of the door that are consistent with the plastic on his driver's license."

"Right, *consistent*. But there are thousands of those laminating kits sold. We can't make a positive match."

"But when you couple it with Donna Alvarez's testimony that he broke in and shot her up, you got burglary at least, furnishing narcotics on top of it."

"We can't prove it, you know that. Donna has a rap sheet longer than my arm, and she's been an addict for years. Who's going to believe her? And she probably wouldn't even testify anyway."

Mike felt sickened, demoralized. "This is terrible. What now?"

"We've got to cut him loose. There's nothing we can do about it."

"How can they just let him go?" Kate asked. "How can they do that? Donna must have been telling the truth about him breaking in. They found the plastic. He had to have done it."

They were sitting on the sofa in the living room. Mike took her hand in his. "They're right. Nobody is going to take Donna's word to convict somebody."

"Why not? Even a prostitute can tell the truth."

"You didn't believe her."

"I didn't know about the plastic."

"Do you believe her now?"

Kate sighed. "I don't want to," she said slowly. "I want to be able to blame her for what happened." She looked miserably at him. "But I don't think it was her fault."

· TWELVE ·

Mike reached outside his apartment door at a quarter to seven the next morning and picked up the *Arizona Republic,* Phoenix's morning newspaper. He laid it on the kitchen table and went back to the stove, where he was frying eggs and patty sausage. He pressed the patties flat with a spatula and the grease crackled. He watched them sleepily for a couple of minutes, then shoveled the eggs and sausage onto a plate and brought it to the table.

He glanced at the various headlines on the front page and froze: RAPE SUSPECT RELEASED.

"Oh, no," Mike murmured. He read the story, which took up all two columns on the left side of the page, and he began to tremble. There was also a photograph from the *Boston Globe* of the wedding couple, Brian and Mary Caitlan O'Dwyer Mulvaney, almost five years ago, cutting the cake.

Kate had a totally different hairdo now, and the corona and veil that she had been wearing partly hid her face. But she was clearly recognizable, and there it all was for the entire world to read about her and her family wealth and annulment and her Christian goodness in seeking to adopt a troubled waif, and the tragedy that had struck like an atom bomb out of the blue.

Mike ran to the bathroom, showered, brushed his teeth, and shaved in the four minutes that it used to take him during basic training in the army. He ran out to his truck and drove to McCormick Ranch.

They had made love and lain together talking until two in the morning, and Kate was late getting up. She rushed around getting ready for school and getting Jennifer ready for Merry Moppets.

When they got to the child-care center, it was seven-thirty, and there were only a half dozen little boys and girls there. Jennifer skipped off to play. Two mothers were standing with Jackie Moreland, the director, in front of the office. They glanced a little oddly at Kate, she thought, but shrugged it off as her imagination.

"Got to go. Late," she called out to Jackie, waving and turning to go out the door.

"Kate, Kate! Can I speak to you a moment?" Jackie called out.

Kate glanced at her watch. Well, she had just enough time. She walked over to the director, and the two mothers slowly faded away.

"Please come into my office," Jackie said, her face atypically drawn and officious.

They walked inside, and Jackie closed the door behind them. She went to the desk and stood, the *Arizona Republic* lying on it.

"I'm terribly sorry," she said.

"About what?"

"You haven't read the morning paper?"

Kate shook her head, suddenly fearful.

Jackie lifted it and proffered it toward her. "It's about you and Jennifer."

Dear God, not this, too, Kate thought, feeling her legs weaken. She walked forward and took the newspaper. She scanned the headlines, saw the rapist story, the wedding picture of Brian and herself, and sank into the upholstered chair beside her. She began reading the story but couldn't finish because tears obscured her vision.

"I want you to know that this is not my decision,"

Jackie said. "Several parents called the owner this morning. I've already had three parents come and talk to me." She paused. "They're afraid to have Jennifer play with their children. They're afraid that if she scratches one of them, even accidentally, they can get AIDS."

Kate breathed deeply, trying to catch her breath. She shook her head. "Jennifer doesn't have AIDS." She wiped her eyes with the tissue that Jackie handed her. "And they're not even sure she has HIV."

"I'm just so sorry," Jackie said. "It's out of my hands."

Kate stood up slowly and steadied herself with difficulty. She left the office and walked up to Jennifer, playing with a little girl.

"Come, honey. Mommy has to take you home."

Jennifer looked up. "Why, Mommy? I want to stay and play." She studied her mother's face. "What's wrong, Mommy?"

"Nothing, honey." Kate reached down and took her hand. "Come, you'll play with Mommy today, and we'll feed the duckies."

Jennifer got up. "Okay. Bye, Emily. See you tomorrow."

She walked out with Kate, and Kate strapped her into the car seat. She got in the driver's seat and sat staring out the windshield, gripping the steering wheel so tightly that her knuckles were white and her fingertips bright red.

Mike pulled into the driveway and ran to the door. He rang, waited impatiently, rang again, then banged on the door. He heard nothing from the house. He glanced at his watch. Seven-twenty. She must have left.

He jumped back into his truck and drove as fast as he could to Merry Moppets. Good. Good! There was Kate's car. He approached more closely and could see that she was in it. He parked beside it and saw both her and Jennifer. Kate was trying to strangle the steering wheel, a dazed look on her face. Oh, God! What he feared would happen had happened.

He got out and opened her car door. She looked around at him and couldn't contain her agony any longer. She burst out weeping, gulping for breath, her chest heaving.

"What's wrong, Mommy?" Jennifer stared at her, very frightened. "Mommy, Mommy." And she began to cry and to struggle in the baby carrier.

Mike ran around to the passenger door and flung it open. He took Jennifer out of the carrier and hugged her.

"It's okay, it's okay. Mommy's just a little sick. Everything will be okay."

Jennifer slowly stopped crying. Mike carried her around the car and knelt down on the dirt beside Kate, put Jennifer on her bosom, and hugged them both. Kate gradually regained her composure, and her shuddering stopped. Mike straightened up and wrapped his arms around both of them, hugging them tightly.

Parents came and went from the parking lot, staring in curiosity at the bizarre behavior.

· THIRTEEN ·

Kate was in a deep torpor that genuinely frightened Mike. He knew from experience that there were times in everyone's lives when the pain of going on seemed more odious than abrupt surcease from sorrow, as the famous poet had put it. He had seen his mother this way, twenty-three years ago, and had it not been for her intense faith in God and belief that everything happened in accordance with His will, she would certainly have taken her own life.

Kate had the same look in her eyes that he so poignantly remembered seeing in his mother's, but Kate neither prayed nor went to church to salve her pain, as his mother had. She just sat rigidly, mute. Nor had Kate gone jogging for days, and the abandonment of that emotional and physical pressure valve was adding to her depression. And now it appeared that at least for a while there would no longer be a daily teaching routine in her life that required her to concentrate on something other than her own sorrows.

Mike called Monsignor Reilly at Saint Daniel's Academy and told him what had happened and that Kate might not be back for a few days because she had to make new arrangements for day care. Kate had Valium, which she seldom took, and then only if she couldn't sleep, but Mike made her take one. Then he called Janice Joslin, and even before he asked her to come out and spend some time with Kate, Dr. Joslin said that she had read the story in the newspaper and would be right over.

When she arrived, Kate was sitting in the big wing chair, staring vacantly at the floor. Mike was on the sofa with Jennifer watching Woody Woodpecker cartoons.

The psychologist sat down on the arm of the wing chair and said, "Why don't we go into your bedroom and talk for a while?"

Kate got up, expressionless, and they walked into her bedroom. Mike heard the door close.

"Mommy's sick," Jennifer said to Mike.

"Yes, honey. And the doctor's here and Mommy will be better."

"She said we were going to feed the duckies."

"Do you want to go right now? I'll go with you. Maybe Mommy will come later."

"Okay." She jumped up and skipped into the kitchen. Mike switched off the TV set and followed.

She pointed. "The food is up there."

Mike took the big plastic bag of stale pieces of bread out of the pantry and handed it to Jennifer. They walked through the patio, across the asphalt path, and down the bank to the lip of the cove. The ducks spotted one of their favorite pals and came paddling to shore. They fluttered around Jennifer and Mike, and she giggled delightedly and threw out crust after crust. The bag was soon empty.

"Can we go on the train?"

"Sure," Mike said.

He took her hand, and they walked to Kate's car, which had the baby carrier. He drove to McCormick Park. There was a little train, just the right size for kids, and Jennifer rode and rode and rode, eating popcorn and then pink cotton candy and then a cherry snow cone.

Mike called the house, and Dr. Joslin picked it up on the first ring.

"She'll be okay," she said. "I had her take another Valium, and it put her to sleep. She's exhausted."

"When do you think we should come back?"

"After lunch is fine. She'll sleep a couple more hours and be a little groggy for the rest of the afternoon, but she'll be just fine."

"Good. Thank you very much. We both appreciate your help."

"It's what I do. And what Kate's going through is perfectly normal. In fact, she's handling it better than most of the mothers I've counseled. She's strong, and she'll be fine. Just make sure she gets plenty of rest and doesn't overdo. And ask her to call me tomorrow. I think she should come in and see me a few more times."

"I will, and thank you again."

Jennifer tired of the train and then spun herself dizzy on the merry-go-round. She rode a golden palomino on the carousel, with Mike holding her so she wouldn't fall. They ate hot dogs and candy apples for lunch and then drove home.

"You like Mommy?" she asked, peering up at him.

"I love you and Mommy."

"You going to be my daddy?"

"Yes," he said.

Mike put Jennifer in bed at two o'clock and sat with her until she fell asleep. When he came out, Kate was in the kitchen, sipping a glass of water, staring out the window toward the lake.

"Is she okay?" she asked.

"Yes, fine. How about you?"

"Stoned but alive."

He kissed her lightly on the lips. "I love you," he said.

"I know," she said. "No matter how crazy I get, don't ever go away from me."

He shook his head slowly.

She studied his face. "You don't look so good."

He frowned. "I don't feel so good. That scum Supremas and whoever was with him aren't even going
to get their wrists slapped for what they did."

"What can we do?"

"I don't know. But we have to do something." He
gritted his teeth and breathed deeply. "The men who
did this to Jennifer and Donna have to be punished.
But now that Big Gun Pete is out of jail, the police
will never find out who did it. I can't let that happen."

The need for justice rose up in him all day and
evening like a swelling river and became so torrential
that at seven o'clock he thought that his chest was
going to burst. He suddenly got up from the sofa and
went into Kate's bedroom. He lay on his back in
Kate's bed in the darkness and tried to calm himself,
but he began to tremble.

What was the psalm that Gwen McLemore had recited to Kate in the hospital? Mike had heard it a
dozen times in Sunday school back in Fort Stockton,
the old priest roaring it out in his hearty baritone:
"God is my rock and refuge. He will repay the wicked
for their injustice; the Lord our God will destroy them
for their misdeeds."

God, if you truly exist, let these men be destroyed
for their misdeeds.

God, if you truly exist, give me the strength to do
what I must do.

Kate opened the door, peeked inside, then came in
and sat down on the edge of the bed.

"My turn," he whispered.

"You're entitled." She put her hand softly on his
cheek.

"I have to find out who did this."

"How?"

"I have to talk to Big Gun Pete."

"Oh, no, you don't," she said. "I don't want you
getting killed. That would really finish me off."

"I won't get killed."

He reached over and switched on the lamp.

She saw the violence in his face. "What are you thinking of doing?"

"I'm going over there."

"Over where?"

"To the shack he lives in."

"You don't even know where it is."

"Yes, I do. It was in the story in the paper this morning. The reporter actually went out there and talked to him."

He sat up in bed. Kate stood up and looked at him in alarm.

"You're serious?"

He nodded and got up off the bed.

"Don't do this. Call Detective Steigman and talk to him."

"Then *I'm* the next one who'll get arrested."

She held him by both arms, looking into his eyes. "Please, Mike, please don't. That man's a lowlife animal. He'll hurt you."

"I grew up on a ranch where the hands shoveled shit all day long and got mean drunk at night. I lost my Boston accent there, and I sure as hell lost my Boston refinement, if I ever had any." He looked soberly at her. "He won't hurt me."

There were no streetlights on the reservation, but the shack was easy to find, despite the darkness. The shack had no front door, and the doorway was covered only by a thin bath towel that had been nailed to the lintel. Dim light bled through it, and the light of the pallid half-moon was barely sufficient to make out the new Camaro parked behind, though its color was indistinguishable.

Mike parked his truck directly in front of the doorway. He reached into the side pocket of the door and took out the Colt .357 single-action army revolver with a seven-and-a-half-inch barrel that he had bought in Fort Stockton when he was seventeen and fancied himself a cowboy. He was six foot four and weighed two hundred eighteen pounds, and none of it had yet begun to hang in a great pouch of fat over his belt buckle.

He was insane, and he knew it. But he was sane enough to know that what he was doing was lunacy. He just didn't give a shit. Only a two-by-four across his head, which he had experienced once before in his life, could have stopped him.

He left the lights on and the motor running, the truck pointed directly at the bath towel door five feet away. He got out of the truck and saw the edge of the towel move, then fall back in place. He walked to the towel and ripped it down. A man was standing just inside holding a foot-long piece of pipe in his fist. Mike lunged toward him and smashed the point of the barrel of his gun into the man's mouth. He fell in a heap, groaning, holding his mouth, spitting out blood and pieces of teeth. Mike took a step toward him and kicked him as hard as he could in the face. The man sprawled over on his side unconscious.

Mike moved past him toward Big Gun Pete, sitting on a black sofa. Pete was reaching underneath it, and he pulled out a sawed-off shotgun just as Mike reached him. Mike slashed sideways with his gun across Pete's jaw, and Pete dropped the shotgun and grabbed his face, groaning.

Mike struck him again across the jaw with the gun, crushing three of Pete's fingers. Blood poured down his fingers and hand. Pete pulled back against the sofa. He lifted his feet up toward Mike to ward off any further blows and stared at him with terror-filled eyes.

"Who did you bring to that house where Donna was living?" Mike's voice was insanely soft and calm.

Pete's eyes opened even wider, as though he was trying to register the question.

"Who?" Mike asked again, stepping closer to Pete, just out of range of his legs.

Silence.

"Your friend there got lucky. He may live. But you're going to end up in a pile of shit in the bottom of that outhouse."

Pete looked at Tony Brown Horse. He appeared to be dead. He looked back at Mike and tried to move his mouth.

"Phil," he mouthed and stopped in pain. "Wilkott."

"There was one more."

Slowly, agonizingly. "Grant." Gasp. "Don't know name."

"If you lied to me, I'll come back and kill you."

Pete shook his head.

Mike left the shack, got back in his truck, and drove to Kate's house. His hands were shaking slightly, but there was no longer any pain in his chest.

She rushed to the door as he came in, saw the look in his eyes, and her torturous worry dissipated.

"I got the names," he said, smiling for the first time in days.

Big Gun Pete sat up slowly on the couch. His jaw was killing him. His broken fingers were paralyzed. He walked gingerly to the three-drawer dresser, reached behind it, and pulled out a small plastic jar taped to the back. He shook out a couple of crack rocks and put them into his glass pipe. He shoved the bit between his lips, lit a small butane torch, and sucked the smoke in painfully. After a few inhales he felt better. A few more, better and better. He moved his jaw to see if he could speak.

"That's good shit, man," he said as clearly as he could, testing his voice. Good enough.

He walked over to Tony Brown Horse and nudged him on the forehead with his boot. Tony was alive, his breathing labored, gurgling through his broken, bloody mouth. Pete walked back to the couch and sat down. He picked up the cellular phone from the floor and dialed Phil Wilkott's home. A Mexican maid answered. She could hardly speak English. Then Wilkott got on the line.

"Listen, God damn you, how many times do I have to tell you not to call me here?"

"Some big fuck jus' tried to kill me." Pete had to speak slowly to make the words come out understandably, but the crack had pretty well anesthetized his jaw.

"What the hell are you talking about? Who?"

"I dunno who. Big guy, white, wanted to know who done them two girls."

"You tell him?"

"No, hell no, man. I tol' ya, ya take care a me, I'm solid."

"I'll take care of you."

"Now, man. I need it now."

"What do you mean now? I have to go to the bank and get it."

"Don' gimme that shit, man. Ya carry a roll on ya bigger 'n my dick. I wan' it now. Get some more tomorrow."

"What the hell is with you? You sound weird."

"I tol' ya, man, this big fuck bent my face. Broke my jaw. I coulda tol' him, man. I coulda said Phil Wilkott 'n some little queer named Grant. But I'm solid."

There was silence on the line.

"Whattaya doin', man? Start talkin'. I'm talkin' t' ya."

"Yeah, yeah, okay. I've got a few bucks on me."

"Bring it."

"I'm not coming over there."

"The hell you ain't. Bring it."

"All right, all right. In a little while."

Phil was having trouble focusing. This wasn't cops that went after Pete, especially not on the reservation. This was somebody connected with the little girl. Shit! This scumbag Pete would eventually talk. He'd get arrested for pushing or pimping and trade Wilkott to the cops for a deal.

It would be only a matter of time, a matter of time. The words played over and over in Phil's head like a popular song you can't get rid of. You hear it on the radio in the car, and pretty soon you're crooning like Vince Gill. A matter of time.

He couldn't let his wife find out about this. She wouldn't be real thrilled, and she'd probably throw his ass out. The money was hers, the house was hers; all he had was the three hundred grand a year his old man paid him. And what about Tom Terrific? Jesus Christ! He'd really love this.

He drove almost in a daze. He had been to the shack twice before to buy cocaine, so he had no trouble finding it. He was cold with sweat. It was seventy degrees, and he was burning up, but his skin felt like it was freezing. He reached into the glove compartment and took out the .25 Colt automatic pistol. Many people in Arizona kept guns in their cars. It was perfectly legal. He held the pistol, but he could hardly feel it. He pulled up in front of the shack. It had no door. There was someone lying in a heap just inside.

Maybe it's Pete, he thought in a sudden flash of hope. Maybe God struck him down for me.

He got out of the car and felt as though his legs were rubber. He walked slowly into the shack and could see that the heap was someone else. Pete was sitting on the couch, his head lying on the top of the back cushion. The room stank of stale crack smoke and brown paper bags of garbage rotting in a corner. It staggered him, but suddenly his nostrils were filled with the odor of his own rank sweat, fear sweat. His face was wet with it.

Phil walked up to the couch. Pete just lay there snoring lightly. A syringe was in his lap. Phil stood close, pointed the pistol at his face three feet away, and pulled the trigger. Shit! Oh yeah, you have to pull the chamber back and let it slide forward to load it. He did it, and the crack of the steel startled Pete awake. Pete tried to focus his glazed, wasted eyes on the handgun. Phil pulled the trigger.

· FOURTEEN ·

The telephone began ringing incessantly at six o'clock in the morning, first from a producer for the Sally Jesse Raphael show, who didn't seem to realize that Mountain Standard Time wasn't the same as Eastern, and then from a steady stream of newspaper and magazine reporters and producers for Oprah Winfrey and Geraldo Rivera and Rikki Lake and a dozen others, who didn't care at all what time it was in Scottsdale. They had a hell of a story to make money from, and that was all that mattered.

Kate said, "No comment," to an endless stream of them and then asked Mike to answer the next dozen or so. When he left the house at eight-thirty, he unplugged all three telephones.

The doorbell rang a few minutes later.

Kate looked through the peephole in the front door, and two gray-haired old women and a much younger one stood there staring back. One of them was Edith Owens, and Kate had seen the other two around the neighborhood at various times. They had always waved at each other. Kate opened the door.

"Yes?" she said.

"Kate," Edith said, "this is Minna Latchman. She lives next to me."

The small, heavy old woman smiled sweetly. "I've often seen you in the mornings, jogging with your baby."

"Yes, I've seen you on your patio. It's nice to meet you."

"And this is Ilse Hodges," Edith said. "She lives across the street." Ilse was perhaps thirty or thirty-two, half the age of the other two, and sturdy and blond like a Scandinavian farm girl.

"Oh, yes," Kate said. "I've seen your husband several times out jogging. He wasn't very happy." Both she and Ilse laughed.

The three women held up the objects in their hands.

"We thought you might like a few home-baked things," Edith said. "I've got a cherry pie, Minna made her special German chocolate cake, and Ilse has some of her famous apricot *kolaches.*"

Kate began to smile, and tears filled her eyes. She wiped them and said, "I'm sorry, I'm a little upset."

"We understand, dear," Edith said.

"Please come in."

"We don't want to be a bother."

"You're not a bother at all. I'm very happy to see you." She held the door wide open for the three women.

Jennifer was on the sofa playing with her dolls and watching cartoons on TV.

"This must be little Jennifer," Minna said. She handed her chocolate cake to Kate, walked over to Jennifer, bent over, and said, "Those are lovely little dolls you have there, dear."

Jennifer smiled and nodded. "This is Cynthia," she said, pointing at the one closest to her.

"Hello, Cynthia," Minna said.

Kate and the other two women walked into the kitchen and set the pastries on the counter. Kate couldn't stop crying. She turned to the stove, embarrassed, and said, "I'll make us all some coffee."

The two women left the kitchen, and Kate breathed deeply to steady herself. She wiped her eyes with a tissue, then filled the Krupps coffeemaker with water and coffee. She cut three pieces of the cake and placed them on a platter along with several kolaches. She brought the platter into the living room and put it on the cocktail table. All three ladies were chatting with Jennifer about her dolls.

They sat down on the sofa and the two chairs. Ilse reached for a piece of German chocolate cake. "Great stuff," she said.

"Try those kolaches," Edith said. "You ever have one?"

Kate shook her head, took one off the plate, and bit off a corner. "Ummm, delicious."

"My mother's recipe," Ilse said. "She's from Czechoslovakia. That's a Bohemy specialty."

"It's really terrific," Kate said.

"We just want you to know," Edith lowered her voice, "that everyone is praying for you."

Kate swallowed and her chin quivered. "I appreciate that," she said hoarsely.

"I was a nurse and a nursing supervisor for forty-seven years," Minna said. "I've seen lots of things in medicine that once would have been considered miracles and became commonplace." She gave Kate an encouraging smile.

"I can't tell you how happy I am that you came over," Kate said. "I'll get the coffee."

She walked into the kitchen and steadied herself at the counter. Thank God for decent people, after what had happened yesterday. Don't lose faith, Gwen kept telling her on the telephone. But a day like yesterday could easily shatter anyone's faith. Thank God for neighbors like these. She took several deep breaths, dried her eyes again, and took four coffee mugs from the cabinet.

The ladies left after an hour, and Kate plugged the telephone into the socket behind the sofa. She put Jennifer down for a nap, then sat on the sofa staring at the two kolaches remaining on the platter, rebuking herself for her weakness. And just as she was reaching for one, the telephone rang.

"Mrs. O'Dwyer?"

"Yes."

"This is Murray Robertson."

"Yes, Dr. Robertson?" she said, very apprehensive.

"I'm sorry to tell you that the PCR test on Jennifer is positive, confirming the presence of HIV antibodies in her blood."

She listened to the words he solemnly spoke, and she was suddenly breathless. She couldn't utter a sound in reply and hung up the receiver.

She sat for minutes, empty, unable to move. Then she telephoned Mike's office, got his answering machine, and left a sobbing message about the PCR test, knowing all the time that it was terrible to be laying it on him in this way, but unable to hold herself back. The doorbell and telephone rang many times during the afternoon, but she ignored them. She and Jennifer played with dolls for hours in the bedroom, and then she hunched, shuddering, on the bank of the cove, watching her daughter feed the ducks.

Mike sat in front of John Steigman's small gray metal desk in his unkempt office at the Scottsdale Police Department.

"I know who did it."

"Great! Who?"

"Phil Wilkott and a Grant something. I didn't get the last name."

John looked at him. Then he wrote the names down on a legal pad.

"How'd you come up with these names?"

"I asked around."

"Asked around?"

Mike said nothing.

"I got a call this morning from Chief Manuelito out at the Salt River Res," John said. "He says Big Gun Pete and a mule of his called Tony Brown Horse are at the Indian Health Services clinic there. Pretty bad shape. He thought it was an odd coincidence."

Mike said nothing.

"Aside from the beating Pete took, he got a bullet through his cheek that's lodged in his brain. He's in a coma. They can't operate and take out the bullet. It would kill him."

Mike's jaw dropped. He stared at Steigman.

"You talk to Pete last night?"

Mike shook his head. "Not that way, I didn't. I'm telling you the truth."

"I called the Department of Public Safety a few minutes ago. They say you have a concealed-weapons permit."

"Sure, I took the course. But I don't carry anything."

"What kind of guns do you have?"

"I have a .357 Colt single-action in my truck. I gave Kate my .38 S & W. That's all."

"The chief says the size of the entry wound through the bone is a .22 or .25 at the largest."

"I've never had a gun like that."

Steigman studied him. "I've been on the job for twenty-eight years. I'm not a psychic, but I don't think you went and shot him. But if I'm wrong, I'm going to rip you a new asshole myself."

"You're not wrong."

Steigman frowned. He looked down at the legal pad in front of him. "What do you expect me to do with these names? I won't even question them under these circumstances."

"But he was telling the truth. Those are the guys who did it."

"And if we arrest them, who's going to tell the judge how this information was acquired, when these guys' lawyers bring a motion to dismiss? You anxious to get yourself prosecuted for assault with a deadly weapon?"

Mike shook his head.

"You know who this Wilkott is?"

"Wilkott and Deets. His father is the senior partner in the second largest law firm in Arizona. Phil is the head of the Scottsdale branch office. I met him once at a Bar Association seminar. A real hotshot."

"Right," Steigman said. "And a sick pervert. He's married, has a couple of kids, and he's been arrested six, eight times for drunk and disorderly and chicken hawking at those queer bars on Seventh Street. He likes his boys real young. Harry Becker over in Phoenix Vice told me he arrested him once in an alley cornholing some fag prostitute. Yeah, Phil is a swell guy. We know him real well around here. Every time we pop him, Richard Haywood comes to the jail two hours later, posts his bond, and the next day the case is dismissed. If you can afford Haywood, you got a pretty good chance of beating a pissant vice rap."

"We've got to get Wilkott," Mike said.

Steigman shrugged. "Got any ideas?"

"How about this? The next time he gets picked up for D and D, instead of your boys giving him an Intoxilyzer to test his breath, have them take him over to County General and get his blood drawn. Perfectly legal. Then you can send some of it to UCLA Medical Center and see if it makes a DNA match with the semen."

The detective began to nod. "That's good. That's ⬛ good. I like it."

⬛about this other guy, Grant somebody? Do ⬛?"

⬛s head. "No, but I'll ask Phoenix Vice. ⬛cker may know him. If not, he'll put the ⬛d out. We'll find him."

When Mike got to Kate's house at a few minutes after four, there were two television news trucks parked in front of the house and two crews standing idly on the lawn. He parked his pickup in the driveway and got out, walking toward them.

"I want you to leave," he said to the woman who lifted a microphone toward him.

"Are you Michael Fallon?" she asked.

"Get off this lawn. This is private property."

"We've been here all afternoon," she said. "Is Ms. O'Dwyer at home?"

"I said I want you to leave," Mike said. "She isn't going to make any statements. All she wants is to be left in peace."

"The world wants to see and hear about this," the reporter said angrily, pushing the microphone toward him.

He pulled it from her grasp and threw it into the street. "To her it isn't a story," he said. "It's her daughter."

"Hey, buddy, that's two hundred bucks—" a cameraman said.

Mike stepped toward him, glaring. "How would you like me to shove that camera up your ass, pal?"

The man backed away. "Okay, okay." He turned to the others. "Come on."

They left the lawn and got into the trucks. "This'll make a great story, asshole," one of them called out.

Mike walked around the house to the patio, saw Kate and Jennifer, and went down to the bank of the cove. He put his arm around Kate's shoulders and held her, closing his eyes tightly to hold back his tears.

Kate sat all evening on the sofa like a zomb[i]ing at the TV screen, her eyes distant a[nd] face soiled by torment.

"They'll never get those animals,"

"Yes, they will," Mike said. "They'll Wilkott up for being drunk, and they'll and it will match semen in either Donn[a] and they'll get him for rape. And then guts about this Grant guy to try to get his sentence."

"Rape? Is that enough? For whoever's the

hurt Jennifer, is that enough? He'll be out of prison before she dies."

"No one can be charged with murder unless the death occurs within one year of the act," Mike told her. "That's the law." Even to him it sounded unconvincing. In a case like this, it shouldn't be the law.

"He deserves to die," she muttered. "Nothing less is right."

Mike sighed and shook his head. "That isn't going to happen."

She glared hotly at him with anger-reddened eyes, then stared again at the television screen.

"I'll put Jennifer to bed," Mike said.

He went into Jennifer's room and helped her put away her toys. He arranged her favorite dolls on the pillow and tucked her into bed, then sat on the edge of the bed and read her favorite story about some pink elephant named Ferdie and a rabbit named Snowy. When the soft purr of her breathing had gone on for five minutes, he tiptoed out of her room, closed the door, and walked back to the living room.

Kate had taken a bath and was sitting in a white terry cloth robe. Her hair was pulled back and banded in a ponytail.

He sat down beside her, leaned to her, put his hand gently on her breast under the robe. She lifted her arm to get his hand away, as though waving away a bothersome bug.

He leaned over again and kissed her cheek. She shook her head, annoyed.

"Please snap out of this," he said softly. "You're going to have to live with what's going on."

She looked at him as though he were crazy. "Easy for you to say. You can just walk away like nothing happened. She's not *your* daughter. You'll find somebody without all this shit going on and it's 'fuck you, sweetie.' That's all I'll ever get from you." Tears fell from her eyes, and she stared back at the TV set.

"Jesus Christ," he said. "Is that what you really think?"

She gritted her teeth and sniffled and fixed her eyes on the TV.

"Kate, you told me yesterday that no matter how crazy you get, I should just ignore it."

"I lied. And I'm not crazy, I'm just sick of everything."

"Come on, honey," he pleaded, "*please* get a hold of this thing. You've got to come to grips with it."

"I can't stand any more of this." Her voice was harsh. "I can't stand any more *loss*. I'm empty. I'm wasted. I'm all fucked up inside."

He reached to her hand, and she pulled it away. "No, don't. Just go."

"Jesus, what are you talking about?" He was becoming angry.

"Why don't you hit me or something?"

"What the hell is with you?"

"I can't take any more of this. Just go."

He breathed deeply, trying to sort out what was happening.

She looked at him, her face taut and hostile. "Go!"

He'd had enough. He got up from the sofa and walked out the front door, slamming it behind him.

She sat on the sofa and tears streamed onto the front of her robe. The tears stopped before the crying did. Her body was running out of water to make tears, she was sure. Soon she would dry up like a sunbaked toadstool and turn to dust. She would just blow away. No one would even know. Oh, God, what have you done to me? I meet a man I really love, and then *you* do this thing to Jennifer, *you* do this thing to *me*. You make it so no sane man will ever stay with me. What did I do to you, God? What did I ever do to anyone? Brian? You didn't like what I did to Brian? Well, what did you expect? Did you think I wouldn't protect my daughter, even against her own father? Is that what you thought? And now this, and now this, and now this, and I can't do anything to protect her.

She rocked on the sofa, gasping for breath, weeping once again a flood of tears that would undoubtedly dehydrate her, kill her. Kill me, kill me, kill me. Please kill me. You killed Jennifer, God, now kill me. She stared listlessly at the TV screen, her lachrymose eyes distorting the images, her ears hearing no sound.

There was a hard banging on the front door. It startled her, frightened her. Had they come back? Had God finally answered one of her prayers and sent those animals back to finish her and Jennifer off? I knew I could count on you, God.

She got up and tiptoed to the door. Three more hard bangs on it made her jump. She peeked through the little viewer hole. It was Michael Fallon's face.

She opened the door a crack. "What?" she called out, hiding behind the door and not looking at him. He pushed the door open, knocking her back, and came into the house. He was carrying a big suitcase. She looked at it, then at him. He closed the door quietly.

"Time for me to take over this little family, ma'am," he said in an exaggerated Texas drawl. "Things're gettin' plumb outta hand."

She dissolved, sobbing, her hands covering her face.

He put the suitcase down and took her in his arms. "I love you," he whispered. "You can't get rid of me."

Her lips quivered and she looked up at him. She threw her arms around his neck and pulled herself up on tiptoes and kissed him fiercely. She had never had such a delicious kiss, salted with tears, long and hard and gentle, and there was nothing in it but love. Not lust, not seeking, not demands or desires, just the most overwhelming, enveloping, satisfying emotion of deep love that she had ever known.

He lifted her into his arms, and she clung around his neck, kissing him, never wanting to let go. He carried her into the bedroom and laid her on the bed.

Her robe fell open, and she pulled her arms out of it and sat up. She reached up and unsnapped the snaps of his cowboy shirt and pulled it out of his Levi's. She unbuttoned the Levi's and pushed them and his shorts down to his ankles. She took him into her hand and mouth, then held it pressed to her cheek and kissed it, whispering, "I love you, I love you, I love you."

He kicked off his loafers and stepped out of his pants, pulled the shirt off, and she took him again in her mouth. Then he lay in bed and held her, and she swung her leg on top of his and pressed herself to him, taking him, all of him, until they both gasped in unison and locked each other in such a powerful embrace that no one could ever break them apart.

· FIFTEEN ·

Grant Felsen had a real thing for blondes. His friends used to kid him that if they brought him a black Labrador and bleached its hair, he'd marry it. Well, that wasn't true. He didn't care much for dogs, even yellow ones. He just plain loved blondes. That was the first thing that had attracted him to Phil Wilkott that night they met two months ago. Phil was gorgeous. Drop-dead good looks will get you places in life, no doubt about it. And couple that with plenty of money and a nice car, you had something going, no doubt about it.

Phil hadn't been around the Bronco Buster for three weeks, since they'd done that kid over in Scottsdale. Man, she was pretty, but brown hair, it didn't turn him on much. And cheerleader? Hell! She was flying so high she must have been riding a two-hundred-dollar-a-day horse. Grant liked them blond, and he liked them awake. Maybe Phil got off on corpses like her, but not Grant Felsen. He liked to feel them move. Like Phil moved. Yeah, really good. Big and wild, man. A guy could settle down with a guy like that.

"Philip," he said softly, "I've missed you."

Wilkott pressed the telephone closer to his ear. He was happy that Felsen had called. "Been out of town for two weeks," Wilkott said. "Tucson. We opened a branch office down there, merged with one of the top firms. I had to work out the contracts."

"Tucson's a drag, man. I spent a week there one night." He mimicked a W. C. Fields voice.

Phil laughed. "You're telling me! No action down there anywhere."

"I read in the papers about that Indian." Felsen paused. "Pity."

"Yeah, a pity," Wilkott said. "But the guy was undependable, a real criminal type. I guess he got what he deserved."

"But now we have to find someone new to get our stuff."

"Shouldn't be too hard."

"So when am I going to see you?" Felsen asked.

"I was planning on tonight. I just got back yesterday, had to spend at least one night at home with my wife and kids, you know, otherwise she gets pissed at me. But I'll try tonight, maybe nine, nine-thirty. You going to be at the Bronc?"

"Yeah, I'll be waiting. I get hard just talking to you."

"Bring it along."

The area around the Bronco Buster, just east of downtown Phoenix, had once been a slum that resembled every other skid row from the South Bronx to Compton, abandoned houses and destitute humans decaying together. Then some businessmen had bought the land cheaply and torn down the ruined brick and wood, trying to transform it from terrible to trendy with shops and cafés and bars painted in cool colors of mauve and gray and pale wine. But it hadn't worked. Cars still stopped at the corners to buy heroin and cocaine and crack from ubiquitous vendors, and male and female prostitutes sat at the little tables of the outdoor cafés, their legs spread invitingly open to the street. The colors of the building facades passed out of fashion, and the city's refuse, unwelcome on Central Avenue and Camelback Road and Scottsdale Road, came here to gather.

If you worked Vice for the Phoenix Police Department, this was the candy store. Any sordid treat that could be bought could be bought here. Plainclothes policemen mingled with the patrons. Plainclothes policewomen sat in short tight skirts and halter tops at the little tables in and out of the cafés. But it would have taken General Patton's Third Army to police an area this large and infested, and the Phoenix Police Department was woefully inadequate for a mission so demanding. And in this day and age of prostitute unions and gay liberation, you couldn't arrest just anybody who pulled his pants down or opened her mouth wide. Somebody was bound to sue you for discrimination or harassment or some such bullshit, and the hassle was too damn much. So most of what you did was to watch and listen and pick up "intelligence," a polite word for doing damn little. But once in a while it did pay off.

At Detective Harry Becker's Thursday afternoon officer call, he had asked if any of them had run into a Grant somebody. Detective Annette Warner, an African-American beauty with an ass and a pair of tits to die for—and most of it hanging out of the short shorts and halter—knew who Grant *Felsen* was. He was a pretty boy switch hitter who hung out at the Bronco Buster and hustled both the men and the women who came in looking for nirvana.

Pay attention to him, Detective Becker had instructed the officers. See if he gets together with our pal Phil Wilkott. The two of them may have raped those two girls in Scottsdale.

Annette Warner had begun hanging out at the Bronc instead of the tables outside the cafés, where most of the girls hustled tricks. The trade inside the Bronc was a little higher-class than the johns who drove by outside, scanning the pickings. In here the men were generally quite well dressed, thin and delicate-looking for the most part, some grossly effeminate, but many just average-looking men who undoubtedly led normal and unrumpled lives outside of this place. Middle-aged women came in now and then, hesitant and a bit fearful at first, sitting alone at tables in the murky corners, waiting for a young boy of twenty-one or -two to come up and take away their loneliness.

Detective Warner was hardly ever bothered in the Bronc. These men weren't after a black whore; they were after each other. She sat quietly at a small table in the corner of the bar, sipping C.C. and 7 very slowly, just watching and listening. She had been there five nights a week for two weeks, and Grant Felsen had also been there most of the nights. But she hadn't seen Philip Wilkott. She knew who he was and had seen him around this area at least a dozen times since she'd been assigned to Vice four months ago, and she had heard all the stories about him. It was a pity. He was beautiful, rich, just the catch that any lucky woman would take a vow for, what his own wife had taken a vow for. Hallelujah! Imagine how blessed she must feel.

He came into the Bronc at a few minutes after nine and went directly to Grant Felsen, sitting at the bar. He walked with a slow sway, as though he was drunk or high on drugs. They kissed briefly, greeting each other with warm smiles and a hug. Wilkott sat down on the high stool with difficulty, almost losing his balance.

Perfect! Bust the pervert for DUI when he leaves, grab some of his blood. Exactly what they were after.

Annette walked into the short hallway with the ladies' and men's rooms and two pay telephones. She dropped a quarter in one and dialed.

"Harry, I got Philip Wilkott here at the Bronc. He's either drunk or high as a kite."

"Bingo!" Detective Becker said. "What's he doing?"

"Licking Grant Felsen's ear."

"Great. Maybe we can get them both. I'll call patrol

right now. There'll be a unit outside in five minutes. They'll take him. You stay out of it, keep your cover."

"Yes, sir."

She went back to the table, sipped on the C.C. and 7, and watched. The two men drank three drinks in the space of twenty minutes. When they got off the stools to leave, Wilkott almost fell down. Felsen wrapped Wilkott's arm around his shoulders and they walked out. Annette waited a moment, then left the bar as well. It was brightly lit under the neon marquee. She stood there a moment looking around. The two men had disappeared. They weren't walking east toward the main area of shops and cafés. On the west was a long apartment building and darkness. She didn't see them. They must have walked down the alley on the east side of the bar or the street to the west.

She opted for the alley, darker and narrower and less visible than the street, a place for lizards and rats and cockroaches like these two. She walked to the edge of the building and peeked into the alley. It was dark, but there was enough reflected light all around to make out two men leaning against a car and caressing. She looked around and could barely discern a Phoenix police car a half block away, across the street, parked with its lights off. She walked toward it. One of the uniformed officers got out and walked up to her, a common occurrence in this area, where uniformed patrolmen regularly rousted street walkers.

"I'm Detective Warner," she said quietly.

"Yes, ma'am," the young officer answered. "Dispatch connected me with Detective Becker. Where are they?"

"Just east of the Bronco Buster in the alley. Wilkott is five ten, one seventy, blond and blue. He's drunk, probably high, too. The other guy is five seven, maybe one forty, brown and brown. It doesn't matter what they do in the car. Just wait till they leave."

"Yes, ma'am. We've been briefed."

She walked west down the street, past the apartment building, into the darkness where her car was parked.

The police car backed up to the street corner, then turned down it to go around the back of the building. It was almost pitch black, the moon curtained by a thin overcast. The police car pulled up slowly to a point where the two officers could see a car parked in the alley pointed toward them. It was about a hundred feet away. They couldn't see anyone inside or outside of it. They pulled their car back to the street corner fifty yards west and parked.

A half hour later, lights went on in the alley. A car pulled out and turned east on the street. It was a new Cadillac Seville. Only the driver was visible. The patrol vehicle followed, and the officer in the passenger seat called for an ID on the license plate. He waited several minutes, holding the microphone in his hand. The Cadillac turned north, then made a right turn on McDowell Road.

"Philip Wilkott," came the voice over the radio. "One-three-seven-five-one North Hidden Valley Lane."

"Ten-four," said the policeman. He radioed Dispatch. "This is Alpha two-four-zero. We have a DUI at McDowell and Twenty-fourth Street going east. We'll be out of the car at that location. We need impound on the vehicle."

"Will advise, two-four-zero Alpha."

"Ten-four." The policeman replaced the microphone in its cradle.

"Is he swerving?" the driver asked.

"Like a full-blown drunk."

"Is he maintaining erratic speed, fast, slow, fast?"

"Affirmative."

"Hit the lights. We got a DUI here."

Phil Wilkott was enraged. He hated it when this happened, and this was even worse than the other times. They dragged him into the County Hospital in handcuffs and sat him in a chair in the waiting room with a bunch of greaser bums and wailing nigger brats. It stunk like used diapers in there. And then some chink or nip bitch who smelled like a pail of rubbing alcohol stuck a needle in his arm and took out half his blood. What the hell right did they have to do that?

"You bastards gonna be sorry," he said, forming his words with difficulty. For some reason he couldn't quite fathom, he was having difficulty speaking. "When Rich Haywood gets done with you, you'll be cleaning flophouse crappers."

The police officers were accustomed to abuse. Arresting scum-bags wasn't exactly like attending your seven-year-old daughter's Thanksgiving play at school, where she wears the pumpkin costume.

Richard Haywood answered the phone on the eleventh ring. He was a heavy sleeper, and he had awakened on the fourth ring and hoped that it would stop. It didn't. Some persistent bastard had the nerve to call him at almost two o'clock in the morning.

"Yeah?"

"This is Phil. I'm in jail."

Haywood swung his legs over the side of the bed and sat up slowly.

"What's the charge?"

"DUI."

"Give me a couple of hours."

Phyllis Haywood rolled toward her husband. "What's wrong?"

"That pervert Wilkott got picked up for drunk driving. I've got to go down and get him out."

"That's what he pays you for."

"Yeah, but I hate having to lose sleep to earn it." He laughed.

He went into the study and sat down at his desk. He called a sleepy James Friedl. The judge said he'd put the handwritten release order in the mailbox by the front door as usual.

Unfortunately, Friedl lived all the way over in Mesa—a long drive. This is one hell of a way to make a living, Haywood thought, dressing in the bedroom in pitch blackness, trying not to wake his wife again.

· SIXTEEN ·

John Steigman called. It was Sunday morning.

"We got him last night," he said to Kate.

"Thank you, thank you," she said. "Did you get his blood?"

"Yes, he's type O. So far, so good. I just called Dr. Van Leisen in Los Angeles. He'll have the sample picked up at the L.A. airport at ten-fifteen and DNA-test it immediately. He should have the results by this evening."

"Thank you, John. Thanks for everything you're doing."

"Is Mike there?"

"Yes. Hold on."

She handed the phone to Mike.

"We did an inventory search of his Cadillac this morning at the impound yard," Steigman said.

"Yes?"

"We got a .25 Colt auto. It was under his seat."

Mike allowed himself to smile. "That's too good to be true."

"Now, if that piece of garbage Supremas will do us a favor and die, we can take the bullet out, get the ballistics, and charge Wilkott with murder."

Mike hung up and told Kate. She felt light and limber and healthy, and she actually felt a surge of pleasure for the first time in weeks. She had been unable to push away the guilt that crept over her, entombed her, guilt at feeling good and loving someone at a time when Jennifer needed her. She knew that it was irrational and that Jennifer had no idea about any of this and was happy. But the guilt threatened to overwhelm her nonetheless.

When Steigman called at seven o'clock that evening, she wept on the telephone, then hugged Mike closely.

"It's him," she whispered. "They got a blood DNA match. He's the one who hurt Jennifer. They're arresting him tonight."

"Okay, don't panic," Richard Haywood said. "Get a hold of yourself."

Phil Wilkott tried to steady and slow his breathing. To no avail. He was shaking all over. His heart was going nuts.

"What the fuck is going on? Get me out of here." He had been released on bail after the drunk-driving arrest last night, and now—suddenly—he was in jail again.

"It's Sunday night," Haywood said. "I can't get you out. You'll have to wait for the initial appearance tomorrow afternoon."

"I gave you fifty thousand dollars, you son of a bitch. You get me out."

Haywood gritted his teeth. "This is going to cost. This isn't drunk driving."

"I'll get it from my father. Just get me out of here."

Haywood hung up the phone. He was sitting on a large upholstered chair in his living room, reading the Sunday newspaper.

"Who was that?" his wife asked. She was watching some music-award show on television.

"Phil Wilkott."

"What's happened now?"

"He's been arrested for raping those two girls in Scottsdale a few weeks ago. You know, the one little girl got AIDS from it."

She looked with concern at him. "I read about it. Did he do it?"

He nodded.

"You're going to represent him?"

"That's why you're wearing that watch."

Last week he had bought her a thirty-five-thousand-dollar Cartier wristwatch with a diamond and ruby bezel. She had been admiring it in a catalogue for years. She had toiled through the lean years with him, and finally he was able to show her his appreciation for what she had been through, and his love.

She took the watch off and laid it on the table, then stared at him.

"Don't be ridiculous," he said. "Everything in this house, the house itself, the cars, the car I just bought for Josh, the prom dress you bought for Candy, it all comes from pimps and whores and thieves and killers and child molesters. It's a business just like driving a cab."

"Not exactly."

"All right, it's a better business. I'm not apologizing."

She put the watch back on. "Sorry."

"I'll be in the study for a while."

She nodded.

He closed the door to the study and sat at the desk. This is ridiculous, he thought. I can't call Jimmy Friedl. He'll tell me to go to hell, and he'll be right.

He put his feet up on the desk and lounged back in the desk chair. Well, I better call his old man and tell him. This is going to make Tom Terrific happy as a bug in a rug. He sat up, looked up the telephone number for Thomas Osborne Wilkott in the telephone book, and dialed.

"He's where?" Tom Wilkott asked, hoping to hear a different answer.

"He's in jail, Mr. Wilkott."

"That goddamn kid. Can't keep his hand off a drink or his dick in his pants."

"It's not that simple this time, Mr. Wilkott."

Hesitation. "What do you mean?" His voice had a tinge of apprehension.

"He was arrested for raping those two girls at McCormick Ranch several weeks ago."

There was silence on the other end of the line. He coughed, and his voice was soft. "My God, no."

"Yes, Mr. Wilkott."

"But he didn't do it. He wouldn't do something so terrible." It was more a question than an assertion.

"Of course not, Mr. Wilkott. But there's apparently an Indian fellow from the Salt River Reservation who claims that he did."

"An Indian? How in hell?"

"I know, Mr. Wilkott. It's ridiculous. But it's happening."

"What are they charging him with?"

"They just arrested him. There's no indictment yet, no formal charges. They'll initial him tomorrow and set bond, probably take it to the grand jury the end of this week or early next week. I'm going to have to get to work on this right away."

There was a long pause. "Yes, yes, okay. I understand. What's it going to be?"

"I believe that a hundred thousand dollars would be fair." He held his breath, not wanting to pant into the telephone.

"Yes, all right. Can you come to my office at nine tomorrow morning?"

"Yes, Mr. Wilkott. And again, I'm sorry about this. I'm sure that it's going to right itself very quickly."

He hung up and smiled, then let out a whoop of joy. His wife opened the door a moment later and peeked in.

"What's the hollering? Are you okay?"

He smiled broadly at her. "Yeah, I'm real okay."

Tom Wilkott had played tennis this morning, as he did every Sunday morning, with Bill Keck, the publisher of the *Arizona Republic*. They had been friends for thirty years, and Bill's oldest son, Matthew, was a partner in the law firm of Wilkott and Deets.

"Oh, my God, that's awful," Bill Keck said.

"But he didn't do it," Tom Wilkott assured him quickly. "He couldn't have done anything like that. I just hired Richard Haywood."

"Well, that's a good start. How can I help?"

"I need a little favor."

"Anything, just ask. You know that."

"I want you to kill the story."

There was a long pause. "You know I can't do that, Tom," he said gently. "I publish a newspaper, not just a bunch of pages that aren't good for anything but wrapping fish."

"But this will destroy him. Even when he gets released and the charges are dropped, the story will live forever. He'll be destroyed."

He heard Bill sighing deeply.

"What if it was *your* son *Matthew* who was wrongly accused? How would you feel then?"

More sighing. "Look, Tom, I don't even know how I could kill it. Somebody's going to pick it up. Then a lot of people are going to wonder why we didn't."

"I've lived in Phoenix for sixty-two years, Bill. I know this place. The TV reporters don't go down to the courthouse unless they read about something in your paper. The *Gazette* comes out in the early afternoon, and they never cover court stuff. They figure that whatever is hot in yesterday's proceedings is reported by you in the morning, and to report it again in the afternoon is old news and won't sell papers."

"Yes, I understand all that, but this is one of the major stories of the year, maybe more than one year. When we ran that story weeks ago on the little girl and her mother, we printed sixty thousand extra papers and didn't even get half of them back. This story is news."

"Come on, Bill." Tom was getting angry, having

difficulty holding his temper in check. "The *New York Times* says, 'All the news that's *fit* to print.' *Fit*. This isn't *fit* to print. It's a goddamn lie."

Again he heard heavy sighing from Bill Keck. "What's the status?"

"He just got arrested earlier this evening. He hasn't been formally charged with anything. He'll make bail tomorrow afternoon."

"When do they have to take it to the grand jury?"

"I'm not sure," Tom said. "I haven't done a criminal case in thirty years. Haywood said probably by early next week."

Bill Keck thought for a moment. "All right, I'll tell you the only thing I'm going to be able to do on this. I'll pull my reporter off the story. But if anyone else picks it up, we have to go with it. And if—God forbid—he actually gets indicted, then we have to cover it. That's all I can do."

"That's all I can ask. Thanks, Bill."

· SEVENTEEN ·

It was not a typical lawyer's Monday morning for Michael Fallon. He had a divorce trial before Judge Sherrill that was a classic. Mike was representing a twenty-one-year-old fellow who had been married for seven months to his twenty-one-year-old high school sweetheart. He was a hod carrier with a construction company, and she slung hash at McDonald's. They each owned a superannuated beat-up little car of indeterminate parentage and the clothes on their backs.

Mike had charged all of three hundred fifty dollars as his fee, initially perceiving the matter as nothing more than a quickie divorce, just pay the filing fees at the court, submit the simple forms, and do a one-page dissolution order for the judge's signature. The filing fees and service of process were a hundred thirty-nine dollars for a tidy little profit of two hundred eleven dollars for an hour and a half or two of work. Well, the best-laid plans of mice and men . . .

The first eye-opener was the negotiation session between husband, wife, and the two lawyers. The young lady had hired an attorney about Mike's age from one of the medium-sized seventy or eighty law firms. Exactly how she was paying his fee, which had to be at least a thousand dollars, was unclear, although she was a pretty woman with a sylphlike body and golden hair, and he had the look of a prospector who had struck gold.

The negotiation session consisted of three hours of screaming, shouting, weeping, wailing, and the husband and the other lawyer almost coming to blows as the stalwart barrister staunchly defended the lady's virtue. The second negotiating marathon was supposed to settle the community property to be divided between them: a Singer sewing machine, vintage 1960 or so, a treasure of inestimable value that had been given by the husband's mother to the wife a day after the marriage ceremony. Husband claimed that it was a loan that still belonged to his mommy and did not constitute property of the marital estate; wife claimed that it was a wedding gift to her and therefore her own property.

Judge Bernard Sherrill presided over this trial of titans as a gathering black thundercloud brooded over the earth below. After each party had testified emotively as to the status of the disputed heirloom, the judge asked both attorneys to join him in chambers. He took his robe off, didn't invite them to have a seat in the two nice oak-tanned leather chairs in front of the desk, and glared at them with reddening eyes.

"Are you kidding me?" he growled.

The lawyers swallowed and shifted their weight to the other foot.

"I have a first-degree murder case starting at ten o'clock, and it's now eleven twenty-three, and I am listening to a divorce case about a *sewing machine.*" The last was said with such passion and fury that both of the attorneys jumped. The judge regained his composure with difficulty.

"I am recessing this trial indefinitely, gentlemen, and the only time I ever want to see either of you again on this matter is to sign a dissolution order. Otherwise I shall have you both disemboweled. Is that quite clear?"

Mike nodded. The other guy nodded. They left the chambers and collected their respective clients. In the corridor, after hearing the judge's sage determination, the husband demanded that Mike give him his money back and threatened to complain about his fee to the State Bar Association. The last glimpse Mike had of the wife was watching her being comforted in the protective arms of her lawyer.

He walked over to the courthouse cafeteria and sat eating an incredibly awful hamburger and a watered-down, bubbleless quasi–Dr Pepper. Harvey Stidham walked up to the table carrying a tray and sat down.

"That doesn't even look edible," he said, jutting his chin toward the half of Mike's hamburger left uneaten.

"This place needs a health department inspection," Mike said. "What's the latest?"

"You haven't heard?"

Mike shook his head. "Been in trial."

"Philip Wilkott is out without bond."

"How in hell did he get O.R.'ed before initial appearances?"

"Haywood asked the chief judge this morning to get the case assigned immediately to a judge so he could bring some accelerated motions, so Judge Hill assigned it."

"Don't tell me."

Harvey nodded. "Yes, sirree. Jimmy the Prick Friedl."

"Damn! Did Haywood ex parte you?"

"Nope. He did it by the book. Called me at eight, said he had an appointment with Hill at eight-thirty. We met in Hill's chambers, and Hill called the court administrator, asked who was the next judge up for a kiddie sex assignment, and it was Friedl." Harvey shrugged. "Luck of the draw."

"Well, he shouldn't have too much trouble with this case," Mike said. "Even Friedl doesn't want to be tarred and feathered and ridden out of town on a rail."

"Yeah, I agree. The guy's a bigoted moron, but this isn't a real tough case." Harvey stabbed at the stubble on his plate euphemistically touted as a Cobb salad. "By the way, you hear about Henry Carpenter?"

Mike shook his head.

"Some of his cell mates apparently didn't cotton to spending their time with a child molester and murderer. Ol' Henry fell out of bed Saturday in the dark hours of the night, got a fractured skull. He's on life support."

"Tell me where," Mike said. "I'll go pull the plug."

John Steigman walked up to the table carrying a pint container of milk in one hand and brandishing a sheet of paper in the other. He nodded to Mike.

"Your secretary said you were down here committing suicide," he said to Harvey, sitting down next to Mike.

"What's that?" Mike asked, looking at the milk.

"That's called a duodenal ulcer, Mikey my boy. Something which I'm sure you'll be enjoying when you're my age."

"When *he's* seventy," Harvey said, "he'll already be dead ten years."

"A mere fifty-three, Harv, though I know I don't look a day over fifty." The mirth left his eyes. "What's this subpoena I just got served with?" He laid the sheet of paper in front of Stidham.

The prosecutor read it. "Haywood's got a motion to quash set for Wednesday morning. I guess he wants to be sure you'll come."

"What the hell kind of testimony does he think he's going to get from me?" Steigman glanced at Mike, then looked back at the prosecutor.

Harvey shrugged. "I don't know. I haven't even seen the motion to quash yet, didn't know he'd filed one until now. We'll just have to wait until I get it. Do you know if anybody else has been subpoenaed?"

Steigman nodded. "Yeah, I checked the praecipes in the file in the Clerk's office: Anthony Waywaykla; Marian Wheatley, one of the matrons out at Black Canyon; Phoenix police patrolmen Skelton and Pozniak; Michael Fallon; and a subpoena duces tecum for the juvenile court records of Donna Alvarez. He also got Friedl to sign a writ of habeas corpus *ad testificandum* to bring the Alvarez girl to court."

"What's an Anthony Waywaykla?" Stidham asked.

"I have a notion he's a guy they call Tony Brown Horse," the detective said. "He hung out with Peter Supremas."

"What's he have to do with this?"

John Steigman looked at Mike, frowned, and leaned over the table toward Harvey. "I don't think we better talk here. Let's go upstairs to your office."

Stidham looked at both men, perplexed, and shrugged. "Let's go," he said.

Kate's face had brightened since learning last night of Wilkott's arrest and the DNA blood match. But now she no longer appeared pleased.

"What's O.R.?" she asked, frowning.

"It means he was released on his Own Recognizance. He didn't have to post a bail bond."

"Is that normal?" she asked.

"Pretty much."

"Then why was there a half-million-dollar bond on that Peter what's his name?"

"Because he had no family, no job, no visible means of support, a prior criminal record, didn't own any property. He was what we call a 'flight risk,' a defendant who has no ties to the community and might simply disappear if he's released. But Wilkott is the opposite. The likelihood of him fleeing is nil, and since he's not charged with murder, he has a right to get out O.R."

"He shouldn't."

"Nobody's proved him guilty yet, and he still is presumed innocent." The theory was nice, but the release of Wilkott didn't sit very well with Mike. But what could you expect from Friedl?

She shrugged and stopped frowning. "Well, he'll be back inside soon enough."

Mike nodded.

"I talked to my dad and mom today."

"Yeah?" Mike said.

Jennifer was asleep, and they were sitting in the kitchen, eating the dessert that they had been too stuffed to eat three hours earlier.

"This is great apple pie," he said. "Did you really make it?"

"Yip. Me sainted mum taught me as a wee girl." She mimicked an Irish brogue.

"She done right fine, ma'am." A thick Texas drawl.

She hesitated. "They want me to come back to Boston, live near them. My dad said that he wants me and Jennifer close so that he can take care of us."

Mike put his fork down slowly. "What did you say?"

"I said it was your turn. You're going to take care of us."

"And what did he say?"

"He said he thought that was an excellent alternative."

A smile spread over Mike's face. He got up and took her by the hand. "Come on, lady, I'm going to ravish your body and then go running off into the night."

She smiled at him. "See, buster? I knew that's what you'd end up doing."

· EIGHTEEN ·

Judge James Friedl disposed of the few matters on his calendar in short order. A sentencing, a motion to reduce bond, an attorney's motion to withdraw as counsel for a client who had proven to be too indigent to pay any of his promised fees. The courtroom slowly emptied. One of the elderly court watchers remained in the spectators' seats along with Mike Fallon, Harvey Stidham, John Steigman, Richard Haywood, Philip Wilkott, and a couple of anonymous-looking women. Donna Alvarez and a matron sat in the jury box. Donna sat stiffly on the edge of the chair, her eyes like a fawn caught in the headlights of a car.

"State versus Wilkott," Judge Friedl said. "Aggravated rape and attempted murder."

Harvey Stidham and John Steigman walked to the prosecution table. Haywood and his client went to the defense table.

"I read your motion to suppress, Mr. Haywood," the judge said. "You've done a fine job of summarizing the law of coerced confessions and illegal search and seizure, but you didn't recite a single fact to relate it to this case."

"May it please the court," Haywood said, "given the short amount of time that I had prior to this hearing, I simply didn't have the opportunity to gather all of the facts into a written memorandum. It seemed to me that my investigation of those facts and the pressing need to bring them before this honorable court and to redress the grievous wrong that has been done to Phil Wilkott before any more public injury could be done to him, these considerations outweighed the formalistic requirement of a written fact statement. In any event, Your Honor, it will rapidly become apparent that the facts are either known to the State or could have and should have been known if the prosecutor and the police had not been so anxious to rush to an unprincipled judgment in this matter."

Harvey Stidham stood up. "May I be heard, Your Honor?"

"Go ahead."

"The State is entirely in the dark about the factual basis for Mr. Haywood's motion. The defendant has made no confession. All of the constitutional scholarship which Mr. Haywood has so eagerly provided this court in his motion has nothing to do with this case."

"Mr. Haywood?"

"If the court would indulge us in the interests of justice a mere half hour, the claimed stupefaction of the prosecution will clearly be proved fictitious."

"All right, let's proceed."

"Defense calls Margaret Pola," Haywood said.

A woman carrying a manila file walked up to the courtroom clerk and was sworn as a witness.

"State your name and occupation."

"Margaret Pola, senior records administrator for the Department of Economic Security Child Protective Services."

"As part of your duties, Ms. Pola, are you responsible for the control and safeguarding of the official records of all juveniles who are adjudicated delinquent?"

"I am. I'm the official custodian of records."

"Pursuant to my subpoena duces tecum served on you on Monday, have you brought to this court any records responsive to that subpoena?"

"I have."

"Whose records are they?"

"Donna Alvarez's."

"In what form are the records?"

"I made a true and correct copy of everything in her file, and I have attached my certification to that effect."

Richard Haywood walked forward and took the file from her hands.

"Defense offers exhibit A, Your Honor."

"Have you seen it, Mr. Stidham?" the judge asked.

"No, sir."

"Let him see it."

Haywood brought it to Stidham. Harvey leafed through it for a couple of minutes.

Harvey stood up. "Your Honor, may I exhibit the file to Mr. Michael Fallon? He's the court-appointed lawyer for Miss Alvarez."

"Yes."

Mike came forward beside Harvey, studied the file for a moment, and nodded.

"I object on the basis of relevance, Your Honor," Stidham said.

"I'll tie it in quickly," Haywood said.

"Do you agree that the file is accurate, Mr. Stidham?"

"It appears to be a true copy, Your Honor."

"Very well. I'll rule on its admissibility once you've tied it in, Mr. Haywood."

Haywood took the file to his table. "That's all I have for Mrs. Pola, Your Honor."

"No questions," Harvey said.

"Michael Fallon," Richard Haywood announced.

Mike walked to the clerk's desk, swore to tell the truth, and sat down at the witness stand. He was nervous and apprehensive, uncomfortable being the answerer instead of the questioner.

"You are Michael Fallon, an attorney admitted to practice in the state of Arizona?"

"That's correct."

"I'm not attempting to embarrass you with my questions, Mr. Fallon, but I am obligated to elicit certain facts and to present them before the court to aid the court's judgment."

Mike nodded.

"You are, let us say, the boyfriend of Mary O'Dwyer?"

"Yes."

"She has a three-year-old daughter named Jennifer?"

"Yes."

"Mary was also, about two months or so ago, awarded temporary custody of Donna Alvarez as her foster mother?"

"Yes."

"Donna Alvarez at that time went to live in the O'Dwyer home?"

"Yes."

"Jennifer O'Dwyer was savagely raped approximately three weeks ago?"

"Yes."

"Both Mary and you were quite understandably traumatized by this terrible crime?"

"Yes."

"Peter Supremas was arrested and charged as the rapist?"

"No. Not as the *only* rapist."

"Explain that, please."

"Donna Alvarez was also raped that night. The semen tests indicated two different perpetrators, because the one who raped Jennifer was infected with HIV and infected Jennifer."

The judge pursed his lips and rubbed his chin and sat back in his chair. Donna began to cry softly in the jury box.

"Donna Alvarez told you that she was raped?"

"Yes."

"Was there evidence of force?"

"She had two bruises on her face—actually, one was

on her temple. She was unconscious when I found her."

"And she had almost overdosed on heroin?"

Mike swallowed. "Yes. She said that she had forcibly been injected."

"Did you believe her?"

"Yes. And I still do."

"You knew that she was a heroin addict?"

"I knew that she had been. She was clean when she was living with the O'Dwyers."

"Did she tell you who had injected her?"

"No."

"Did she ever mention the name Philip Wilkott?"

"No."

"Do you know Anthony Waywaykla?"

"No."

"Perhaps you know him as Tony Brown Horse?"

"I have been told by Detective John Steigman that they are one and the same. I don't know that of my own knowledge."

The courtroom door swung open, and Thomas Wilkott came in. He sat down in the first row of the spectators' pews. Judge Friedl glanced at him out of the corner of his eye. He had never met him, but he had seen his photographs dozens of times, in the *State Bar Journal*, in newspapers. There were always photos of him at charity events, or shaking presidents Reagan's or Bush's hands, or laughing at a dinner table with his old pal Barry Goldwater. Nobody doesn't know Tom Terrific.

"Was the criminal case against Peter Supremas dismissed as a result of blood tests which proved that it was not his semen that was recovered from either Jennifer or Donna?"

"Yes."

"Did that cause you anger?"

"Yes."

"Did you believe that Mr. Supremas had brought the two rapists to the O'Dwyer home?"

"Yes."

"Did you go to see Mr. Supremas?"

"Yes." Mike's cheeks reddened.

"Did you enter his home without invitation and by use of force?"

"Yes."

"Did you beat Tony Brown Horse so severely that he required hospitalization?"

"Yes."

"Did you beat Peter Supremas severely?"

"Yes."

"Did you shoot him?"

"No."

"Did you in the course of that beating demand that he give you the names of two rapists?"

"Yes."

"Did he?"

"Yes."

"What are those names?"

"Philip Wilkott and Grant. He didn't know Grant's last name."

Haywood sat down.

Judge Friedl was frowning. "Mr. Stidham, your witness."

"Thank you, Your Honor," Harvey said.

"Just one thing, Mr. Stidham," the judge said, leaning forward on the bench and scowling. "Has this witness been charged with aggravated assault or attempted murder?"

"No, Your Honor," Harvey said, standing up.

"Is there a reason?"

"Yes, Your Honor. The county attorney himself made the determination Monday afternoon that Mr. Fallon had sufficient legal justification to preclude the state from prosecuting him."

"Has the county attorney referred Mr. Fallon to the State Bar Association for disciplinary proceedings?"

"We have not, Your Honor."

"Well, Mr. Stidham," Friedl said. "I think that it is

quite appropriate for me to refer this to the bar." He settled back in his chair. "All right, let's get on with it." He noticed out of the corner of his eye that Tom Terrific was smiling.

Harvey Stidham sat down at the table. "Mr. Fallon, were you instructed, asked, told, urged, begged, or any other word that might come to mind, by me or any prosecutor or John Steigman or any law enforcement officer to go get those names from Peter Supremas or to hurt him in any way?"

"No."

"That's all I have, Your Honor," Stidham said.

"You're excused, Mr. Fallon," Friedl said. "Rest assured that this court is not as unmindful of the rights of innocent citizens as the County Attorney obviously is."

"Defense calls Detective John Steigman," Haywood said.

John was sworn, took the stand, and answered the preliminaries.

"How did you receive the name Peter Supremas, being the man whom Donna Alvarez claims injected her with heroin?"

"We got 'Big Gun Pete' from Donna Alvarez. I then got his true name from the chief of police at the Salt River Reservation."

"Did Donna tell *you* that name?"

"No, she refused to talk to me. She told Kate O'Dwyer."

"That's Mary O'Dwyer?"

"Yes."

"You asked Mary O'Dwyer to get the name or names from Donna?"

"That's right."

"How many times?"

John shrugged. "Several."

"Did you set up her meeting with Donna at the Black Canyon Detention Center?"

"I did."

"And isn't it true that without your intervention, she would not lawfully have been permitted to visit Donna?"

"No. She was Donna's foster mother. She had the legal right-to visit."

Haywood lifted the Child Protective Services file off the table, flourished it in front of him, and stood up. "May it please the court, may I show this exhibit to the witness?"

"Very well."

Haywood walked up to Steigman, opened the file, folded back several pages, and handed it to the detective.

"Please read the heading of this court order."

Steigman took a pair of readers out of his suit coat pocket, perched them on his nose, and read. "In the matter of Donna Alvarez, a Juvenile. Severance of custody of foster parent."

"Would you please read the sentence here?" Richard Haywood pointed.

"On motion of Child Protective Services, and good cause appearing, subject minor is remanded to the custody of the State Department of Juvenile Corrections, and without objection, the appointment of Mary Caitlin O'Dwyer as foster parent is set aside and all custodial rights severed."

"What is the date of that court order, Detective Steigman?"

"April 26."

"On what date did Mary O'Dwyer visit Donna Alvarez?"

Harvey Stidham turned his head toward Mike and rolled his eyes.

"I don't remember."

"Let me refresh your recollection, Detective." Haywood picked up the file, turned a few pages, and handed it back to John. "This is the visitation order issued by the director of the Black Canyon facility. Would you read it for the court?"

"At request of Detective John Steigman, Scottsdale Police Department, Donna Alvarez will be permitted visitation with M. C. O'Dwyer on Friday morning, April 28." Steigman's lips blanched as he pressed them together.

"Now I ask you again, Detective Steigman, was Mary O'Dwyer the foster mother of Donna Alvarez on April 28?"

"It appears not."

"Did Mary O'Dwyer have the legal right to visit Donna Alvarez on April 28?"

Harvey stood up. "Objection, Your Honor, calls for a legal conclusion."

Friedl waved him back to his seat. "Overruled. Answer the question, Detective, if you know."

He cleared his throat nervously, his voice weaker. "It would appear that she did not."

"And once again, Detective, just so I'm quite clear on this, you set up the visit and urged Mary O'Dwyer to go and find out who Donna claimed was responsible for the terrible crime?"

"Yes, but I had no idea whatsoever at that time that Kate O'Dwyer's parental rights had been severed."

"Did any evidence at all point you to Peter Supremas before you received his name from Mary O'Dwyer?"

Steigman shook his head, his cheek twitching. "No."

"And you would not have learned of any other names had you not first learned the name of Peter Supremas?"

"I don't know that. But at *that* time we had no other leads."

Haywood sat down.

Stidham remained seated. "Did you ask for or provide any compulsion that Donna actually answer Mrs. O'Dwyer's questions?"

"No, none at all."

"That's all, Your Honor," Harvey said.

Steigman sat down beside the prosecutor. Both he and Harvey appeared crestfallen.

"May I have a moment, Your Honor?" Harvey asked.

"You may."

Harvey walked over to Mike, sitting in the spectators' section. "Did you know that her custody had been terminated?" he whispered.

Mike shook his head. "No. And I don't think Kate knew."

"We've got us a little problem here," Harvey said. He walked back to the table and sat down.

"Defense calls Marian Wheatley," said Haywood.

The matron in the jury box stood up, was sworn, and sat in the witness chair. She was in her late fifties, wore her dark gray hair in a bun, and weighed at least a hundred eighty pounds. In the white short-sleeve uniform shirt and blue twill trousers, she didn't look fat.

"You are Marian Wheatley, a matron at Black Canyon Detention Center, is that correct?"

"Yes, sir."

"You took Donna to the attorneys' interview room on April 28 to speak with a visitor?"

"Yes, sir."

"You heard loud noises from the interview room?"

"Yes, sir. Like a fight, yelling."

"What did you do?"

"I entered the room and seen the woman pulling the juvenile's hair and screaming at her, and there was red marks like slap marks on the juvenile's cheek."

"Did you hear the woman say anything?"

"Not really. Just real angry, you know, real wild-eyed. She just up and left."

"Did you ascertain her name?"

"The sign-in log had a Mary C. O'Dwyer."

Mike Fallon sat at the end of the front spectators' pew and leaned against the wall. The breath left his lungs.

"Move the introduction of exhibit A, Your Honor," Haywood said.

"Yes, admitted," said the judge.

"Defense calls Donna Alvarez," Haywood said. "Your Honor, it will be okay if she's sworn right there and testifies from the jury box."

The clerk told Donna to raise her right hand, and Donna did it hesitantly, obviously terrified. She was sworn.

"You are Donna Alvarez," Haywood asked.

"Yes," came the whisper.

"You heard Mrs. Wheatley testify. Do you agree with what she said?"

Donna looked around for help. She looked at Mike Fallon, her eyes pleading.

Mike stood up. "Your Honor, I'm the court-appointed counsel for this girl, and I have not had the opportunity to interview her on this matter. I had no idea for what purpose she had been writted here."

Judge Friedl eyed him distastefully. "You certainly had plenty of time to see her before this hearing, Mr. Fallon."

"And what would I have talked to her about, Your Honor?"

Friedl stared at Mike with disgust and shook his head. "Come up here and talk to her." He pointed at the jury box.

"That's not exactly a confidential interview, Your Honor. I would request five minutes in the attorneys' conference room."

"Request denied, Mr. Fallon. You should have done your job *before* coming to court. *Whisper* to her, and we'll wait a couple of minutes." He settled back in his chair and looked imperiously around the courtroom, glancing quickly at a pleased-looking Tom Terrific.

Mike sat down on the chair next to Donna. He leaned over and whispered close to her ear, "Don't be afraid, Donna. Nothing is going to happen to you."

"I don't care about me," she said. "I'm not going to hurt Kate."

"Just tell the truth, whatever it is."

"I won't hurt Kate. She didn't mean it." Tears began to spill over her eyelids. "She was just real upset."

"Just tell the truth," Mike whispered. He settled back in the chair and nodded to Judge Friedl.

"Continue," the judge said.

"Answer my question," said Richard Haywood. "Is what Mrs. Wheatley said true?"

Donna clenched her jaw and looked at her hands.

"Answer yes or no, Donna," the judge said sternly.

"I don't remember," she said, her voice tremulous.

"Did she hit you before or after you told her the name?"

Donna shook her head, sniffling, crying. "I don't remember."

Richard Haywood sat back in his chair and shrugged. He nodded to the judge.

"Mr. Stidham?" the judge said.

"No questions."

"Defense calls Patrolman Dennis Pozniak, Your Honor," Haywood said.

Mike whispered an inch from Donna's ear, "You're a very nice girl."

She turned her face to his and looked into his eyes. "Please tell her I'm sorry. Please tell her I wish it was me."

He wanted to hold her in his arms and comfort her, but he couldn't. He walked back to the spectators' area, sat down on the front bench, and rubbed his eyes hard.

The bailiff left the courtroom and returned a moment later with a uniformed Phoenix policeman. He was sworn to tell nothing but the truth and took the stand.

Haywood remained seated. "You are Dennis Pozniak, the driver of the marked police car which stopped Philip Wilkott on suspicion of drunk driving on Saturday night?"

"Yes, sir."

"Were you instructed to wait near the Bronco Buster, to identify Philip Wilkott, and to stop him for drunk driving?"

"Yes, sir."

"Who so instructed you?"

"Dispatch. It was on the orders of Detective Becker from Vice."

"How did you know who Wilkott would be, how to identify him?"

"A Detective Warner was doing surveillance in the Bronco Buster. She came out and described him for us, said he was drunk, was in a car in the alley next to the bar."

"Would you have stopped him or even been following him had it not been that you were assigned to do so?"

He shrugged. "No, sir."

"Describe the driving behavior of Mr. Wilkott."

The policeman squirmed a bit, looked around, and pursed his lips. "He was weaving, driving inconsistent speeds."

"Were your instructions to arrest him, no matter how he was driving?"

Again the officer squirmed. "Our instructions were that if Detective Warner said he was drunk, we were to arrest him no matter how he was driving."

"That's all, Your Honor," Haywood said. "Defense rests."

"Mr. Stidham?" the judge asked.

"No questions, Your Honor."

"You're excused, Officer Pozniak," Judge Friedl said.

The policeman left the courtroom.

"Any witnesses, Mr. Stidham?"

"No, Your Honor. May I address the court?"

"Argument?"

"If the court please."

"Well, why don't we hear Mr. Haywood first? It's his motion."

"Thank you, Your Honor," Haywood said, rising. "I think it is crystal clear beyond any doubt that the evidence in this matter which resulted in the arrest of Philip Wilkott was illegally seized. Mary O'Dwyer could not legally have visited Donna Alvarez, since she was no longer her foster mother. The Scottsdale Police Department sent Mary there *as its agent* for the purpose of conducting the interrogation of a minor who had refused to speak with the police. She did speak to Mary, but apparently only as a result of coercion by physical violence at the hands of Mary O'Dwyer. Even had she voluntarily spoken, it was an illegal interrogation by an agent of the police, and every bit of information that led to Peter Supremas was illegally seized. Under *Wong Sun* versus *United States*, all of it is fruit of the poisoned tree and must be suppressed.

"Even more shocking is the conduct of Michael Fallon, an officer of the court, beating two men almost to death, shooting Peter Supremas, and thus acquiring the name of Philip Wilkott. How much credibility do we lend to such a name? Supremas could just as easily have said Richard Haywood or James Friedl.

"Then police officers, armed with this illegally seized information, lie in wait for Mr. Wilkott and arrest him on the pretext of drunk driving. And such is the evidence upon which the state of Arizona arrests Philip Wilkott. This is shocking to the conscience of every decent human being. The warrant must be quashed. This case must be dismissed." He sat down.

Harvey Stidham stood up. "May it please the court, Mr. Haywood has missed the point here. The Phoenix Police Department did not arrest Philip Wilkott when Mike Fallon informed Detective Steigman that he got the name from Supremas. There is no question that Mike Fallon was *not* an agent for the state; he was not asked or induced by anyone to question Supremas. He was a private citizen acting entirely on his own volition and with no one's knowledge. The Supreme Court has ruled that evidence illegally seized by a private citizen who is not an agent of the state *may legally be used*. Even so, Detective Steigman declined to arrest Philip Wilkott at that time.

"The subsequent arrest of Wilkott was completely legal. He was arrested for drunk driving by two Phoenix patrol officers in the normal course of their duties. His blood was lawfully taken at Maricopa County General Hospital, and it revealed a .22 alcohol level, more than twice the legal limit. He was lawfully arrested and charged with DUI. His blood type was determined by the hospital and the criminalistics lab to be the same as that of the rapist who had attacked Jennifer Mulvaney in this case. A sample of his blood was sent to the UCLA Medical Center, which had DNA-tested the semen taken from both of the raped girls. A DNA match was made of Mr. Wilkott's blood with—"

"Your Honor, I most strenuously object to this improper argument by the prosecutor," Richard Haywood roared as he jumped up from his chair. "This is a motion to quash an arrest warrant as the direct fruit of an unlawful search carried out by Mary O'Dwyer as the agent for the state. No more, no less. This scurrilous character assassination by the prosecutor must not be permitted to proceed."

Friedl leaned over the bench. "All right, gentlemen, settle down." He spoke mildly. "I realize this is not a pleasant case for any of us, Mr. Stidham, not for you, not for me, not for Mr. Haywood. But *Wong Sun* is the law of the land, and the evidence from this witness stand seems to me to be unimpeachable. Notwithstanding any other fact, notwithstanding the heinous nature of the crime committed, this court is bound by the law. Do you have anything further to present to this court bearing on the visit that Mary O'Dwyer had with Donna Alvarez at Black Canyon?"

Harvey Stidham shook his head. "No, Your Honor. But the drunk-driving arrest breaks the nexus of illegality. It was an independent arrest, lawful, made on the grounds of drunk driving, which indeed proved to be true. It is the evidence from that lawful arrest alone that is being used in the prosecution of Philip Wilkott."

"Mr. Stidham," the judge said. "I do not agree with you that the arrest for drunk driving was legal. I do *not* believe the testimony of the patrolman who made the stop that he did it on the basis of Mr. Wilkott's poor driving. I believe that it is perfectly clear that he was instructed to make the stop no matter what, and DUI was simply the pretext. The fact that Mr. Wilkott later turned out to be DUI does not retroactively make the pretext stop legal. Let me ask you a simple question to illustrate this. How many arrests per month do the Phoenix police make of drunk-driving suspects?"

"I don't know, Your Honor. Probably hundreds."

"Yes, so let's say two hundred just for the sake of argument. And of these, how many alcohol determinations are made by the drawing of blood as opposed to breath testing with the Intoxilyzer?"

"I don't know, Your Honor. Perhaps it's rarely done. But it is perfectly legal to do so both under state law and the United States Supreme Court case of *Schmerber* versus *California.*"

"Indeed it is, but let's zero in on the point at hand. How many blood samples from the four hundred drivers arrested these last two months have first been analyzed for alcohol and then sent to the UCLA Medical Center to be DNA-tested against the semen collected from the two rape victims?"

"That has no bearing on whether Wilkott has *standing* to assert a defense of illegality possessed by Donna Alvarez alone."

"I'm not addressing the issue of *standing,* Mr. Stidham. It is clear to me from the demeanor of Patrolman Pozniak on the witness stand that the DUI arrest was illegal, and the blood sample was taken from Mr. Wilkott only because of the illegally seized evidence secured from Donna Alvarez. Otherwise, the officers would simply have had him blow into the Intoxilyzer, like they do with everyone else. Otherwise, the state would never have sent his blood to UCLA to be tested. Under these circumstances, I find that the nexus of illegality was not broken." He paused, nodded, and closed the file in front of him. "The motion to quash is granted, and the defendant is released from custody." He banged the gavel and walked off the bench into his chambers.

Phil Wilkott shook his lawyer's hand and slapped him on the back. They walked out of the courtroom, Tom Wilkott smiling and leading the victory parade. The matron took Donna out the side door of the courtroom. The two women filed out followed by the elderly court watcher.

Mike sat with his arms folded on the railing before him. His face rested on his arms. Stidham and Steigman slumped in their chairs at the table.

"Goddamn thing is," Stidham muttered, "the devious little prick just made his ruling dependent on a basis that no appellate court is going to overturn on appeal: his own determination of whether the policeman was telling the truth. We're dead."

Mike got up, breathed deeply, and walked out of the courtroom. John Steigman patted Harvey Stidham on the shoulder. He stuffed his hands into his jacket pockets and slowly left the room.

Stidham opened his briefcase on the floor, reached inside, and withdrew a brown kraft envelope. He walked through the rear door of the courtroom into the judge's chambers. Friedl was talking on the telephone.

"I'll get back to you," he said, hanging up. He

looked harshly at the prosecutor. "Don't try to back-door me. I made my decision."

"I wouldn't do that, Judge. I just need to talk to you for a minute about a personal matter."

Friedl squinted at him quizzically. "What?"

"That stuff about you referring Mike Fallon to the state bar ethics committee."

"What the hell do you care?"

"He's a good guy. He doesn't deserve shit like that."

"The guy is dangerous. I'm referring him."

"No, you're not. I'm not going to let you shove your foot up his ass."

Friedl looked at him and his face turned ugly. "Who the hell do you think you're talking to?"

"This little prick," Harvey said, "the little piece of shit who did this." He took five sheets of paper out of the kraft envelope and tossed them one by one on Friedl's desk.

The judge glanced at them, his eyes twitched for a moment, and he looked up at Stidham. "Where'd you get these?"

"Not very hard to find. I went over to the jail yesterday afternoon after one of my pals at the Sheriff's Department called me and told me that Wilkott got out at two o'clock Sunday morning after the DUI arrest. My pal said it was against jail policy, but a lawyer delivered a court order, so they had to cut him loose."

"I did nothing illegal."

"How about the other four times? Same scenario."

"It's perfectly proper. It's fully within my inherent powers as a judge. How did you get these release orders?"

"They're all kept in the jail log. All I had to do was run Wilkott through the computer, find out the dates he was booked. It goes back two years. Lo and behold, I found one of these for each of his DUI and drunk and disorderly arrests. The originals are in my office, by the way."

"Are you trying to blackmail me?"

"Is Wilkott giving you bribes?"

The judge started to sputter. "I-I-I acted legally, you-you-you scum, you lowlife."

"How about the local rules of criminal procedure which Chief Judge Hill put into effect three years ago: no release until the initial appearance."

"There are valid exceptions."

"Yes, two times when juveniles were improperly locked up in the jail; their parents complained to the sheriff, and they were released by Judge Hill's order and transferred to juvi. The only other five times are these. You and your pals Wilkott and Haywood."

"It's within my power." Friedl's voice had lost its certainty.

"I'll tell you what I'll do for you. I'll keep the originals of those in a safe place. If you ever turn Mike Fallon's name into the bar for misconduct over this case, I'll personally give a copy of those release orders to Judge Hill and bring the originals down to Judge Velasco in Tucson. He's the head of the Committee on Judicial Qualifications, in case the name doesn't ring a bell, and I'm sure he'd like to know about your little peccadilloes. After you get thrown off the bench, you'll probably be able to get a swell job sorting books in the law library, you know, something that puts your legal training to good use."

"You two-bit piece of shit! You'll still be stealing seventy-five grand from the taxpayers for losing cases, and I'll be making a half a million bucks with one of the big firms."

"Wilkott and Deets?"

"You're threatening me?" Friedl screamed. "You fucking bastard!"

Harvey left the judge's chambers through the secretary's office, leaving the door open.

She stared at him, shocked, the judge's screams echoing through the door.

• NINETEEN •

"There ain't no joy in Mudville," Mike murmured under his breath. He was driving down Camelback Road toward Scottsdale. There was a baseball game in Mudville one day, and they had a really good batter named Casey who always came through in the clutch and won the games for the joyous people of good ol' Mudville. Well, one day he came to bat and didn't come through, and they lost the game. And there was no joy in Mudville.

"Ain't that a sha-a-a-ame, my tears fell like ra-a-ain,
Ain't that a sha-a-a-ame . . ."

Can you imagine how the good ol' people of Mudville would handle this? If a goddamn baseball game threw them into the doldrums, watching Phil Wilkott walk out of the courtroom a free and joyous man would have them jumping out of tenth-story windows.

"Ya hear a lonesome whippoorwill,
he sounds too blue to fly.
The midnight train is whinin' low,
I'm so lonesome I could cry."

Hank Williams was twanging on the car radio. Mike always listened to the country western stations. It was a habit from Texas, but the songs really had soul. They talked about the life that people actually live. Poor ol' Hank, a barefoot country boy who came from dust and returned to it at the ripe old age of twenty-nine.

Mike was having a dissociative reaction—well, sort of. He knew about such things. He'd had some clients who had them. He'd get appointed to a criminal case and go to the jail to interview his new client, and the guy would be real weird. God told him to shoot the guy, or Arab terrorists had injected him with a quart of muscatel and they were after him, so he had to drive fast to escape, and he didn't even see the old lady in the crosswalk; or a fifty-year-old blown-out junkie who spread her legs and pointed and whispered confidentially, "They get in through here and then they come up here"—she pointed at her stomach— "and they do awful things to me."

Mike would go to court and request a "Rule 11," and the judge would order that they be examined by a state psychiatrist. The report always said something like, "Subject suffers from dissociative reaction," meaning that his or her personality was breaking up, disjointed, their grip on reality was slipping. In other words, their brains were mush, and their heads were on backward.

So was Mike's. How do I tell Mary Caitlin O'Dwyer about this?

> *"Ya ever see a Robin weep,*
> *when leaves begin to die?*
> *Like me he's lost the will to live,*
> *I'm so lonesome I could cry."*

Tell 'em, Hank baby, tell 'em. Tears came to Mike's eyes. It wasn't even noon yet, and Kate would probably be by the lake or at McCormick Park. He wiped his eyes hard with the sleeve of his suit jacket. Better not be so weepy when she sees me, or she'll fall apart for sure.

He went to an Italian restaurant near the Safari Hotel on Scottsdale Road. He drank two Jack Daniel's and sodas and forced down some forkfuls of mustaccioli. He added enough tabasco sauce to the tame tomato sauce to sting his tongue and make him think for about ten seconds that he was still a sixteen-year-old kid in Fort Stockton in a simpler, gentler life. He had two more Jack Daniel's, and he felt sufficiently anesthetized to go see Kate and Jennifer. He wasn't drunk or even very high, but if he got stopped, he knew that he'd blow a .15 and get arrested. So he drove carefully, right at the speed limit.

He had his own key now and an electronic gizmo that remotely operated the garage door. Her car was there, and he pulled his pickup beside it and pushed the button to close the garage door. Neat little gadget. He walked into the laundry room of the house, took off his tie and jacket as he walked, and slung them on the upholstered chair in the living room. The house was silent. Kate's bedroom was empty, as were Jennifer's and the kitchen. He rolled up the sleeves of his white dress shirt, gathered his resolve, and walked through the kitchen door onto the patio. They were sitting at the table under the orange trees eating lunch.

"Hi, Mike," Jennifer called out.

Kate turned around and smiled at him. He bent down and kissed Jennifer on the cheek, then sat down across from them. Kate studied his face.

"What happened?" she asked.

"We ran into a problem."

She wrinkled her brow.

"We went to the petting zoo. Mommy let me pet the baby goats."

"That's great, honey," Mike said, happy for the interruption. He should have prepared better for this. Having a pleasant schizophrenic episode in his truck and guzzling a barrel of sour mash whiskey hadn't worked very well.

"He's not being held on these charges," he said quietly.

She flinched and stared at him.

"There may have been a technical mistake made in the investigation, and the judge released him from custody."

She tilted her head and her eyes opened wide.

"There's a little doggie in the pet store, and Mommy says I can have him if I promise to clean up after him." Jennifer looked very serious. "I promised."

"Well, good," Mike said. "I think we need a puppy around here."

It was hot, probably ninety-five degrees. April wasn't spring in Scottsdale, it was the beginning of summer. Beads of sweat broke out on Mike's brow.

Kate got up from the table and walked into the house.

"Mommy told the man in the store that we'll come back tomorrow and get her. She's real cute. She's all soft and her eyes are real pretty. And she licks me all over."

Mike forced himself to smile. He wanted desperately to go inside with Kate, but he couldn't leave Jennifer alone. She finished the rest of her hamburger and chattered excitedly about her new puppy. She'd name her Brassy, because she was the color of the doorknobs on the house, and Mommy said the color was called antique brass.

He took her by the hand, and they walked into the house. Kate was sitting on the living room sofa. She looked at him, searching his face. Mike took Jennifer into her bedroom to play with her dolls.

"Tell me what happened," Kate said softly.

He sat down close to her. "It's what's called a Fourth Amendment violation, an unconstitutional search and seizure. The judge ruled that all the evidence seized was illegal."

"Please speak English."

He sighed and nodded. "Did you know that your foster parent relationship with Donna was terminated by the juvenile judge?"

She thought for a moment. "I guess so. I remember a Child Protective Services caseworker called me one afternoon sometime right after the rape. My parents were still here, and I wasn't thinking very straight yet. And she asked me something like would I fight the termination of my status, and I was confused and so upset, and I asked her what that meant, and she asked me did I want to have Donna back after she got out of detox, and I told her no. That's all I remember. I haven't heard anything since then. Why?"

"The judge entered an order terminating your foster parent status on Wednesday, April 26. Two days later, on Friday, Detective Steigman set up a visit at Black Canyon between you and Donna."

Kate shrugged. "So?"

"You were no longer legally permitted to visit Donna."

"I didn't know that."

"I know, but it's against the rules of the State Department of Juvenile Corrections. So you were technically there as an agent for the Scottsdale Police Department, as though you yourself were a police officer."

She gave him a look of astonishment. "Me, an agent for the police?"

"Yes. Believe it or not. And when you talked to Donna, you were technically conducting an illegal interrogation. Whatever information you learned from her was tainted—we call it 'unconstitutionally seized'—and it wasn't legal for the police and me to make use of that information and ultimately arrest Philip Wilkott as a result of it."

The breath went out of her, and she gulped. She stared at him, shocked. "You mean the case was thrown out because of *me?*"

He grimaced and rubbed his nose and mouth

roughly. "No, there was another problem, too. I made a mistake of thinking we could get away with a pretext stop, especially in front of Friedl."

"Oh, dear God," she gasped. "God, oh God, oh God. What have we done?" She looked at him. "Isn't there *anything* we can do? Anything?"

"I'm not sure," he said.

She began to cry, softly at first, then trembling all over. She put her face in her hands and sobbed.

Mike wrapped her in his arms and held her tightly, and his tears fell on her hair. They sat silently for several gloom-filled minutes.

"I talked to Donna for a few seconds," Mike said quietly.

Kate looked up at him.

He could hardly get the words out. "She said to tell you that she wished it was her, not Jennifer."

Kate squinted her eyes tightly shut and breathed deeply to steady herself. "Dear God," she murmured, then made the sign of the cross. After a minute she looked at Mike, her eyes pleading.

"What has happened to us, Mike? What happened to the people who make the laws? The nuns used to tell us that the most basic law of all was what the prophet Amos said: 'Let justice well up like a river, and righteousness like a torrential stream.' Doesn't justice mean that somebody who commits a terrible crime must be punished? What happened? Tell me what happened."

He shook his head. "I don't know."

"You're a *lawyer*. You deal with this stuff every day. Tell me what's happened to us," she implored.

He shrugged, pursed his lips, searched for an answer. Was there an answer? Were there twelve answers?

"I guess that complexity happened," he said. "Two and a half thousand years happened. The prophets talked about justice, and the Ten Commandments were the laws of God and the law of the land. The people lived in little villages where everybody knew everybody else, and the laws were part of everyone's life. The laws grew up with the people and were simple and straightforward, and if you took an eye, you gave your eye, and if you took a life, you gave your life. But then the villages evolved into enormous cities, and people became anonymous, and the laws were imposed from above by kings and dictators and tyrants and legislators, and laws became as complex as the societies that they applied to. And just like medicine is no longer simply a bag full of leeches and a stethoscope, the law has become a huge library full of books and fifty legislatures and a Congress and a Supreme Court and a thousand other courts and a million men and women who earn money from it every day. And maybe the concept of justice is buried under all that stuff, and the only thing we know about it anymore is that it's the saying that's engraved into the cement over the front doors of the courthouse."

Kate stared at him, and her eyes showed her deep frustration. She shook her head slowly and frowned.

Mike knew that philosophical explanations, no matter how handsome, were inadequate salve for a wounded soul. He and Kate, like all normal people, knew in their hearts what was just and what was unjust. They knew what was right and what was wrong. And it wasn't so hard for anyone to figure out that what had happened to Philip Wilkott was wrong.

Some wag once said that if society applauds bad philosophy because philosophy is an exalted calling, and it scorns fine plumbing because plumbing is a menial trade, then it will have neither good philosophers nor good plumbers. Neither its pipes nor its theories will hold water.

The handsome theory that had freed Philip Wilkott didn't hold water. But it was the law. And it was a travesty of justice.

· PART ·
TWO

Let justice well up like a river and righteousness like a torrential stream.

—AMOS 5:24

• ONE •

Mike telephoned Harvey Stidham the next day. Harvey told him that John Steigman was coming to his office at five o'clock to see if there was some other angle they could use to get Wilkott. Mike was free to come if he wished.

He wished. He got there at five on the dot. Steigman arrived five minutes later, and they walked into Harvey's office. They were all still bruised from the day before.

"We can't go directly after Wilkott," Harvey said. "No matter what we do, it all goes straight back to the visit Ms. O'Dwyer made to Donna Alvarez."

"How about going after him on a murder charge if Big Gun Pete dies?" Mike said. "If the bullet matches his gun, we've got a case."

"I wish we could, but Peter Supremas died yesterday morning. The pathologist did an autopsy this morning and retrieved the bullet. He sent it over to the forensics lab, and this is the report." He picked up a sheet of paper from the desk and handed it to Mike.

Item numbers S-2897-0495 and S-2898-0495 are two fragments of lead which upon microscopic examination demonstrate an almost perfect joint when placed together as depicted below. Fragments together weigh 25 grains and are a .25-caliber bullet. Bullet struck rear interior of victim's cranium and is too distorted to present identifiable rifling for any ballistics comparison.

"Damn," Mike mumbled, handing the sheet back to Harvey.

"That blows everything we have on Wilkott," Steigman said.

Mike nodded. "How about targeting Grant Felsen? He's sure to get popped one of these days."

"What good would it do? Even if he raped Donna, we can't charge him. No jury will convict. He'll just say he paid her. With her record, we lose."

"No, I was thinking of something a little different," Mike said. "What if he gets arrested for lewd and lascivious or 'the infamous crime against nature'?"

"They're only class-three misdemeanors," Steigman said. "All he gets is thirty days in jail."

"Yes, but he gets one year probation, and if he gets arrested again he gets four months in jail. And even thirty days for a punk like him is probably a death sentence. Those guys will pass him around a few times, and he'll end up choking to death. And I'm sure he knows that."

"Okay," Harvey said, "so we get Felsen killed. What's that have to do with Wilkott?"

"I don't want Felsen killed," Mike said. "I want to twist him."

Harvey looked at him for a moment and his face brightened. He looked at Steigman. "Not bad."

"Not bad at all," John said. "Give him a deal if he agrees to testify against Wilkott. Then we can legally arrest Wilkott, send a blood sample to UCLA, and take him down."

"Not bad at all," Harvey said. "It may take awhile, though. The guy's only been arrested once. L and L a year ago. Got probation. He's learned how to stay out of the limelight since then."

"No matter how long it takes," John said. "No matter how long it takes."

"I hope it happens before I get disbarred," Mike said. "I may have to move back to Texas and shovel shit for a living."

"Oh, I wouldn't worry about that," Harvey said. "I think the little prick was just blowing smoke out his ass to impress Tom Terrific. I don't think he'll refer you to the bar."

"I wish I felt secure about *that.*"

"Ease your mind," Harvey said. "I know the little prick pretty well. He was just blowing smoke."

• TWO •

"Have a seat, Donna," Jeanette Goldstein said. She was a tall, thin widow in her late thirties with three teenage children. She had worked for Children's Protective Services as a caseworker for twelve years.

Donna Alvarez sat down on the metal folding chair in the CPS office in the Black Canyon Detention Center. She was sullen and combative.

"You're being released today."

Donna looked up in surprise. "How come?"

"You committed no crime by being addicted to heroin. Possession would have been a crime, selling would have been a crime, but not being an addict. So eight weeks of 'status offender treatment' here in the detox unit is all we can hold you."

"Are you sending me somewhere else?"

Mrs. Goldstein shook her head.

Donna smiled for the first time in over two months.

"We're sending you back home. Your mother's parental rights have never been severed."

"Home?" Donna scowled.

"That's all we have the legal right to do." She shrugged apologetically.

"There's no foster home that wants me?"

"I'm sorry, Donna. I tried." She reached into her purse on the desk. "Here's twenty dollars." She handed the bill to Donna. "It's your seed money for a new life. I'm sorry it's so little, but it's all I can afford."

Donna nodded. "Thank you very much, Mrs. Goldstein."

"If you wait until noon, I'll drive you back home."

Donna shook her head. "I don't want to hang around this place another two hours."

The caseworker smiled. "Okay, I understand. Let me see if I can get you on the transport to the Juvenile Court Annex. From there you can get buses back to the reservation."

She picked up the telephone and punched three numbers. "Has the JCA van gone yet?" She listened a few seconds and hung up.

"It's leaving in five minutes. It's at the front. I'll walk you out."

She walked with Donna down the short corridor to the front entrance. Donna had no clothes or personal belongings at all, so she had to wear the denim shorts, white sneakers, and blue chambray work shirt of the detention center. Mrs. Goldstein stood with her outside the front doors.

"Here's my card." She handed it to Donna. "It has my work phone and home phone. Before you think of taking drugs or going on the streets again, I want you to call me. Understand?"

Donna nodded.

"You're a pretty girl, Donna. Your tests show that you are very bright, very intelligent. Be somebody, Donna. Do something with your life. Get a job, earn some money, go back to high school at night." She looked intently at Donna. "*Be* somebody."

Donna nodded, her face somber. She climbed into the small bus and sat down in the rear. The windows had steel mesh coverings. There were a half dozen other juveniles in it, all going to court for one reason or other.

Be somebody, she says. Oh, God, how I want to be somebody. Tears came to her eyes, and she rubbed them quickly away. You didn't want to let anybody see you cry in this dangerous place. They'd take you for a pussy and rip your throat out. There were fifty ways to get yourself fucked up here. Get into a fight with one of the Chicana gang bangers, and you'd wake up at midnight with a knife in your chest—if you woke up at all. Mouth off to one of the girls on work detail, you'd get your head stove in with a bucket full of floor wax. Get caught hoarding a little food in your cell from the mess hall, they'd send you to the disciplinary barracks for a week to scrub floors for a dozen hours at a time and dig holes in the yard and fill them in again and again.

Be somebody. How? What do I do? She had looked at herself in the mirror this morning and become morose. Her skin had become grayish in this place. Her eyes were dull and flat. Her hair had lost its sheen from being washed with some horrible brown soap all the time, the only soap they were given.

"I am a rose of Sharon, a lily of the valley," she murmured under her breath. She stared out the window through the wire mesh.

How can I get a job looking like this and wearing this prison shirt? And what will I do? What can I do? I don't know how to do anything.

Four bus trips and an hour and a half later, she walked up Thomas Road to the shack where her mother sat decaying on the rickety porch, listening to Hank Williams, sluggishly swatting flies with a slat of wood torn from a vegetable crate. Her mother was bleary-eyed and stank of sweat. An empty half-gallon jug of Gallo zinfandel was by her chair.

"Mama, you stopped taking the Antabuse?"

She looked up at Donna, aware of her for the first time. Her eyes appeared to register no recognition. Donna went inside to the bedroom where she and Louise and Janet slept. Louise's stuff was gone, her clothes, her makeup kit, everything. Donna sat on the edge of the bed, wondering what to do now. She looked around the filthy bedroom. It smelled of sweat and pee and cat shit. Flies buzzed around a pile of shit in the corner. She was totally destitute. Her life was no more important than that stinking pile of shit. With her mother drinking again, there wouldn't even be enough of the welfare money left for food. Suddenly she felt nauseated. She would die there if she remained.

The shirt she was wearing had BCDC stenciled in black letters on the left breast. She had a little over sixteen dollars left after bus fares and a hot dog. Not enough to buy anything. She had to find Louise, get something to wear. She couldn't walk around the rest of her life with her hand over her breast.

She walked out on the porch again. "Mama, where's Louise?"

Her mother slowly looked up. "OD'd last month," she said in her hoarse, thick voice.

Donna was jolted, but only for a moment. It would have to happen to Louise sometime. She had been on heroin and crack and had freebased for five, six years. Donna shook her head for a few seconds, the only grieving that she would do for her seventeen-year-old sister, and crossed herself like the priest had taught her.

She walked down Thomas Road in the hundred-degree June heat. The sky was cloudy and faded baby blue, bleached almost to white by the dazzling sun. There was no door on Big Gun Pete's shack, no cars around it. She looked inside, and there didn't appear to be anyone around. She walked inside, and the place was bare. No furniture, nothing.

She remembered that Michael Fallon had testified that he beat up Pete and Tony Brown Horse so bad that they had to go to the hospital. Maybe they were still there and people had stolen everything. Or maybe they took off because it was too hot around here, the cops knowing about them and all.

Thinking about Mike Fallon brought back memories

of Kate and Jennifer. But she didn't want to think about them again and get all teary and miserable and wish that the terrible things hadn't happened. They had. Wishing wouldn't help. And Donna had lost the only chance she would ever have in her life to be a person, a real human, a lady.

She walked down Thomas Road to Country Club Drive. Can you imagine that? she thought. Country Club Drive in this place? There was an old lady who lived there up by Montecito Avenue. She sold old clothes whenever she had them. Maybe Donna could find a shirt without BCDC stenciled on the pocket. And then what? And then what?

"You jus' got out, huh?" the old woman said. The skin of her face was the color and texture of a walnut. She was short and humpbacked and scrawny, at least seventy-five years old, though she wasn't sure, and had short white hair like the pelt of an ermine.

Donna nodded. "I need a shirt."

"Yah, I got six a dem BCDC"—she pointed at Donna's shirt—"but only two, tree udders." She spoke with the familiar accent of many of the old people, native speakers of the Pima-Maricopa language that was rapidly becoming extinct.

"Fi' doller." She held up a faded red polo shirt that could easily fit a two-hundred-fifty-pound man. Donna shook her head.

"I got, I got," the old woman said. She limped into another room and came out with a short-sleeve shirt dress, white cotton with pale pink buttons down the front and a white cotton belt with a pink buckle.

"Twel' doller," she said.

It was actually a nice dress. "I don't have that much. I need money to eat."

The woman studied her, tilting her head sideways and wrinkling her nose and cheeks. "What you need it, de dress?"

"I have to work."

"Do what, be who', be sell drug?"

Donna stared back at her, saying nothing. What the hell business was it of this old bag?

"Yah, I see you girls, pretty like you, young, you got ever'ting, ever'ting come to nutting."

Donna turned to leave.

"I gi' you dress free, you work for *me*."

Donna turned back to her. "You want me to be a whore for *you?*"

The old woman shook her head. "No, no, no. You get cloding."

"What?"

"I got little pickup truck. Runs okay. But I got bad joints." She pointed at her swollen, crooked wrists and fingers, her distorted ankles. "Don' drive so good, don' do nutting so good. Gotta get help to get cloding so I can sell, den buy food. You drive, you go get cloding, you live here wi' me." She pointed at a side room. "My two dodder gone, marry, jus' me." She nodded energetically at Donna.

"I don't have a driver's license. I never even drove before."

"I teach you, I teach you. It be okay, easy." She waved away the problem. "Come, I show."

She took Donna's hand and pulled her through the living room to the side room toward which she had pointed. The living room furniture was old but clean, and there was a TV set on a wooden table. The floor of the small cinder block house was wood planks worn smooth and polished by a million footsteps. The little bedroom was neat and attractive, an oak chest against the wall, flowered chintz curtains on the window, and a small bed covered with a multicolored patchwork quilt. Donna felt the cool air coming out of the cooler vent.

"That's all I have to do? Learn to drive and then go pick up clothing?"

The woman nodded. Her black eyes gleamed, and she smiled, displaying toothless gums.

Maybe there's still a tiny bit of hope, Donna thought. With a pretty dress like this and a truck, she could drive by Kate's house, maybe even bump into her by accident. Maybe a miracle could happen twice.

"Okay," Donna said. "Okay."

· THREE ·

"Dr. Stilb called me today," Mindy Wilkott said. "My father called him and told him that if he didn't talk to me about you immediately, he'd sue him for malpractice. He told me you've been HIV positive for three years."

Your eyes are real weird, crazy-like, Phil thought. You deserve it, bitch. You deserve whatever happens.

"You didn't tell me?" she whined. "You didn't tell me? How could you not tell me?"

They'd been over and over this for an hour now. First with Mindy screaming and yelling like a shrew, and now with her sitting in the pink satin wing chair acting like a weepy wishy-washy old woman. Piss on you. I've had enough, Phil thought. You can have the goddamn house your daddy gave us. You can have the goddamn Bentley. There's only so much that a man can do to make a bitch happy. This is the last straw.

"Who'd you get it from? That little queer you've had around here a couple of times, you told me he was your client? Grant something. Was he the one with you when you raped those two little girls?" She burst into tears.

It had been Phil's father who had told her. God damn you, Phil thought. You kept it out of the papers, you prick, but you ran and told my wife. She didn't have to know. Were you concerned more about her than about me, your own son?

Mindy and Phil had both gone to a private clinic in Laguna Beach for PCR tests, and both their tests had been positive. Not Hopalong Cassidy's millions, not even all the money in the world, could cure her. Phil's father had come over the next evening to comfort her, and he had wept for her.

I've got it, too, Dad. I've got it, too. Don't you care about me dying? But his father had only glared at him in disgust.

Phil walked out of the house and got into his Cadillac in the garage. He sat there trying to think where to go. This shit about Grant was getting serious. Everybody was beginning to figure it out. Grant was great in the sack, but he was fickle. Phil had wanted to put him up in an apartment, have him all to himself, but Grant didn't want to be tied down. He didn't mind taking Phil's money, and plenty of it, but he liked a little variety. Girls now and then, black guys, the fourteen-year-old Mexican boy who hung out at the Bronc sometimes. Phil was jealous, but that was the way it was. Grant was hung like a donkey, and if you wanted a piece of it, you had to share it now and then with somebody else.

But this had all gone too far. Phil had never done any criminal cases, but he had been a lawyer for five years, and he knew enough about police procedure to realize that he had a big problem. That Fallon bastard had testified that Big Gun Pete had given him Grant's first name. It didn't take a rocket scientist to know that one of those undercover cops down on Seventh Street must have heard the name Grant from time to time. And Grant Felsen was the only person in the world who could walk Philip Wilkott back into court.

He drove down Lincoln to Twenty-fourth Street, south to Washington, and west to the Bronco Buster. He didn't want to be seen leaving with Grant, but he had to talk to him. He had gone down to Tucson three weeks ago to buy a gun at one of those firearms-collectors shows they had at the Pima County Fairgrounds every couple of months. You could buy any kind of gun you wanted down there without registration or waiting. He had bought a little .32-caliber Smith & Wesson revolver. Ever since the cops had taken his gun, he had felt kind of unsafe. After all, there are all kinds of dangerous creeps lurking out there. You have to protect yourself.

It was only a little after eight o'clock, and the Bronc hadn't started jumping yet. There were a few pretty boys scattered around at the tables and one really stunning black whore with a great pair of tits and amber skin that glowed. Phil had been coming here for almost a year—this was where he'd met Grant about six months ago—and he'd never seen a nigger whore in this place. Who the hell would someone like that hustle *here?* But all of a sudden this one had started showing up. She must be a cop. Although everyone else must have realized it, too, nobody really cared, because the cops never arrested homosexuals for L and L or sodomy anymore. The queer liberation groups would start screaming, and the mayor would start sniveling. But Phil didn't want the nigger cop to see what he knew she must be there to see: him. That must be how they had gotten him for DUI that night.

He left the Bronc and stood near the alley for fifteen minutes to see if she would follow. She didn't. Maybe he was wrong. Was he getting paranoid? Well, better to be safe than sorry. He got into his car and wondered where he might find Grant. It was twenty-five minutes after eight. Maybe he was eating supper. A little late, but who knows?

Grant always liked a fancy sports bar and grill down near the Civic Center just a few blocks away. There were a lot of hunks around, and he had gotten lucky three or four times and picked up a good piece of change servicing them.

Grant was there at a small table eating a steak. Phil walked up to the bar and caught Grant's eye. He tilted his head toward the door, then walked outside into the darkness down the block. A few minutes later Grant came out, standing in the restaurant light and squinting unseeing into the darkness. Phil whistled low, and Grant walked up to him.

"What's with the cloak and dagger?" Grant asked.

"The black chick's a cop."

"What black chick?"

"The one that's been hanging out at the Bronc the last couple of months."

"So what? She never does anything."

"I think she's the one who got me arrested."

Grant shrugged. "Okay, I'll stay away from there for a while."

Phil stepped toward him and kissed him on the lips. "I've missed you the last couple of weeks," he whispered.

"Me too," Grant breathed.

"My car's over here." Phil pointed.

They walked down the sidewalk. Phil suddenly had an epiphany. He knew precisely what he had to do, and his annoying indecision vanished. He took a pen-knife out of his pocket. He had bought it at a fancy knife store a couple of years ago. It was a Puma with a single two-and-a-half-inch blade, and the reason he had bought it was because it cost two hundred dollars. Anybody could buy a twenty-dollar knife, thirty, fifty even. But a two-hundred-dollar knife? Only a Philip Wilkott could afford such a trinket.

He opened it quickly, swung his right arm across his body, and plunged the knife blade into Grant's ear canal. He had seen it in a movie once, navy Seals or Special Forces or frogmen or something like that, battling Middle East terrorists or Japanese ninjas.

It worked. Grant went down without a sound. There wasn't any blood. Phil knelt by him and tried to pull out the knife. It wouldn't budge. It was embedded somehow. He yanked on it, and the blade broke off at the hilt. Now blood began to flow. He leapt back from the body, put the handle of the knife in his pocket, and ran to his car.

A long way east on McDowell Road he pulled into a drive-in liquor store and bought a fifth of Jim Beam. He drove all the way into Scottsdale on McDowell and pulled off onto the north shoulder of the road beside a little sandstone hill called Barnes Butte. He drank several swigs of the cheap bourbon, dropped the knife handle into the bottle, put the cap back on, and swished it around to obliterate any fingerprints or whatever else might be on it.

There was too much traffic here. He pulled back on the road and drove along the Pima-Maricopa Reservation to the Beeline Highway, then south to the bridge over the Salt River, a wide, dry bed of sand and rocks. He slowed and tossed the bottle out of the window as far as he could and heard the distant tinkling of shattering glass. He turned east on McKellips all the way past downtown Mesa to Hawes Road and turned north. It led away from any housing areas up to the edge of the Usery Mountains and dead-ended at a locked gate, preventing four-wheel drives and motorbikes from assaulting the unsullied terrain.

He got out of the car and took off his beige linen trousers. He walked down the hill into a deep arroyo, tossed the pants behind a huge boulder, and lit them with a match. They burned completely in a minute or two. He walked back to the car, took out the light gray silk suit trousers that he had forgotten to drop off at the cleaners, dressed, and drove back to Scottsdale.

No use going back home and getting screamed at by the wicked witch of the west. He checked into the Hilton Hotel, ordered a bottle of Glenlivet scotch from room service, and felt enormous relief that his troubles were over. He got pleasantly potted.

The telephone rang at quarter to seven in the morning, waking both Mike and Kate.

"Damn, I thought the reporters had stopped calling," he mumbled. He groped for the telephone. "Yeah?"

"It's about Grant Felsen."

Mike recognized John Steigman's voice and immediately became wide awake. "You got him?"

"Not exactly. He's dead."

Mike sat up slowly. Kate watched him with growing concern.

"How?"

"He got a knife in his ear down near the Civic Center. Homicide detective friend of mine just called me. Says the blade was broken off. A Puma blade. That's all they have."

"Nobody saw anything?"

"No. It was a couple of blocks from that new sports bar. Nothing but trees and bushes. It happened some time between eight and nine, pitch black. The private security down there makes hourly rounds, found him at nine-thirteen."

Mike felt Kate's eyes on him and didn't want to display to her what he was feeling. This would really be the last straw for her.

"I'll have the pathologist send a blood sample to UCLA," John said. "At least we'll be able to verify if he's the one who raped the Alvarez girl."

"Good."

"I don't know where else we can go from here," John said.

"I guess it's over, huh?"

"Looks like it," said the detective. "I think we just struck out."

"Yeah," Mike said bitterly. "Still no joy in Mudville." He hung up.

Kate was staring at him.

"Grant Felsen's been murdered," he said. "The police have no leads."

She rolled over on her side toward the wall. "And there's no way they can ever touch Wilkott," she said. It wasn't a question. "I knew this would happen. I just knew it would happen."

· FOUR ·

Kate hadn't been sleeping well for many days, and especially since the ultimate bad news about Felsen. She was up drinking coffee and reading the newspaper every morning long before Mike or Jennifer got out of bed. She had stopped jogging months ago.

Mike came into the kitchen, his hair wet and glistening from the shower. "What's that sour look on your face?" he asked.

Kate had the Sunday *Arizona Republic* open in front of her on the kitchen table. She pointed at the story in the society section.

"Mindy Wilkott filed for divorce," she said.

"Philip Wilkott's wife?"

She nodded.

Portrait photos of each of them graphically demonstrated that he was a lot prettier than she. Kate had never seen him before, and looking at him now, staring back at her with his handsome face and perfect smile, she wanted to stop him from smiling. A shudder radiated through her.

" 'Philip Wilkott moved to Tucson just last week,' " she read. " 'He has been made the managing partner of the branch of the Wilkott and Deets law firm in Tucson. It has thirty-seven lawyers and is the premier firm in southern Arizona. Phil has been practicing law for only five years, but it is not his father's position as senior partner that has facilitated Phil's rapid rise to managing partner in Tucson. It is Phil's superb credentials and high legal skill.' "

"Superb credentials and high legal skill?" Mike scoffed, sitting down at the table with a steaming mug of coffee. "I don't even think he's ever really practiced. Tom Terrific just gave him an office and a secretary so it would look like he had some sort of career. I never heard anyone say they'd ever had any dealings with him on legal matters. And now he's the managing partner in the Tucson office? Man, I bet they're all jumping for joy down there."

"Why do you think he left Scottsdale?"

Mike shrugged. "I don't know, maybe his old man just got sick of looking at him. After what he saw in court, he couldn't have been very thrilled. A father may do whatever is in his power to help his son when he gets into trouble, but that doesn't mean he has to be real happy about it."

"Somebody should shoot him," Kate mumbled.

"I don't want to hear you talking that way," Mike said with a stern voice. "You've got to live with it. You can't let it eat at you and consume you."

"It's going to consume Jennifer." She looked up at him and raised her hands in a halt gesture. "Okay, okay. I'm sorry."

Jennifer came into the kitchen rubbing her eyes and yawning. A little antique-brass-colored cocker spaniel pranced behind her, its long ears almost bouncing on the floor.

"Brassy did somefing naughty, and it's not on the paper."

"Uh-oooh," Kate said. "Time for emergency girl to whip into action."

Jennifer giggled.

"What do we get?" Kate asked.

Jennifer looked thoughtful. "Wet paper towas and dry paper towas and Windek."

"Perfect!" Kate smiled at her daughter. "Let's go."

*   *   *

"Don't lose your faith, Mary Kate," Gwen said on the telephone. "Faith in God is all you've got to hold on to at a time like this."

"I can't return to Saint Daniel's Academy to teach, because there's no day-care center that will accept my HIV-infected little girl. I have to remain at home with her. Sundays no longer begin with mass at Our Lady of Perpetual Help Church, because the very name of that church seems to me to be a lie, an affront to reality."

"I hate listenin' to you talk this way, Mary Kate. It makes me sad deep inside."

Kate's voice was morbid. "Monks debase their flesh and whip their own backs bloody in the name of God, and nuns remain celibate and seclude themselves in prayer their entire lives for love of God. I just don't have any of that kind of faith anymore—or maybe any faith at all. The only thing I think about doing all day is watching Philip Wilkott die."

"Please stop, Mary Kate. It's hatred talkie'. You can't let this hate destroy your soul."

Kate sighed deeply, trying to cleanse the bitterness from her voice. She didn't want to hurt Gwen. Gwen didn't deserve it.

"I'm sorry, Gwenny, I really am. But I never felt this horrible in my life. It just keeps getting worse and worse, and I'm beginning to feel hopeless. I just don't know what to do."

"I'll come visit you."

"I'd love you to, but I won't let you. You're doing your first defense of your doctoral dissertation in two weeks. You have to concentrate on that now. And there's nothing you can do here anyway. Honest."

"Dissertations don't matter at a time like this."

"Oh, yes, they do! If you came here and it caused problems with getting your degree, how do you think I'd feel?"

Gwen sighed. "Promise me, Mary Kate, promise me you'll do nothin' stupid."

"I promise. I really promise. I'm sorry I said that about Wilkott just now. It was just talk."

Kate hung up after reassuring Gwen several times that she really had herself under control and that everything would eventually settle down.

Just a few minutes later the telephone rang.

"Hello," she said, answering it hesitantly.

"Mrs. O'Dwyer?"

"Yes."

"My name is Howard Slocum. I'm with the *Enquirer.*"

Kate frowned. "I really don't want to talk about what's happened."

"We're pleased to be able to offer you fifty thousand dollars for your story, Ms. O'Dwyer."

"I don't need the money, Mr. Slocum. And I don't want a story about Jennifer and me in your trashy magazine."

"How about the Alvarez girl? We'd be willing to offer her a very nice price for an exclusive."

"Why don't you just give her a ring, Mr. Slocum? She's either at the juvenile detention center or who knows where." She slammed down the phone, seething over the offhand callousness of these people, and ripped the plug out of the wall.

"Even today, Muslims maraud and Sikhs sack in the service of God," Kate said to Mike late that evening. He was busy trying to clean a Kool-Aid spot off the cream-colored carpet in front of the TV set. "Crusaders once killed thousands upon thousands of Muslims in the name of God. If a noble-minded Crusader glorified God by murdering perfectly innocent Muslims, how much more do I glorify God by killing an animal like Wilkott?" Her voice was cold and strained with fury.

He looked up at her and sighed huskily. "The Crusades were a thousand years ago, Kate. I think things have changed somewhat, don't you?"

"Have we become so civilized," she said, undaunted, "that there's no punishment for these animals? Big Gun Pete doesn't even get prosecuted, and now that Felsen's dead, nothing will ever happen to Wilkott."

The look on her face was no longer grief, it was hate. Her eyes danced with flame. He had seen a box of .38 cartridges that she bought yesterday, and today it was gone.

He got up off the floor and stood towering over her in front of the sofa. "It's okay to learn to shoot well for your own protection," he scolded her, "but don't you be thinking about going looking for Philip Wilkott. That would be murder."

"He murdered Jennifer."

"You can't murder him. Then not only her life but yours is destroyed as well."

She just shrugged, walked into the bedroom, and slammed the door. She sat down on the edge of her bed and slowly opened the bedstand drawer, staring at the .38 Smith & Wesson revolver. She breathed deeply and swallowed, then closed the drawer softly and lay back on the bed.

"Mr. Wilkott," his secretary said, "I have a woman on the line who wants an appointment for a divorce."

"Mrs. Macklin, I hate doing divorces. I have enough trouble with my own."

"Well, she says she read about you in the Sunday *Republic,* and she needs you to represent her. Her husband is quite wealthy and influential, and she needs the best."

Flattery will get you somewhere. "What's her name?"

"Annette Jencks."

"Jencks? That's the doctor who owns the private psychiatric hospital?"

"She didn't say, Mr. Wilkott."

"Where's she live?"

"She said in Cobblestone."

Cobblestone was the most expensive area in Tucson. High in the foothills of the Santa Catalina Mountains, most of the homes ranged from at least a million dollars on up. There was one huge estate up there that Phil had always admired. It was perched on a long hill, covering the whole top, and had to be at least ten million dollars, maybe twelve.

"All right, I'll speak to her." He punched the blinking button. "Mrs. Jencks."

"Yes. Mr. Wilkott."

"Right, call me Phil. Everyone calls me Phil. What can I do for you?"

"Well, it's really very embarrassing. My husband has been fooling around with some young girl."

"How old is your husband, Mrs. Jencks?"

"Fifty."

"And how old are you, Mrs. Jencks?"

"I'm twenty-six, and this trashy girl is nineteen."

"I'm very sorry to hear that, Mrs. Jencks. Men can be very foolish. Is your husband Dr. Jencks, the psychiatrist?"

"No, no. My husband is *Dennis* Jencks. He owns an electronics plant in Palo Alto, California. They make computer chips and some software. It's an exceptionally good business. He patented a new type of chip he developed two years ago that's already brought in almost a hundred million dollars."

Phil swallowed. A patent awarded during a marriage was community property. Jesus! This woman could be worth more than Mindy the monster!

"Well, perhaps the courts in Tucson won't have jurisdiction over the divorce. Are you a resident here?"

"Oh yes, sure. We've lived up here in Cobblestone for four years. We were married right here on our patio three years ago. My husband goes back and forth."

"Do you have any children, Mrs. Jencks?"

"Yes, a two-year-old girl and an eleven-month-old boy."

He spun in his high-back chair and looked out the picture window at the Catalina Mountains. She was good not only for millions in community property as well as alimony in high numbers, but also at least seventeen years of child support.

"Well, I'll certainly be pleased to meet with you, Mrs. Jencks."

"Thank you, Phil." Her voice was a delicious purr. "I'll have to call tomorrow to set up an appointment. My schedule is in a real mess these last couple of weeks. Would that be okay?"

"Oh, yes, of course, Mrs. Jencks."

"That's just fine." She sounded like a cat meowing.

He was very disappointed. He hoped that she wouldn't go shopping for another lawyer to represent her. Women like her didn't fall into your lap very often.

"Have you gotten any bites on your house yet?" Kate's father asked.

"No, not serious ones. The best offer so far was six seventy-five last month. I didn't even counteroffer."

"Well, don't get discouraged. It could take a year, even longer, to sell an eight-hundred-thousand-dollar house. Be patient."

"Oh, I am, Dad. I'm not as unhappy living here as I was at first, anyway. Maybe I'll just take it off the market. I'll see what Mike says."

Brendan O'Dwyer hesitated. "Honey, your mother and I are just a little worried about you. You can't blame us for that."

"I know, Dad," she said into the telephone receiver. "But you don't have to worry. I've told you that. I'm doing as well as I can under these circumstances. I'm learning to live with what happened to Jennifer. Sure it's hard, and sometimes I just get real blue thinking about what will be with her. But I certainly wouldn't be any better off back in Boston. Mike Fallon looks after both of us, and I couldn't leave him. I just couldn't."

"Has he asked you to marry him?"

"Not in so many words, Dad. But he will. Don't be so old-fashioned. We don't need a long engagement and all of that. One of these days I'll just show up at your door on my honeymoon with my daughter and my new husband in tow."

"Promise me you're doing fine."

"I promise."

"I just want to look into my little girl's eyes for a few minutes so I can see for myself," her father insisted.

"Okay, I'll tell you what I'll do. I'll come visit you and Mom for a few days. All right?"

"Yes, wonderful."

"Okay, I'll call you and let you know when."

"I'm going back to Boston just for a couple of days," Kate said. "I have to look my father in the eye and assure him that Jennifer and I are okay. He's not totally convinced."

"Sure," Mike said. "Are you taking her with you?"

"No. I asked her, and she's kind of scared of flying. Anyway, it's five hours in the air each way and then the traffic hassles and all. I think it's a little too much for her to cram into two days. Do you mind watching her?"

"Of course not. I'll have to take her downtown with me tomorrow, though. I've got a justice court trial at eleven. Remember, I told you about it last week. The fire in that apartment complex. It should only take an hour. I'm sure that one of the secretaries or bailiffs over there will be happy to look after her."

"Good, that's great."

"When's your plane?"

"Eleven-thirty."

He frowned. "I'm really sorry, but I won't be able

to take you. I can't get this particular matter continued."

"Oh, that's all right. I'll drive myself. Then you won't have to come pick me up."

Phil Wilkott was reclining in his black leather desk chair, throwing M & M's one by one into the air and catching them in his mouth. His feet rested on the top of the huge walnut burl desk that had cost the firm twenty-three thousand dollars. This would take a good half hour if he strung it out well enough, and then he could go have lunch at the Mountain Oyster Club and have a couple of Glenlivet shooters and a nice steak. His telephone intercom rang.

"Yes, Mrs. Macklin?"

"It's Mrs. Jencks. She asked for an appointment at four o'clock this afternoon. I told her I'd have to check with you."

He beamed with pleasure and glanced at his empty appointment calendar. "That'll be fine. Tell her you'll find a way to squeeze her in between appointments."

"Yes, sir," Mrs. Macklin said. She punched the button. "That's just fine, Mrs. Jencks. Mr. Wilkott said to fit you in no matter what. You may not have very much time with him today, he's running a little late. But we'll do our best. I'll see if I can cancel his four-thirty meeting."

• FIVE •

"Mommy, Mommy," Jennifer said, running to Kate as she walked into the living room, "I, missed you."

Kate picked her up and hugged her. "Mommy missed you, too, honey, very much."

Jennifer giggled. "What happen your hair? It's all funny-looking."

"Mommy just colored her hair brown, honey. It'll be blond again in a couple of days."

Mike sat on the sofa smiling at her. "Did your father and mother talk you into being a brunette?"

"No, not exactly," Kate said. "I'll tell you in a minute. Isn't it time for Jennifer's nap?" She looked into her daughter's eyes. "You look tired, sweetie."

"Oh, Mommy, I don't need no nap."

"Well, let's just go into your bedroom and put you on the bed and see if you need just a teeny nap. Where's Brassy?"

"She was naughty. She was chewing on everything. And I said, 'Brassy, if you don't stop that, Mommy going to be real mad at you.' But Brassy wouldn't stop. Mike put her in the kitchen."

"Okay, that's a good place for her."

"Can I have her with me for my nap?"

"How about right after your nap, honey? Brassy probably won't want to sleep, and she'll be jumping all over and keep you up."

"Okay," Jennifer said.

Kate carried her into the bedroom. Five minutes later, she came out, closed the door, and sat down on the sofa next to Mike. He leaned toward her and kissed her on the cheek.

"How about us taking a little nap, too?" he said. "I missed you."

She turned toward him. "I'd better tell you something first."

He studied her eyes. "What's up? You find a new boyfriend in Boston?"

She shook her head. "No, I wasn't in Boston. I was in Tucson."

He wrinkled his brow and tilted his head slightly.

"Philip Wilkott is dead."

He flinched visibly but said nothing.

"I went down there to kill him."

He stared at her, his eyes wide open.

"But I didn't kill him."

He swallowed. His voice was oddly hollow-sounding. "I'm not following this very well."

She sighed. "I know. I'm sorry. I'll tell you exactly what happened."

She took a deep breath and began reciting.

"I knew you were going to be in court at eleven o'clock the other day. That's why I told you I was leaving for Boston at eleven thirty, so you wouldn't be able to drive me to the airport."

Mike blinked and watched her.

"I went over to the place I get my hair done at noon and had Ginny put a dark brown rinse in my hair and give me long bangs. She promised that the color would wash out in a few days. I had called Wilkott at his office on Monday from a pay phone, so it wouldn't be traceable to my phone bill."

Mike rubbed his mouth and chin hard. Jesus Christ! She had really *planned* this.

"I told Wilkott I wanted a divorce and told him my name was Annette Jencks, and my husband ran an electronics company in Palo Alto and was really rich, that I was twenty-six years old and had two little babies. I figured he would jump at the chance to get a date with a young woman who would be good for millions in community property and years and years of child support. And I was right. I drove to Tucson two days ago and went to his office yesterday afternoon, and he hit on me just like I figured. He was practically stepping on his tongue when I talked about how lucrative my husband's business was and that we had a three-million-dollar house in Cobblestone."

Mike shook his head. "What were you planning to do?"

"I took your gun with me. I had it in my purse. I was going to get him to ask me out for dinner, get him drunk, go back to his place in my car, and shoot him."

Mike's mouth dropped open, speechless. Kate looked away from him.

"So anyway, he asked me out, and I went to dinner with him, and he got drunk—I mean, *really* drunk. We finished at around nine o'clock, and he says let's go to his place. He was too drunk to drive, so I say we have to go in my car. We were at a restaurant on Campbell Avenue in the foothills, a place called Anthony's, and he tells me to drive south on Campbell to River Road. Well, the road there is very dark and windy and goes up and down a bunch of little hills, and—" She gasped, losing her composure. Her alabaster skin turned pink and blotchy, and perspiration beaded on her forehead.

"So?" Mike said.

"So he started pawing me," she gasped and began to cry, "and he was all over me and put his filthy hand under my dress, and I was pushing him away as hard as I could with my one free hand," she paused and wept loudly, "and nothing would stop him, so I was going about thirty-five miles an hour, and we got to the bottom of one of the hills, and I hit the brakes real sharply, and it jolted him, and he sat up and looked around, real drunk, and I guess he figured the car was out of control or something"—she gulped for breath and wept loudly—"and he grabbed hold of the wheel and jerked it, and the car went out of control and veered off the road and hit a big stone wall head-on."

She was crying too hard to continue. Mike was so shocked he couldn't move, couldn't speak. Kate took a tissue out of her purse on the end table and wiped her eyes.

"He flew through the windshield. His head was totally destroyed. The airbag opened on the steering wheel and kept me in my seat, and the only thing that happened to me was I got a bad bruise on my shoulder from the seat belt." She rubbed her left shoulder and looked timidly at Mike.

He closed his mouth and tried to find his voice. He cleared his throat several times. "The police must have come, ambulance?"

She nodded. "The people from the house behind the wall I hit came out and took me inside. I was really shook up. And they called the police and emergency ambulance, and a bunch of policemen showed up. One of them searched around the car and found my purse. I guess it had fallen out when the man yanked my door open to help me out. And the policeman brought it to me and asked to see my license, and I opened my purse and your gun fell on my lap."

She blinked back more tears and looked away from Mike again.

"Holy shit!" Mike gasped. "Did they take it?"
She nodded.
"What'd they do to you?"
She shook her head. "Nothing. He just said he had to hold on to the gun because I didn't have a permit, and he asked me if I was injured and wanted to go to the hospital, and I said no, I was fine, and he questioned me while he filled out an accident report, and then he just drove me back to the La Paloma hotel, where I was staying, and dropped me off. He told me

how sorry he was that my friend had died like that."
She shrugged. "That's all."

"Jesus Christ," Mike mumbled. "Jesus Christ al-
mighty." He shook his head. "Tom Terrific isn't going
to let you get away with murdering his son."

"I didn't murder him. God did."

"I don't think Tom is going to see it that way."

"Fuck him."

Mike breathed deeply. "Look, the shit's going to hit
the fan here for real any minute now." He got up off
the couch.

"Why? The police didn't do anything to me in Tucson. It was just an accident."

"Yeah, it's just an accident until they find out your
connection to Phil Wilkott. And they'll ask around up
here and find out you're really a blonde, and you used
a phony name to get an appointment with him, and
they've got the snub-nosed .38 you were carrying
around in your purse, and it isn't going to take even
a congenital moron more than about a minute and a
half to figure this out."

"Figure what out? I didn't kill him. It was an
accident."

"Jesus, Kate!" he exploded. She flinched. "Don't
you get it? You planned a first-degree murder. You
would have killed the guy if you hadn't had the accident." He glared at her. "I told you not to even think
about it. I told you, God damn it!"

She sat back on the sofa, exhausted and morose.
Mike looked toward Jennifer's door. It was closed.
The shouting hadn't awakened her.

"All right, I've got to figure out what to do," he
said, trying to calm himself. He rubbed his chin and
frowned. "By the way, how'd you get back up here?"

"I went over to the Chrysler dealer this morning,
bought a '95 Le Baron, same thing I had, just a year
newer."

He nodded. "What name did you use at the La
Paloma hotel?"

"Annette Jencks."

He winced. He paced back and forth for several minutes, then glanced at his watch. "Damn! It's almost two o'clock. I wonder if it hit the *Phoenix Gazette* yet. I'm going down to the Circle K to get the paper."

He ran through the living room and laundry room into the garage. He got into his pickup, backed out, and screeched down Via Frontera. At the Circle K, he stood reading the front page story and main headline: UNPOETIC JUSTICE. It was the newspaper's lead story, all three columns on the right side of the front page and continued for two full columns on page two. It regaled the whole thing from the foster parenting of Donna Alvarez, the rape of the two girls—"or at least one of them"—the arrests and releases of Peter Supremas and Philip Wilkott, Wilkott's blood match to the HIV-infected semen in Jennifer, and the auto accident last night. The story was fair and balanced.

Mike jumped into his pickup truck and sped back to the house. He ran inside.

"Get Jennifer. I'll get Brassy. We're going to a hotel right now."

"It's in the paper?" Kate asked.

"Yes, and everything's in there. They're calling it 'unpoetic-justice,' but believe me, the cops and the Pima County Attorney aren't going to see it that way."

She got up from the sofa and ran to Jennifer's room. She came out holding the sleeping child. Mike came out of the kitchen with the puppy in his arms.

"But what good is it to run and hide?" Kate whispered.

"I need some time to think," Mike said. "I don't want you giving any statements or getting arrested till I've thought this through."

"Arrested?" She appeared alarmed for the first time.

"Yes," he said.

They went through the laundry room into the garage. The baby carrier was in the truck, strapped in the center of the bench seat.

"Come on, we'll take the truck," he said.

They got into it, and Kate buckled her sleeping daughter into the seat. Mike laid Brassy on Jennifer's lap. He pressed the electronic button, and the garage door opened. A tan late-model Ford was parked in front of the house. Two men in light-colored suits were coming up the walk toward the front door. They stopped, and one of them waved his arm at Mike as he backed the truck out of the driveway. Mike braked to a stop and rolled down the window.

"Is that Ms. O'Dwyer?" the man asked. He was middle-aged, short, bulky, with a puffy face.

"You got a warrant?"

He shook his head.

Mike rolled up the window, pushed the button to close the garage door, and drove away without speeding. He could see the two men standing on the walkway, staring after the pickup.

Victor Hodges was mowing his lawn across the street, and his wife, Ilse, was on her knees by the sidewalk, planting a row of striped red petunias. Victor and Ilse both waved at them as they drove by. Kate waved back feebly and forced a small smile.

"I guess they haven't seen the newspaper yet," Mike said. "Otherwise, they'd be running for their shotguns."

"I don't think that snide remark is very funny," Kate said, shaking her head and frowning. "We're not exactly fugitives from a chain gang."

"Not yet, anyway."

She ignored him and stared out the window. "Who were those men back there?" she asked after a moment.

"I don't know for sure, but my guess is they're either police or County Attorney's investigators from Tucson."

"Were they here to arrest me?"

"No. They didn't have a warrant. They can only arrest you if they have a warrant signed by a judge. They were just here to talk to you."

"Well, I eventually have to talk to them, don't I?"

Mike shook his head. "No, you can take the Fifth Amendment."

"You mean like all the gangsters do?"

"I mean like anybody who just murdered somebody does."

She grimaced and bit her lip. "I told you God did it. I had no intention of crashing into a wall." Her voice was hard with anger. "At least *you* could be on my side."

"All right, all right," he said. "I *am* on your side. But I'm about to have a goddamn heart attack. Let's just both be calm and quiet till we get to the hotel. I've got to think."

Grief furrowed Thomas Osborne Wilkott's face. He sat in his office reading the story in the *Phoenix Gazette*. It was two o'clock in the afternoon.

Perhaps Philip had deserved to die. Perhaps he had committed unspeakable crimes that should have operated to forfeit his life. But the law had taken its course, the law had taken its best shot at him, and the law had pronounced him a free man. Nobody, not even an angry and aggrieved mother, had the right to spit on the law and take his son's life.

The world will grieve for Jennifer O'Dwyer. She will at least have that. Her mother will at least have the honor and knowledge of the pity of the entire world. But who will grieve for Philip Wilkott? I grieve for you, my son, my poor, pathetic, sick son. *I* grieve for you, *your mother* will grieve for you when she hears of this, *your sons* will grieve for you when they are told of this. But *the world?* The world will laugh and clap its hands and shout in one great swell of voices, "Justice has been done! The Lord of Hosts has visited rightful vengeance upon this tool of Satan."

They will dance and sing "Hosanna to the highest" as the pallbearers lay your coffin in the earth.

This cannot be. I cannot let this be. For all and all, he is my son. He was my son. He was Philip Marshall Wilkott, the son of Thomas Osborne Wilkott.

Hatred fulminated in him, making him lightheaded as he read the story over and over.

Mike left the Phoenician Resort at four-thirty in the morning, drove to an all-night convenience store on Camelback Road a half mile away, and stood reading the *Arizona Republic*'s lead story just outside the swinging glass doors. The headline read: MYSTERIOUS ACCIDENT TO BE PROBED. The story was all of the right side of the first page and all of page 5. It referred to the auto accident repeatedly as *"accident"* in quotes and italics. Again the wedding photos of Kate and Brian. But this story did not include any mention of the fact that Philip Wilkott's blood had been matched to Jennifer's assailant. What it did include at great length was the glamorous life story of the only son of one of Arizona's great families as well as an interview with Thomas Osborne Wilkott, Republican king maker, lawyer extraordinaire, family man, and philanthropist.

"The fundamental underpinning of our system of justice in America," Tom Terrific said, "is the absolute prohibition against people taking the law into their own hands. The law must operate exactly the same for everyone at all times; otherwise, *someone* ends up deciding when and to whom it applies. That is dictatorship, not democracy. That is tyranny, not justice. Mary O'Dwyer must be brought into a court of justice to answer for what she did to my son."

Mike steadied himself back against the doorjamb. He slowly gathered his strength and drove to Kate's house to pack some of their toiletries and clothes. They were going to have to stay at the Phoenician for a while. Maybe he could figure out what to do about this mess.

" 'Ye shall know the truth, and the truth shall make you free,' " Kate said.

"Come on, honey." Mike was frustrated and deeply worried. "This isn't catechism class, this is criminal law. The truth doesn't play much of a role in it."

"That's about the most cynical thing I ever heard *anybody* say."

"I'm sorry, but I've been a lawyer for eighteen months now, and real life isn't much like the gospel of Saint John. Do you think that if O. J. Simpson had walked into a police station and told the truth, he'd be anywhere but sitting on death row right now?"

"That's different. I didn't kill Philip Wilkott."

"But you *attempted* to."

"But I didn't *do* anything, I never got the chance. I didn't attempt to kill him."

Mike opened the Arizona Criminal Code, which he had picked up at his office earlier that day. There had been a handwritten note taped to his office door asking him to call John Steigman, but Mike hadn't thought that would be such a good idea.

He thumbed the pages. "Let me read you one of the statutory definitions of 'attempt.' This is Title 13, Section 1001: 'A person commits attempt if, acting with the kind of culpability otherwise required for commission of an offense, such person intentionally does anything which is any step in a course of conduct planned to culminate in commission of an offense.' "

"Oh, my God," she murmured.

"You *wanted* to kill him—that takes care of the culpability part—you *planned* to kill him, you made all the *preparations* to kill him, you *embarked* on a *scheme* to kill him, you had a *gun* in your possession to *kill him with*. You disguised yourself, used a false name, and checked into a hotel under it. That adds up to a lot of steps planned to culminate in the commission of first-degree murder, and *that's the truth*. Even if you convince everybody in the world that you didn't plan the accident, the truth is that you *attempted* to murder him. It's a Class 2 dangerous felony, so the judge will be compelled by law to impose a minimum of seven years' imprisonment. Because there's a gun involved, you won't be eligible for parole. With good time and a little luck not getting knifed by one of the bull dykes in the women's prison in Florence, you'll be out in time to see Jennifer graduate from the third grade."

"Jennifer will never graduate from the third grade."

"And do you want to spend the rest of *her* life seeing her only for two hours on Sundays?" Mike asked very gently. "I don't think the truth will make you free."

"Gwen, it's me."

"Mary Kate, thank God you called. Your mum 'n da' are sore frantic."

Kate swallowed. "Was something in the newspapers?"

"Aye, the front page of all the Boston rags. You know, the daughter of Brendan O'Dwyer."

Kate rubbed her eyes. "Hold on a second," she said. She put the telephone receiver down and walked into the bathroom. She took a tissue, wiped her eyes, and blew her nose. She tried to compose herself, breathed deeply, and returned to the telephone.

"I don't want to talk with my parents just yet. I'll just break down on the phone, and Daddy will have a heart attack. Would you please go over there and tell them I'm? fine?"

"First I want you to tell me you really are."

"I am. I didn't kill him, no matter what the papers say."

"The papers are sayin' that you disguised yourself and seduced him to take you out to dinner and got him drunk and ran into a stone wall. Only your side of the car had an air bag."

"Oh, my God," Kate groaned. "That just isn't so. I *did* plan to kill him. God help me, I *did*. But he was drunk and jerked the wheel of the car and it was really an accident. I *didn't* plan that."

Gwen spoke soothingly. "Okay, darlin', take it easy." Pause. "What's goin' to happen?"

"I don't know. Nothing has happened yet, but Mike thinks that the police in Tucson may charge me with murder or attempted murder."

Gwen gasped. She crossed herself. "God forbid such a terrible thing will happen," she murmured.

"Will He forbid it?"

There was heavy silence for a moment.

"Well," Gwen said, "what with that Bobbitt woman getin' off scot-free cuttin' her husband's thing off just for bein' a philanderin' shit, I can't imagine any judge or jury coin' anything to you for *not* killin' a man who *deserved* to be killed."

"What if they think I *did* kill him?"

"Then they'll *sure* be of a mind that he got the proper punishment for his crime."

"I hope there are twelve of you on the jury."

Gwen sighed. "So do I, Mary Kate darlin'."

"Will you go see my parents?"

"Of course I'll go. Right away. And I'll tell them that you sound just fine and you didn't do a damn thing wrong."

"Thank you, Gwen. I'm at the Phoenician Resort in Phoenix. Daddy has the number."

"Do you want me to come out and stay with you for a while?"

Kate thought for a moment. "Maybe it's best not. We'll be going back to the house tomorrow or the next day, and Mike says there's going to be problems for a while. I think my parents will need you there."

"Okay, darlin'. I'll go right over now to see your mum 'n da'. My heart is with you, Mary Kate. And may God watch over you."

Kate had too big a lump in her throat to respond.

She hung up and sat unmoving on the upholstered chair. The hotel room was luxurious, but it wasn't home. It was small and stuffy, becoming a jail cell. Mike had taken Jennifer over to the playground when he got back from his office at three o'clock, just to give Kate a little time by herself. They had been gone a half hour, and they'd probably be gone another half hour. The room was suddenly claustrophobic. Kate had to do something, go somewhere, feel her body and try to settle down the volcano building in her mind. Soon the top of her head would blow off or her eyes would explode. She hadn't been jogging in many weeks. She put on sweat pants and running shoes and a short-sleeve sweatshirt and left the room.

There was a cinder path outside the bungalow that led toward the golf course. It was a weekday afternoon, quite warm, and not many golfers were on the course. The path was uncluttered with carts. She hadn't felt like jogging since Jennifer had been raped, but suddenly she needed it—she needed physical exhaustion and release from the chains tightening around her. She began running in a rhythm, loping, her breasts bouncing, her thick hair trailing her head like a palomino's silky mane. Men stopped practicing their swings on the tees and watched her, turned from their sand trap shots and stared at her, looked up from the greens and admired the tall beauty with the great body and the gliding elegance of a thoroughbred racehorse.

She saw nothing, no one. She just ran, faster, faster; perhaps she could outrun the terror that lurked behind her. What will happen? What will happen? What will happen? Her footfalls on the cart path were as rhythmic as a railroad train on tracks. What is that kid's refrain? "I think I can, I think I can, I think I can. . . ." What will happen? What will happen? What will happen?

It was all ambiguous. It was all muddy and uncertain. *Intolerance of ambiguity,* a psychology professor had once lectured about in a psych class years ago. Intolerance of ambiguity can make you go nuts. People need certainty, answers, they cannot stand to have the most serious problems in their lives go unresolved day after day. It is destructive to the mind, destructive to the ability of a human being to keep his life in order, to forge ahead day by day.

Kate needed answers, resolution. How could she go on just waiting for the sledgehammer to drop, for the doorbell to ring, for the police to come and take her away. Would they? Why not just go to them and tell them the truth? Oh, God, things were once just that simple. At least that's what they taught you in school: the simplicity of the truth. "I cannot tell a lie, Daddy. I cut down the cherry tree." "How nice of you to tell the truth, Georgie dear. Well, that's okay. Just don't cut down any more." "Yes, Daddy."

God, was it really ever that simple? All you had to do was go say you were sorry and everything was suddenly okay. I want to go say I'm sorry. "I'm sorry I attempted to murder Philip Wilkott, Mr. Policeman. I apologize, and I promise it won't happen again." And he'll look at me with gentle eyes and say in a wonderfully soothing brogue, "How nice of ya t' tell the truth, Katy dear. Well, that's okay. Just don't plan any more murders." The only problem is that I'm not sorry, and if the bastard were still alive I would still be planning to kill him.

She stumbled on some loose gravel and almost fell. Tears were streaming down her cheeks, and men were no longer looking admiringly at her, but with odd stares. What the hell is this hysterical woman doing? She was suddenly aware of them.

She ran back to the hotel room as fast as she could, unable to stop crying, unable to shield herself from the disturbed, quizzical stares of the golfers. Thank God Mike and Jennifer weren't back yet. She stripped and turned on the shower, cold water. She stood under it and shivered, not knowing if the water rushing down her face was tears, not knowing if her shoulders were shaking and her legs were weak because of the cold water or because of her struggle to maintain her sanity.

· SIX ·

Agnes Ishpia didn't want a daughter, not at her age, seventy-eight, seventy-nine, something like that. She already had two. She needed a servant. She needed someone to wash the floors and do the laundry, clean the bathroom, and drive around to the Salvation Army stores and the various charitable agencies and foundations in Phoenix and Scottsdale and Mesa and pick up donated clothing.

But Donna didn't mind scrubbing the floors of the little house. She had scrubbed them at the Home of the Good Shepherd and the Black Canyon Detention Center, and that was much worse. There was always a guard watching, and you couldn't take a break when you wanted to—just ten minutes every two hours—and they treated you like a dangerous animal, a coyote or wildcat or rabid dog.

Agnes was good to her. That was all that mattered to Donna. Agnes shared everything she had with Donna, her food, whatever few dollars she made from the clothing, and the clothing itself. And for the first time in her life, Donna had clean, decent clothes and some money in her pocket and no need to spend it on heroin or crack. Donna had found the second place in her life that was actually a home.

There had been heavy coverage of the death of Philip Wilkott on television, and Donna had watched every news broadcast that she could and switched back and forth. She had driven to the Circle K down on Thomas Road the evening that the news first broke and bought a *Phoenix Gazette.* The story was sympathetic to Kate and detailed Philip Wilkott's crime and his HIV infection. The memory of it all, as much memory as she had of that night—but mostly the memories of Kate and Jennifer and then losing everything—brought tears to her eyes. But she quickly rubbed them away and chided herself. All of that was gone. It was just plain gone. There was nothing she could do about it.

The next morning she had bought an *Arizona Republic,* and the story seemed like it was all on Wilkott's side. She read that Grant Felsen's blood had matched the semen removed from her, and then the story dwelt at great length on her sordid life and the opinion of "highly placed investigators" that "the Alvarez girl had sold the three-year-old baby for heroin."

She flared with anger, sitting in the truck in front of the Circle K, and tore the vicious story to shreds. Why couldn't they just leave her alone? But at least nothing had happened to Kate over the weeks—no arrest, apparently no further investigation. Donna was very happy for that.

On Sunday afternoon she had been switching channels on the TV set, trying to find something to watch. As she flashed through one interview program, she heard the name Wilkott, so she switched back to it immediately. It was Thomas Osborne Wilkott, Philip Wilkott's father and a bigwig lawyer—she had remembered his name from the story in the *Republic*—and the Maricopa County Attorney, she didn't catch his name, being interviewed about "the administration of criminal justice."

They were talking about all kinds of things that Donna really didn't care about. How to reform sentencing, how to correct the huge backlog of cases jamming the system, stuff like that. But then it began to get mean and personal.

"There are county attorneys," Wilkott said, "who are supposed to prosecute criminals and uphold the law, but who really care only about reelection. They're just callous politicians. The Pima County Attorney hasn't brought charges yet against Mary O'Dwyer even though she clearly murdered my son."

"Come now, Mr. Wilkott," said the interviewer, "that's not quite fair, is it? Your son raped a three-year-old girl and infected her with HIV, and there is an almost statistical certainty that the little girl will die of AIDS within six or eight years. He sentenced her to death. Mary O'Dwyer sentenced him to death."

Donna clapped her hands. Wilkott's face got real mean. Apparently not too many people talked to him like that. He got up and walked off the TV set.

"Well, this being a live show," the interviewer said, looking into the camera, "I guess we'll just have to soldier on." He smiled at the viewing audience.

The Maricopa County Attorney gave the interviewer an amused look and said, "I've heard that you're outspoken, but I didn't realize you were suicidal."

"I've been a newspaper and TV reporter for twenty-six years, Mr. Shreve, and I believe that our job is to bring the truth to the public, not to let it be covered over with obvious nonsense because we fear the consequences to ourselves. 'Ye shall know the truth, and the truth will make you free.' Now, let's move on to another matter of great fascination to all Americans, the O. J. Simpson case. What is your read on what has happened?"

"Well, the thing that most fascinated me all along is the public's view of our justice system. From the very beginning of the case all of the evidence pointed to Simpson, and all of the polls said that most Americans believed him to be guilty. And as the trial progressed and more evidence came out, the great majority of people became convinced that he was guilty. But that same majority of Americans believed that he would get off. This simply means that the vast majority of Americans believe that our system of justice stinks, and they have no faith whatsoever that guilty people will be punished. And they were dead right in the Simpson case.

"I believe that's why we have crime in this country that is so out of hand and brutal and beyond control. The criminal justice system is so out of joint that nobody believes that a criminal will really be punished for whatever he does. What other lesson can anyone draw from O. J. Simpson, the Menendez brothers, Lorena Bobbitt, the first Rodney King trial, the Reginald Denny case? I mean, how much worse can it get when you have a terrible crime committed against a human being with a video camera recording the entire thing, but our justice system still sets the criminals free or merely slaps their palms with a ruler?"

"Pretty scary stuff," said the interviewer.

"It doesn't bode well for the administration of justice in America," said the county attorney. "And as the public sees more of these televised trials and more of these incredibly unjust results, the public is going to rise up with one voice screaming, 'The lunatics are now running the asylum.' "

"And then what will happen, Mr. Shreve?"

"Then there will be a growing number of people taking the administration of justice into their own hands, and cases like the death of Philip Wilkott, at least brought about to some degree by a grieving mother, will become commonplace. Because people feel deeply in their hearts that terrible criminals need a terrible punishment, but they also believe that the justice system is no longer capable of making that happen. And when these cases occur—where a mother, father, sister, brother, or loved one exacts retribution against some killer or rapist—how do we punish the mother or brother or whoever? How? I am the Maricopa County Attorney, but I don't have the answer to that fundamental conundrum."

Donna stared at the TV set, fascinated, but lost in the big words. Agnes came out of the kitchen wiping her hands on a dishrag.

"What all dis talk-talk?" she said. "Is Ed McMahon Star Search time. No understand all dis bullshit." She switched the channel.

"I'm going to church, Mrs. Ishpia," Donna said.

"Yeah, go, go. Is okay."

Five o'clock on Sundays, Father Oldenham did a mass in an old abandoned cotton shed down on McDowell Road near the Salt River Indian Agency. He was an old priest, short and real overweight and almost totally bald, but he seemed to care about the kids. The word was that he had been banished to this bottom of the barrel post because he was part of a group of priests and nuns who did not oppose abortions and had often said as much from the pulpit of his parish in Mesa. The bishop had gotten pissed off at him and busted him and sent him to the Pima-Maricopa Reservation as a warning and to do penance. But none of that mattered to the Indians, who needed a priest and yearned for the refuge of the church for their poor and sometimes hopeless lives.

The kids especially took to him. He had convinced Anna Luhan to get off the streets and go to detox in Mesa and had given her a job cleaning the old shed that served as the church. She could sleep there at night and didn't have to sell herself to get money for food. He got a seventeen-year-old hair spray and glue sniffer a job with a gardening business in Scottsdale. He got a nineteen-year-old alcoholic off booze and into the marines.

The five o'clock mass was always short, because Father Oldenham knew that the first reason that so many people turned out for it was that there was always a lot of free food afterward, provided by one or another of the Catholic church women's groups from Phoenix or Scottsdale or Mesa.

Donna was no longer hungry. Agnes was a good cook and was teaching Donna how to cook. So for Donna it was not the food that was so attractive, it was the mass. The story of Jesus and how he had saved people and cured them cried out to her soul. It was magic, something she could cling to and cherish no matter what she had done, no matter how low she had crawled. Mary Magdalene had been a whore, sold herself to half the Roman garrison of Jerusalem. But she had seen Jesus, and she had recognized him as the Christ, and she had been made pure by God himself, who had loved her for the untainted beauty of her soul. Jesus had absolved her of the sins that she had committed.

That's what Donna wanted, desperately needed, prayed for, wept for. Love me as you loved Mary Magdalene, Jesus. Let me have a chance to live and be clean. Dear Jesus, make me clean again. When I did those things, I didn't care about *me*. When I did those things, I didn't know about *you*. Help me, dear God, help me be clean.

She even went to confession. It was at six o'clock, after the food was all gone, and Father Oldenham sat on one side of a latticework wooden screen, and she sat on the other, and she told him everything, weeping and gasping. She told him of the heroin and the crack and the intercourse and blowjobs and sodomy. And when she finished, his voice cracked, and he told her that God absolved her of her sins, and they said a Hail Mary together, and then he came around the screen and hugged her close to him. He wept, and his tears washed over her hair and cheeks, and she felt them scrubbing her soul clean.

She walked back home, to her new home with Agnes, and she felt strong and purposeful. Her steps quickened as she reached the little house. She rushed inside to the bathroom to see how she looked, how the confession and the priest's tears had changed her.

She stared at herself in the mirror, studying the new woman who peered back.

"Thou art all fair, my love"—she whispered her favorite lines from the Canticle of Canticles. *"There is no blemish on thee."*

• SEVEN •

"She didn't kill him, John," Mike said.

"Tucson Police Department thinks maybe she was planning to," Detective Steigman said.

"Well, I don't know about that. All I know is she sure didn't plan to run head-on into a stone wall. He jerked the wheel, and the car went out of control."

Mike stared at Kate while he spoke to the detective on the telephone. They had been in the hotel for five days, and her hair was once again strawberry blond. She looked back at him with fear-filled eyes.

"So meet with them and tell them that, Mike. I greased the skids for you with them. They know the whole story, and they're sympathetic. I sent down all our investigation and the lab reports on Supremas, Wilkott, and Felsen."

"So why are they pushing it?"

"They're not. I got them just about willing to close the thing out, but the longer you hole up out of sight, the worse it looks."

Mike thought for a moment. "All right, here's what I'm willing to do. We'll go back to Kate's place, and we'll meet with them. But all she's going to say is 'Hi, how are you?' I'll do the talking."

"I don't know if that's going to be enough."

"That's all they get. I can't give her worse advice than I would give any of my clients. This situation is too rough."

"Okay, let me pass it on. The guy I've been talking to is Hugh Milletti. He's the captain in charge of Homicide."

"Thanks, John."

As they drove up, the doorjamb of Kate's house appeared as though it had been painted yellow. Mike parked in the garage and went around to the front door. The jamb was covered with little yellow Post-it notes, mostly from TV, radio, and newspaper reporters. Mike pulled them all off. Three of them were from Detective Max Cohen of the Tucson Police Department. Mike crumpled them all into a ball.

He unlocked the front door and walked into the house. Jennifer was busy taking her dolls out of the valise and laying them carefully on the floor in front of the TV set. He could hear Kate puttering around in the kitchen.

The telephone rang. Mike answered it.

"Hello."

"Hello, is this Michael Fallon?"

"Yes, it is."

"This is Captain Milletti, Tucson Police."

"Yes, John Steigman told me you'd call."

"You have a good friend there."

"We know that."

"I'd like Ms. O'Dwyer to have a talk with one of my men, Max Cohen. He's been trying to reach her for several days. He's the one who was walking up to her house when you pulled out."

"Well, he didn't have a warrant."

"Yes, absolutely right. I'm not saying you did anything wrong."

The silence on the line was uncomfortable for Mike.

"Will Ms. O'Dwyer be willing to meet with Detective Cohen?"

"She's willing to meet, but she won't say anything. I'll do the talking."

"Are you her attorney?"

"At the moment, yes."

There was another moment of discomfiting silence.

"Well, I don't know if that's such a good idea. Detective Cohen is going to want to talk to you about your role in this."

"My role?"

"The .38 Smith that was in her purse is registered to you."

"Yes, it was in the bedstand where I put it."

"Look, Mr. Fallon, don't get hot. I'm just telling you there are a lot of loose ends here that we have to tie up."

"I'll be happy to talk to your detective. Ms. O'Dwyer will not speak to anyone, on my instructions."

"All right. I'll have Cohen call you."

"Will he be bringing a warrant or a grand jury subpoena?"

"No."

"Is that straight?"

"It's straight. This is strictly Tucson Police Department. The county attorney isn't involved, at least not yet."

"Okay, have him call."

Mike hung up. Jennifer was talking to Raggedy Ann, tucking her into her little baby carriage. Kate was standing behind Mike, and he turned to her.

"You mean, I'm going to sit here like an idiot, and you'll do all the talking?" she said.

"Absolutely not. You're going to sit here like a beautiful woman, and I'll do all the talking. Men like looking at beautiful women."

"What's that you were discussing about the gun?"

"They want to know how it got from me to you."

"That's all?"

"No. I suppose they're working on a conspiracy angle. Since I was, let's say 'active,' in finding out about Wilkott and Felsen, I'm sure they figure that I engaged in some activity in bringing about his death."

"Oh, Mike. I'm sorry." She put her hands on his

shoulders. "This is awful. I never thought you'd get in any trouble."

"I'm not in any trouble."

"What if they don't believe you?"

He shrugged. "Then I'm in trouble."

"Honey, how can you be so cavalier?"

He kissed her on the forehead and the tip of her nose. "How else can I be?"

They kissed softly.

"Mommy and Mike is kissy, Mommy and Mike is kissy," Jennifer sang out and giggled.

Mike stepped to her and picked her up, setting her in the crook of his arm. He walked back to Kate, and all three of them hugged. Kate kissed her on the lips and then kissed Mike.

"Now we're all kissing," Kate said.

"This is a free talk," the detective said. "Off the record. What either of you say to me, I don't write down. I'm here to close this case if I can."

Homicide detective Max Cohen had an endearing smile and searching brown eyes. He was in his early fifties, overweight, medium height, and had a short cropped fringe of graying brown hair around a bald spot like a tonsured monk. He reminded Kate of Friar Tuck from the Robin Hood movie that Errol Flynn had done forty or fifty years ago. She had fallen in love with Robin Hood when she was fourteen, and she'd watched the movie fifteen or twenty times since then, every time she could when it was on television.

It was three o'clock in the afternoon, and Kate had just put Jennifer down for a nap. She and Mike and Max Cohen sat at the kitchen table.

"No one has to convince me or Captain Milletti that this maggot Wilkott was a piece of garbage who deserved to die. But I don't think the boss will let me close this file without hearing what happened from you." He smiled at Kate.

She looked at Mike, her eyes pleading. She trusted this man, and she wanted to tell him the truth.

"Are you wired?" Mike asked.

"No," said Cohen. He stood up, took off his suit coat, and draped it on the back of the chair. He turned around in a circle, his arms outstretched. His white shirt clung damply to his heavy chest and stomach and back. He sat down again.

"And what happens," Mike asked, "if the county attorney decides to do a grand jury investigation on this and you get subpoenaed as a witness? Are you going to commit perjury?"

Cohen pursed his lips and shook his head. "No, but if Milletti closes the case, there won't be a grand jury on it. It hasn't happened in the eleven years I've been in Homicide. Ted Garland's been the Pima County Attorney for fifteen years. If Milletti tells him it's not a case, that's the end of it."

"Listen, Detective Cohen," Mike said, "what you're saying is exactly what we want to hear. You know it, and you know that we know it. Ms. O'Dwyer wants to talk. She knows in her heart that she hasn't done anything wrong. But you're very good at your job, I can see that, and it's obvious why you're sent out to do these kind of interviews. In fact, you're a lot more experienced in this stuff than I am. But I'm not going to throw out three years of law school and a year and a half of practice and tell my client to have a nice chat with a homicide detective. I'd deserve to be sued for malpractice for advice that bad."

Cohen frowned. "Is that final?"

"That's final. Ask me anything you want about what role I played in any of this mess, but Ms. O'Dwyer will decline to be interviewed, on my instructions."

"Did you take any part in planning the murder of Philip Wilkott?"

"No."

"How did your gun get into Ms. O'Dwyer's purse?"

"I don't know. The last time I saw it, it was in the bedstand in the main bedroom here."

"Your side or hers?"

"I don't have a side. I have my own apartment."

"Do you spend time in the bedroom here with Ms. O'Dwyer?"

"Ms. O'Dwyer and I intend to get married. We maintain a relationship that is normal these days for such individuals."

"Well, I wouldn't call any of what's happened to you folks the last few months 'normal.' I hope to God something like this never happens to my two daughters and three granddaughters. I guess I'd be looking for someone to kill, too." His face was kind, his eyes limpid.

"It's nice meeting you, Ms. O'Dwyer," Cohen said, standing up at the table. "You have a good man here."

She smiled at the detective. "I know."

"There's a Thomas Osborne Wilkott on the telephone for you, Ted," said the Pima County Attorney's secretary over the intercom.

"Aw, shit!" he muttered. "Tell him I died."

"I don't think he'll believe me."

"Okay, I'll take it." He watched the button blink on the telephone for a moment, frowned, then pressed it. "Ted Garland here."

"Yes, Mr. Garland. This is Tom Wilkott, perhaps you've heard of me?"

"Of course, Mr. Wilkott. And may I offer you my deepest condolences over the death of your son."

"Yes, thank you so much. It's been awfully upsetting. I'm sure you can understand."

"I do, sir."

"Call me Tom."

"Certainly."

"I was wondering, I'll be passing through Tucson

tomorrow on my way back from L.A. Would it be an imposition for me to drop by around two o'clock?"

An imposition, no, Garland thought. A goddamn headache and a half, yes. "No, not at all. I'll be happy to meet with you, sir."

"Fine, fine. See you then."

Garland cradled the receiver. "Shit," he mumbled. "Here it comes."

"I understand that you're getting a bit restive down here," Thomas Osborne Wilkott said. He sat in one of the brown leather upholstered armchairs in front of Theodore Garland's desk in the Pima County Attorney's office on the ninth floor of the Great American Building in downtown Tucson.

Ted Garland combed the fingers of his right hand casually through his wavy silver-blond hair. He was forty-five years old, tall and slender, and attractive enough to have had a dalliance or two or three over the years, the most notorious of which had been with a *Tucson Citizen* reporter who had taken to coming to his office most afternoons for months on end to conduct in-depth interviews. It had become clear to a lot of office employees after a while that her coming was often associated with groaning, and whatever they were mining in-depth on the sofa was not his life story or his theories of jurisprudence.

"What does 'restive' mean, Mr. Wilkott?" Garland, a Democrat in a Democratic county, had the assured air of a professional politician who had been elected to four terms as county attorney. He had taken on all comers, Democrat and Republican alike, and whipped them handily.

"Call me Tom. Just that I've heard through the grapevine that you're thinking of running for the United States Congress next year."

"Who told you that, Mr. Wilkott? In my experience, grapevines don't talk." He chuckled.

Tom smiled and laughed. "Oh, some of the boys at

the Phoenix Country Club were babbling. You know how it is. And I was thinking that there wouldn't be much chance of a Tucson Democrat defeating Jim Kolbe for the House. Jim's a reliable Republican in a district that pretty much votes Republican. He's beaten back Democratic challenges three times now, and there aren't enough Democratic votes in Pima and Cochise counties to get you very far. You're going to need some Republican backing."

"Maybe I'll have to switch parties."

"Well, then everybody would just brand you a turncoat and you'd lose anyway."

"What is your interest in my career, Mr. Wilkott?"

"Tom, please call me Tom. It just crossed my mind that an endorsement from me and maybe even from the Arizona Republican party, of which I happen to be chairman, might give quite a boost to your aspirations, could even help you raise some seed money for your campaign."

"*You* are going to abandon Jim Kolbe for *me?*" Ted Garland chuckled.

Wilkott smiled. "Things happen."

"Yeah, and I guess what you're here to suggest to me next is that things ought to happen with respect to your son's unfortunate accident."

"I won't combine the two subjects. That might appear unseemly."

"Yes, it might."

"So let us simply leave that first matter on the table and move over to this 'accident,' as you call it, which claimed my son's life."

Garland nodded, his face sober.

"I think that the proper administration of criminal justice requires that Mary O'Dwyer be tried for murder."

"Mr. Wilkott, I have the reports of a police captain and a senior homicide detective who have recommended to me that justice appears to require quite the opposite."

"It is not their decision, Ted, it is yours." There was no more affability in Wilkott's face or voice.

"Yes, that's true. And I simply haven't decided yet. This is a very troublesome case. This woman's daughter is going to die of AIDS. Philip Wilkott raped and infected a three-year-old girl with HIV. He was freed primarily on a very technical search-and-seizure error. And while I agree with you that Ms. O'Dwyer had no right to take his life, there is no evidence whatsoever that the accident was anything but precisely that, an *accident.*"

"Clearly she intended to kill him: a disguise, a phony name, a dinner date where she got him drunk, a gun in her purse."

"I'm just not certain in my own mind what to do about all of this. It is the most unsettling case that I have seen in my fifteen years as county attorney."

"Let a jury decide. That's what the administration of justice is all about."

"But before I can ethically charge her with a crime and bring her before a jury, I have to be convinced that it is the proper thing to do. The facts about your son make that very difficult."

"I certainly understand your concern, Ted. I respect that in an honorable county attorney. Such a man of character is clearly someone we could use in Congress."

"Let's knock off the bull, Mr. Wilkott. I would love to serve in Washington, but if I prosecute Mary O'Dwyer for anything, I won't be able to be elected dog catcher next year. In fact, my wife would probably lock me out of our house. There just aren't too many people who think that it would be justice to punish Mary O'Dwyer."

Tom Wilkott stood up. His eyes were bloodshot, his face drawn.

"I didn't think that my presence here constituted *bull,* Mr. Garland."

The county attorney stood up, looking contrite. "I

apologize for that, Mr. Wilkott, and I'm sorry for your loss. Truly I am. Just give me some more time to think about this."

Wilkott gritted his teeth and left the office.

Ted Garland sat back heavily in his chair. "Shit," he mumbled. "That son of a bitch will bury me." He clasped his hands behind his head, swiveled his chair around, and stared out the window at the clear cerulean sky.

• EIGHT •

Kate sat on a redwood bench in the backyard, shaded by a thick-leafed orange tree, and watched Jennifer wheel her baby carriage around and around on the patio walk. Jennifer was telling bedtime stories of her own imagination to her new doll, Candy. Brassy had been prancing around for an hour, playing with Jennifer, and now slept sprawled at Kate's feet, jerking and moaning now and then with some doggie dream.

This must be what they mean by the "dog days of summer," Kate thought. The only thing you want to do in this heat is lie in the shade and dream of chasing rabbits and hope that autumn will come soon.

Three weeks had passed since Detective Cohen had come to the house. Neither Kate nor Mike had heard anything from anyone since that day. Reporters still called occasionally, but Kate would simply say "no comment" and hang up. A producer from *Hard Copy* had offered her $100,000 for an interview with her and Jennifer and Donna together, and Kate had slammed down the receiver so hard on the cradle that the earpiece broke off.

John Steigman had stopped by last Sunday afternoon with his four-year-old granddaughter and a big box of See's chocolates. He hadn't heard anything from Cohen or Milletti, either. Given the length of time that nothing had happened and the fact—verified by Harvey Stidham—that the Pima County Attorney's office was not conducting a grand jury investigation, it was fairly certain that the case had been closed. But investigations were never formally closed, Mike cautioned her. They simply ceased to be active, and after a while they were *presumed* to be over.

Last week she had gone to Saint Daniel's Academy to speak with Monsignor Reilly about getting her fifth-grade teaching position back. Reilly was a small man of forty, very thin, with deep blue eyes and rust-colored hair. They had sat in his office and had a nice talk. He told her how devastated he had been to read of the tragedy that had befallen Jennifer. He asked Kate if prayer was helping her, and she admitted that she had lost faith in prayer, and even her faith in God had suffered.

Monsignor Reilly came around the desk, took her hand, and they walked down the hallway to the school chapel. They both touched the holy water in the font, genuflected, and walked past the communion railing in front of the altar. He knelt on the first padded step of the altar and gestured to Kate to kneel beside him. He clasped her hands in his, his eyes intense.

"O Mary, Mother of Sorrows, I beg you on behalf of your servants Mary Caitlin O'Dwyer and Jennifer Catherine Mulvaney, by the bitter agony you did endure at the foot of the Cross, offer to the Eternal Father, in their names, your beloved Son, Jesus, all covered with blood and wounds, in satisfaction for our sins . . . Amen.

"O Mary, Mother of Sorrows, grant peace of spirit to Mary Caitlin and purity of body to Jennifer Catherine. Glory to God in the highest. Amen."

He kissed her hands and released them. They crossed themselves.

"Is there a prayer you can summon from your soul, Kate? God is here in this place, now. He reaches out to you. Reach to Him, Kate, let your spirit fly to Him."

She could think of nothing but the opening words of the mass. She began to whisper.

"In nomine Patris, et Filii, et Spiritus Sancti, Amen." She crossed herself. "I will go to the altar of God. Deliver me from unjust and deceitful men. For you, O God, are my strength, why have you forsaken me? And why do I go about in sadness, while my enemy afflicts me?"

She was crying. Monsignor Reilly wrapped his arm around her, his head bowed, his eyes tightly shut.

"Pray with me, Kate," he said. "Oh, my God, I am most heartily sorry . . ." She joined in the act of contrition.

They both crossed themselves. Monsignor Reilly took her face in both of his hands and looked gently into her eyes. " *'I am wounded, but I am not slain. I'll lie me down and bleed a while, then I'll rise up and fight again.'* Those are very important words to live by, Kate." He stood up. "Stay here. You are in the company of Mary, our Mother of Sorrows. She also suffered the loss of her only child. Speak to her, Kate. Speak whatever is in your heart."

He left the chapel.

"Father, Father, I have sinned before Thee," she whispered. "I thought that it would be all right for me to take a man's life. I forgot that You alone are the giver and the taker of life. But Father, my beloved God, I would do it again. Isn't there a time when your people, your creation, must be permitted to punish evil, to destroy those who would destroy? Wasn't this such a time? O Mary, Mother of Sorrows, isn't your sacrifice enough to last all eternity? You are the Mother of God, and He died for all of our sins. I am only the mother of a little baby. Why must she be a sacrifice?"

Kate wept. She got up slowly and genuflected, then left the chapel and went to the girls' rest room. Her eyes were red, her mascara had run, and she looked like she had been beaten with a stick. She removed the makeup with tissues and water and drove home.

An hour later, Monsignor Reilly called. He told her that he had faxed her application for reinstatement to Chancellor Berne at the diocese office in Phoenix. The chancellor wanted her to come to the office next Wednesday at four o'clock to fill out the various insurance and tax forms.

"I am delighted to have you back, Kate," Monsignor Reilly said.

Kate had hired a lovely older woman, a grandmother a dozen times over, as housekeeper and nanny. Mrs. Gadarian was good with Jennifer, and Jennifer had quickly become accustomed to her. She no longer cried when Kate left.

Kate drove into Phoenix on Indian School Road and stopped off at the travel agency near Forty-fourth Street to pick up the tickets she had ordered yesterday for her and Jennifer to go to Boston for a visit. They were leaving early tomorrow. She had wanted Mike to come with them, but his law practice was growing, and he had a burglary trial beginning tomorrow and a contract dispute arbitration on Thursday. Good for him, she thought. Someday he will be the senior partner in his own firm.

It was a hundred-ten-degree day, so hot that even the bold sunflowers were drooping, as though they were trying to shield their faces from the acetylene torch rays of the pitiless sun. The kaleidoscope of goldenrod, purple larkspur, orange and yellow daisies, and scarlet hummingbird bush that had grown wild in the spring and graced every available piece of dirt just six weeks ago had wilted and dried up and blown away in the searing afternoon winds. But the grounds of the diocese of Phoenix were beautiful. A narrow strip of rich green Bermuda tiff grass was bordered by lavender Mexican primrose. Sunlight through the mist of water spraying from the sprinklers created a low rainbow over the lawn and against the front wall of the building.

The chancery was a pink plaster Spanish colonial two-story building with a reddish mission tile roof. Kate parked in the big lot behind the rear entrance. She had been to the chancellor's office last year to fill out the same set of papers, so she knew where it was and went up the stairs to it. It was a gaudily decorated office with a burgundy carpet, a Louis Quatorze copy cherrywood desk inlaid with gray leather, and Chippendale copy side chairs in matching cherrywood and gray leather.

The chancellor, Monsignor Paul Berne, was a young priest on the rise in the diocese. He studied Kate like a Jesuit examining the shroud of Turin. "The bishop would like to meet with you for a moment, Ms. O'Dwyer. If you don't mind."

"No, not at all."

He pressed a buzzer on his desk, and the lock on the carved wooden door across the room unlatched noisily.

"Come right this way, Ms. O'Dwyer." He escorted her into the bishop's office. It was even more tasteless than the chancellor's. The walnut desk was huge and inlaid with red leather panels. The red leather chair behind it was framed in carved wood like a throne. There were two camelback red leather sofas against the side walls and a white satin upholstered Chesterfield in front of the desk. Official photographs of recent popes hung on the walls.

Bishop Losiento looked like Pope John XXIII, roly-poly and jovial, beaming with good humor. He remained seated and extended his hand, palm down, his apostolic ring toward her. She bent over the desk and kissed it dutifully. He gave her a cherubic smile and folded his pudgy hands together on the bulb of his stomach.

"Good day, Your Grace," she said.

"I'm delighted to meet you, Ms. O'Dwyer. Please

have a seat. May I offer you some tea? Paul, bring Ms. O'Dwyer a cup of tea, will you please?"

The chancellor covered his lower face with a brittle smile. "Yes, Your Grace."

"No, nothing for me, really," Kate said.

The chancellor left the office and closed the door behind him. The bishop opened the file on his desk.

"You're the young lady for whom I received a letter of recommendation from Cardinal Gerrity, I see." He scanned a document in the file.

"Yes, Your Grace."

"A fine man. I was delighted to see him join the college. He's not one of the stodgy old ruddy duddies. We have too many of them." He laughed.

Kate smiled.

"I see that you'd like to return to teaching?"

"Yes, very much."

He settled back in his chair and shook his head sadly. "I'm afraid that our Board of Trustees has acted negatively on your application."

Kate blinked and swallowed. "I don't understand, Your Grace."

"This is a hard time for the church, Ms. O'Dwyer. The archdiocese of Santa Fe, of which we're a part, has been sued for as much as fifty million dollars because of improprieties by some of our priests and nuns. I'm sure you're aware of that."

She nodded.

"Our school trustees are very fearful of having a teacher who has been involved in a criminal case, such as the situation between you and that Wilkott fellow who died."

She stared at him. "That's correct. He died. I didn't do anything to hasten his death."

"I'm not judging you, Ms. O'Dwyer. I'm not even suggesting that you did anything wrong. But what I am passing on to you are the profound concerns of our trustees that if any little thing were to happen to one of your students, God forbid, a boy falls off the monkey bars or a girl's dress gets torn or you have to discipline a child—or God forbid, you are actually charged with some crime over this Wilkott matter—some parent is going to sue this diocese for hiring you as a teacher. That would be wrong, the parent would be misguided, but we would nonetheless be facing the expense of lawyers and the shame of being sued." He paused for a moment.

"These are perilous times for the church, Ms. O'Dwyer," he said soothingly. "I wish that it were not so. I wish that I could overrule the recommendation of the board of trustees."

She looked at him, and she saw cunning eyes in that soft, round face. Behind the burgundy carpet and the burl walnut and the red leather and the black silk suit was a practiced church politician.

"What we are doing to you is wrong, Ms. O'Dwyer. I have prayed for God's grace to forgive us. But I cannot risk even a wrongful lawsuit against this diocese. To do so would be an injury to Mother Church, and the church is more important than any one person."

She spoke in a low, bland voice. "Seamus Cardinal Gerrity used to tell me that the church is only as strong as each person in it." She stood up. "But I do understand *you,* Your Grace."

He extended his hand to her. She walked out without kissing his ring.

She stopped at the travel agency on her way home and returned the airplane tickets. She couldn't look her parents in the eye right now. They would take one look at her and beg her not to return to Scottsdale. She didn't want to live in Boston again. And she didn't want to leave Michael Fallon.

She got home and telephoned Manchester by the Sea and talked to her mother. She told her that she was awfully sorry, but Mike had his first big trial coming up, and she really wanted to watch him. She didn't tell her mother about what had happened in the bishop's office. She promised that she and Mike would both come to Boston over the July Fourth holiday. That seemed to mollify her.

Kate called Gwen next. She had talked to her dozens of times in the past few months, but she hadn't seen her since that awful week.

"It's hot as hell here, Mary Kate darlin'," Gwen said.

Kate laughed. "It's hotter than hell here. Why don't you come out so we can get sunburned together?"

"What a marvelous notion," Gwen said. "But I haven't a farthing."

"I'll prepay your ticket, Sister Gwenny. I never took a vow of poverty."

"Thank God for that," Gwen said.

They both chuckled.

It was a pleasant day of a mere hundred degrees when Gwen arrived, and she and Kate took Jennifer to McCormick Park and then down to the duck cove. They all swam among the gabbling ducks in the pleasantly cool water. Jennifer had long ago learned to swim, but she still wore inflated "swimmies" on both arms. They got out of the water, and Kate rubbed number 30 sunscreen all over Jennifer. Gwen, protected by an olive complexion, applied coconut oil to her arms and chest. Kate put sunscreen on her fair skin. Then they lay back on towels on the bank and sunned for an hour.

Mike went back to his apartment while Gwen was staying in Kate's house. Kate hadn't asked him to, and she hadn't even wanted him to, but he felt a little funny sleeping with Kate with a nun in the next room. Not that Gwen resembled any of the nuns whom he had known, but just the fact of her *being* a nun.

He came over to the house every evening, and they barbecued hamburgers on the patio the first night, ate at Houston's the second night, and struggled through Kate's second bravura attempt at lasagna the third.

The next day, Kate took advantage of the presence of Gwen to build up her courage to go into the small bedroom next to Jennifer's. Kate hadn't been in Donna's old room since that terrible night months ago. She had simply closed the door and excluded it from her world. At first it had been a relentless reminder of her own pain and agony and hatred for what had happened. And then, when she finally became fully convinced that Donna had been as much a tragic victim as Jennifer, the unsettling pain of constant guilt made her want to push all reminders of that terrible time away. And even if Donna was really just a pathetic victim, and even if her life would not be the same ever again, there was only so much that a human being could do for another. Kate could not do any more for Donna.

She opened the door and surveyed the room. The quilt was still lying crumpled on the floor. The bedsheet and mattress pad had been removed by the police to test for semen and vaginal secretions. There had been none. The mattress was still bare. Seeing it made Kate's skin tingle.

She walked inside and sat down gingerly on the bed, looking around the little room, suddenly feeling very depressed. Gwen sat down on the bed and looked around uneasily. The other side of the bed was pressed up against the wall, and wedged between was a book. Kate reached over and pulled the book free. It was the Bible that the sister from the Home of the Good Shepherd had given to Donna in the Juvenile Court Annex the day that Kate was appointed Donna's foster mother.

Kate stared at the Bible and swallowed. She put it on the bed and opened it, and the pages flipped almost automatically to the Canticle of Canticles, because Donna had read it so many times that she had broken the spine of the book in that place.

"Look at this," she said to Gwen. Gwen moved close to Kate, and Kate turned the Bible so that both of them could read it.

There were penciled underlines of some of the verses: *"I am the rose of Sharon, and the lily of the valleys."* And a little handwritten note in the margin next to it: "What's Sharon?" And other verses underlined:

"The flowers appear on the earth; the time of the singing of birds has come, and the voice of the turtle-dove is heard in our land."

"Arise, my love, my fair one, and come away."

Kate flipped some pages, and there was a passage underlined in the book of Job:

"Why was I not stillborn, why did I not perish when I came from the womb? Why was I ever laid on my mother's knees or put to suck at her breasts? Why was I not hidden away like an untimely birth, like an infant who never saw the light?

"For now I should be lying in a quiet grave, asleep in death, at rest."

"Dear Lord," Gwen gasped.

Kate's chin quivered. She flipped some more pages, and there was a photograph of herself and Jennifer on Singing Beach by her parents' home in Manchester. It had been taken about a year ago, and Kate had kept it in a beautiful small leather frame she had bought at Mark Cross. She had put it on one of the shelves of the entertainment center in the living room, and now that she thought about it, she *had* noticed some time ago that the frame was empty. But given all the terrible things that were happening day after day, she had never really registered it, never really wondered about the photograph and looked for it.

She held it up and looked at her and her daughter's smiling faces. The photo was etched from the other side, as though someone had written on it. She hadn't.

"Look at the writin' on the back," Gwen said softly.

Kate turned it over. In the same carefully penciled

handwriting as was in the Bible, was written, "My mom, my sister."

Kate squinted back her tears, and Gwen hugged her.

"Perhaps the girl deserves a second chance at a real life," Gwen whispered. "Can it be, Mary Kate, that you judged her too harshly?"

"Dear God, I wish I knew what to do. I feel so terrible about her."

"Mommy, why you in Donna's room?" Jennifer said, standing in the doorway and staring at Kate. "Mommy, you sick again?"

Kate held out her arms, and Jennifer ran to her and jumped up. Kate caught her and held her in her lap.

"Do you remember Donna, honey?"

"Yeah, Mommy. Donna was my sister. But she went away. Is she coming back?" She looked at Kate with big blue eyes.

Kate looked intently at her daughter. "Would you like that, Jenn?"

"Oh, yes, Mommy. She's my big sister." Jennifer nodded vigorously.

"My mom, my sister," reverberated in Kate's mind over and over again, like a blacksmith's hammer striking a steel anvil. She sat in the living room distractedly watching TV with Gwen until Jennifer's nap time, and then Gwen went to the guest room for a nap. The heat of Scottsdale had enervated her.

The idea had been forming in Kate's mind, since she had seen the photograph, that she had to see Donna. It hadn't been Donna's fault. That was clear enough now. But Kate was nonetheless forcing Donna to pay the same price as Jennifer: she was losing everything. Kate felt a deep guilt over abandoning her.

Donna had told Kate where she lived on the reservation, described the shack to her in painful detail. Kate drove east on Thomas Road and recognized the small, decaying, ramshackle wooden box that had been home for Donna's parents and dozen brothers and sisters. It was straight out of a Ma and Pa Kettle movie, but there was nothing humorous about *this*.

She parked on Thomas Road, treaded gingerly through the garbage-strewn ditch marking the edge of the road, and walked up the rickety porch steps. There was a radio tape boom box on the porch next to a rocking chair. The player was on, and Hank Williams was twanging out one of his signature songs. Several empty bottles of Gallo muscatel lay around the chair. Kate knocked on the partially unhinged screen door. The front door was open.

The woman who stumbled drunkenly toward her was immense, much shorter than Kate but at least two hundred pounds heavier, clad in a filthy muumuu with huge sweat rings under the arms and in the folds of her breasts and belly. The smell coming from the house was a mixture of rotting garbage and piles of cat shit, which Kate could see in various places on the wooden floor of the shack.

"You from the welfare?" the woman asked.

"No, I'm a friend of Donna's."

"Donna ain't got no friends," the woman said, her voice thickened from drink. "She got tricks, but they ain't no friends." She stared at Kate, trying to focus her dead brown eyes. "You got some money for me?"

"Is Donna living here?" Kate swallowed, trying to keep from gagging at the smell of filth and the sense of despair that poured through the screen door like a biblical plague.

"Naw, she ain't here. I told 'er about Louise dyin' from a overdose, and she just took off. Fuckin' bitch. She's down t' the Civic Center doin' niggers for twenty bucks a blowjob. Never even gimme a dime. And me her mama. If you see 'er, tell 'er her mama asked after her, needs a few bucks for food. Ain't nice a daughter goes runnin' off like that, 'specially after niggers. She ain't got no self-respect." She started coughing from the strain of talking and almost gagged.

Kate backed up, nausea rising in her throat. She turned around and ran off the porch, stumbled, regained her balance, and ran back to her car.

• NINE •

Late in the afternoon of July Fourth, in the midst of the huge picnic on the grounds behind her parents' mansion in Manchester by the Sea, Gwen McLemore read the look in Kate's eyes and took her into the house, into the library, and closed the door.

"They mean well, Mary Kate," she said.

Kate's eyes filled with tears. "I know. I just don't know how much more of their well meaning I can handle. I'm about to lose it."

Gwen sat Kate on the leather sofa and sat down next to her. "Be tough, darlin'. Keep smilin'."

"I never thought that I could feel this low here," she said. "My old friends look at me and Jennifer like they're sizing us up for coffins, and they leer at Mike like they'd like to take him off for a tryst on the couch."

"I think those are only projections of your own heartache and frustration, darlin'."

Kate breathed deeply and nodded. "I understand, Madam Psychologist. But I feel like we're living inside a thermos, and nobody *really* wants to touch us or talk to us, like they'll get some horrible disease if they do."

"There's nothin' they can do but pat you on the back and smile. That's all they *can* do to show their affection and concern."

Kate nodded. She opened her purse and repaired

her eye makeup, then went back into the backyard and put on as brave a face as she could.

They had gotten to Manchester on Friday morning, and she and Mike were in bedrooms in separate wings of the huge house. Not that Brendan and Catherine O'Dwyer were such prudes as to mandate the chastity of their unwed daughter, but there were four servants in this house, and gossip was their perfervid pastime.

The July Fourth bash ended in the late evening after seven hours of bountiful food and drink, and Kate and Mike walked languorously on Singing Beach. The moon was veiled behind thick clouds, and most of the beach revelers had gone home. Just a few lay under blankets or towels here and there, bodies close together, and there were telltale sounds of passion or lust and even an occasional snore.

Singing Beach was so named because the locals who lived in the sumptuous mansions on the bluffs near the beach liked to say that when the wind was just right and the moon was in the proper phase, thrumming the rolling water with celestial yellow light, the beach sang exotic melodies. Manchester by the Sea and Singing Beach were certainly the kinds of places where extraordinary things seemed possible, things of richness and opulence and rarity. But listen as they might, and concentrate on the sounds as they did, Mike and Kate heard no exotic melodies. Perhaps it was because the moon was hiding, or maybe it was too skinny or fat, or the emanations coming from it were too timid or bold; but whatever it was, they heard no songs.

They walked to the stone breakwater, delighted and relieved at last to be alone and to be able to touch. Mike leaned back against a smooth, sloping boulder. The water washed up a few inches around his feet, and he sank into the sand. He put his rubber flip-flops on a small ledge in the rock. He was wearing loose white cotton shorts and an old faded blue polo shirt, and Kate crawled her hand up his thigh and touched him.

"Yikes!" he said. "A sand crab."

She kissed his cheek and he untied the loose knot of her halter top around her neck, and it fell. She was wearing wide-legged short shorts and she lifted her leg up and pressed her knee high against the rock. She pulled his shorts down around his thighs.

"This is the way they do it in the Trobriand Islands," she breathed.

"Oh, yeah? Where are they?"

"South Pacific."

"How do you know?"

"Anthropology class. I read it. Bronislaw Malinowski—" She caught her breath.

"Who?"

"An anthropologist—" she gasped.

"Were there pictures?"

"Uh-uh."

"Oh, heck. I would have liked to see the pictures. Well, I think he knew what he was talking about," Mike whispered, his breath short and wheezy. "This is definitely the way to do it by a rock."

They rocked together for moments in a tight embrace, then tensed and gasped in unison.

"Good old Bronislaw," she said, lowering her knee. "A man after my heart."

"Your heart?"

"Well, there are many ways to a woman's heart."

"So many ways, so little time," he murmured.

They laughed, both feeling the welcome release of the tension of the past few days. And suddenly, magically, they could hear the exotic melodies of Singing Beach.

Seamus Cardinal Gerrity had been in Washington, D.C., on Tuesday, at the National Cathedral, unable to make the O'Dwyers' July Fourth picnic as he had done most of the past twenty years. But the next morning he telephoned Kate and asked her if he could come out and visit her. "Of course," Kate said, delighted.

He arrived in a black Mercedes sedan, and the monsignor's chauffeur opened the door for him. The monsignor was in his black suit and dickey and white collar, but the cardinal was dressed in a joyously garish Hawaiian shirt with a vermillion background and huge flowers of yellow and white and blue. He smiled with genuine pleasure when he hugged Kate and then surveyed her.

"I wish I had known earlier that you were coming, Father Seamus. I would have asked Michael Fallon to stay here to meet you. He went into Boston with Daddy this morning."

"Yes, it's really a pity," the cardinal said. "Not *black* Irish, I pray."

"No, no, Father. He's Catholic."

Gerrity squinted at her and laughed. "And quite handsome, too, so I'm told."

It was three o'clock in the afternoon. Catherine O'Dwyer busied herself with Jennifer in another part of the house. Kate led the cardinal down the long hallway to the study. It was filled with overstuffed brown leather chairs and sofas and paneled in gleaming walnut. A wet bar took up a corner of the room. Kate went to it and poured Black Bush whiskey into two glasses, added ice cubes from an ice bucket already prepared, and handed one to the cardinal. She sat down on the sofa next to him, and they took a sip from their drinks.

"It is an awful tragedy you have met with, Mary Kate," he said quietly, his face suddenly solemn. "May God watch over you and little Jennifer in this terrible time."

She sighed. "I don't think He's doing so well, Father."

"I know, my dear. I know. But we are not given to understand all His ways."

She nodded, and her chin quivered.

"Don't abandon Him, Mary Kate."

She looked at him, just a bit sheepishly, then shook her head. "How can I still believe, Father?" she whispered.

He put down his drink on the cocktail table. "I wish I had the answer," he said softly. "Have you abandoned Him?"

She shook her head slowly. "I don't think that *I* have abandoned *God*," she said. "I think it's the other way around."

Gerrity nodded and frowned. "I'll tell you a story, and it's the only thing I have I can say to you. I was a chaplain in the navy in Vietnam for twenty-six months, two tours, from 1966 through 1968, the heart of the war. I was stationed on a hospital ship, the *U.S.S. Mercy.* I saw terrible things there, men with the most terrible wounds."

He swallowed and looked hard at her. "And each time I leaned over one of those boys, I said, 'Dear God, what have *You* done?' And it wasn't only the ones who died who caused me this pain, it was also the ones who lived: destroyed faces, paraplegic, quadriplegic. And they would say to me, 'Why me, Father? Why did this happen to me?' And I would cry myself to sleep at night because I could no longer pray, and I had no answers."

Kate watched him intently, captivated as always by his burning eyes.

"Have you seen the movie *Born on the Fourth of July,* came out a few years ago?"

She nodded.

"A terrible true story," the cardinal said in his gentle Irish accent. "Here was a boy who joined the military because he was full of patriotism and feelings of duty, and then look what happened. The war turned out to be a cynical exercise in death and adventure by dishonest politicians, and over fifty thousand young men died for no apparent reason, and hundreds of thousands were maimed and disfigured and crippled. And for what?"

Cardinal Gerrity looked at Kate and wrinkled his brow, then answered his own question. "For God's will," he said resolutely. "For God's will."

She stared at the cardinal.

"That terrible Vietnam War was like every other terrible war. In the Second World War, if men had not died and been maimed in battle, would we all still be here in the same way as we are today? What would the world have become if we feared the loss and injury of our loved ones and the Nazis had simply taken over the world?"

"But isn't that different, Father?" she said. "The Second World War seems to us a *just* war, a war of good and decency over evil and tyranny. Men came back in boxes or with parts gone, but it was for a purpose that we can understand. But Vietnam? Where's the purpose that we can understand?"

Gerrity nodded. "Perhaps the purpose was that it caused a revolution in the way that our own citizens viewed the authority of the government of the United States, and this led directly to a huge change in our fundamental understanding of politics and politicians and literally destroyed a corrupt president and his administration. Would the Nixon presidency have weathered the storm of protests if the grassroots revolution in this country had not dramatically changed our willingness to be misled and manipulated?"

Kate was silent.

"But of course, during the Vietnam War none of this had yet happened. We had no idea what would be the outcome of the yippies and the student protests and ultimately the grassroots revolution that swept our land. But in view of that, in view of what we now realize has since occurred, isn't *Born on the Fourth of July* really very narrow-sighted, short-sighted? Of course it's a tragedy when an innocent young man is struck down in the full flower of his youth. To him or his loved ones there can never be any justification. But to see in it none of the greater meaning that so many such sacrifices have is to lose sight of the forest for each tree."

Kate was confused, far more uncertain than before. "And Jennifer?" she asked weakly. "What greater meaning can there be, Father Seamus? Will HIV-infected rapists be put to death? No, that certainly hasn't happened. Will her death enhance the quality of life for me, for Mike, for Arizona, for the United States?"

"I don't know. We cannot know, because nothing has happened yet to show us the purpose of this tragedy in God's plan. But as with the death of an innocent man murdered by Nazis in a *just* war, as with the crippling of an innocent man in Vietnam in an *unjust* war, we cannot yet see the good that God's will shall bring forth from it."

Kate sighed. The compassion in Seamus Gerrity's face was genuine. And so was the ache in her heart.

· TEN ·

It was just over six months since Jennifer had been raped, and the day finally arrived that had been set for Kate to take Jennifer to the laboratory at Good Samaritan Hospital in Phoenix to have blood drawn for the ELISA test. It was the next-to-last step in confirming the presence of the HIV virus that had been diagnosed by the PCR test five months ago. The doctor had told Kate that in the many thousands of cases of HIV infection, where the date of the infecting episode could be pinpointed, no individual had ever contracted HIV whose blood was untainted after six months. In other words, if Jennifer had no HIV infection after six months, then she had in fact *not* been infected by the rape.

It was Kate's last hope for her daughter. But she had forced herself not to hope, not to be crushed by the extremely probable confirmation of the positive diagnosis provided by the PCR test. She sat with Jennifer on her lap, told her to close her eyes, and the technician inserted the needle in Jennifer's brachial vein in the inside of her elbow. She wailed in pain, and Kate comforted her as much as she could. The technician covered the pinprick with a cotton ball and a Band-Aid that had *Peanuts* characters on it. Kate promised Jennifer that there wouldn't be any more needles.

*   *   *

"Kate?" Mike said.

"Yes, honey?"

"Will you marry me?"

She turned to him on the sofa and lowered the volume on *Seinfeld* with the clicker. "What brought *this* on?"

He shrugged, a little embarrassed.

"Why are you blushing?" she asked.

"I haven't done this very much before."

"Well, I'm happy for that."

"I want to marry you."

"When?"

"How about tomorrow?"

"How about during Christmastime in Boston?"

"Why?"

"My parents want to be at our wedding."

"Oh. How did they know we were going to get married?"

"I guess I mentioned it to them when we were there over the July Fourth holiday, maybe even a couple of other times."

"Oh."

"You want to be married by a cardinal?" Kate asked.

"I didn't think them li'l ol' red birds could even talk," Mike drawled, "let alone perform weddin's."

She smiled. "Very cute. Answer the question."

"How are we going to manage that?"

"My father says if we come between Christmas and New Year's, Seamus Cardinal Gerrity would be happy to marry us."

"Well, I'm not sure I want to marry *him*."

She scowled at him. "Will you be serious?"

"Okay, sorry. Yes."

"You sure?"

"I'm sure."

"You sure you want to?"

"Yes."

"You don't look it."

"I'm sure, God damn it."

"Okay, okay. Just asking. Can my parents invite a few guests?"

He eyed her askance. "I'm afraid even to ask how many."

"Just a few, honest. Mom promised just a few."

"Jesus, I can just picture it: five thousand lace curtain Irishmen crowded into Saint Paddy's Cathedral. Whoopie!" He winced. "My mom's got to be there. There's got to be one more of us shanty Irish just to balance it out."

"I'll ask Daddy to send her a ticket."

"I'll send her a ticket myself," Mike said. "What day?"

"Saturday, December the thirtieth. At my parents' place in Manchester, in the backyard. And your mother will stay there."

"Good. Sounds like fun."

"It *will* be fun. It'll be the most fun we've ever had."

He put his arms around her waist and drew her close. "Well, I don't know about that," he said.

Kate coughed and cleared her throat. "Are you sure?" she said into the telephone as strongly as she could.

"Yes," Dr. Burkenheim said. "I had them do three independent ELISA's. We drew plenty of blood. Dr. Shilton, the chief microbiologist at Good Sam, did the tests himself, and I just got off the telephone with him."

"Oh, dear God. Oh, dear God." She could hardly think. Her thoughts were flitting around in her head like a swarm of bees. She began to cry, caught her breath after a moment, and gasped, "What else?" into the phone.

"Just one thing more, Ms. O'Dwyer."

"Yes?"

"Dr. Shilton is doing a Western Blot Test to confirm the results of the ELISA's. I'll call you just as soon as he calls me."

"Thank you," she murmured.

She didn't think that there were any more shocks that could knock her off her feet. She thought that she'd about had the course, but Dr. Burkenheim's telephone call left her speechless, weak in the knees, and she sank to the sofa.

She gathered herself after a few moments and telephoned Mike's office, but his new secretary said that he was doing a motion in court. She telephoned her parents' home in Manchester, but for some reason no one answered the phone. Then she was relieved that she hadn't been able to reach anybody. Why lay this on them? Everybody had been through enough. Better wait for the final verdict on the Western Blot Test.

She got up and walked absently onto the patio. Mrs. Gadarian must have taken Jennifer down to the duck cove. It was ten o'clock in the morning, and autumn had finally arrived in Scottsdale, always a welcome guest. It was just eighty degrees, and now, in early November, the temperature wasn't likely to climb much higher. A gentle breeze was coming off the lake.

Jennifer was tossing pieces of dried bread among the always gleeful ducks. She burst out in laughter as a big, long-necked goose waddled up to her and swatted her with her long tail feathers, annoyed that Jennifer was wasting these treasures on other ducks. Jennifer ran away squealing, with the big goose in hot pursuit.

Kate sat down beside Mrs. Gadarian.

"She's a wonderful little girl," Mrs. Gadarian said. She looked at Kate, and her voice was wistful. "I lost a little one, too. My four-year-old boy, Alan. He had leukemia. Nothing anybody could do. I never understood why. I guess there isn't any why. All you can do is hope nothing like that happens, and when it does, you just have to accept it and go on and hope it doesn't happen again." She crossed herself and kissed her thumb.

Kate nodded.

Jennifer was crying. "Mommy, Mommy, the big duckie bited me."

"Where, honey?"

"Right there." She pointed at a little red mark on her calf.

"Here, Mommy will kiss it and make it better."

Jennifer sat down on the grassy bank, rolled over onto her tummy, and cocked her leg up. Kate leaned over and kissed the red mark.

"Better?"

"Yop, all better," Jennifer said. She jumped up and ran back to the ducks.

"Don't let the big ones get too close," Kate called out.

It just so happened that Dr. Burkenheim called Kate with the results of the Western Blot Test about two minutes before she got a telephone call from one of the genuinely persistent and pesky reporters for the Phoenix CBS television affiliate, Channel 10. Kate simply couldn't say "no comment" for the thousandth time in the past six months, avoiding hundreds of reporters and cameramen. She was too full of emotion, too much off her guard.

"My baby, Jennifer, does *not* have any trace of HIV infection," Kate gushed. "Three ELISA tests and a Western Blot have absolutely confirmed it."

"Oh, that's wonderful news," the reporter said. "I think the whole world would love to hear this, and not just secondhand from me. All anyone has ever seen of you is that old grainy wedding photo in the newspapers. Don't you think it would be wonderful to be on the news and let everyone know about it yourself?"

"Well, I'm certainly no newscaster. I wouldn't know what to say."

"Don't worry about that, Ms. O'Dwyer. I'll ask you questions. All you have to do is respond."

"I don't want to be on live TV. I'd be too scared and embarrassed."

"That's perfectly all right. Can I bring a cameraman out to your house? We can tape an interview."

Kate was feeling too expansive and ebullient to say no. Why not? she thought. They've all heard the worst. It's time for everyone to hear the best.

"Okay, fine. Can you be here soon?"

"Probably a half hour or forty-five minutes, depending on traffic."

"All right."

Kate called Mike's office and asked Mike's secretary to have him call as soon as he came in. Then she called Manchester and told her mother, who wept loudly and long; but Kate was too happy at the moment to shed even one more tear.

She called Gwen, got her answering machine, and left a long, rambling message. "You were right, Gwenny," she said. "You were right."

She went into the bedroom and looked appraisingly at her clothing in the closet for the first time in months. She put on a simple raw silk short-sleeve shirt with a scoop neckline and a long, loose pleated silk shirt in a dark green and orange and yellow small floral print. She wore black suede granny boots. She spent fifteen minutes in front of the bathroom mirror, putting on enough green eye shadow, brown eyebrow pencil, and black eyeliner and mascara so that her soft green eyes wouldn't disappear in the bright lights of the TV camera. She had read about that in *Vanity Fair* once. She looked into the mirror and beamed at herself, almost burst into exuberant tears, but forced herself to be calm.

The telephone rang, and she spoke to Mike for several minutes. He began crying, and tears wet her eyes. She daubed them with a tissue and listened to him babble effervescently for a few moments, and he said he'd be home by six and they'd all go over to the new French restaurant on Fifth Avenue in downtown Scottsdale for the splashiest dinner money could buy.

"By the way," she said, "a TV reporter just called me, and I told her about it, and I'm going to be interviewed."

He paused. "Well, I don't know if that's such a good idea. Maybe it's best not to."

"I really feel like telling the whole world myself," she said. "For Jennifer. Jennifer deserves it."

"I know how you feel, but it's a lot safer not to."

"I won't say anything about anything but Jennifer. I'm just too happy to hold it in."

"Okay, then just be very careful."

"Don't worry."

She went back into the bathroom and repaired the damage to her eye makeup, couldn't do much about her slightly bloodshot eyes, put some blusher on her cheeks, and applied fire-engine red lipstick with a pencil. She brushed her hair full and bouncy around her face, got the jewelry box out of the floor safe in the closet, and put on ruby and gold bead earrings and the matching one-strand necklace, a very expensive present from her parents when she had graduated from Wellesley just a few years ago in what seemed another lifetime.

Another look at herself in the long mirror on the closet door elicited a nutty peal of laughter from deep within her. She began to murmur the morning prayer, trying to calm herself: "Oh, my God, I adore you, and I love you with all my heart. I thank you for having created me, having saved me by your graces, and for having preserved me through the dark night."

The doorbell rang. She looked sternly at herself in the mirror. "Don't get crazy," she whispered.

Mrs. Gadarian had taken Jennifer to the petting zoo, and they were going to stop off at McCormick Park and have lunch and then ride the little railroad. They wouldn't be home for at least an hour.

Kate opened the door, and Laura Casterleigh introduced herself and the cameraman. She was prettier in person than on TV, dark brown, wavy hair, dark blue eyes, and tennis court tanned skin with an almost luminous sheen. She also had a very kindly smile. She was formally dressed in a cream-colored light wool suit. The cameraman, in contrast, was about the reporter's age but had a straggly beard and wore Levi's, a faded black polo shirt, and tennis shoes. But he was also very gracious and congratulated Kate on the wonderful news.

"The whole world will breathe a sigh of relief when they hear this," Laura said, smiling. "Everybody at the station is so happy and excited for you."

Kate didn't want to start crying again, and she didn't trust her voice at the moment. So she simply smiled and nodded.

"Come, let's have us here on the sofa," Laura said. She sat down and Kate sat beside her, both turned to each other.

The cameraman spread his tripod about six feet away and switched on a bank of four very bright lights supported on another tripod. He busied himself with a light meter against Laura's shoulder, then Kate's. Laura took a steno pad and Mont Blanc fountain pen out of her purse, put the purse on the floor, opened the pad, unscrewed the cap off the pen, and poised the pen officiously over the pad.

"Ready?" she asked the cameraman.

"Try it."

"Testing one, two, three. This is Laura Casterleigh."

"Hold it a second." The cameraman adjusted the bank of lights, squinted into the camera again, and said, "Go."

"The entire country has followed the tragic story of Mary Caitlin O'Dwyer and her three-year-old daughter, Jennifer," Laura said, looking into the camera. She gave a very brief recital of the facts of the crime, the dismissal of the criminal case against Philip Wilkott on a technicality, and his death in an automobile accident while Ms. O'Dwyer was driving. Then she turned to Kate.

"Just today you've heard some wonderful news, for a change."

"Yes," Kate said, her voice strong and under control. "Jennifer's doctor called me and told me that the initial testing of Jennifer's blood, which detected the HIV virus, was a false positive. The four tests that have just been administered to Jennifer have demonstrated conclusively that she is free of any infection. There is no chance that she contracted HIV or will contract AIDS as a result of the attack on her."

Laura asked some questions about Jennifer's average day, and then whether she understood anything about what had happened.

"No, she was unconscious at the time Wilkott attacked her. She's never had any memory of it or bad dreams or anything like that, and the doctors assure me that she never will."

"There was a good deal of violence associated with this case. Your boyfriend, Michael Fallon, learned the name of Philip Wilkott only by beating two men, one of whom subsequently died. Do you regret any of that?"

Kate looked at the camera, then at the reporter, and suddenly felt trapped. Mike had been right about this. "I really don't want to talk about any of that. I just wanted to tell everyone that my daughter is going to be fine."

"Do you believe that what Michael Fallon did was right?"

Kate had never been interviewed before and wasn't skilled in whatever art was required to answer carefully or deftly avoid answering. It suddenly made her feel resentful of these questions on this day when only good news should be discussed. She felt herself blushing and becoming combative, but she held herself in check.

"I told you that I just don't want to discuss those things now."

"Do you have any regrets about the death of Philip Wilkott?"

"It was an unfortunate accident."

"Well, Ms. O'Dwyer, the police determined that you visited him in disguise, that you had a false story about needing a lawyer for a divorce, that you seduced him into a dinner date, got him drunk, and that you had a .38-caliber revolver in your purse."

Kate desperately wanted to throw Laura Casterleigh out of her house, but she knew that she could not do that on CBS television.

"Miss Casterleigh, you told me that this interview would be about Jennifer."

"Do you think that you would have acted in the same way if you had known at the time that your daughter was not HIV-infected?"

Kate stood up and extended her hand for a handshake. "Thank you so much for coming, Miss Casterleigh."

The reporter stood up, all smiles and charm, and shook Kate's hand. "Well, I'm sure that the entire nation shares your joy in the news about your daughter, Ms. O'Dwyer. And I'm sure that you'll be happy to return to a normal life."

"Yes, of course," Kate said, forcing a pleasant smile.

Jennifer was with her dolls in the bedroom, and they were telling each other stories. Jennifer was even using different voices.

"How'd the interview go?" Mike asked.

Kate shrugged, her face unhappy. "I don't know. She just got me at the precise moment that all of my defenses were down. I wasn't thinking of anything but how happy I was and that everybody should hear about Jennifer. It didn't even occur to me that the other stuff would come up. She seemed so sweet and caring."

"Maybe she is, but she's a reporter. Controversy makes news, and there's enough controversy in this mess to get some reporter a Pulitzer prize." He frowned. "Better see what it looks like on TV." He switched it on. "Do you remember exactly what you said? After these folks edit it, you might not even recognize it."

Kate grimaced. "She shook me up so badly, I can't even remember what I said."

The news started, and the anchor introduced Laura Casterleigh with the lead story. She sat at the anchor desk with him and did a segue to the taped interview. Mike sat on the edge of the couch, watching and listening intently. When the segment ended, he turned to Kate.

"Was that the whole interview? Was it edited?"

"I think that's the whole thing."

"Well, that isn't bad at all. You kept your cool and didn't say anything that'll backfire. I'm proud of you."

She smiled for the first time in four hours. "Thanks. I'll never do that again."

"That's good advice," Mike said and kissed her on the cheek. "Wow, you smell delicious and you look spectacular. I'm really hungry."

"You still want to eat at the French place?"

He nodded. "And I want you for dessert."

She put her arms around him and hugged him. "Thank God it's all over," she said.

• ELEVEN •

"Here's a nice bundle for you, Donna," Mrs. Joseph said. She handed Donna a big white bulging laundry bag. "I put some pretty good work clothes in there, average men's sizes, and also a whole bunch of dresses from a rich family. They're like new."

"Thank you very much, Mrs. Joseph."

Donna's last stop to pick up old clothing was usually the Latter Day Saints' Family Welfare Outreach in Mesa near Second Street and Ashland, two blocks from the huge Mormon Temple. For some reason the Mormons had a thing for Indians, thought they were some kind of kin to early Mormons from the Holy Land. Something like that, anyway. Donna wasn't quite sure, but for whatever reason, the Mormons treated her better than most people who knew that she was from the reservation.

Mrs. Joseph, the elderly woman who ran the Outreach, was as fat as Donna's mother, but she didn't smell like she was rotting inside or look like she'd been pickled in booze.

"How are you coming along?" Mrs. Joseph asked.

"We're doing real good."

"Have you read any of that book I gave you?"

Donna shrugged, embarrassed. "I tried, Mrs. Joseph, but the words are so big, and I can't really understand."

"Why don't you come to one of our study sessions

for teenagers, Donna? Every Sunday evening at the Stake Meeting Hall over on Kimball. You'll meet some other youngsters, and Bishop Smith is terrific at explaining the marvels and wonders of the holy books."

"I'll try, but Mrs. Ishpia usually wants me go with her to the Catholic church by the Indian agency on Sunday evenings. They hand out free food there." As she said it, she lowered her eyes self-consciously, feeling a twinge of shame at the abject poverty of her existence.

"That priest is no good." Mrs. Joseph shook her head emphatically. "I understand he got thrown out of his parish here for advocating abortion. He's not the kind of man you should be listening to."

"I can't help it. Mrs. Ishpia makes me go," Donna lied. "Anyway, he never says anything about that. He just talks about Jesus and the Apostles and how we should be like them."

Mrs. Joseph's scolding look softened. She nodded.

There was a twelve-inch color television set on the end of the short counter a few feet from Mrs. Joseph, and she had always been glued to it when Donna had seen her. She was distracted by something on it now, and Donna looked over at it. A very pretty reporter named Laura Casterleigh was talking about an interview she'd had earlier that afternoon with Mary Caitlin O'Dwyer, the Scottsdale woman whose baby had been raped and who everyone thought was stricken with AIDS by the assailant.

"Did you hear about that terrible thing?" Mrs. Joseph asked rhetorically, glancing at Donna, then turning quickly back to the TV set so that she wouldn't miss anything.

The interview played, and Mrs. Joseph steepled her hands together prayerfully. "The Lord has worked a miracle," she said. "Praise the Lord, praise the Lord."

Donna felt lightheaded. She crossed herself.

"Baby Jesus has watched over that little girl," Mrs. Joseph said, her voice and face reverent.

Donna nodded and smiled. "Thank you for the clothes, Mrs. Joseph." Her voice sounded weak and far away. She needed to be by herself now; she needed to think about this miracle that had happened to Jennifer.

Mrs. Joseph smiled at her and went back to watching the evening news. Donna walked out of the Outreach office and got into the old truck. She started it and immediately tuned the radio to the station that was always broadcasting CNN news. She pulled slowly away from the curb and was almost broadsided by a car coming down Second Street. The man at the wheel swerved, beeped his horn, and threw her a finger. She decided that she'd better get herself settled down before she caused an accident. She pulled to the curb.

She sat there, the engine running, radio playing, pressed her hands to her eyes and wept with joy.

CNN carried a brief synopsis of the interview with Kate, and Donna stopped crying, but she couldn't stop beaming with exhilaration. She dried her eyes, looked in both rearview mirrors to make sure that no cars were coming, and pulled into the street. She drove up Country Club Drive, over the Salt River bridge, and slowed as she reached McDowell. She didn't want to go home right now. It was too confining. She wanted to drive, to feel free, because she felt as though she *had* just been freed from the evil demon that had clawed its way into her soul six months ago and been eating it away bite by bite ever since.

She turned left on McDowell, toward Scottsdale, and suddenly felt the need to see Kate and Jennifer. An overwhelming rush of pleasure made her hands shake and her breath come shallowly and fast. Maybe now, maybe now, maybe now, maybe now. God, God, God, God, maybe now, maybe now.

She drove faster, with a mission, with a purpose. She wanted to see Kate and Jennifer. Kate would feel differently now. She wouldn't blame Donna for killing Jennifer. Jennifer was going to live to be a hundred.

As she reached Indian Bend Road, the sun lost its grip on the sky and slid below Mummy Mountain, and the horizon over the mountain was ignited by vermillion and lavender and lemon yellow light. She drove a mile or so to McCormick Parkway and turned into the luxurious development of rich homes and greenery and man-made lakes.

Suddenly she became aware of where she was, that she was driving a beat-up old pickup truck in a residential neighborhood of Cadillacs and Jaguars and Mercedes. Strollers on the asphalt walking and biking paths were casting suspicious looks at her as she drove by. She turned left on Via Camello del Norte to go to Via de Frontera, and in her rearview mirror she could see a black and white car with lights on the top. She gulped and stared at it. She had no driver's license, and if she got stopped, the cop would take her down to juvi, and then she'd be heading back to Black Canyon for sure.

The car turned off on Via Arbor, and she saw that it had been some kind of emergency vehicle, not a police car, and her heart stopped squishing uncontrollably. But the odd looks of the strollers didn't stop. She neared the turn to Via de Frontera and saw what looked like Mike's pickup truck heading toward her.

It was. It was rapidly becoming dark, as it always did in the autumn very soon after sunset, but she could see through the windshield of the truck that Mike was driving and Jennifer was in her car seat in the middle and Kate was on the other side. They all had their mouths open and happy smiles on their faces, obviously celebrating today's miracle.

Donna turned her head quickly to the other side, suddenly embarrassed, confused, frightened. She pulled to the curb as the truck went by. What in hell was she thinking? She was the junkie whore who Big Gun Pete had shot up with heroin and fucked in the kitchen and shot up again the next day and then been had by someone else while a three-year-old baby was being raped just fifteen feet away. What was she going to do? Run up to the child's mother and throw her arms around her neck and kiss her and hug her and announce, "I'm back!"? And what would Kate O'Dwyer do? Just kiss her sweetly and say, "Oh, golly jiminy gosh, it's so good to have my own little heroin addict whore back living in my house next to my daughter so the next time one of her former pimps comes calling, Jennifer actually *will* get AIDS."

The adrenaline rush that had brought her here bled away. She rubbed her face hard with both hands, washing away the childish dream that had driven her for the past twenty minutes. She took several deep breaths, made a U-turn, and drove slowly toward the reservation. She didn't want to go back there, but where else was there to go? Downtown to the Civic Center? Maybe that was all she was good for anymore.

"Are you planning to do anything about Donna?" Mike asked.

Kate's face sobered, and she looked over at him. "Yes. I'm going to go see her. First thing next week. I've just got to rest for a few more days, get myself together. Then I'll go to the reservation and see if I can find her."

Jennifer was in the car seat between them, not paying attention to what her mother and Mike were saying. She was singing "Itsy, bitsy spider," in her tiny voice and was engrossed in twisting her hands together, showing the spider crawling up the water spout.

"I already tried to find her once," Kate said. "It was when Gwen was here."

"You didn't tell me."

"I didn't tell anyone," she said quietly. "I guess I felt a little funny about it."

"What did you do?"

"I went out to the reservation and found the shack where Donna's mother lives. Donna had told me where it was and described it. Her mother is a huge woman who just sits on the porch and drinks wine and listens to Hank Williams tapes."

"At least she has good taste in music."

Kate rolled her eyes. "God, it was awful. You wouldn't have believed how low people can get."

"Yes, I would," Mike said.

"And she didn't have any idea where Donna was. Said she'd come home from Black Canyon and found out her sister had just died of an overdose, and she took off again right away. She said she was down at the Civic Center doing niggers for twenty bucks a blowjob." She looked at Mike, her eyes incredulous. "Can you imagine the girl's *mother* saying a thing like that?"

Mike gritted his teeth and shook his head grimly.

"And then she asked me for some money, and I started to walk away, and she yelled out that if I see Donna, I should tell her to bring some of the money home for mama."

"Great life Donna's had," Mike said.

"It's a wonder she's still alive. I'll go out there next Monday, see if I can find her. If not, I'll get the name of her CPS caseworker and see if she knows where she is." She paused and frowned. "I hope to God she's okay."

"Are you going to take her back?"

Kate sighed deeply. "I think so." She turned her head and stared out the side window of the truck. "I have to see her and talk to her, find out what's in our hearts."

There were at least fifty reporters and cameramen on the street and the lawn in front of Kate's home in the morning. She had unplugged all of the telephones and refused to answer the door, but none of them left.

The party on the patio of Kate's home was spontaneous. Mike had stayed home from his office, idling around the house, whistling and occasionally bursting out singing various show tunes, "June Is Bustin' Out all Over," and "Memories," and "My Boy Bill." He puttered around the house fixing drips and tightening loose screws that had long been ignored.

At about ten o'clock in the morning, people just started showing up through the patio gate. Edith, Kate's best friend in the neighborhood, came over with a huge chocolate cake. Minna Latchman, one of the neighbors who had brought Kate and Jennifer pastries, brought even more. Another neighbor brought candy and yet another showed up with a bottle of fine brandy. At eleven o'clock Suzy Marren from Merry Moppits and her mother came over and then four more little girls and their mothers twenty minutes later. Victor Hodges, Kate's "jogging buddy" from across the street, came at noon with his wife, Ilse, and two bottles of Dom Perignon.

The reporters and cameramen observed the growing throng of visitors going around to the rear of the house and began edging back there as well, filtering through the crowd in the backyard. Neither Kate nor Mike cared any longer, though Mike cautioned her to give no formal interviews to anyone.

At one o'clock Monsignor Reilly came with three other teachers from Saint Daniel's Academy. Father Baedecker and two nuns came over from Our Mother of Perpetual Help, and then more neighbors drifted in, carrying bottles and platters of this and that. John Steigman and Harvey Stidham and their wives showed up at a few minutes after six with two Super Whopper pizzas covered with anchovies, onions, Italian sausage, pepperoni, and mushrooms.

Kate hadn't been drunk since her third year at Wellesley, when she had experimented with six or eight different whiskeys, just for the hell of it, and hell she had paid for it. This time she felt too jubilant to care, and she simply wandered around the patio chatting merrily with everyone and sipping drink after drink. By the time the last celebrant had left at eleven o'clock that night, Mike had already carried Kate to bed and tucked her in hours before.

· TWELVE ·

Thomas Wilkott and Theodore Garland sat in the darkened conference room adjoining the Pima County Attorney's office in Tucson. Wilkott had brought with him the newspaper stories from the *Arizona Republic,* the *Phoenix Gazette,* a videotape copy of the Casterleigh-O'Dwyer interview, which he had obtained directly from the general manager of Channel 10, and a dozen other news snippets he had himself taped from various broadcasts, including shots of the party on Mary O'Dwyer's patio.

Ted Garland had read the stories and just now had watched the interview and the other TV coverage. There had also been front-page stories in both of the Tucson newspapers, although neither was as long and as detailed as those in Phoenix, where the powerful Wilkott family lived.

He switched on the overhead lights. "Okay, Mr. Wilkott. So what's on your mind?"

"Please call me Tom."

"Why don't we go back into my office? It's much more comfortable there."

They walked into Garland's office and sat down. Garland clenched his hands on the desk blotter and studied Wilkott.

"Now that it is proven that my son did not infect the little girl, do you still believe that the death penalty inflicted by a private citizen without judge or jury or appeal was an appropriate sanction? And do you think that such a person should be permitted to celebrate so cavalierly?"

Garland pursed his lips thoughtfully. "Perhaps not."

"I think you see, Ted, that the very integrity of the administration of criminal justice cries out here for the laws of our state to be enforced."

"And how would you propose that the laws be enforced?"

"I'm not asking for blood, Ted. I'm not asking you to do anything whatsoever that would be unlawful or improper or unethical for a chief prosecutor to do. I think that while the public's sentiment was probably in favor of the O'Dwyer woman when the false information about HIV and AIDS distracted everyone from the crime she committed, I think that now the public is in a far more reflective mood. Good people everywhere abhor an attack on a little girl. But she will never even know that it happened. And I think that good people everywhere, in this day of violent crime, rampant, insane killings and mayhem, good people will hear the facts of this case and say that Mary O'Dwyer had no right to take the law into her own hands."

Ted Garland sighed and nodded. "That may well be true. I don't know."

"The only way to know is to charge her and let the people speak out, let a jury judge her. That is what justice is about: the informed and well-considered voice of the people speaking out above the screams and cries and threats of the criminals whose acts would hold us all hostage. This is a nation of law and justice. Let the people exercise their right to render justice according to law."

"Well, that's quite an eloquent statement, Tom, very eloquent indeed. I can see why we elected you president of the State Bar twice." Garland appeared quite sincere.

"Thank you, Ted. I cherish the confidence that men

and women of our profession have placed in me over the years. And I fully expect even more confidence to be placed in you when you tackle that congressional race next year.''

Garland looked hard at Wilkott. ''I'm certainly counting on your confidence to be expressed openly and with conviction, Tom.''

''You have my solemn pledge on the matter.'' He nodded reassuringly.

''Well, the truth is that I think the underlying facts of this case have changed radically and now warrant an official inquiry by this office. I'm confident that it will result in charges against Ms. O'Dwyer. We'll let the people decide whether Mary O'Dwyer should be punished.''

They shook hands warmly. Tom Wilkott left the county attorney's office feeling buoyed by the spirit of justice that had soared there like a golden eagle, the very symbol of American greatness. He could feel it. He could see its proud head and beak and widespread wings, steadfastly sweeping into the pristine heavens. You will be avenged, my son. The world will not piss on your grave.

He walked past the faux marble pedestal in the foyer with a bronze statue of the blindfolded lady of justice resting upon it. The lady held a sword in her right hand and a balance scale in her left. Under her foot she was crushing a deadly snake against a book of the law, the cornerstone upon which all of society was supported. Her eyes could not see whose cause came before her to be weighed in the scales, for justice must be blind to the individual. She must not see tears. She must not be swayed by beauty. She must not see through the eyes into the soul beyond, for none of that mattered. She must only weigh the act that had been perpetrated and determine from objective evidence alone the culpability of the perpetrator.

The blindfolded lady had a tranquil smile on her

lips, and Thomas Osborne Wilkott knew that the smile was for him and his son, Philip.

"What do you think?" Ted Garland asked.

"It sucks," Dan Emerick said. He was the chief criminal deputy county attorney and had headed the criminal division staff of some fifty prosecutors and eight investigators for nine years. "I never saw anything like this before."

"We're going to prosecute and let a jury decide."

"It doesn't feel right to me, Ted."

"We're doing it. Just tell me how you want to handle it."

When the Pima County Attorney himself ordered a prosecution, and there were clearly provable facts to support it, you could argue for a while, but the ultimate decision was his. No matter how uncomfortable you felt, you worked for the county attorney, and he was the boss.

"We've got to treat her exactly like we would any murder suspect," Garland said. "No favoritism."

Emerick frowned. "You mean arrest her, no bail, the whole nine yards?"

Garland nodded. "Did you talk to Captain Milletti?"

"Yeah. He said that he talked it over with Cohen, and Cohen thinks that the HIV positive on the little girl at the time and the fact that Wilkott's DNA tested as a match to the infected semen was legal justification, particularly in light of the fact that Wilkott was released on really bullshit technicalities."

"Since when does Cohen decide what's justification and what isn't? That's for a jury."

"He told Captain Milletti he didn't want anything to do with the case."

"What's Milletti say?"

"He backs him a hundred percent. Says Cohen's the best investigator he's got. If he says no go, it's no go."

"Shit!" Garland hissed. "That goddamn bleeding

heart Jew bastard. I'm gonna keep that son of a bitch in mind." He frowned. "So how do we do it?"

"We'll have our own investigators make the arrest, and one of them can read all the relevant police reports into the record at the preliminary hearing. No big deal. She's cold for attempted murder, maybe even first-degree murder if the magistrate thinks she planned the accident knowing about the airbag and there not being one on his side. Maybe that's why she was driving *him* and not vice versa."

"Okay, sounds good. But let's not go to a justice of the peace. They're a bunch of scared rabbits. Let's arrest her on a first-degree murder warrant and get one of the superior court judges to stipulate to hear the preliminary hearing."

"Who?"

"Who's got a good pair of balls and will bind her over without giving a damn about what the public thinks?"

Emerick shrugged. "Who's not up for reelection next year?"

Garland thought for a moment. "Kellman. White. Marstad, I think."

"Kellman. He's the best judge in the courthouse, keeps on getting the highest ratings in the Bar polls. He's well respected, well liked, and he'll do what's right without worrying about a nasty editorial or some squealing bunch of feminist cunts."

"Good. Kellman it is. Draft a complaint and let's get it going."

Ted Garland wanted to get the most mileage out of Tom Wilkott that he could from this case. He'd throw the whole load of shit at the O'Dwyer woman and let a jury decide. That's what the jury system was for. And the best thing to do to keep her in jail at least for a few days would be to arrest her on a Friday night. Most people can't make bail on a weekend, since any substantial bail often entails obtaining mortgage documents and other financial instruments from banks, which aren't open until Monday.

Garland and Emerick drafted a criminal complaint and had it signed by county attorney senior investigator Marvin Trillker. It set forth the facts surrounding the death of Philip Wilkott and charged Mary Caitlin O'Dwyer with murder in the first degree. That charge technically encompassed all lesser included offenses of which she could be convicted: second-degree murder, manslaughter, negligent homicide, and the attempt to do any of them.

Judge Aaron B. Kellman, presented with the persuasive facts set forth in the complaint, signed an arrest warrant at four-thirty Friday afternoon. Senior investigator Trillker knew from the reports in the file that the O'Dwyer woman had a three-and-a-half-year-old daughter and no other relatives in Arizona. Trillker therefore drove to Scottsdale with a female county attorney's investigator, Peggy Nix, and a child protective services caseworker named Hattie Simmons, who would take the little girl into protective custody.

Peggy Nix was tall and stocky, in her mid-forties. The men around the office occasionally referred to her as the "butch bitch" behind her back. Trillker knew her very well, and it had never bothered or concerned him that she was a lesbian. She had been living with one or another girlfriend for years and was a retired sheriff's deputy, as was Trillker, who was fifteen years her senior and a former lieutenant. Once she had hidden her relationships fearfully, referring to her live-in friends as roommates when anybody asked. But in the past few years things had changed. Nobody threatened to fire you anymore as long as you did your job well and kept your home life private.

Marvin Trillker had served in the army in the Korean War and won two silver stars and a distinguished service cross. Since then he had been in law enforcement. He had a wife of almost forty years, two daughters in their thirties, and seven grandchildren.

Hattie Simmons was a short, slender, thirty-year-old African American with a master's degree in social work and a second master's in developmental psychology. She had been involved in three hundred seventy-four cases in which a child had been taken from its parents. But never one like this.

The three law enforcement officers drove up the driveway of Kate's house in Scottsdale at eight o'clock that evening. Mike Fallon answered the door. Jennifer was on the floor in front of the TV set playing with a set of big colored plastic ring tosses.

"Yes?" Mike said.

The investigator held up his opened badge wallet. "Is Ms. Mary O'Dwyer here?"

"Why?"

"Who are you?" Trillker asked.

"I'm Michael Fallon, her lawyer."

The investigator handed Mike the arrest warrant. He read it. "Oh, no," he muttered.

Kate came out of the kitchen. "Who is it, Mike?" She watched the two investigators and the CPS caseworker push past him into the living room. The big woman came quickly up to her, and Kate stepped back, lifting her hands defensively.

"We have a warrant for your arrest, ma'am," Peggy Nix said.

Kate was dumbstruck. "I-I don't, I—" she began to stammer.

Nix quickly handcuffed her. Kate gaped at her arms stretched in front of her, the steel cuffs on her wrists.

"Hey, come on, you don't need to do that," Mike said, stepping toward them.

"Take it easy. It's just standard procedure," Marvin Trillker said, holding Mike's right wrist tightly. Mike was much larger than Trillker, and the investigator pulled his revolver from his belt holster.

Jennifer began to cry. She got off the floor and ran toward her mother. "Mommy, Mommy!"

Kate reached out for her, but Hattie Simmons swept

her up into her arms, hugged her, and tried to soothe her. "It's okay, honey. Mommy is okay. You're going with Mommy, don't worry."

"Leave the child with me," Mike said hoarsely.

"Can't do that, sir," said Hattie Simmons. "You aren't a relative or a legal guardian. I have to take her into protection. She'll be at the Casa de los Niños in Tucson, and she'll be very well taken care of. Don't worry."

The woman gave Mike a truly sorrowful look, then walked out of the house with Jennifer in her arms. The investigators walked Kate toward the door.

"We're not happy about this, sir," Trillker said. "But that arrest warrant is signed by a judge, and we're just doing our job."

Mike called out, "I'll be at the jail first thing in the morning, Kate. I'll have a petition for you to sign to appoint me guardian for Jennifer." His voice faltered.

Kate heard him, but the words were unclear. She stumbled to the car, supported by the investigators. At the rear door, the big woman unlocked the handcuffs, turned Kate around, and cuffed her arms behind her back.

Kate wanted to slip out of this unbearable reality to a place where nothing caused her pain or pleasure or even impinged on her inner silence. She sat in the rear seat of the tan Ford with her hands cuffed behind her back and stared out the window at nothing. Jennifer was belted into a car seat next to Kate. She was whimpering, and Kate couldn't bear to look at her. Their eyes were too full of tears.

Kate attempted to focus on the darkened land passing by, trying to make it stop blurring so that she could fix her mind on something, anything. She began to block out the sound of Jennifer's cries, the pain in her own wrists and arms, the fact of where she was and where she was going and what would happen to Jennifer.

"I have walked in evil and my foot hath made haste

to folly . . . but let Him weigh me on the scales of justice, and He will know my innocence."

She saw Gwen's face reflected in the car window. "Believe on Him," the nun whispered, her eyes sparkling and fervent. "Believe on Him, Mary Kate, and be damn sure ya believe in yourself. *A woman of valor, who can find? Her worth is far greater than rubies."*

Kate stared at Gwen's face and nodded. She breathed deeply, forced herself to stop crying, stiffened her body, and sat up straight in the seat.

Mike drove to his office in a fever, his head throbbing painfully. He looked up the guardianship statutes and frenetically began typing a petition. Then he glanced at his watch. It was almost midnight in Boston. Damn! The other time he had called Kate's parents, it was in the middle of the night and he had to report a genuine tragedy. They would soon spontaneously begin to shudder every time they heard his voice.

Brendan O'Dwyer answered the telephone on the first ring. "I was just getting into bed," he said. "What's wrong?"

No beating around the bush this time. "Kate's been arrested for murder, Mr. O'Dwyer. I guess as soon as they found out that Jennifer was HIV negative, they decided that she'd have to stand trial."

The breathing was heavy on the other end of the line. "I was afraid of something like this," Brendan said, his voice thick and drained of animation. "I guess Wilkott's father pulled out all the stops on this."

"I'm sure that's true, Mr. O'Dwyer."

"What happens now?"

"Well, they took Jennifer into protective custody—"

"Oh, sweet Jesus, how could they do such a thing?"

"They really didn't have a choice. It's the law when there's no legal guardian or family."

"Well, Catherine and I will be there tomorrow. We'll take custody."

"Yes, sir. That's fine. Now as to Kate, they're holding her on first-degree murder. That's a non-bailable offense in Arizona, meaning that she's going to have to stay in jail at least until a preliminary hearing or grand jury hearing."

"When will that be?"

"Within ten days."

"And then what?"

"If she's bound over or indicted on first-degree, she'll have to stay in jail until the trial. If she's charged with something less, she'll be entitled to bail."

"Okay. We'll be in Tucson as soon as we can, and we'll be staying at the Loew's Ventana. Do you know it?"

"I'll find it."

"Okay. Sometime tomorrow. Where will you be staying?"

"I don't know. Downtown near the courthouse, I guess."

"Leave a message at the Ventana."

"Okay," Mike said.

They hung up. Mike wouldn't need the petition for guardianship with Jennifer's grandparents coming in tomorrow. He would drive them over to Casa de los Niños, wherever that was, and CPS would release her to them. Now all he had to worry about was Kate.

He began to feel less frantic and decided to take along his portable typewriter and some pleading paper to Tucson. Then he could take care of any emergency between now and Monday. They'd have to hire a criminal lawyer. Mike couldn't represent her. He'd be too fearful. But he didn't know anybody in Tucson. He'd call around Monday, see who was supposed to be the best.

He got into his truck and drove to Scottsdale to pack some clothing for Jennifer and himself. He was too wired to sleep at all. He climbed back in his truck and headed for Tucson.

Marvin Trillker drove the tan Ford onto the shoulder of Interstate 10 under a bridge and parked. Kate watched the three people in the front seat. They had begun to argue hotly.

"Come on, Marv," Hattie Simmons said. "Take the cuffs off. She's got no way to get out. There aren't any door handles or window cranks back there."

The three law enforcement officers were separated from Kate by a Plexiglas screen, but she could hear their muffled voices.

"It's not SOP," he said.

"Screw SOP," Peggy Nix said.

"We can't comfort the child with her mother back there like that," Hattie Simmons said. "Quit being an asshole. We've got two hours of driving left. We can put the cuffs back on when we get to Tucson."

"Shit," Marvin mumbled. He took the keys out of the ignition and handed them to Peggy.

She slid the Plexiglas sliding window open. "Turn around," she said to Kate.

Kate twisted her body and brought her arms up. Peggy unlocked the cuffs.

"Thanks," Kate said. "Thanks."

Kate picked up Jennifer and hugged her to her bosom. The child was exhausted and soon fell asleep in Kate's arms.

"We'll go to the Casa first," Hattie said. "Let her own mother put her to sleep, it'll be much easier."

"Can't do that," Marvin said. "What if one of the caseworkers reports that she was there, no cuffs? My ass is grass."

"Nobody will report anything, Marv. I'll take care of it," Hattie said.

"Uh-uh," he said, shaking his head vigorously.

"Cut the crap," she said. "This is a lowlife deal, and

you know it. You read the stories about what happened?"

"Sure, I read them. So what? I just work for a living. Couple more years I get my pension."

"You'll get your pension, Marv," Peggy said. "You'll be the happiest fat man on Seal Beach, drinking beer and belching and chewing hot dogs all day. And this'll be the one moment you remember in your whole life when you did the right thing."

"Shit," he muttered. "When they let broads into law enforcement, they really screwed up."

Kate carried her sleeping daughter into the Casa de los Niños "crisis nursery." There were several other babies in cribs in the small room. Jennifer no longer slept in a crib at home, but here it was necessary, to keep the toddlers from wandering around when they awoke. Kate laid her gently in an empty crib. She and Hattie stood and watched Jennifer snore softly.

"She'll be okay," Hattie whispered. "The women here are wonderful."

Kate turned to her, and they hugged.

"Good luck to you, Ms. O'Dwyer," Hattie whispered.

"Thank you for what you did. I'll never forget it."

"I hope you'll soon forget this whole terrible thing," Hattie whispered.

It took an hour to book Kate into the Pima County Jail. She was fingerprinted and her mug shots taken. A matron brought her into a shower area and ordered her to undress and take a shower with soap. The matron, a two-hundred-pound Mexican woman bulging out of her tan uniform shirt and pants, sat on a creaking folding chair reading a comic book. When Kate finished and dried herself, the matron took a rubber glove out of a can on the wall.

"Bend over and grab your ankles," the woman said.

"What for?"

"Ya don't ask no questions here, O'Dwyer," the woman barked. "Ya do what I say."

Kate bent over. The guard shoved her dry gloved forefinger into Kate's vagina and then her rectum. Kate gasped with pain.

"Fold your clothes and go to the wooden counter."

The matron walked into the clothes room, got a green shirt and pants and white rubber slippers that looked like surgical garb, and handed them to Kate.

"Drop them other clothes in here," the matron said, holding open a large plastic garbage bag.

Kate put her clothes into it, and the woman taped the top of the bag while Kate dressed.

The matron took her by the arm and led her down the corridor through three metal doors operated by electronic buttons in a glass-enclosed control booth with two male guards. They stared with interest at Kate, and she looked quickly away. The matron brought her to a cell with about twenty other women. Three-tiered bunks lined the walls. One woman was vomiting in the corner. Another was sitting nude on a toilet, staring vapidly into space. Some were leaning against the bars, others lying in bed weeping, others sleeping. The place reeked of shower soap, vomit, urine, defecation, and the rotten breath of a dozen drunks and drug abusers. The barred cell door cranked noisily open two feet, the matron pushed Kate inside, and the door clanged shut.

Kate walked into the attorneys' interview room at a few minutes past eight o'clock. The matron closed the door to the small room. Mike stood and came toward her, searching her eyes. He smiled and embraced her.

"Are you okay?" he asked. He stood back from her and studied her eyes again.

"I wouldn't exactly call it okay," she said. "How's Jennifer?"

"I just left her. I was over there at seven-thirty, and

she was already up, playing dolls in a big playroom with some other little girls."

"They let you in to see her?"

"Yes, but only through a one-way glass thing. I flashed my bar card, said I represented you. It works like magic."

They sat down on metal chairs at a small card table. "Your parents are coming in sometime today. They'll be at the Ventana hotel. I'll get Jennifer released to them. She'll be fine."

"I don't want Dad or Mom coming here to see me. I'm too miserable, and it would only hurt them more."

"Well, you can't have visitors until after the initial appearance, anyway, and that won't be till Monday afternoon. By then we'll figure out what to do."

"Okay. What did they charge me with?"

He breathed deeply. "First-degree murder."

She gasped. "And what's going to happen?"

He shook his head resolutely. "Not a thing. Not a damn thing. You'll be found not guilty."

"Is that Mike the man who loves me, or Mike the lawyer?"

"Both," he said. "I wouldn't feed you a lot of false hope. One way or another, you'll be free. If they let you out on bail, we'll go live in Timbuktu, and to hell with everybody. If they lock you up in prison, I'll hire six of my clients and we'll break you out."

Kate smiled thinly. He was dead serious. "What about bail?"

"No bail on first-degree murder," he said.

She nodded and swallowed. "So how long will I be here?"

"Just three and a half months. I won't waive your 'speedy trial' rights. They have to bring you to trial within ninety days after you enter your plea, and that has to be after either a grand jury or preliminary hearing within the next ten days."

"Well, that's swell," she said. "It'll give me and a

couple of the girls just enough time to make some chintz curtains for the cell doors."

He studied her face. "You okay?"

She grimaced. Then she rolled her eyes. "Yeah, I'll live. Just make sure Jennifer is okay. I don't want my parents taking her back to Boston. I want to be able to see her."

"Don't worry. If there's any chance of that, we'll petition to have me appointed guardian, and we can get married right here in jail, if that's what it requires. No one will take her from you—or me."

She nodded. "I love you, Michael."

"I love you, Kate."

They leaned over the table and kissed. Then they sat back and looked at each other.

"They'll do your initial appearance this afternoon by remote TV. I'm going to have to spend all day tomorrow at the law library researching my motion. First thing Monday, I'll bring a motion to set bail in front of whatever judge I can get to hear it. But it probably won't be granted. Then we'll get you the best criminal lawyer around."

She looked surprised and hurt. "You won't do it?"

He shook his head. "I'd be too scared of making mistakes, and I'd probably make bad mistakes as a result. Like a heart surgeon operating on his own son or daughter. You need somebody detached and objective."

She sighed. "Okay," she said.

• THIRTEEN •

Mike telephoned Loew's Ventana hotel every half hour after leaving the jail. He couldn't go there and wait, since he had to be at Kate's initial appearance at one o'clock. He sat on the bed in his room at the Marriott Hotel directly across from the Pima County Courthouse. It was a modest hotel with modest prices, and from his small room he looked out over the Tucson Convention Center. He needed to go to the law library at the University of Arizona law school, but he was too nervous at the moment. After he had picked up Kate's parents and gotten Jennifer out of jail, he would worry about preparing the motion. Nothing could be done until Monday morning, anyway. There was plenty of time.

He watched some sitcom reruns on television and didn't even know what he was watching. He scanned the tourist guide in the bedstand drawer three times through and then picked up the Gideon Bible. The Bible had never seemed to him to be a source of comfort, as it did to so many, his mother principal among them. He had read most of it, maybe even all of it at one time or another, and he realized that it contained fine poetry and family stories and history and lofty phrases, but comfort he had never found.

In a humanities class he had taken in college seven or eight years ago, the first few weeks had been spent reading sections of the Old and New testaments. The

Bible was written in a simpler time, the professor had said, when the four horsemen of the Apocalypse were the most fearful scourges of mankind: famine, pestilence, war, and greed. But how many scourges were there now? The same, only magnified by the complexity of society? Or whole new ones: drive-by shootings, inner-city riots, deterioration of the family, loss of faith in God and justice, loss of hope that "progress" still survived. Were things getting better? Really?

Who was still optimistic for the starving, wretched people of Haiti, for the Rwandans and the Somalis and the slum dwellers of the South Bronx and Detroit and Compton? Who believed that schools could really be made to teach and to nurture, that parents really could instill moral values, that churches really could shelter the poor and the helpless? Who still had a lingering faith that the meek would inherit the earth in the fullness of time? Who still truly believed that America was a country with liberty and justice for all?

Who was optimistic for Mary Caitlin O'Dwyer?

Mike flipped through the pages of the Gideon Bible. He was freaked out, his brain was shit. Kate had been charged with first-degree murder. The fact that she had been driving and that her car had only one air bag made for a persuasive case of murder. No, she wouldn't get the death penalty. No judge would do that. But life? Twenty-five years? Seven at the very least?

The telephone rang. Mike tossed the Bible back in the drawer and rubbed his face roughly.

"Hello."

"Mike. This is Brendan. We got your messages."

Mike breathed deeply to steady himself. "Yes, sir. I'm glad you're here."

"What do we do?"

Mike glanced at his watch. It was almost eleven. "I'll be out there in a half hour. We'll go right over to the place where they're keeping Jennifer and get her. She's fine. I saw her this morning."

"And Kate?"

"Solid as a rock."

"All right. We'll be in the lobby."

Brendan O'Dwyer hugged Mike in the lobby. His eyes were red from no sleep, as were his wife Catherine's.

Gwen McLemore was with them, and her eyes were always the same, sparkling brown. Mike nodded to her. Wherever it came from, there was a palpable strength in her and a toughness that somehow bolstered his own courage just to look at her. He knew nothing about her—except that Kate loved her—and he was beginning to understand why.

"Tell us how bad it is," Catherine O'Dwyer said. She hugged Mike and then studied his eyes.

"It's bad," he said. "I can't imagine any judge or jury convicting her of first-degree murder. But there's certainly a possibility of attempted murder or even second-degree murder. I don't want to mislead you. The fact that Jennifer isn't HIV-infected puts a whole new complexion on the case. Public opinion may no longer be on Kate's side."

Torturous pain was evident in both of their faces.

Gwen shook her head sadly. "From a miracle comes tragedy," she said quietly.

"I'll say just this," Mike said, trying to lessen the jolt. "I think none of that will happen. I think that when the jury hears the truth about what happened and the kind of animal that Philip Wilkott was, they will set Kate free. I really believe that."

"May God grant the fulfillment of your faith, Michael," Gwen said, her eyes steady and intense.

Mike nodded. "Come, we'll go get Jennifer."

Jennifer was thrilled to see Mike and Gwen and her grandparents. Mike told her that Mommy had gone on a little trip and would be back in a couple of days, but that Grandma and Grandpa were here to look after her. She was a bit whiny for a moment, unhappy that Mommy wasn't around, but she quickly snapped out of it and started telling them all about her new friends Bonnie and Joyce and the toys in the playroom.

Brendan carried Jennifer in his arms to Mike's pickup and strapped her on his wife's lap. Mike had forgotten to take the baby seat out of the car back in Scottsdale.

All of them cheered up noticeably on the drive back to the Ventana hotel. Jennifer was garrulous and happy.

Mike told Brendan that nothing could happen until Monday morning, and Kate couldn't receive any visitors except her lawyer until Tuesday. Brendan nodded and frowned and followed Gwen, Catherine, and Jennifer into the hotel.

Mike drove downtown to the courthouse, waited in the initial appearance room for an hour, and announced himself as attorney of record for Kate when she sat down in the defendant's chair and looked into the closed-circuit TV camera. She was surprisingly composed and pretty. She spoke her name in a strong and steady voice and listened to the reading of the criminal charges against her. The magistrate told her that the preliminary hearing would be held in ten days and that she was not entitled to bail.

The entire initial appearance was over in three minutes. She stood up and walked out of the camera's view.

Mike spent all afternoon at the law library, then ate dinner with the O'Dwyers and Gwen at the hotel that evening. He stayed with them in their suite until nine o'clock, when Jennifer went crabbily to bed, then drove to a liquor store, picked up a pint of Jack Daniel's, returned to his hotel, and drank himself to fitful sleep. When he awoke early in the morning, he was nauseated and had a headache that lingered for two hours.

He went directly to the law library at nine o'clock and stayed there until two. He then returned to his hotel and hacked away at his portable typewriter for three fevered hours, ignoring the numerous typographical errors.

Again he spent the evening in the O'Dwyers' three-bedroom suite at the Ventana hotel, but this time he was unsuccessful in putting on a brave face. He was preoccupied with what would happen tomorrow, and he sat quietly on the sofa, his forehead deeply lined, a jabbing pain behind his half-closed eyes. He was barely cognizant of the conversation among Catherine, Gwen, and Brendan.

He left the hotel after putting Jennifer to bed and sitting with her until she fell asleep. He didn't buy any whiskey to put himself to sleep. Sleep or no, he had to be unhampered by a hangover in the morning.

• FOURTEEN •

"I got a chicken," Donna Alvarez said, walking into the house. She smelled something foul, like rotten meat or a dead squirrel. It almost made her vomit.

"Agnes?" she called out again, stopping in the middle of the living room floor and listening for her. She didn't hear her in the kitchen. It was five o'clock, and she had bought a roasting chicken at Basha's Market. She went into the kitchen and put the chicken in the sink.

"Where's that awful smell coming from?" she mumbled, wrinkling her nose. She walked through the living room and saw that the bathroom was empty, then knocked on Agnes's bedroom door. No answer. She opened the door a few inches and peeked in. The stink was heavier. She curled up her nose and walked into the bedroom.

Agnes lay at the foot of the bed. Her head was twisted toward Donna, her eyes open wide and white. Her forehead had a wound on the side that had poured blood down her face and puddled under her on the wooden floor. The end of the frame holding up the bed was a piece of metal that stuck out two inches from the lower box mattress. It was covered with blood.

Donna put her hands over her mouth. She stood rigidly for several moments. "Dear God," she gasped, crossing herself several times.

The old woman was obviously dead, and by the looks of her it must have happened much earlier in the day. Donna stumbled into her bedroom and sat down on the edge of the bed. She tried to calm the hammering of her heart, to push away the panic that was constricting her throat. A jumble of conflicting thoughts were rolling around in her head like bowling balls. She took several deep breaths and stiffened her body, focusing on a little picture she had cut out of a magazine and thumbtacked to the wall. It was a beautiful, nude, white-skinned woman with blond hair swinging on a swing tied to the branch of a big tree. It had reminded her of Kate.

"Dear Jesus," she whispered aloud, "please tell me what to do. Please, please." Somehow, talking to herself out loud made her feel calmer, as though someone else were with her to protect her. "If I go tell the police, will they think I killed her? With my record, what else will they think? Should I just drive off in the truck and keep going as far as I can till my money for gas runs out? But then they'll think I killed her to steal her truck. And they'll go looking for the truck. And if I get stopped for anything, I don't even have a driver's license. We were always going to go get it but just never quite made it."

Her voice sounded frail to her, like she was sick. She rocked back and forth on the bed, rubbing her shoulders, suddenly feeling chilled, although it was seventy or seventy-five degrees. "I need a fix," she said, then lowered her voice as though she might be overheard. "I need a fix. That guy who lives up on Pima Road, the one everybody calls Gordito. He always has some H to sell, maybe some crack. I see him all the time in that big black Cadillac."

She went out to the pickup truck, drove to Pima Road, and turned left toward the small house where she had often seen the Cadillac parked. It wasn't there. Damn, damn, damn. Now what? She turned the truck around and drove slowly back up the road, not knowing what to do, where to go.

"Better do something quick about Agnes," she mumbled, her face sour. "I can't leave her there to rot. I have to move her, bury her so nobody finds her."

She drove back to the house and ran inside. The stink of death shocked her like an ammonia inhaler. She stood stiffly at the door to Agnes's bedroom. "Cut this shit out. Stop being a criminal," she chided herself. "I have to stop thinking like a junkie whore. I didn't do anything wrong. I better go to the health clinic and ask them to send an ambulance. Or whatever they use for dead people."

There was no telephone in the house. She drove to the clinic a few blocks away on Osborn Road and ran inside. She came out after several minutes and returned home to wait.

The old ambulance arrived about a half hour later. Donna watched two young men roll Agnes nonchalantly onto a stretcher, not saying a word or even seeming interested, and carry her out to the ambulance.

"Bye, Agnes," Donna said as they drove off. She crossed herself.

She walked out onto the porch and closed the front door to get away from the smell. She sat down on the wooden porch step and stared into space. Bright orange flowers cluttered the honeysuckle bushes Agnes used to tend so carefully in the front yard. The wonderful fragrance of tiny white grapefruit blossoms from a nearby tree mingled with the cloying odor of rotting garbage in the ditch that ran beside the road.

"I better not clean the bedroom yet," she said. "If Chief Manuelito comes to investigate, he has to see the room just like I found it, to prove that Mrs. Ishpia fell and hit her head, that I didn't hit her with a hammer or something."

It got dark, a purple sky like a huge eggplant and

cotton candy clouds and bright, twinkling stars. The moon was hidden behind one of the big clouds making it luminous. It was a songwriter's night:

> "*The silence of a falling star,*
> *   lights up a purple sky.*"

One of Hank Williams's songs her mother always listened to:

> "*The moon has gone behind the clouds,*
> *   To hide its face and cry.*"

But Donna didn't feel like crying. And she wasn't so lonesome that she could cry—or die. Agnes had been good to her. She liked Agnes a lot. But it wasn't like losing Kate or Jennifer. She pushed that thought away. She had to keep her composure.

Tonight she would get a hamburger at McDonald's. She had about eight dollars, maybe nine. And Agnes kept a ten-dollar bill in a jar on her dresser. "Mad money," Agnes always called it and laughed. That would be enough.

"I'll get a blanket out of the house and sleep in the bed of the truck tonight," Donna said to the moon, which was now beginning to peek out from behind the clouds. "And then tomorrow I'll go see Chief Manuelito and make sure everything's okay."

She got up and walked into the house, holding one hand over her nose and breathing shallowly through her mouth. She got the quilt off her bed and hurried outside.

As she walked toward the pickup, an Indian Police Bronco turned the corner on Country Club Drive and came toward her. Her heart leapt and started pumping furiously. She couldn't help it. Cops had never been her friends. They had rousted her, busted her, robbed her twice, and fucked her a few times, but they had never been her friends.

"Hey, Donna," Henry Manuelito said, getting out of the Bronco and walking up to her. "You found her, huh?"

Donna nodded. Panic muted her. Manuelito had been chief of the reservation police for as long as she could remember. He was a Navajo from way up north, and everyone said he'd been a cop up there on the reservation for a long time before coming here. He had come to her house and arrested her father more times than she could count, but he'd never rousted her.

"I was just at the hospital," he said. "Doctor says she died of a stroke. Went like that." He snapped his fingers. "Didn't feel a thing."

Donna's heart slowed enough for her to speak. "I guess she hit her head on the bed thing when she fell. There's blood all over in there."

He nodded. "You know where her daughters live?"

She shook her head. "I never saw them, and Agnes didn't say. I think she once got a letter from one of them."

"Can you look for me?"

"Yes, sir."

The chief waited outside. Donna went into the reeking bedroom, stepped gingerly around the blood puddle, held her nose, and rifled through the top drawer of the dresser, then the middle drawer. She took out a torn-open envelope with a folded letter sticking out of it. The return address was "Mrs. Mildred Tellez, 1413 Gravina Avenue, Goodyear." That was a little town way out west of Phoenix.

Donna brought the letter outside and handed it to the chief.

"What are you going to do?" he asked.

She shrugged. "Same thing, I guess."

"What if the daughters come?"

"What do you mean?"

"Well, the truck, the house. They belonged to Agnes, and she probably didn't leave a will. Her two daughters will inherit everything, sell it for whatever they can get, and split the money."

"I don't know anything about that stuff," Donna said, shaking her head. She looked at him with sudden concern. "Does that mean I have to leave?"

"Yeah, maybe. It'll be up to the daughters. They're okay. I knew them years ago. Must be in their fifties or sixties now. Come on, maybe you'll get lucky. Maybe she gave you something in a will."

They walked into the house. *"Chihuahua!"* he said, grabbing his nose. "This stinks. Where'd she keep her papers?"

Donna shook her head. "I don't know."

He walked into the bedroom. Donna waited in the living room. She heard drawers opening and closing, the closet door open. He came out a moment later holding his nose with his left hand and a Folger's coffee can in his right.

"Come on," he gasped. He walked quickly out the door and emptied the can on the hood of the Bronco. There were some folded papers. He unfolded one, looked, and put it back in the can. The next one he left on the hood. Several more into the can. The last, a big envelope, on the hood.

He took the truck title out of the envelope and studied it. "A 1963 Ford," he said. "What do you think it's worth?"

She shrugged.

"Probably a hundred bucks," he said. "I'm going to tell them to give it to you. You worked hard for their mama."

Donna's eyes opened wide. "You can do that?"

"Yeah, sure. I want to see you get a chance. You got a good little business riding around with those clothes. You keep doing it, hear?"

She nodded. "Yes, sir. Thank you."

"I'm going to get ahold of Mildred here, and we'll get everything sorted out real fast. The tribal judge can sign over the title to you. I'll bring it over when he does. You got a license yet?"

She shook her head.

"You get it, okay?"

"I'm too young. I've got to have my mother with me, but she won't go anywhere. She just sits."

"Yeah, I know." He frowned. "Okay, I'll bring you over a parental consent form when I bring the title. I'll sign her name. Nobody'll know the difference. See you later." He got into the Bronco and drove away. The Bronco raised smoke signals of dust on the dirt road.

· FIFTEEN ·

At eight o'clock Monday morning, when a woman turned the key in the lock on the floor-selection panel, permitting the elevator to stop at the county attorney's main reception area on the ninth floor, Mike had already been riding it up and down for ten minutes. At least it gave him something to do. He got out on the ninth floor and handed a document to the receptionist.

"This is a motion for an accelerated hearing on a bail application and a motion to set bail. They're for Mr. Emerick," he said. "I'll be in Judge Kellman's office and will attempt to see the judge as soon as he comes in."

He left the building, walked two blocks, and entered the courthouse through the east doors. He emptied his pockets, went through the metal detector, put everything back in his pockets, and located Kellman's chambers on the directory. He took the elevator to the fourth floor and went to the courtroom door. It was locked. He went through the swinging doors at the end of the hall, then down a much narrower corridor to a locked door.

There was a video camera mounted overhead. He pushed the button on a small speaker on the wall.

"Show your bar card," came a voice through the speaker.

Mike took his card out of his wallet and held it toward the camera. The door unlatched, and he walked down the corridor to a doorway over which was a wooden sign with etched black letters: HON. AARON B. KELLMAN, CHIEF, CRIMINAL DIV.

The door was open. A powerfully built Mexican was sitting at a small desk just inside the secretary's office.

"How ya doin'?" he said to Mike.

"Fine. I'm here to see Judge Kellman."

"Whattaya got?"

Mike handed him several sheets of paper.

"You notify the county attorney?"

"Yes, I just dropped copies of each of them off for Emerick."

"Okay. Judge has been in there"—he gestured to the closed door—"for an hour with a coupla other lawyers. As soon as they're done."

Mike nodded. He sat down on one of the three chairs in front of the secretary's desk. Five minutes passed. Ten. A man of average height and build, with a thick salt-and-pepper beard and a thin-lipped frown, walked into the office.

"Hey, Manny," he said.

"Whattaya say, Dan?"

"I say the day is starting to turn to shit real early." The bailiff chuckled.

"You Fallon?" Dan Emerick asked.

Mike nodded.

"What the hell kind of deal is this, you throwing a motion for an accelerated bail hearing at me at eight o'clock Monday morning? I got seven goddamn motions in three different courts. I haven't got time for this shit."

Mike stared at him.

"What the hell are you doing representing her, anyway? Half the evidence in this case is going to be about you."

Mike stood up and laid his papers on the chair. He walked toward Emerick and glared down at him. Manny stood up at his desk, ready to come around and stop a fight. It didn't happen very often, but it happened.

Mike extended his hand. "Mike Fallon. Glad to meet you." His face was somber.

Emerick was taken aback. He extended his hand mechanically, almost a reflex. They shook hands.

"We'll let the judge decide what's right and wrong here, Mr. Emerick," Mike said quietly. "That's *his* job."

Emerick stepped back.

The judge's office door opened, and two men came out, one smiling pleasantly, calling out, "Thanks, Judge," the other silent and subdued.

Manny walked into the judge's chambers with the papers that Mike had delivered and closed the door. He came out a moment later and closed the door again.

"The judge is reading it. If he'll see you on this, he'll let me know in a minute." He sat down at his desk. Emerick stood leaning against the wall. Mike sat on a chair in front of the secretary's desk.

The secretary came in a few minutes later, a pleasant-looking woman in her early forties, said a cheerful hello, and sat at her desk. She picked up a letter opener and began opening and reading the mail and hand deliveries.

The judge's door opened, and he leaned out a few inches. "Hi, Rhonda. What do we have this morning?"

"Twenty-three motions, one sentencing."

"Get me the court file on *State* versus *Mary O'Dwyer,* please."

Judge Kellman sucked in his cheeks and pursed his lips. He looked at Mike and then at Dan Emerick. Kellman was in his early sixties, slightly built, average height, with cropped graying brown hair. His face appeared morose, and his pale blue eyes were weary. Under his eyes were slightly purple pouches.

"Well, boys," he said, "let's talk about this little matter."

He opened the door and walked to his desk. Mike followed, and Emerick came in last, closing the door behind him.

"Sit," the judge said, pointing at two aged oak-tanned leather armchairs in front of the desk. He sat behind his desk in a swivel chair of the same cracked leather.

"Your Honor, I most strenuously object to this proceeding. I have had only fifteen minutes' notice, and Rule 7.4 of the Criminal Rules calls for bail motions to be done only when the case has been transferred to Superior Court."

"We're in Superior Court now," the judge said.

"I beg to disagree, Your Honor. You have agreed to act as the magistrate for the preliminary hearing. That doesn't move the case out of the Justice Court's jurisdiction."

The judge shrugged. "Maybe so, Dan."

"I think this is an unethical attempt by counsel, who happens to be very personally involved in this matter, to skirt the proper legal procedures available to him and to illegally attack the validity of the criminal charges against this woman."

The judge nodded and gave Mike a hard glance. Then he looked back at Emerick.

"I read his motion, Dan." The judge held it up off the desk. "Did you get a copy?"

"Yes, I did, Judge. But I haven't even had the time to read it."

"Well, it's a mess. Typos every two words. I guess Mr. Fallon didn't read the rule about what kind of paper these motions are required to be on and how they have to be set up: white, opaque, unglazed paper, two-inch top margin first page, one and a half inches all subsequent pages, inch on the left, half inch on the right, no goddamn typos. I almost got cross-eyed."

He took a ruler out of the center drawer of his desk and measured in various places on the motion. Mike was getting angry and embarrassed and felt himself on the verge of exploding.

"Don't you know that us judges can't handle anything that comes up unless it's in proper form?" He looked at Mike.

Mike cleared his throat. "I tried, Your Honor, but I only have a portable typewriter, and it's real hard to adjust right. And it doesn't have any correcting ribbon. It's just a cheap little thing."

"Well, I'm going to have to notify Chief Justice Rehnquist at the United States Supreme Court about this. If you can't type a motion, you just have no business being a lawyer." The judge frowned.

Mike was confused. Chief Justice Rehnquist? What kind of crap is this?

There was an unmistakable twinkle dancing in Kellman's eyes.

Mike nodded, pursed his lips, and said, "The chief justice will really be pissed, Judge. Please give me a second chance."

"What do you think, Danny? Does he get a second chance?"

"I don't think he should've had a first chance."

"Well, painful and unjust as it may seem to you, Dan, please read the motion."

"But, Your Honor, I object—"

"Come on, Dan, let's not get testy so early in the morning. Just read the damn thing."

Emerick started reading. Judge Kellman lit a cigarette and inhaled deeply. He coughed a grinding, gravelly cough, and inhaled deeply again. A small cumulus cloud of smoke drifted lazily upward. He leaned back in his chair.

The judge's secretary came into the office, handed him a file, and left.

Emerick flipped the last page over and nodded. "Okay."

Kellman sat up, the cigarette hanging out of his mouth. "He says in the motion that none of the admitted and uncontested facts support any charge of murder. He says they'll only support attempted murder at the very most. What's your position?"

Emerick shrugged. "None of that is relevant for a bail motion, Judge. The only issue on setting bail is what amount of money or property will secure the defendant's presence at trial. But in this case she's charged with first-degree murder. You signed the arrest warrant and the complaint yourself. She's not entitled to any bail."

"I didn't ask you that. I asked you whether the facts of this case, as set forth by Mr. Fallon in his motion, are true."

Dan Emerick was angry. "Maybe all of it's true, I don't know."

"Well, it's *your* goddamn case, isn't it?"

Emerick nodded.

"I want to know why you didn't have Marv Trillker present me with *these* facts when he came in here to get the arrest warrant signed."

"Because they're not relevant to the charges against this woman, Judge, certainly not at *this* stage of the proceeding. If these facts are going to be her defense at the trial, so be it. But our office is under no obligation to state the facts of the accused's defense when we prepare the warrant. Anyway, the story has been in the newspapers a dozen times and on the TV news more than that. I figured you knew what this was about."

"God damn it!" Judge Kellman slammed his hand down on the desk, and everything jumped, including Mike Fallon and Dan Emerick. "I didn't put the two things together at all! And I damn well expect your people to fill me in on *all* the facts before I sign a warrant. That's what's supposed to happen." He flipped the pages of the court's file to the arrest warrant and held it up, pointing at the bottom line above his signature. "See here, where it says 'The Court, *being duly advised in the premises,* and good cause appearing,' et cetera, et cetera? That's just not legal-ese bullshit! That means that whoever comes after the warrant tells me *all* the relevant facts." His face was fierce.

"Well, if you're unhappy with this thing, we'll move it over to another court," Emerick said, his cheeks and the tip of his nose beet red.

Kellman flipped to another page in the file in front of him. "Is this the stipulation assigning the prelimi-nary hearing to me, signed by Daniel Emerick, Chief Criminal Deputy County Attorney?"

Emerick nodded and swallowed.

"Well, I guess you're bound by it, unless Mr. Fallon stipulates to a reassignment. Mr. Fallon?"

Mike shook his head. "Reckon not, Judge."

"Well, Dan, you're stuck with me. All right, let me get the court reporter."

He walked to the door and opened it. "Rhonda, please call the court administrator and ask her to reas-sign my motions calendar. I've got an emergency pre-liminary hearing this morning. Ask Jean to come in."

He left the door open and returned to his desk. A few minutes later, a harried-looking woman came in carrying a steno machine. She was young and attrac-tive. She set the machine down next to the desk and pulled a chair to it from the table.

"In the matter of *State* versus *O'Dwyer*," the judge recited. "The defendant's attorney, Michael Fallon, has filed a motion for an order shortening time to hear a bail application. Mr. Fallon is present in chambers. Mr. Emerick is present. I am treating Mr. Fallon's motion to set bail as a motion for an immediate pre-liminary hearing. I am making a specific finding that this is in the interests of justice and that good cause is completely set forth by the fact statement in Mr. Fallon's motion, which the county attorney has not disputed. If the facts alleged by Mr. Fallon are true, then Mrs. O'Dwyer cannot be held without bail on a charge of first-degree murder. Mr. Emerick has asked

me to remove myself from this case, and Mr. Fallon
has objected based on the stipulation. I have declined
to remove myself. Over the objection of the county
attorney, I am ordering that this preliminary hearing
commence in thirty minutes at nine o'clock. Mr. Emerick, I order the State to produce all available police
reports and evidence at that time in support of its
charge of first-degree murder. If the State fails to present sufficient facts to maintain its charge of first-
degree murder against Mrs. O'Dwyer, then she is entitled to have bail set and to be released from jail pending the trial on whatever criminal charges I determine
to be legitimate against her. I am also ordering the
sheriff, whom I will now telephone, to produce Ms.
O'Dwyer in this courtroom at nine o'clock. Is there
anything else, gentlemen?"

Emerick was breathing heavily, his lips a tight gray
line. He stared at the wall behind the judge. Mike
shook his head. His heart was squishing so loudly that
he was sure that the secretary could hear it through
the wall.

"Jean, please type that up immediately so we have
a formal order in the file before we commence."

She nodded and stood up.

Emerick stormed out of the office. The judge picked
up the telephone. Mike left, leaned against the wall
out in the hallway, and waited for his breath to return.

"You okay, *amigo?*" asked the bailiff, coming into
the hallway.

"*¡Ya lo creo, amigo! Me siento come nuevo.*" You
bet, pal! I feel like a new man. Eleven years on a
Texas ranch with a dozen Mexican hands hadn't all
been for naught.

The bailiff laughed and unlocked the rear door to
the courtroom.

Mike walked through the courtroom to the landing
by the elevators where the pay telephones were located. It would be unfair not to tell Brendan O'Dwyer

that the preliminary hearing would be held this morning. Mike telephoned the Ventana, assured him that it was good news rather than bad, and Brendan said that he'd take a cab downtown immediately.

Mike hung up and looked at his watch. It was 8:35, and it would take Brendan at least forty minutes to get there. He would miss a few minutes of the hearing, but that couldn't be helped. Mike walked into the courtroom and sat down at the defense table, always the one farthest from the jury box.

Courtrooms are lonely places when they are empty, Mike thought, looking around somewhat uneasily. When a judge is on the bench and court is in session, the judge wears a black robe, there is a bailiff keeping order, a clerk makes notes of all proceedings, and a court reporter makes a verbatim record of those matters that must or may by law be reported. Courtrooms are places where enormous power is wielded, where men and women can be financially aggrandized or decimated in a minute, where men and women are imprisoned or sentenced to death, where marriages are severed and children uprooted from one place to another with the rap of a gavel.

With the rap of a gavel, the power of the state will be executed on one of its citizens, Mike thought. No, no! "Executed" is a lousy choice of words. Kate O'Dwyer's fate would be decided by a stranger in a black robe with world-weary eyes. Who was this man? Was he honest or venal, competent or incapable, fair and just or malicious?

The judge, the font of enormous power. Who is the judge? He or she is a lawyer who has practiced at least five years and then either runs in an election for office or is appointed to the bench. The lawyer need not possess competence or even common decency to be a judge, and many were notoriously incompetent or failed lawyers looking for a sinecure. As soon as he or she donned the black robe, the new judge was transformed from an average nondescript human into a mighty legal colossus, wielding power like a professional wrestler doing flying leaps off the ring ropes and slamming his opponent to the mat. "Robitis," lawyers called it, an unfortunately common affliction.

Heavy thoughts for a morning like this, Mike thought, perched uncomfortably on the unpadded oak chair at the defense table. He was actually frightened, even more so than the time he had appeared in Judge Diller's court and been publicly rebuked by the judge for being two minutes late for the hearing—although he had been detained by another judge in another courtroom—then humiliated by Diller for wearing tennis shoes to court. "An affront to the dignity of the court," the judge had said.

"But they're black, Your Honor, and I thought they blended in quite well with this charcoal gray suit."

"The next time you appear in *my* courtroom, Mr. Fallon, do not display such open contempt for the court."

Diller had died in a scuba-diving mishap in the West Indies. Mike was sure that some stalwart lawyer had cut his air hose. A proper reward.

The back door of the courtroom, where the incarcerated defendants entered, creaked open. Kate shuffled into the courtroom in a belly chain attached to handcuffs and ankle cuffs. An armed sheriff's deputy followed her. She was dressed in the wrinkled green jail uniform and rubber slip-on shoes. Her hair was pulled back in a ponytail and she wore no makeup, but despite everything Mike was once again arrested by her natural beauty.

The deputy told her to stand by the empty chair next to Mike at the defense table. She appeared bewildered, and she looked at Mike with doe eyes. The deputy removed her restraints, and she sat down at the table. The deputy sat in a chair six feet behind her in front of the spectator section railing.

"What's happening?" she whispered.

"We're having a preliminary hearing in five minutes," Mike said quietly.

"I don't get it." She searched his eyes.

"The judge signed an arrest warrant and a criminal complaint charging you with first-degree murder, which doesn't permit you to be released on bail. Now he's going to require the prosecution to prove that they have sufficient evidence to make you stand trial on that charge, or he's going to set bail for you."

"Is this good?" she asked.

"I think so," he said. "I don't know the judge, and I have no feel for what he'll do, but if what happened in chambers is any guide, then I think he's going to throw out the first-degree murder charge and bind you over on something much less, probably attempted murder. Then you can make bail this afternoon."

She sighed and nodded. "God willing," she whispered. "But I thought you weren't going to represent me."

"I wasn't, and I shouldn't. But this happened so fast, I didn't have any chance to locate somebody. I'll do it after you get out of jail."

"I'm glad you're my lawyer."

"I'm not," he mumbled. "I'm too scared."

She leaned over and kissed his cheek.

"No physical contact," said the deputy.

"Is Jennifer okay?" Kate asked.

"Yes. Just fine. She's at the hotel with your mother."

"Good. That's a tremendous relief." She paused. "Will I get to testify in this hearing?" Kate said.

Mike frowned at her. "Absolutely not."

"But I want to. I want to tell the judge exactly what happened. I didn't do anything wrong."

Mike shook his head. "Don't even think about that right now. Just stay cool and silent. Today isn't the time for you to testify."

The rear door opened, and the court reporter and clerk came in. The reporter was the same one who had been in the judge's chambers. The clerk was a skinny, tall, middle-aged bleach blonde in an incredibly tasteless purple wool suit with two great big burgundy buttons on the low-cut jacket. A broad strip of lace of a lavender undergarment showed on her chest.

Dan Emerick opened the main door of the courtroom and walked in, followed by Marvin Trillker. Emerick sat down at the prosecution table and stared straight ahead, his jaw fixed. Trillker sat down beside him and nodded to Kate and Mike.

"Top o' the mornin' to ya, Counsellor," Trillker said.

"And the rest o' the day to you, me lad," Mike said, trying to appear and sound calm and assured. Just another merry day in court for a light-hearted lawyer.

The rear door creaked open, and the bailiff came in. "All ready?" he asked.

Emerick nodded. Mike said, "Ready."

The bailiff pressed a buzzer on the judge's bench, picked up the gavel next to it, and rapped three times on the small block of wood.

"All rise," he said.

Judge Kellman came through the door directly behind the elevated bench and sat down in the black leather swivel chair. "Be seated," he said.

He opened the file on the bench and looked up. "This is the preliminary hearing in CR-1018754, *State* versus *Mary Caitlin O'Dwyer.* Announce your appearances, please."

Emerick stood up. "Daniel Emerick for the State, Your Honor. I object to this hearing and move to continue. It is illegal, and the State has not had sufficient opportunity to prepare."

Kellman frowned at him. "When did the death of Philip Willcott occur?"

"Several weeks ago, Your Honor."

"Have you received and reviewed all D.R.'s from the law enforcement agencies involved?"

"Yes, sir, I think so."

"Is there further investigation that you need to conduct in order to establish probable cause?"

"Well, Your Honor, we certainly need more time."

"Mr. Emerick, your investigator, Mr. Trillker, signed a criminal complaint under oath avowing probable cause for the issuance of a warrant for first-degree murder. How can your office have had probable cause on Friday afternoon and not have it today?"

"Your Honor," Emerick said, "this hearing is being conducted in violation of the Rules of Criminal Procedure. This court has no jurisdiction to convert a bail-reduction motion into a preliminary hearing."

"This court has the inherent power to treat any motion in the manner that the interests of justice require. I have determined that the interests of justice require the preliminary hearing at this time. Your motion to continue is denied."

Emerick sat down.

Mike stood up. "Michael Fallon for the defendant, who is present in court, Your Honor." He sat down.

"Very well," the judge said. "Call your first witness, Mr. Emerick."

Marvin Trillker walked up to the clerk to be sworn. She stood and raised her hand. The main door of the courtroom slammed open with a boom. A tall, attractive man in an expensive-looking black wool double-breasted suit strode into the courtroom, brandishing a document in his hand. He marched down the side aisle and stopped directly in front of the judge's bench.

"Mr. Garland," Kellman said, "you appear to have something exciting to share with the court."

"Yes, Your Honor." He handed the document to the judge.

Kellman read it carefully, and his face showed no sign of emotion. He looked up at Mike Fallon.

"Mr. Fallon, the chief judge of the Court of Appeals has issued an interlocutory stay order preventing me from continuing with this hearing."

Mike flinched.

"You and Mr. Emerick are ordered to appear before Division Two of the Court of Appeals immediately so that the court may determine whether to enforce the stay order pending a formal hearing on the State's Special Action."

Kate looked at Mike, and there was fear and disappointment in her eyes.

Don't sit here like a goddam idiot, Mike thought. *Do* something. What? Do *something*, damn it!

Mike stood up. "May it please the court, has the typed order from the hearing in chambers reached the file?"

The judge looked down at the file. "Yes, Mr. Fallon."

"Would the court inquire of the court reporter how much time she would need to prepare the transcript of these proceedings?"

Kellman looked over at the reporter. "Jean?"

"At least a half hour, Judge."

"We do not have a half hour, Your Honor," Ted Garland said. "That stay order is for an *immediate* hearing at the Court of Appeals. This court has been formally divested of jurisdiction over this case at this time."

The judge nodded. "He's got me there, Mr. Fallon," he said lightly.

Mike grabbed for a straw. "Your Honor, my understanding of Special Actions in a case like this is that they are not primarily directed at defendants such as Ms. O'Dwyer, but they are directed at the judge. They must allege that the judge abused his discretion or acted in excess of his jurisdiction."

Kellman nodded.

"So the essential issue to be determined by the Court of Appeals is whether Your Honor's decisions this morning are proper."

Again Kellman nodded.

"Perhaps the only way to prove to the Court of

Appeals that Your Honor acted justly and to vacate the stay order is to have your court reporter accompany us to the Court of Appeals so that she can read to it a verbatim record of Your Honor's decisions."

The judge shrugged and pursed his lips. "Out of the mouths of babes," he said and laughed. "Jeannie dear, please put on your hiking boots and take a stroll with these handsome gentlemen down the block to the Court of Appeals to defend my virtue."

She nodded and smiled.

"Your Honor," Mike said, "may the defendant remain in the courtroom pending this determination so that there will be no delay in proceeding with the preliminary hearing if the stay is lifted?"

"Yes," said the judge. He looked at the deputy. "John, keep her here until we sort this out, huh?"

"Yes, sir."

"Court is adjourned subject to call," Kellman said. He stood up and left the courtroom through his private door.

"I don't know what's going to happen," Mike whispered to Kate. "It won't take long. I'll be back in probably forty-five minutes."

"Come on, Fallon," Ted Garland said.

"I don't know what's going on," Kate whispered.

"I'll explain it later. I've got to go." He followed the others out of the courtroom.

Fifty minutes later, Mike returned to the courtroom. Brendan O'Dwyer and Gwen McLemore were sitting in the first row of spectator seats, leaning over the railing talking to Kate. She was sitting directly in front of the railing where the deputy had been. He was standing fifteen feet away by the water fountain.

"Hello, everybody," Mike said, not stopping. "We won." He held up a sheet of paper victoriously and went through the rear door of the courtroom to the judge's chambers.

Emerick and Trillker came into the courtroom, followed by the court reporter. A moment later Mike returned to the defense table.

"So far, so good," he said, smiling at Kate and her father.

The deputy came toward his seat, and Kate returned to the table.

The clerk came into the courtroom, followed by the bailiff. He buzzed, gaveled, everyone stood up, and the judge sat down at the bench. Everyone sat down.

Judge Kellman lifted a sheet of paper and read: "Court of Appeals, Division Two, Order. The interlocutory stay is lifted. Relief sought by Petitioner is denied. Signed by all three judges." He put the sheet in the file. "Let's proceed, Mr. Emerick."

The chief deputy stood up. "Your Honor, I respectfully request a half-hour continuance so that Mr. Garland can petition the Supreme Court for a stay. He's in his office on the telephone to Phoenix right now. The county attorney's office feels that it is our duty to exhaust all of our remedies in this matter."

"Well, Danny boy," Kellman said, rubbing his left eye with the back of his hand, "a guy's gotta do what a guy's gotta do, and I gotta get this P.H. going. From the size of that file in front of Marv, he'll be reading D.R.'s into the record for the next two hours, so I think there's plenty of time for Mr. Garland to try to get another stay. If he does, we'll just terminate the P.H. at that time. Call your witness."

"But, Your Honor—"

Kellman slapped the top of the bench and cut Emerick off. "Call your witness," he said gruffly.

Emerick breathed deeply and bit his cheek. "Marvin Trillker."

The investigator once again walked up to the clerk and was sworn. He took the seat in the witness box and adjusted the microphone closer to him. He removed a two-inch packet of documents from an Expando file and laid them before him. He took a pair of readers out of his plaid shirt pocket and adjusted them on the end of his nose.

"You're Marvin Trillker?" Emerick asked.

"Yes, sir."

"How are you employed?"

"Senior investigator for the Pima County Attorney's office."

"How much experience do you possess in the field of law enforcement?"

"Three years M.P., United States Army, one of them in Korea. He was my C.O." He pointed at Judge Kellman.

The judge nodded and laughed. "The good old days," he said.

Emerick didn't change his dour expression.

"Then I did six years with the Los Angeles Police Department, moved here to Tucson, twenty-two years with the Pima County Sheriff, retired as a homicide lieutenant, and the last fourteen years with the County Attorney."

"Have you obtained all police reports from Phoenix and Tucson concerning the murder of Philip Wilkott?"

"Objection, Your Honor," Mike said, standing. "Describing the act as 'murder' assumes facts not in evidence."

"Right, Mr. Fallon," Kellman said wearily. "But we're all friends here, and this is just a preliminary hearing. Let's get on with it before I die of old age."

Mike sat down, embarrassed in front of Kate and her father.

"I believe that I have all the reports, Mr. Emerick," Trillker said.

"In your expertise as a peace officer, do you believe that the reports establish probable cause for first-degree murder?"

Mike leapt up from his chair. "Your Honor, I—"

Kellman waved him back to his chair, casting him an annoyed look. Mike was embarrassed again. He was making proper objections, but the judge was treating him like a wet-behind-the-ears novice. The "out of the mouths of babes" comment had really rankled him. He was glad that Kate's father hadn't heard it.

"Dan," the judge said, "you're getting on young Mike's nerves, and you're about to get on mine. I'll decide if there's probable cause. Knock off the crap and let him start reading."

"Thank you, Your Honor," Emerick said. "Mr. Trillker, please read the relevant reports to the court."

Trillker started reading. There was nothing about the rapes of Jennifer and Donna. There were seven Phoenix Police and Maricopa County Attorney's reports about the investigation of Michael Fallon for the murder of Peter Supremas and the severe beating of Anthony Waywaykla. Mike was afraid to look back at Brendan O'Dwyer or Gwen McLemore. He thought that this was most likely the first time that they were hearing about this. It didn't sound very savory.

The judge glanced at Mike from time to time with looks ranging from shock to anger to censure. Mike wanted to slide out of his chair under the table and hide. Without the background facts that gave rise to the attacks on Big Gun Pete and Tony Brown Horse, the attacks appeared to be grossly criminal and unjustified. Trillker didn't read the report by the Maricopa County Attorney summarizing the background of these attacks and determining that they had been justified by extreme provocation. He also didn't read the subsequent report that determined that the bullet which killed Supremas had most likely come from Philip Wilkott's gun, and there was no probable cause to believe that Michael Fallon had killed him.

The reading droned on for twenty minutes, thirty. A young man came into the courtroom and sat in the rear. He opened a steno pad and started writing. Two women came into the courtroom and also sat down and opened steno pads. Mike assumed that they were reporters. He hadn't seen either of the Phoenix newspapers since Kate's arrest, but he was sure that Tom

Terrific would have crowed like a rooster to the press, and he could just imagine the spread that this story had been given, particularly by the *Arizona Republic.* Neither the Sunday nor this morning's *Arizona Daily Star,* the Tucson morning newspaper, had picked up the story yet. Tucson's courthouse reporters apparently didn't work on weekends.

Ted Garland slammed into the courtroom again, making everyone stop in his tracks and take note. This asshole likes to make waves in front of an audience, Mike thought.

"Well, Mr. Garland," Kellman said, "has the Supreme Court broken my cherry?"

The Pima County Attorney frowned, shook his head, and sat down beside one of the female reporters, a very pretty one.

"Well, I reckon I'm still a virgin," the judge said and chuckled. "Continue, Mr. Trillker."

The investigator read for another hour, including a report of an interview with Hank Strump, salesman for Ed Moses Chrysler-Plymouth, Inc. "Mr. Strump stated," Trillker read, "that a Mary O'Dwyer purchased a 1995 Chrysler Le Baron through him. She specifically wanted a '95 because it had dual air bags. There was a new '94 available in exactly the same color and with the identical options package, and it was three thousand dollars less than the '95, but Ms. O'Dwyer said she had enough of one air bag cars, and this time she wanted two."

Kate glanced at Mike. He was studying his thumbnail.

The final report that Trillker read was his own summary of the facts of the case and a detailed analysis of the specific, provable acts of Mary O'Dwyer that gave rise to probable cause to believe that she had committed the premeditated murder of Philip Wilkott. In the report there was a lengthy elaboration of the rape of Jennifer Catherine Mulvaney, the medical finding that she was infected with HIV virus by the assailant, and the steps that occurred in determining finally that Philip Wilcott was the rapist. A motion to suppress, precipitated by the wrongful interrogation of an in-custody juvenile by Mary O'Dwyer and the ultimate pretext arrest of Wilkott, had been the grounds for Wilkott's release and the dismissal of all charges against him. Mary O'Dwyer had then planned the murder of Philip Wilkott and apparently carried it out perfectly. Shortly thereafter, it was conclusively determined that Jennifer Mulvaney had not been infected by Wilkott with the HIV virus that he carried.

Emerick sat down.

It was a devastating list of acts of preparation for murder. Mike felt as though he had been hit over the head with a pail of cement.

"Mr. Fallon, you may cross-examine." The judge's demeanor was no longer light.

"Thank you, Your Honor." Mike's voice was hollow. He cleared his throat. He stood up slowly and walked around the table to the well of the courtroom in front of Trillker and the judge, doing it just to gain time, to think of something to do to combat the overwhelming evidence of Kate's guilt.

He pursed his lips and rocked on his toes for a moment.

"Mr. Fallon," the judge said, fixing him with a stern glare, "are you going to dance or get on with this case?"

Don't piss the judge off, Mike scolded himself. The son of a bitch has Kate's life in his hands. "I apologize to the court," he said.

"Don't apologize, son. Just get on with it." The judge's voice was harsh.

There was a giggle from the rear of the courtroom.

"Mr. Trillker, by your background I would think that you have often been asked to testify in criminal courts as an expert witness. Is that correct, sir?"

"Yes. Maybe forty, fifty times."

"And surely some of those times have involved the investigation of homicides?"

"That's right. Probably ten, twelve."

"Good. Good. Why don't we review some of these facts of Mary Caitlin O'Dwyer's alleged first-degree murder?"

"Sure."

"She disguised herself with a new hair color and much different hairdo and unusually heavy makeup, and she was so successful at the disguise that Mrs. Macklin, Mr. Wilkott's legal secretary, was unable to identify the photograph of Ms. O'Dwyer as being the same woman who visited Wilkott to hire him for her divorce."

"That's correct."

"And that was a photograph which I had taken of her at a park, the photo supplied by me to the Phoenix police, showing Ms. O'Dwyer as she appeared, blond and very little makeup, some three months ago, just as she looks now?"

"Yes, that's right."

"And as we know, this very well-disguised woman used a fictitious name, Annette Jencks, so that she would not reveal her true identity to either Mrs. Macklin or Mr. Wilkott?"

"Yes."

The judge leaned over the bench and said, "Mr. Fallon, would you come here for a second?" His face was stern, and he crooked his finger at Mike.

Mike walked up to the bench and leaned toward the judge.

"Listen, son," the judge whispered, "I know you're trying to do your best for your client, but I'm getting the impression that you aren't very experienced in this kind of work. If you ask any more questions like those, we might as well just move the electric chair in here this afternoon and get it over with."

Mike clenched his jaw. He was enraged and humiliated, but you didn't tell a preliminary hearing judge to go to hell, because it would be your client whom he sent there. Mike said nothing and nodded. He walked back toward Trillker, and out of the corner of his eye he could see Garland smiling happily. Even Emerick wore a grin. Kate was crying, and Brendan O'Dwyer looked like a lion with a thorn in his foot.

Mike took a deep breath and continued. "This same well-disguised woman was registered at the Westin La Paloma under the false name Annette Jencks, obviously to avoid detection?"

"Correct."

Judge Kellman, his eyes narrowed, stared at Mike.

"It is quite clear from this objective evidence that Ms. O'Dwyer, who was indeed this woman, had meticulously planned to murder Philip Wilkott and devised an excellent means of escaping undetected back to Scottsdale, one hundred twenty-five miles away, where she could immediately wash the makeup off, rinse or bleach the color out of her hair, and no one would be the wiser."

"I think you've stated that very well, Mr. Fallon."

"Yip, very well," said the judge in a sarcastic grumble.

Emerick laughed.

Mike gritted his teeth. He walked back to his chair at the defense table and stood staring at Trillker.

"Given all of that brilliant planning to commit murder with her automobile and get away with it, why did Mary Caitlin O'Dwyer drive her car headlong into the patio wall of a residence? Why did she have only her true driver's license in her purse and not a phony one in the name of Annette Jencks? Why didn't she have a getaway car parked nearby? Why didn't she switch the license plates for stolen ones and use acid to obliterate the Vehicle Identification Number on the engine block? And why was she illegally carrying a concealed weapon in her purse?"

Mike sat down slowly, leaned over the table, folded his hands, and stared at Trillker.

The judge waited a moment for the investigator to

answer. Trillker looked hard at Emerick, then at Garland.

Judge Kellman leaned over the desk and smiled at Mike. "Mr. Fallon, I owe you an apology." He turned to Emerick. "Mr. Emerick, further questions of this witness?"

Emerick shook his head. He had no grin.

"You may step down," the judge said.

Trillker took his seat at the prosecution table.

"Any further evidence, Mr. Emerick?"

"None at this time, Your Honor."

"Well, I think it's pretty clear, Mr. Emerick, that you do not have probable cause for murder here, not first-degree, not second, not manslaughter. The accident appears to have been just that: an accident."

Emerick stood up. "But there is also no question that she planned to murder Philip Wilkott and to escape detection. She clearly intended to kill him with a gun, probably in his home, since that's the direction the car was heading, and he lived only a mile from the accident scene. There can be no legal doubt that these facts amount to *attempted* murder, as defined by A.R.S. 13 Section 1001."

Judge Kellman pursed his lips and nodded. He reached for a statute book and pulled it out of the bookshelf built into the bench. He flipped the pages, hunched over the bench, and then said, "You mean this subsection, Mr. Emerick? 'A person commits attempt if, acting with the kind of culpability otherwise required for the commission of an offense, such person intentionally does anything which is any step in a course of conduct planned to culminate in the commission of an offense.'"

Emerick said, "Yes. All the facts fit it."

The judge nodded and turned to Mike. "Mr. Fallon, you've done quite well so far. How are you going to do on this?"

Mike stood up. "Well, Your Honor, I'm a little bit at a loss for words at the moment."

Kellman rolled his eyes, his expression grave. "I can understand that, Mr. Fallon. Do you have any evidence that the court should consider before making its determination?"

Mike shook his head slowly, feeling his shoulders sag.

Kate tugged on the sleeve of his suit jacket. "I want to testify," she whispered urgently.

Mike pulled his sleeve away. "Nothing, Your Honor."

Kate stood up next to him. "I want to testify," she said.

"Kate!" Mike whispered sharply. "Sit down!" He tried to take her arm, to push her down. She pulled away from him. "Keep your mouth shut, Kate!" Mike said.

"I want to testify, Judge." Her voice was strong. Tears were on her cheeks. Her eyes glistened with them.

"Young lady," the judge said, looking at her like a testy schoolteacher, "you take your lawyer's advice. He knows what he's doing."

"I want to testify."

"Your Honor," Mike said, "may I have a few minutes to talk to my client? I think that she is extremely overwrought from what she's been through."

"I want to testify," Kate said loudly.

"You talk to your lawyer, Ms. O'Dwyer. You take his advice. Court is recessed for five minutes." He walked off the bench and through his private door.

Mike turned to the deputy. "Is there an attorneys' conference room?"

"Yeah, in the back hallway. Come on."

Brendan O'Dwyer leaned over the railing, his face and eyes distorted with worry. "Kate, you listen to Mike. Don't be stupid."

Gwen sat rigidly, her eyes boring into Kate's. She nodded her head almost imperceptibly at her.

The deputy put handcuffs on Kate and led her

through the back door of the courtroom and down the hallway. Mike followed them. The deputy unlocked the door, turned on the light, left the small, windowless room, and closed the door behind him.

Mike stood close to her. "Are you nuts or something?"

"I'm going to testify," she said, not looking at him.

"God damn it, Kate! You'll testify yourself right into prison. The judge is going to bind you over on attempted murder. If you get on that stand, whatever you say is going to be used at your trial, and it *can't help* you. And Judge Kellman might change his mind and charge you with first-degree murder."

"I'm going to testify," she said. "If I've got to stand trial, I've got to tell the truth. I've waited too long. I should've done it sooner. *A woman of valor, who can find? Her worth is far greater than rubies.*"

He frowned. "This isn't the time to start spouting the Bible at me, damn it!"

"When *is* the time if not now?" She looked into his eyes.

"Jesus!" he muttered in exasperation. He threw up his arms and rolled his eyes.

"Gwen used to tell me that. It's from Proverbs."

"But Gwen isn't going to stand trial for *murder!*"

"Right now I have to believe in myself and do what *I* believe is right." Kate's voice was strong and resolute.

"Damn! What the hell did they teach you in that parochial school? That it's *good* to end up like Joan of Arc?" He shook his head at her, deeply frustrated. "Don't be a martyr. What good is being dead? I keep telling you that *the truth will not set you free.*" He put his hands on her shoulders, imploring her. "That's not a priest out there, and the courtroom isn't a confessional. Get a hold of yourself. You'll be out on bail in two hours, I promise you. Then we'll talk."

"I'm going to testify."

He glowered at her. "I'll punch you in the jaw, and

you'll have to be hospitalized, before I let you take the stand."

She frowned at him.

The deputy opened the door. "Judge wants us back."

Mike followed Kate into the courtroom. At the defense table, the deputy unlocked the handcuffs. The judge was sitting at the bench, his hands folded.

"Well, I'd sure like to get to lunch, folks," he said. "This court determines that the evidence establishes sufficient probable cause to bind the defendant over for trial in Superior Court on a charge of attempted murder. Anything further?"

Kate was still standing. "I want to testify."

The judge shook his head. "Young lady, I've already made my ruling. I think it would be an awfully bad idea for you to testify."

"I want to, Judge."

Emerick stood up at the prosecution table, eager to have her testify. It was the almost always unrequited dream of every prosecutor to have the defendant testify, so that the defendant would convict himself with his own words. But the Fifth Amendment prevented the prosecutor from ever compelling a defendant to testify. If one voluntarily chose to, it was manna from heaven.

"Your Honor," Emerick said, holding an open statute book before him, "Rule 5.3 says that the court '*shall* allow the defendant to present the offered evidence,' unless the court determines that there's no chance that anything she says could possibly alter the court's determination of probable cause."

Kellman shrugged. "How could I determine that? I have no idea what she's going to say."

"Exactly, Your Honor," Emerick said. "Then the court is required to permit her to testify."

Kellerman rubbed his chin and looked at Kate. "Do you really want to testify?"

"Yes, sir."

"Do you relize the seriousness of this? You may very well say things that constitute a confession, perhaps to a crime even more serious than attempted murder."

"I'll only tell the truth."

"Your Honor, I cannot permit my client to testify," Mike said.

"Well, Mr. Fallon, I'm afraid that you can't do that. Your client has the absolute right to testify whether you or I think it's wise or not. And I do not." He looked at Kate, "Please go to the clerk and be sworn."

Brendan O'Dwyer gasped. "Oh, sweet Jesus!" he murmured. "No, Mary Kate, please," he pleaded, standing up.

"Please ask the gentleman to be seated," the judge said.

The bailiff got up from his desk ten feet away and walked toward Brendan.

"Sir, be seated," he said.

Gwen put her hand gently on Brendan's arm. He sank into his chair, tears misting his eyes.

Kate was sworn and took the witness stand.

"You have a right to remain silent," the judge said. "Do you give up that right?"

She looked at him steadily. "Yes."

"You have your own attorney. Have you discussed it with him?"

"Yes."

"Do you realize that the court reporter is taking down every word you say, and a transcript of this may be introduced against you in any subsequent proceeding?"

"Yes."

"Do you still wish to testify?"

"Yes, I do."

"The court finds that the defendant has made a knowing and intelligent waiver. All right, Mr. Fallon, do you have questions for this witness?"

"Not one, Your Honor."

Kellman turned to Kate. "You may testify on direct examination in narrative form, Ms. O'Dwyer, with no questions being asked of you. When you finish, Mr. Emerick will be permitted to cross-examine you. Do you understand?"

"Yes, I fully understand."

"All right. Proceed." Kellman leaned over the bench and watched her closely.

Kate was suddenly unsure of what to say. But she had to tell the truth. She had to confess to God. She had to confess to man. They had to know why she did this.

"I love six people in the whole world," she said, trying to keep her voice strong and her eyes dry. "I love him, my father"—she pointed at Brendan, slumped in his chair and looking compassionately at her. "I love Gwen McLemore, my very dear friend." She nodded at Gwen, who smiled softly. "I love him"—she pointed at Mike. He was resting his chin on his open palms, tears in his eyes, not looking at her. "And I love my mother. And I love Seamus Gerrity, he's a friend of mine from Boston. A very good man." She paused, catching her breath. "And I love my three-year-old daughter, Jennifer Catherine." Try as she might, she could nor squeeze back the tears. They began to roll down her cheeks.

"But although I love these other people with all my heart, it is different from the love that I have for Jennifer. I love Jennifer more than my own life." Her chin quivered, and she paused for a moment.

"You are men, and I don't know if you really understand that a mother's love for her child is something which has no equal in the whole range of emotions and human relationships. Men, I think, are a little different. They are physically stronger than women, and they can try to protect their children with strength that a woman simply lacks. She can only protect her child with love."

She breathed deeply to steady her voice and looked at Mike. He was looking back at her, his face sad.

"Donna Alvarez and Jennifer were raped, and when we were told that Jenn had contracted the HIV virus from the rapist and that she was at least eighty percent certain to die, I almost died. Mike almost died. All the love in the world could not make Jennifer whole again.

"We wanted to kill whoever had done this. When Peter Supremas was arrested and then released because he wasn't one of the rapists, we knew that he knew who the rapists were. He had brought them to my home. Michael Fallon was so deeply injured that he did the only thing he knew how to help heal his family, me and Jennifer. He went to Supremas and beat him up, and he found out the names of the two rapists."

She looked at Emerick and then Trillker. "You could not have found out, because the only way was the way Mike chose." She looked at the judge. "If the police had beaten Supremas and gotten the names, it would have been an illegal act, and you would have thrown out the case. But Michael is a private citizen. He *could* find out, even if he had to break the law to do it.

"Philip Wilkott was arrested, and his DNA matched the infected semen in my daughter. But suddenly he was released from custody because of a mistake *I made,* just by talking to Donna Alvarez, a girl who had been my foster child. I didn't know I couldn't talk to her. I didn't know I had suddenly somehow become the same as a policeman. And because of that Wilkott walked out of jail a free man."

Her voice was rising. "Nobody was going to do anything. *The law* said that the murderer of my baby had to go free." She washed her hands together. "Just wash it all away. Move on to the next case. Poof! It's just some meaningless little three-year-old girl. Who cares? Who gives a shit?"

She rested a moment, trying to regain her composure. "But what would you do if she was your daughter? *You,* Judge Kellman. *You,* Mr. Emerick. God damn you, you smug lawyers," she screamed, "what would you do?" She burst into tears again and wept for minutes. Everyone in the courtroom was silent, unmoving.

Kate looked up again and around the courtroom. "Didn't God cry out for justice to be done? Didn't a voice from heaven scream out for punishment of such an animal? Isn't there a still, small voice in each of us that tells us when a terrible injustice has been committed?"

She looked straight ahead, her vision once again opaqued by tears, and rubbed her eyes. She swallowed and looked down at her hands. "That's all," she mumbled.

Kellman's mouth and chin were squeezed hard in his hand, and his rheumy eyes glistened. He cleared his throat and looked at the prosecutor. "Questions, Mr. Emerick?"

"Just a few, Your Honor." He remained seated. "Ms. O'Dwyer, do you regret your action in attempting to murder Philip Wilkott?"

"No." She shook her head. "No."

"Do you agree that what you did fits the definition of attempted murder that the judge read a few moments ago?"

She looked at her father and Mike, then at her hands in her lap. "Yes," she said, "it sounds like what happened."

What more did Emerick need? She had just confessed, convicted herself.

"Ms. O'Dwyer," he said, "is there anything that you would like to add?"

She studied her hands, and tears once again came. She looked up, looking straight ahead, seeing nothing.

"I am very ashamed of myself," she said, her voice thin and hoarse. "I am very ashamed that I wore a disguise and used a phony name. That was cowardice. That was shameful and inappropriate. If I had it to do again, I would simply walk into Wilkott's office and kill him."

Mike slumped at the defense table. "Oh, my God," he murmured. He heard Brendan O'Dwyer crying behind him.

"And the only other regret I have," she said, hardly more than a whisper, "is that I won't be seeing my daughter or Michael Fallon every day for a while." She closed her eyes and bowed her head, and her body heaved with sobs.

Emerick sat down.

The courtroom was sepulchral. Judge Kellman rubbed his eyes roughly, reclined back in his swivel chair, and stared at the ceiling. He waited several minutes for Kate to stop crying. Then he coughed and cleared his throat and said, "You may step down, Ms. O'Dwyer."

Kate walked to the table and sat down. Mike straightened up and looked at her, his eyes forlorn. She touched his shoulder lightly and smiled. The deputy did not order her to remove her hand.

The judge closed the file on the bench. He looked around at the stunned, silent people in the courtroom and began to recite his order.

"The law, in one of its most fundamental, centuries-old, and widely accepted concepts, requires that to convict a person of first-degree murder or attempted murder, the judge or jury must find that the person committed the act of killing or attempting to kill with *malice aforethought*. In fact, that is the very instruction I give to the jury before it retires to deliberate in a murder case. The classic legal definition of an act of 'malice' is an act which is 'the dictate of an abandoned, depraved, and malignant heart.' I have searched for that in this case. Mary Caitlin O'Dwyer wanted to kill Philip Wilkott, and she planned to kill him. Yet I cannot make the necessary finding that her state of mind was the dictate of an abandoned, depraved, and malignant heart.

"If a mother had come home and found a rapist in the act of raping her three-year-old daughter, or just finished and leaving through the window, we would praise her for getting a gun out of her bedstand and shooting him in the back. We would not question for a moment whether the rapist had HIV or AIDS and had infected the child. The act itself is so atrocious that we happily applaud his death. But if he escapes, and even if everyone knows who he is, suddenly everything changes.

"One of the oldest laws of mankind is that punishment must be equal to the crime: an eye for an eye. If a man takes a life, his life shall be taken. If he takes an eye, his eye shall be taken. In this case Ms. O'Dwyer genuinely believed, on all available evidence, that Philip Wilkott had taken her daughter's life. While our law today does not condone vengeance by individuals and instead requires the state to exact vengeance, in this case the state failed. The law, if it is to be respected, must not ignore the moral outrage that ordinary people experience when a terrible criminal simply avoids any consequences of his crime because a tiny mistake was made in following some of the arcane and complex laws of criminal procedure. Do we really believe that it is justifiable to set Philip Wilkott free because Mary O'Dwyer questioned Donna Alvarez about who the rapists were or because his arrest was the result of a carefully planned pretext? In an ordered society, the law must be considered by its subjects to be fair and just. Was it fair and just to set Philip Wilkott free?

"John Rawls, a Harvard philosophy professor and scholar of the theory of justice, tells us that 'an injustice is tolerable only when it is necessary to avoid an even greater injustice.' Let us say for a moment that Ms. O'Dwyer's attempt to kill Philip Wilkott was unjust. She had no right to do that. But wasn't the heinous crime committed by Wilkott, and the failure of the state to punish him, a far greater injustice? And is not Ms. O'Dwyer's injustice thereby made tolerable?

"For this court to hold Ms. O'Dwyer to answer for any crime under these circumstances would be an inexcusable outrage to morality and compassion. The lady of justice, who holds the scales in her hand, is blind*folded,* but not *blind.* She is blindfolded to prevent her from showing favoritism to either side. Everyone must be judged alike. But she must never be blind to the morality of the people who come before her and the true nature of the acts which they commit. She must never apply the letter of the law blindly and without fairness and mercy. There is no evidence in this case to establish that Ms. O'Dwyer had an abandoned heart. In fact, I find quite the opposite.

"The court finds that no probable cause exists to establish the crime of murder in any degree or attempted murder.

"It is ordered that Mary Caitlin O'Dwyer be forthwith discharged from custody. This case is dismissed."

He looked at her, into her eyes, and smiled. He left the bench. The bailiff didn't bang the gavel, and everyone was too stunned to rise.

Kate began to sob breathlessly, her face in her hands, and Mike wrapped his arms around her and held her tight.

The two female reporters clapped, joined after a moment by the young man. Ted Garland stood up, his jaw tightly clenched, and waited for Emerick and Trillker. They walked slowly out of the courtroom.

"It's over," Mike whispered to her. "The nightmare is over." He looked back at Brendan and Gwen and smiled. "It's all over."

Gwen buried her face in a handkerchief. Brendan beamed at him and wiped his eyes with the sleeve of his camelhair sports coat. He breathed wheezily.

"You were terrific, Michael," he said. "Terrific!"

"The judge just about ripped my head off a couple of times."

"He'll never do that again, believe me. Not after what you did today."

Kate straightened up wearily and began to smile. "I can't believe it's all over. I couldn't have taken much more."

Mike kissed her on the lips. "You were wonderful."

She smiled, then turned to her father and Gwen. "Let's go see Jennifer and Mom."

"You want to pick your clothes up at the jail?" Brendan asked.

She shook her head vigorously. "I don't ever want to go near that place again. I can buy a blouse and shorts and sandals at the Ventana hotel. I'm sure there's at least one nice boutique there."

"You're going to walk in there like that?" Mike jutted his chin toward her wrinkled green pullover shirt and baggy pajama pants.

"Yeah, sure. They'll think I'm a gynecologist."

They laughed.

· SIXTEEN ·

Sunday night, before going to sleep in the bed of the pickup, Donna had opened all the windows in the house and scrubbed the blood off the floor and the bed frame with Pine Sol. In the morning the foul smell was gone. She took a shower and put on a pair of faded baby blue Levi's and a tight-fitting, almost new, bright blue Polo knit shirt that some skinny rich lady had donated to the Mesa Outreach.

She drove by the Circle K on Rural Road and decided to get a donut. She parked in front of the convenience mart and glanced at the *Arizona Republic* in the newspaper machine as she walked by. O'DWYER CHARGED WITH MURDER was the headline.

Donna gulped and stared at the newspaper. She put thirty-five cents into the machine and took out a paper, then walked back to the truck and read the story. She sagged against the door of the pickup and felt breathless and weak, as though she had been punched in the stomach. Oh, God, no. How can this happen? This is too awful.

She read numerous high-sounding quotes about justice from Thomas Osborne Wilkott and the Pima County Attorney, and her knees almost buckled under her. "No citizen can take the law into his own hands," the county attorney said, "because the only result of that is lawlessness." Then from Wilkott, "Our criminal justice system is the most cherished protector of our liberty." And, "Only society can judge the acts of a fellow citizen, and the way that is done is through the hallowed jury system."

The story was mean, again asserting that "Donna Alvarez had sold the three-year-old baby for heroin." She gritted her teeth, and her arms were suddenly covered with goose bumps.

"Those dirty liars," she muttered. "Why can't they stop?"

She opened the door of the truck slowly and threw the newspaper inside. She took several breaths to clear away her dizzy feeling. "I have to see Kate, to tell her that I love her. I've got to see her and help her."

She got into the pickup feeling hopeless and helpless. In her entire life she had had just two weeks of hope with Kate and Jennifer and four months of hope with Agnes Ishpia. In all her sixteen years.

How can I help her? she thought. I can't help her. I can't help anybody. I am a stinking pile of cat shit in the corner of the bedroom of my mother's shack. It's where I came from and where I'll end up. It's only a matter of days before Agnes's daughters throw me out of the house. Then where can I go but back to my mother's, or the Civic Center?

She started the engine, and suddenly she had to see Kate. Despite everything she needed to see Kate, to talk to her, to tell her she was sorry. She glanced at the gas gauge, and there was plenty. She drove down Rural Road to the Superstition Freeway, hoping that the pickup would make it.

Donna had never been to Tucson. She exited I-10 a little after noon on a street that looked like it was near the center of the downtown, where all the tall buildings were clustered, and pulled into a gas station. She pumped ten dollars of gas into the tank and asked the attendant where the women's jail was. He didn't know exactly where the *women* were held but said that the main jail was just up at Twenty-ninth Street, a couple of blocks to the right.

It took her another three minutes to get there, and she parked in the parking lot. She went to the entrance and rang a buzzer below a sign that said every visitor had to ring it. A voice asked her what she wanted, and she said to visit a woman inmate. The lock shot open on the big steel door, and she walked inside to the long counter, behind which were several uniformed sheriff's deputies. Donna was suddenly frightened. All these cops, a jail.

"I'd like to visit Kate O'Dwyer," Donna said, trying to make her voice calm.

The guard checked a roster. "She's down at the courthouse."

"Where's that?"

"Downtown, Congress Street."

"Is it far?"

"Are you family?" asked a female guard.

Donna shook her head.

"You got identification?"

Donna shook her head and swallowed.

The guard looked at her oddly. "You'd better haul ass outta here. You ain't gettin' in to see nobody."

Donna backed out of the jail, watching the guards, and pushed the steel door closed. Would they come after her? What the hell was she doing here? She felt naked and vulnerable in this strange city. She ran to the pickup truck, wanting to flee from Tucson as quickly as she could. She started the engine and pulled out of the parking lot with a screech of tires, turned left on Twenty-ninth Street, and gunned the engine toward the highway overpass that she could see just two blocks away. As she got to the intersection, the light turned yellow, then red. She sped up to get through it, then turned left on the access road to I-10.

Behind her almost immediately were blinking blue and red lights. She was terrified. She had no license. Juvenile hall. No, no, no. She sped up, but the ancient pickup was no match for the new Ford sedan. She heard the siren behind her. She knew that she had to pull over.

She parked on the dirt shoulder of the access road, and the police car parked behind her, the siren off but the lights still turning. The cop sat there for several minutes, and she watched him through the rearview mirror talking on his radio. A few minutes later another police car drove up and parked in front of the pickup. Both officers got out of their vehicles. The one in front withdrew his handgun and held it by his side, looking at her through the windshield.

The one behind came to the driver's door and opened it.

"Get out, please," he said.

Donna stumbled out and steadied herself back against the rear fender.

"May I see your license, please?"

She was petrified. She couldn't speak.

The officer looked into the cab of the truck. He signaled the other officer, who holstered his gun and came around to the passenger door. He opened it and looked into the glove compartment, then looked at the other cop next to Donna and shook his head.

"You got registration?"

She said nothing, her eyes blinking wildly.

"You steal the truck?"

She could hardly breathe. She couldn't answer.

He took her by the arm, turned her around roughly, and patted her down, his hands lingering on her breasts and between her legs. Then he handcuffed her. "I'll take her down," he said to the officer by the passenger door.

He put her in the rear seat of his car, caged behind a metal mesh partition. He drove into the downtown area just a few blocks away and parked behind a big building by a sign that read PROCESSING.

A plain tan Ford drove up and parked next to the marked police car. Two plainclothes policemen got out of the front of the car, and the driver held open the rear door. A young Mexican got out, handcuffed.

The uniformed policeman opened the rear door for Donna to get out. She swung her legs out and stood up.

"Hey, Max," said the uniformed patrolman.

One of the plainclothes officers said, "Whattaya say, Jim?" He stared at Donna Alvarez, then looked at the uniformed officer. "You got a hard case here?"

The patrolman chuckled. "Yeah, big time. No license, no registration, tried to outrun me in a thirty-year-old Ford pickup."

Max Cohen turned to the other plainclothes officer. "Can you process this maggot, Fred?"

"Sure, Max." He came around the car, took the young Mexican by the arm, and led him through the double doors.

"You're Donna Alvarez?" Cohen said, walking up to her.

She glanced at him, her eyes wide open with alarm, then looked away, and nodded. She stood shuddering.

"I know this girl," Cohen said to the patrolman.

"Yeah?" he answered. "You bust her before?"

Max shook his head. "Just saw her picture. Let me have her."

The patrolman gave him an odd look. "What?"

Max nodded. "She was one of the two kids raped in the O'Dwyer case."

The patrolman screwed up his face, thought for a moment, then looked quizzically at Cohen. "You mean the woman they arrested for the Wilkott killing?"

Cohen nodded.

The officer shook his head. "I just can't cut her loose. No ID, no registration, fleeing a law enforcement officer. Bill Freeling's out at Twenty-ninth and the I-10 access waiting on a tow truck."

"Tell him to hold off. I'll take her up to the 2-A interrogation room and make a couple of calls. If she stole the pickup, she's yours, but she's a juvenile, she'll have to go out to Ajo. Otherwise, cut her loose in my custody."

He nodded. "Okay." A patrolman didn't buck the orders of a detective sergeant unless the sergeant was doing something illegal. Here there was nothing improper. He got back into his marked vehicle and began talking on the radio.

"Come on, kid," Max Cohen said. He led Donna through the double doors into the rear of the police station and up the stairs to the second floor. He walked her into a small room, bare but for a rectangular metal table bolted to the floor and four metal chairs. He removed the handcuffs with the universal handcuff key issued to all Tucson policemen. He pointed to a chair. Donna sat down slowly, staring at him through twitching eyes.

"I know your picture from the investigation of the Wilkott case, Donna. I was in charge of it."

She nodded slowly.

"Did you steal that truck?"

She shook her head vigorously.

"Whose is it?"

"Agnes Ishpia," she said, her voice reedy. "I lived with her. She died yesterday."

"Who can prove that, Donna?"

She thought for a moment. "Chief Henry Manuelito on the reservation."

Cohen nodded. "Okay, I'll be back in a minute."

Donna slumped in the chair. She glanced around at the pornographic graffiti covering almost every inch of the age-grayed walls.

Cohen returned a short time later with the uniformed patrolman. The patrolman picked up his handcuffs off the table and left.

"Okay, I talked to Chief Manuelito. Why are you in Tucson?"

"I read in the papers this morning that Kate O'Dwyer

was in jail." She stared at the floor. "I just wanted to see her."

"Well, she isn't in jail anymore."

Donna looked up at him, startled. She straightened in the chair. "How come?"

"She had a hearing this morning, and she was released from jail about an hour ago."

Donna began to smile. "She . . . she's not . . . she's not going to have to stand trial?"

Cohen shook his head. "No. No charges."

"That's great," she said. "That's really great."

"Come on," Cohen said.

She looked at him, fearful again. "You taking me to juvi?"

He shook his head. "Nope. I'm taking you over to Motor Vehicle Division Licensing. I have a friend over there. Let's see if we can get you a license, make you legal."

She began to smile, then nodded happily.

They passed by a Coke machine in the corridor. "You want one?" Cohen asked.

"Can I?" she said.

He put three quarters into the machine, punched the button, and handed her a can of Coke.

It took ten minutes to get to the MVD. Max Cohen told her to wait in the huge, crowded lobby and walked through a door marked PRIVATE, AUTHORIZED PERSONNEL ONLY. He came back into the lobby five minutes later and gestured for Donna to come over. He led her into a private office down the hallway.

"I have to have my mother—" she said.

He cut her off. "I took care of it. Just study this booklet on driving rules. Come down the hall to the door marked 'Director' when you're ready." He left the office and closed the door behind him.

Donna studied the little booklet for a half hour, and when she took her written test in the MVD director's office, with him and Detective Cohen chatting together like old friends, she missed only one answer.

Her driving test in Cohen's unmarked police car went equally well, and suddenly she was a legal driver.

It was the first achievement that she had ever experienced in her life, and it made her glow with pride. She held the little laminated card carefully in both hands and stared at it lovingly as though it were a precious gem.

Cohen grinned at her. "Come on, kid. I'll take you back to your truck."

He drove her to the pickup parked on the shoulder of the I-10 access road. "Good luck, Donna."

"Thank you, Mr. Cohen." Her eyes were sparkling with tears, but there was a wide smile on her face.

He waited for her to get into the truck and pull away, then drove slowly back to the police station. She was a pretty girl, a frightened and sad girl. And she didn't have much chance in the world. It made him feel very bad, but he'd been doing this job for almost thirty years, and you couldn't let yourself feel heartache for all the sad things you saw. Otherwise, you had nothing to take home with you at night to your family except your misery.

• SEVENTEEN •

"How the hell can he do that?" Garland grumbled. "She goddamn confessed! All that horseshit about an abandoned heart? That's for the jury to decide, not for him!"

"He can do any damn thing he wants. He's the judge," Emerick said.

"I'll tell you, we've got to get decent judges on the bench. This is outrageous, loose cannons like Kellman."

Emerick shrugged.

"Let's appeal it," Garland said.

"We can't win an appeal. We'll take it to the grand jury. That's a lot surer, anyway."

"Can we?"

"Yes. *Wilson* versus *Garrett,* a case I had twenty-five, twenty-six years ago."

"Who's got the grand jury now?"

"Julie Harcourt and Derrick Kahn."

"Good," Garland said. "Let's get the Harcourt woman to do it. A woman after a woman."

"Yeah, and she's a Nazi, too. She'd prosecute her own mother for spitting on the sidewalk."

Garland laughed. "My kind of girl. Go get her, will you?"

Emerick left the office. Garland stared at his telephone, Well, it had to be done. But at least he could soften the blow. He opened the center drawer and took out the business card that Thomas Osborne Wilkott had given him. On the back was the number of his private line, which rang only in his office. He dialed.

"Tom, this is Ted Garland."

"Yes, Ted. I've been waiting for your call."

"Well, Tom, we ran into a little trouble with this judge."

Pause. "What kind of trouble?"

"He didn't think we had probable cause."

"What?" Wilkott growled. "I thought you had the son of a bitch in your pocket." *What kind of powerless pansy am I dealing with here? They told me this Garland had some juice and knew how to use it.*

"So did I. He's usually reliable, but today he suddenly got a wild hair up his ass."

"Fucking incompetent judges we got," Wilkott muttered. "I'm telling you, Tom, there just aren't enough good men on the bench. It's a damn shame, but I have to say it. For the good of the bar, Ted, for the good of decent people, we've got to put you into Congress. At least we'll be able to get some decent judges on the *federal* bench." *Take the bait, you prick.*

"Well, I appreciate that, Tom." *But where are the endorsements you promised me?*

"Now, knowing you, Ted, you're not going to take this in the shorts without a fight. Where can we go from here?" *Don't quit on me, you bastard.*

"I'm putting it together right now, Tom. My chief deputy is bringing one of our grand jury team in for a chat. She's a top-notch prosecutor, about thirty years old, two or three kids, her husband's a Department of Public Safety lieutenant. She's our kind of people."

"You vouch for her?" Wilkott asked.

"Yeah. First-rate. She'll do the job. We have a hell of a lot more control over the grand jury than we do over the judges, even the friendly ones. The O'Dwyer woman testified today in court, broke down and confessed."

"You're kidding."

"Nope. I'll send you a transcript of it when the court reporter gets it typed. You won't believe it."

"And the judge still cut her loose?"

"Yes. She's really a beautiful woman, cried for a goddamn hour like she had shower heads for eyeballs. I guess the judge felt sorry for her."

"Felt *sorry*? He's a goddamn judge. He's not supposed to let that affect his decisions. Jesus, what terrible shape our justice system is in!"

"Yeah, well, the grand jury will take care of it." Garland hesitated. "But you understand there's a different procedure involved this time. We can't arrest her until she's indicted."

"Why not? I want that bitch to rot in jail without bond."

"To do that we have to file a criminal complaint and get a warrant. But it's illegal for us to do it again after the same complaint has been dismissed by a magistrate or a judge."

Wilkott's sigh was audible. "Well, you just have to do the best you can. If a grand jury is all that's legally available, then we have to take the bitter with the sweet. When they indict her, she'll rot in jail until the trial."

Garland swallowed. "Well, I'm going to suggest to you, Tom, that it might not be wise for us to indict her on a capital, nonbailable crime."

"What do you mean? Not charge her with first-degree murder?"

"I think we better just charge her with *attempted* murder this time." Ted Garland cleared his throat. "I don't think that the facts are going to support murder, and we'll be more certain to get a conviction if we don't overreach."

"But the bitch murdered my son." If you let me down on this, you bastard, the only way you'll ever get to Washington is on a tour bus.

"Listen, Tom, I've investigated this thoroughly, and

I've just listened to the testimony in court. We have her cold on *attempt,* but we just might not have murder. She did *plan* to murder him, but with a *gun.* The accident in which your son tragically died was probably just a genuine accident."

There was a painfully long silence. "That woman was strapped into her seat and harnessed and protected by an air bag. She got my son drunk, and she should have made damn sure he was using his seat belt and shoulder harness. Then he wouldn't have died." He paused. "I'm just a little too emotional about this thing to talk about *attempted* murder."

"Yes, Tom, of course you're right. Who wouldn't be just as upset as you are? And I'm going to do my best for you, I want you to know that and believe it."

"I do, Ted. I do."

"Thank you, Tom. Believe me, we're going to give this absolutely top priority."

"Good. I have faith in you, Ted." With a congressman like you, we'd risk running the whole goddamn county right into a rattlesnake pit. "When do you think you can indict?"

"Well, first we've got to get the preliminary hearing transcript. It'll only take a couple of days. I told the court reporter we'd pay extra if she'd expedite it. I'll use O'Dwyer's in-court statement instead of putting her on the stand to testify. That way the grand jurors won't see her and watch her weep for an hour. It's a whole lot easier for them to indict a statement on paper than a real live woman like O'Dwyer. Our grand jury meets on Tuesdays and Thursdays, and the presentation will only take a couple of hours. I'll tell our grand jury deputy to do it next Tuesday morning, providing we have that transcript."

"Okay, Ted. I'll wait to hear from you." He hung up.

Well, that wasn't so hard, Garland thought. When I call him about the indictment, I guess it'll be just about the perfect time to talk about a little campaign fund—

A knock on the door interrupted his musing. It opened. Dan Emerick came in with Julie Harcourt.

Garland stood up and extended his hand to her. "How nice to see you again, Julie."

"Nice to see you, Mr. Garland." She sat down in one of the desk chairs, perched expectantly, her knees close together in her tight black wool skirt.

"Call me Ted. Please." He had met her twice before in the five or six years she had been in the County Attorney's office. Once for a hiring interview. Once at a Fraternal Order of Police annual banquet two or three years ago.

He smiled pleasantly at her. "Dan tells me that you're doing a marvelous job with the grand jury."

"Thank you. I appreciate that."

"We've got a little matter that needs priority attention."

She nodded.

"It's a murder case."

Her smile faded. "Mary O'Dwyer?"

"Yes. You know about it?"

"Who doesn't know about it?"

"Well, we had a little trouble with old Aaron Kellman this morning."

"Yes, I heard. Everybody's talking about it."

"What are they saying?"

She shrugged. "You know the office. The Nazis think she beat the rap, and the Jews think we tried to railroad her."

Garland maintained his pleasant smile with difficulty.

"Where do you fit on that spectrum?"

"Usually I'm a Nazi. I think criminals should be severely punished. But this case? I've read about it in the papers, seen reports on TV. I grant you that it's a very tough case. But Mary O'Dwyer is not a criminal."

Garland looked over at Emerick, and Dan pursed

his lips and shrugged. "I told you, Ted. This one is not everybody's cup of tea."

"We're not having a tea party here, my friends." Garland kept control of the professional smile and the smooth voice. "We are not the judges and the jurors. Our sworn duty to the public is to bring a person who commits an arguably criminal act into court so that a judge and a jury can determine whether the act is sufficiently coupled with a criminal mental state to allow that person to be convicted of a crime. Mary O'Dwyer has to be judged by a jury of her peers."

"Peers?" she said. "Are there any peers who have been through what she's been through, Mr. Garland? How many women can we put on the grand jury whose three-year-old daughters were brutally raped by an HIV-infected pile of shit?" She smiled sweetly at the county attorney.

Garland smiled back at her, fighting the intense urge to grab her throat and choke her to death.

"I have a two-year-old son and a four-year-old daughter, Mr. Garland. What do you think I would do if that happened to my son or daughter, and the attacker was set free like Wilkott was?"

"I don't know, Julie. But you wouldn't kill the man in cold blood."

"I'm not so sure. I'm not sure of that at all. How does anyone know what she would do in such a terrible situation? I have a strong feeling I would try to kill him."

"Well, then you'd be in the same position that Mary O'Dwyer is, waiting to be judged by a trial jury, for society to determine whether you acted properly. You may think you did right; I may agree with you. But the whole purpose of the justice system is to prevent *us* from making the ultimate decision. That decision is in the hands of society. And that's our obligation as prosecutors, to present the case to them for *their* judgment, whatever it may be."

"But haven't we already fulfilled our obligation to

society?" she asked. "The first step for a criminal case to go through before it's taken to a *trial* jury is either a *grand* jury or a preliminary hearing. We just presented the charges against Mary O'Dwyer to Judge Kellman in a P.H., and he dismissed the case. What is there left for *us* to do?"

"I think we have to bring it to a grand jury."

She wrinkled her brow and looked at Emerick, then back at Garland. "Can we do that? Is it even legal?"

"Dan assures me that it is. He prosecuted the very case that decided the issue back in the early seventies."

She rolled her eyes. "I've never seen a case before where we got blown away in a P.H. and then took it to a grand jury. It doesn't seem fair."

"Listen, Julie. I need a favor on this, and I'm counting on you. You don't have to love the assignment, and I don't blame you, but I'm giving it to you. You're one of the real comers in this office, and you'll make it to the top a lot faster than most of your contemporaries. I've had my eye on you for a long time." He smiled reassuringly.

He could see her eyes brighten with the bullshit. "Can I count on you, Julie?"

"Of course you can, Mr. Garland."

"Good. Good. That's just what I've come to expect from you." He looked at Emerick. "Dan, you were right. She's the right one for this job."

Emerick sat still, staring blandly at Garland. You lowlife prick, Ted, you two-bit scumbag.

"Okay," Garland said, standing up and extending his hand to Julie Harcourt. "Dan will give you the file and tell you how to present this one. I really appreciate your help, and I don't forget."

She smiled warmly at him, shook his hand, and walked out the door being held open by Emerick. He followed her out and closed the door behind him.

Twenty steps down the corridor she looked at Emerick and said in a low voice, "This is a shit deal."

He shrugged. "Welcome to real life."

"We shouldn't do this to Mary O'Dwyer. She's been through enough. Kellman cut her loose, and he's a damn good judge. It's not fair to take her to the grand jury. You know what's going to happen. They rubber-stamp whatever we give them. If I put an indictment in front of them, they'll vote eighteen to nothing to indict her and not even give it a second thought."

They stopped in front of Julie's office.

"And that's what you're going to do," Emerick said. He looked soberly at her. "It's legal, it's within the county attorney's jurisdiction and power, and you've been ordered by Ted Garland to do it. You'll either do it, or you'll be typing up job applications tomorrow."

She swallowed and frowned. "Come on, I don't deserve this shit," she said. "I've worked for you for almost seven years. I've never bucked anything before. But this is just unfair. It's *wrong*. I won't be able to look those grand jurors in the eye when I hand them the indictment."

"Then look the other way." He glared at her. "I just spent two and a half fucking hours in purgatory. Unfortunately, it's not the *first* time. And you're about to have your baptism in fire. And unfortunately, it won't be your *last* time."

Two deputy county attorneys walked by them. One of them clapped Emerick on the back. "Whattaya say, Dan?"

"Howdy, boys," he said jovially. They kept walking down the corridor. He waited until they were far enough away not to hear.

"Just do it. Okay? I don't want to lose you. You're a damn good prosecutor." He kept his voice low.

She nodded, her face somber.

"If you go into the grand jury room and come out without a true bill, Garland's going to know you fucked him. Then I won't be able to protect you around here. Understand?"

"Yes, sir," she mumbled. "I'll get it done."

"Be in my office at three o'clock. I'll give you the file and tell you how to present it. Nothing to it."

"Yes, sir."

Dan Emerick walked down the corridor toward his office. Julie walked into hers, closed the door, and sat down at her desk. She expelled the air that she had been holding in her lungs. She put her head back on the chair, stared at the ceiling, and wondered what her kids were doing at day care. It made her tremble for a moment.

· EIGHTEEN ·

Kate opened the door and froze in shock.

"Don't worry, Ms. O'Dwyer," Marvin Trillker said, holding up his hands. "I'm not here to arrest you. I'm just serving a subpoena." He handed a sheet of paper to her.

She stared at it.

"Sorry, ma'am. I really am." He turned and walked back to his car.

She was paralyzed, trying to understand the writing on the paper, but she couldn't. She slammed the door shut.

She studied the paper again. It said "Subpoena," and the box in the upper left corner said, "76 Grand Jury 95, In the matter of the Investigation of Mary Caitlin O'Dwyer." The short paragraph that formed the body of the document read: "You are hereby directed to report to Room 312, Pima County Superior Courts Building, 110 West Congress Street, Tucson, to testify in this matter." It was for next Tuesday at ten o'clock in the morning.

What can *this* be about? she thought. What in the world can this be about? She went to the phone on the lamp table and dialed Mike's office. Thank God he was there. She read him the whole subpoena.

"What the hell?" he said after a moment of complete perplexity. "Hold on. Let me get my Criminal Rules." He came back on the phone a moment later and talked to himself. "Let's see, grand juries, Rule 12, yeah, here, let me just check through them." Silence. "Shit," he grumbled. "Rule 12.6: 'A person under investigation by the grand jury may be compelled to appear before the grand jury. . . .' Damn it! Those sick bastards down there are starting this whole thing all over again, this time by grand jury indictment instead of a preliminary hearing."

Kate shook her head and squeezed her eyes shut. "You mean they're still trying to charge me with murder?"

Mike swallowed. "Sure looks like it. I didn't know they could do that, get thrown out at a P.H. and then go to a grand jury. I never heard of that. I'm going to call Harvey Stidham. If he doesn't know, I've got to go over to the law library at the courthouse. You going to be home?"

"Yeah," she said weakly.

"I'll call." He hung up.

Kate sat staring at the phone for several minutes, afraid to blink so that she wouldn't miss his call. Finally it rang and she grabbed it.

"Harvey says it's legal. It's rare but legal. Damn! What gives with those people down there?"

Kate sighed and let out a long breath. "Come home. Can you come home?"

"I'm leaving now."

"They didn't subpoena you because they need you to testify. They already have your statement, which they'll read to the grand jury. They just want you conveniently there so they can arrest you and don't have to go through all the hassle they had last time."

"You mean just arrest me while I'm sitting there waiting to testify?"

Mike nodded. "They wouldn't want you actually to testify to the grand jury, anyway. The same thing's liable to happen that did with Kellman. This way the bunch of old farts on the grand jury sleep while Trillker reads reports for two hours, and then the grand jury foreman signs whatever indictment the prosecutor hands him or her."

"That's the American way?" she said acidly.

"Yes. Believe it or not. Thomas Wilkott must have something awfully important that the county attorney down there wants. Otherwise, this wouldn't be happening."

"Is there any way to find out, to stop it?"

He shook his head, his face grave. "I'll tell you what I *think* the law is. I'm not sure, and I'm going to research all this stuff tomorrow. But I think the law is that if there are sufficient facts to support a criminal charge against you, then it doesn't matter what reason the prosecutor has for bringing charges. In other words, if you did the crime, you do the time. And if he took a bribe to indict you, then you can put him in jail for taking a bribe, but it won't get you out."

"Level with me. How does it look?"

He grimaced. "Terrible. Grand juries are just rubber stamps for the prosecutor."

"So why didn't they go that way the first time?"

"They wanted to put you in jail without bond and hold you for ten days until formal charges were filed. They never thought a judge would throw it all out. But when they do it this way, they can't arrest you until the grand jury indicts you, and then you can get bond set immediately and be out in a couple of hours."

"But not if they charge me with first-degree murder again?"

"I don't think they'll do that. They don't have the facts to support it, and after what Judge Kellman did, I think they'd be afraid to charge you with first-degree just to be able to hold you without bail until we could get that charge dismissed. It might even amount to prosecutorial misconduct, and they'd risk having the case thrown out."

"I hope you're right."
"So do I."

Mike found two twenty-five-year-old case precedents that legitimized the procedure being used by the Pima County Attorney's Office to attempt to charge Kate with a crime. Oddly, it didn't appear to have been used since that time. He spent another two hours searching for cases on the elusive issue of "selective prosecution," the technical term for a prosecutor's vendetta-like pursuit of a particular criminal suspect. Unfortunately, he had been right about what the law was in that area.

Kate didn't want her parents to have to go through this mess again. Her father's flushed face and labored breathing at the Ventana hotel last Monday and Tuesday had frightened her. This time, Mike had assured and reassured her, she would not be held without bail. So she called her father and broke the news to him as gently as she could. He handled it with as much aplomb as he had, almost fainting on the phone. But he got hold of himself, for there was nothing else to do, and they discussed it. He immediately wired a quarter of a million dollars to her account for bail. Who could say how high it would be set, and he didn't want her having to languish in jail any more time than absolutely necessary.

Mike didn't go downtown to his office on Thursday. He had to talk to Kate about Jennifer while no one was around. At eleven o'clock Mrs. Gadarian took Jennifer to the fourth-birthday party for Suzy Marren, a girl who had been one of Jennifer's close friends at Merry Moppets months ago.

Mike made a couple of hamburgers on the barbecue in the patio and brought them to the table under the orange tree.

"We've got to talk about what's going to happen with Jennifer," he said.

She wrinkled her brow and looked at him. "Why? Why can't she stay with you?"

"She probably can, if we do a petition to appoint me *guardian ad litem*."

"What's *probably* mean?"

He looked soberly at her and put down his hamburger. She hadn't touched hers yet.

"It means that your ex-husband, Brian, is going to have priority over me or even your parents if he petitions the court for custody."

"Oh, no! I'm not letting that alcoholic drug addict near Jennifer again. He's totally irresponsible."

Mike shook his head. "It's not really going to be up to you."

"God damn it!" she screamed. "God damn it! She's my daughter. I want her safe. Brian is dangerous." She burst out in tears.

Mike sat for several minutes staring morosely at the slumbering ducks on the bank of the cove.

"Okay, I'm calmer now," Kate said hoarsely. "What can we do? Let's just get married right away. Then they can't take her away from you. You'll be her father."

He shook his head. "No, I'll be your husband, but Brian will still be her father. The only sure way is if I adopt her."

"Well, then adopt her."

He shrugged. "That also isn't easy. If I file the petition and Brian contests it, there's going to have to be a court hearing over it, and that could take months. He'll still have priority for custody during that time."

She put her face in her hands and rubbed her eyes. "Oh, God, will this terrible nightmare ever end?" she whispered. She stiffened in her chair, broke a little piece of hamburger off, and chewed on it absently.

"Why don't we just take the money Daddy sent and take off? We can go live in Ireland, France, Germany, Italy, Spain, wherever. They'll never find us."

"What would your father say?"

"He'd be perfectly happy."

"Okay," Mike said. "If that's really what you want to do, I'll help you pack the suitcases right now."

She looked into his eyes, and he was absolutely serious. She put her hand on his on the table and smiled softly. "You really would, wouldn't you? Just throw everything away for *me*."

"I wouldn't be throwing anything away."

She leaned over and kissed him lightly on the lips. "Well," she said, sighing, "I guess we really don't have to decide that right now. If I do get indicted for attempted murder next Monday, they'll set bail. Right?"

"Yes."

"Then we can decide after that. There'll be time. Right now I'd like you to do the petition for adoption. With Brian's record, I don't think he'll get any judge to deny the petition and grant him custody. At least I hope not. And I bet he won't even fight. He's been paying me fifteen hundred dollars a month for child support for over a year, and knowing Brian, he'll be thrilled to be able to stop sending it to me and be able to buy more cocaine. Let's try."

He nodded. "I'll go to my office and draft it right now."

"Okay." She squeezed his hand.

Mike got up from the table and went into the house. Kate pushed the hamburger away, having no appetite for anything. It was a very pleasant day, sunny and comfortable. She thought for a moment that she would go jogging, try to run off some of her frustration. But she didn't have the energy for it. She didn't have the energy for anything right now. It was strenuous enough just standing up, deciding what to do next.

She walked aimlessly through the patio gate, looked around as though she were surprised to be there, then walked across the asphalt path and sat down on the bank with the ducks. A couple of them quacked crankily, then tucked their beaks under their wings and immediately went back to sleep. She sat slumped forward, her arms wrapped around her drawn-up knees, immersed in anxiety over what would happen to Jennifer. The immersion became choking, then drowning, and she gasped repeatedly for breath. Ducks began fluttering their wings, running away from her and waddling into the water.

Kate stood up, felt dizzy, steadied herself for a moment, then walked up to the path and began to jog. She was wearing shorts and a halter top and tennis shoes, and she tried to empty her mind, to run so fast and so hard that the only thing she could think about was the pain in her lungs and the need to breathe.

She slowed down after ten minutes and then stopped, bending over with her hands on her hips and trying to catch her breath. Then she began walking, and she walked for three hours, around and around the lake area and then the golf course. But nothing could drive from her mind the realization that had finally taken firm hold of her: she was about to lose Jennifer.

Talking and brooding about these things endlessly all day Thursday, exploring the labyrinth of contingencies involved in the various steps that had to be taken, trying rationally to discuss with Mike all of the ramifications of Kate's conviction and Jennifer's custody, finally took its toll. Kate was still sleeping at one o'clock Friday afternoon.

Mike asked Mrs. Gadarian to take Jennifer to the Phoenix zoo and to Fantasy Island at Encanto Park. Then he went into the bedroom, sat down on the edge of the bed, and touched Kate's shoulder softly. She didn't move, but at least he could hear her breathing normally. He shook her shoulder harder, and she came drowsily awake.

"Honey, you've slept thirteen hours," Mike said. "I think that's enough."

She blinked at him as though she didn't recognize him, then nodded and sat up slowly. She seemed to be confused and disoriented, as though she were genuinely uncertain about who she was and what was happening.

He helped her into the bathroom, and she looked around vacantly. He turned on the bath water, only lukewarm, and ran it half full. They stood together watching the water, and he held her around the waist.

"Come on, honey. Take a bath." He slipped her short nightgown over her arms, picked her up, and laid her gently into the tub. He knelt beside the tub and washed her, her thighs, her loins, her tummy, her breasts, then splashed water gently on her to rinse her off.

He lifted her out of the tub, sat her on the edge, and helped her dry off. He brought her beige linen shorts and a white cotton T-shirt to put on. She absently went to the sink and brushed her teeth, more out of habit than intent, then walked into the living room and sat down on the sofa. He switched the TV on and sat next to her.

Her almost complete lethargy continued for hours. She was unresponsive and physically slow, and Mike became increasingly fearful for her. He looked in the bathroom for the small bottle of Valium, but there were none left. He tried to reach Dr. Joslin on the telephone, but she was responding to a rape crisis call at Good Samaritan Hospital in Phoenix. Her secretary told him that she would have Dr. Joslin call as soon as she came in.

Kate sat unbudging, staring dully at the television set.

The laundry room door from the garage suddenly banged open, and Jennifer came skipping into the living room. She bounded into Kate's lap, almost knocking her mother's wind out.

"Mommy, Mommy, guess what the big red oranny-tan did?" She giggled. "She peed straight out sitting on the tree and just kept on eating the banana. Everybody laughed. It was so funny." She laughed.

It was the jolt that Kate needed to come back from whatever dark place she had been headed. She hugged Jennifer close, burying her face in her daughter's platinum curls.

After a few moments she loosened her hold on Jennifer and smiled at her. "Well, I guess you had a good time, huh?" She kissed her little girl on the tip of her nose.

Jennifer nodded enthusiastically. "Can we go tomorrow, Mommy? You and me and Mike, so we can see the orannytan?" She looked from Kate to Mike.

"We'll see, honey. I don't know why not."

Mike began to relax for the first time in hours. He took a deep breath and slumped against the back of the sofa.

• NINETEEN •

"She said, 'Hell, no, it's *my* hundred bucks,'" Henry Manuelito said, shaking his head. "I couldn't talk her into it. She says she don't know you from nobody and she don't owe you."

"I have to give back the truck?" Donna's smile suddenly fell away, and the sides of her mouth turned down.

He nodded. "Don't be scared. You're going to be okay. You can still peddle the stuff on foot."

She grimaced, then reluctantly handed him the keys. "Where am I going to live now?" she murmured.

"Why don't you go over to the church? There's a bed, little stove. At least you can stay clean."

"I can't. Anna Luhan's living there."

Manuelito shook his head. "Uh-uh. Not anymore. She's over in the clinic."

"Detox?"

"No. She grabbed a couple of extra bucks from her pimp. He cut her nose off."

She gasped. Tears came to her eyes. "Oh, Jesus," she whispered.

"Yeah, real bad. I told her stay off the streets. I told her." He shrugged. "She wanted money, some fancy clothes. Now she's got no nose." He grimaced. "You stay off the streets."

Donna nodded.

"Come on, I'll give you a ride over to the church.

I talked to Father Oldenham. He's happy you're coming."

"I've got to get my stuff."

"Yeah, okay. I'll help you."

It was an eight-feet-square room attached to the rear of the old wooden shed that was the church. There was no electricity, and the only light was an old kerosene lantern. The room had walls of corrugated tin and a roof of desiccated slats of wood covered with tarpaper. The floor was hard-packed mud. The bed was an old, collapsible canvas army bunk with no mattress. There was a thin gray army surplus blanket, but with nights still mild, that was no problem. The bathroom was a two-feet-square wooden outhouse ten feet away. A hose spigot and a plastic bucket outside the church supplied water.

Donna had left her Bible at Kate's house, and Kate had probably thrown it out or burned it. But Father Oldenham had happily given Donna one of his own. It was old and had black, soft leather covers. Donna had picked through it for a couple of days, reading and trying to understand more of it than just the Canticle of Canticles, and she had read about Jesus, God's own son, being born in a stable. She looked around her and realized that however little she had, it was a lot more than a stable. She felt better about herself. And every day she would throw the laundry bag full of used clothes over her shoulder and walk the lower part of the Pima-Maricopa Reservation, selling clothes door to door.

When she ran out of clothing after three days, Father Oldenham loaned her his newish little car, some little Japanese thing, and she drove to the Goodwill store in Phoenix and the Mormon Outreach in Mesa and picked up a couple of bundles of clothes.

There was very little work around the church. It was too small. Just an altar and sanctuary and about forty metal folding chairs. So she had plenty of time to peddle her inventory around the reservation. In less than a week she had almost eighty dollars. Half of it she spent on food and gas for the priest's car when she drove it, most of the rest on cosmetics and some nice new clothes over at a real bargain place on Rural Road.

Someday she'd be the richest kid on the reservation. She looked at herself in the small hand mirror she had bought, and she knew that she was becoming a very pretty young woman.

"I am a rose of Sharon, I am a lily of the valley," she said to herself in the mirror, smiling. *"Thou art all fair, my love. There is no blemish on thee."*

Anna Luhan was waiting for Donna on Saturday afternoon. Donna gasped when she saw her. In the place of her nose was a little white plastic triangle and under that a small patch of gauze that fluttered when she breathed.

Anna saw the horror in Donna's eyes and cowered, hiding her face with one hand. "What am I gonna do?" Anna whined.

Her voice was real odd, lacking resonance and depth. It scared Donna.

"Isn't there plastic surgery or something? I read about it in a magazine. They make noses and chins and ears and everything."

"IHS won't do nothin'," Anna said. "Say it's not covered by federal funds, they got no doctor like that."

"How about the county hospital in Phoenix?"

She shook her head.

Donna looked at Anna's wasted eyes, and she began to cry. She couldn't help it. This could be *her* sitting there. She made the sign of the cross.

"You gettin' into all a that religious shit?" Anna asked. She stared with dead eyes at Donna. "I done it awhile. Lookit me."

Donna looked away.

"Ya got money?" Anna asked.

Donna nodded. "Ten, twelve."

"I gotta have it. I need a bottle. I need it bad. It hurts alla time."

"I've got Father's car. I'll take you over to the drive-in."

"Naw, I can't go. If the priest sees me, he throws me out. He said I was a bad example. Said I spit in God's face when I went back on the streets. You go, huh? Bring me back a bottle."

Donna nodded. She still had Father Oldenham's car from the afternoon. She had borrowed it to go get some used clothes in Phoenix. He lived a couple of miles down McDowell in a nice little house, and he was in his late sixties. He never went anywhere at night, and he wouldn't mind not having his car back for a while.

Donna wiped her eyes on a frayed towel. She got into the car and drove to the drive-in liquor place just outside the reservation. It was dark, she was hidden in the car, and the old guy that owned the place would sell a bottle to anybody old enough and rich enough to have ten bucks.

She drove back, brought it in to Anna, who was sitting torpidly on the cot, and drove down to Father Oldenham's house to drop off the car. His front door was never locked. She knocked, he called out, "Come in," and she went in. He was sitting in a big reclining chair reading. A radio was playing.

"Thanks, Father," she said, putting the keys on the lamp table.

"Sure. You need it tomorrow?"

"No. I don't think so."

"If you do, just come by. I'll be here all day. My arthritis is killing me. I'm all stove up."

"Okay, Father." She kissed him on the forehead and left.

It took her about forty minutes to walk back to the shed. When she got there, the lantern was off and it was dark. She reached down just inside the door, felt around for the lantern, took matches out of her pocket, and lit it.

Anna was on the cot, the entire fifth of Four Roses empty on the floor beside her, and blood dripped off the cot into a huge pool seeping into the mud floor.

Donna held the lantern high and edged toward Anna. She had cut the big blood vessels in the right side of her neck with a razor blade.

Donna vomited. She stumbled outside, vomited again, fell to her hands and knees, and dropped the lantern. The glass mantle shattered, oily fuel splattered on her Levi's, and several splashes landed on her polo shirt and right cheek. Flames leapt up from her knee to her chest, and her face was on fire. She slapped at herself frantically.

She was in excruciating pain and couldn't think. The flames billowed out from her Levi's. She slapped her thighs, got up, and started running wildly. She fell headfirst into a muddy irrigation ditch. She rolled around in the mud extinguishing the flames. The pain was so intense that she passed out.

· TWENTY ·

The sole legal qualification mandated of grand jurors was that they were registered voters in Pima County. Period. They didn't even have to prove that they could read. The second qualification was practical. Since the term of each grand jury panel generally lasted four months, and the panel met at least every Tuesday and Thursday, the jurors were generally retired people who preferred the heady task of deciding the fate of fellow human beings rather than wiling away mindless, deadening hours of boring inactivity watching *General Hospital* and *The Price Is Right*.

Julie Harcourt was an expert in the care and handling of grand juries, and Harry Young was Julie's favorite foreman in the two years that she had been stroking grand jurors. He was the paragon of a foreman, virtually a gift from God to an ambitious prosecutor. He was seventy-one years old, a former farmer from the incredibly medieval town of St. David some seventy miles southeast of Tucson, where arch right-wing, devoutly religious Mormons periodically invaded the elementary and high school libraries, seized immoral and trashy books like *Tarzan* (two folks living together out of wedlock) and *To Kill a Mockingbird* (a nigra having the shocking chutzpah to contest the allegations of an obviously lying white girl that he had raped her), and ceremoniously burned them in the little grassy square by the American flag in front of the historic, roughhewn granite block jailhouse.

Harry possessed all of the qualifications of a model grand juror: he was a registered voter in Pima County.

He had moved to Tucson a few years ago so that his ailing wife would be close to excellent and well-equipped hospitals. But he hadn't forgotten his roots. He was a grumpy old bastard with a full head of pure white hair, a fat belly bulging his shirt buttons, and a thick, jowly face with tiny broken capillaries all over his cheeks from years of field labor under southern Arizona's pitiless sun.

Julie loved him. Every true bill she handed him came back signed with a unanimous vote of the grand jurors. Criminal misconduct in Harry Young's world was the equivalent of pissing on the Book of Mormon in the Stake Hall, an affront to God who had created the world and all that was therein and commanded man to "let justice well up like a river and righteousness like a torrential stream." Harry the grumpy old bastard knew damn well what that meant. He had no legal training and not a hell of a lot of education and didn't read much, but he did read the Good Book every evening for an hour, and he had a fair t' middlin' notion of what society needed to do to whip the assholes into shape.

Mike sat with Kate on an unbalanced wooden bench in the hallway outside of Room 312. It rocked each time one of them moved.

As Kate watched the grand jurors straggle one by one into their lair as ten o'clock approached, she became increasingly despondent. These sixty- and seventy-year-old men and women, with just a sprinkling of forty- and fifty-year-olds, weren't going to do anything but sleep through the whole damn thing, just as Mike had predicted. And then it would take them all of about one minute of "deliberation" to indict her for attempted murder.

Panic seized her. She would soon be taken away from Jennifer again. For how long? A day? A week? Seven years? Oh God, oh God. Why?

Jennifer was with Mrs. Gadarian in Scottsdale. Kate's essential toiletries were in a bag in the car out in the parking lot, just in case, and the $250,000 had been transferred into Mike and Kate's joint checking account so that he could go to the First Interstate Bank two blocks away and get a cashier's check for the bail. All these arrangements are so mechanical, so impersonal, Kate thought. But what could be more personal than going to prison, than not being with the people you love for year after year?

Mike put his arm around her shoulders. "You okay?" he asked.

She swallowed and nodded.

Marvin Trillker came out of the elevator carrying an Expando file under his arm. He glanced at Mike, walked by, and stood forty feet away at the end of the hall, staring out the window. A moment later an attractive woman, perhaps five or six years older than Kate, came out of the elevator chatting volubly with a tall middle-aged man carrying a stenographic machine. Neither of them looked at Mike or Kate, apparently having become immune to the range of expressions and emotions exhibited by accused persons and their lawyers. They walked into the grand jury room.

It was exactly ten o'clock.

"Ladies and gentlemen of the grand jury, today's first matter is '*In re* the Investigation of Mary Caitlin O'Dwyer,'" Julie Harcourt said, standing behind her small table and addressing the eighteen jurors. Sometimes use a little Latin on them, she knew. Latin lends the case an aura of special importance.

"We'll only have one witness for this matter, Mr. Marvin Trillker." She walked to the door and opened it, leaned into the hall, and called out, "Marv." She glanced at Kate, and their eyes met. Kate stared at her, and the prosecutor looked away, her cheeks reddening.

Trillker walked into the room, and he closed and locked the door behind him. Only the prosecutor, her witnesses, and a court reporter were allowed in the grand jury room with the eighteen jurors.

Foreman Young held up his hand, swore Marvin to tell the truth, and resumed his slumped position in the uncomfortable metal chair with an inadequate seat cushion. His heavy-lidded eyes began to glaze over in preparation for the reading of reports.

"You are Marvin Trillker, senior investigator with the Pima County Attorney's Office?"

"Yes, I am."

"Have you brought official police reports with you this morning *in re* the first-degree murder investigation of Mary O'Dwyer?"

"I have."

"Would you please read them to the grand jury, omitting inessential matters, and giving logical sequence to the investigation without reading any such report out of context?"

"Yes." He took out a package of reports and started reading. He droned monotonally in an intentionally soporific voice that generally succeeded in putting most of the grand jurors to sleep.

After about an hour, Mrs. Thurman in the back row raised her hand. She was a seventy-three-year-old retired schoolteacher who had a little bladder-control problem and always needed to go pee. Julie halted Trillker's reading, and everybody waited, fidgeting and annoyed at yet another Thurman interruption, until the toilet in the adjoining rest room hissed and sucked and Mrs. Thurman came out looking sheepish as always. Julie gave her a daughterly smile and told Trillker to proceed, rotating her finger horizontally to signal him to speed it up. She didn't want anyone to die of boredom in here. Finally he finished.

"Do you have other evidence to present to the grand jury today?" Julie asked.

"Yes. I have a recorded statement of Mary O'Dwyer given in open court eight days ago before Judge Kellman and transcribed verbatim."

"Please read it to the grand jurors."

Marvin started reading. Julie looked around at the faces of the men and women seated before her. Most of them did not change expression at all. Some had their eyes closed, probably asleep. Several were yawning. Harry Young was tapping his fingers lightly on his knee and staring out the side window at a pigeon shitting on the ledge.

Marvin did not drone the statement. It was too good to read to a sleeping bunch of jurors. He wanted them awake. It was a literal confession, at least to attempted murder.

"Thank you, Mr. Trillker," Julie said. It was almost noon. "Does any grand juror have a question of Mr. Trillker?"

No one raised his hand, though several of the jurors stirred in their chairs, realizing that the morning's labors were about to cease, and they would soon be gobbling lunch at the county's expense in one of the beaneries across the street.

"You're excused, Mr. Trillker." Marv left the room.

"Ladies and gentlemen, I have many times read you the statutes that deal with first-degree murder and all lesser included offenses. I have a copy here of the instructions I read to you about two months ago at our first session. I am incorporating them by reference into the record of this proceeding and giving them to your foreman so that you may all familiarize yourself again with the law during your deliberations, if you need to. I am also handing the indictment to your foreman at this time. It was prepared by my office. It includes counts charging Mary O'Dwyer with first-degree murder, second-degree murder, vehicular homicide, and attempted murder." She handed the papers to Harry Young.

"Do you wish to have any further legal advice from me?"

No one responded. Harry Young sucked his cheek and gave her his usual chauvinistic "I have a granddaughter your age" look. She knew that he was thinking, "Why ain't ya home bakin' pies like ya oughta be doin'?"

"All right," Julie said. "There being no further evidence to offer before this grand jury in this matter, the court reporter and I will retire while you deliberate in private. Please bang on the door three times when your deliberations are completed."

She left the room, avoided looking at Mike or Kate sitting on the bench, and went to stare solemnly out the window with Trillker at the end of the hall. The court reporter leaned on the wall outside Room 312 and absently whistled the theme song from *Beauty and the Beast*.

Not five minutes later, there were three bangs on the door. Kate and Mike both jumped. He put his arm around her shoulders and held her tightly. She stared at her hands folded in her lap, her lips trembling.

The court reporter walked into the grand jury room followed by Julie Harcourt, who locked the door behind her. She walked up to the small table and faced the grand jurors.

"Have you voted as required by law on the true bill?"

Harry Young stood up slowly, shaking the stiffness from his joints like an awakening bloodhound. "We have." He walked to Julie and handed her the indictment.

The signature line for the foreman was filled in with Harry's illiterate scrawl. She read the grand jurors' vote tally above it. It was a typed line that had three underlined blanks to be filled in by the foreman to record the vote, as required by statute. The line read:

"The grand jurors vote *18* to *0 not* to return a true bill."

She blinked her eyes rapidly. Her mouth dropped open. She looked up at Harry Young, still standing before her table, and studied his pouchy face.

"What do you think you're doing?"

"Just what we're supposed t' do."

Her voice grew angrier, louder. "You have legal obligations. This is not *legal*. You all took an oath to uphold the *law*. You can't do this. That woman *confessed*! You can't just ignore that! You just can't let her go!" Oh, God! Garland's going to have my ass for this.

"Young lady," Harry the grumpy old bastard Young said in the tone of a disappointed father counseling his misbehaving child, "we can do whatever we think is fair. That's our job. They ain't a one a us that thinks this is fair." He nodded toward the indictment in her hand.

"But the *law*!" she whined. "She broke the *law*."

He stared back at her and shook his head, disgusted. "Didn't they teach ya nothin' in law school?" He pointed at his chest and swung his pointed finger around at the grand jurors. "*We're* the law," he said. And then he pointed straight overhead. "And *He's* the law."

He walked out of the grand jury room, followed by the seventeen other qualified grand jurors, mostly old folks, registered to vote, residents of Pima County, and bored watching *General Hospital* and *The Price Is Right* day after day. And they didn't even have to prove that they could read.

· TWENTY-ONE ·

"I'm so glad the shit finally stopped hittin' the fan," Gwen McLemore said in her marvelously earthy brogue.

Kate laughed heartily. Gwen had just come to Scottsdale to visit Kate and Mike and Jennifer. They had picked her up at the airport an hour ago, and Mike had gone to his office.

"Aye, an' that lad a yours got a pair a buns on 'im to die for, an' he's about the cutest thing I ever did see."

Kate roared, wiping tears from her eyes. "If ya don't stop prattlin' on this way, Gwenny me lass, I'm gonna havta call yer mother superior an' report that ya've been blas*phem*in'!"

Gwen shook her finger at Kate. "Admirin' a gorgeous man's bottom ain't blasphemy."

They clasped each other hard together and laughed.

"What am I supposed to call you now, by the way? Dr. Sister Gwenny?"

Gwen shrugged. "Oh, just Saint Gwen would be fine, darlin'."

Again they both roared with laughter.

"I see the For Sale sign is gone from in front of the house."

Kate nodded. "There's nothing to fear here anymore. Everyone is dead who crossed that threshold in evil." She jutted her chin toward the front door. "Now the place seems charmed instead of jinxed."

"And what's with the adoption?"

"Oh, I didn't get a chance to call you. It just came through yesterday afternoon. Brian didn't even contest Mike's adoption. His only response to the petition was a sweet card he sent to me."

Kate got up from the sofa and walked into her bedroom. She came back a moment later and handed it to Gwen. The front was a photograph of a handsome, young, well-muscled man holding his large erection in his hand, and the sentiment inside, FUCK YOU. Under it Brian had provided his own personalized message: "Good riddance to bad rubbish."

Gwen pursed her lips, closed the card, and stared at the photo on the front. "Do ya happen t' know where this young fella lives?" she asked sweetly.

Kate exploded with laughter.

"So you're teachin' again at Saint Daniel's Academy?"

Kate nodded. "Yes. Bishop Losiento called me himself and groveled, told me how sorry he was about the Board of Trustees' decision, as though it wasn't his ultimate decision to make in the first place. A real man of God."

"They can't all be Seamus Gerritys."

"I know. And unfortunately, most of them aren't. But I finally got Mike to go with me to mass last Sunday at Our Lady of Perpetual Hope. Father Baedecker is a good pastor."

"And Michael? Did he behave himself?"

"Oh yes, he prayed like a Jesuit. And when we left the church, I asked him if his faith in God had been restored, and he got real philosophical with me."

"Aye?" Gwen said, interested. "And what did he say?"

"Well, I want to be sure I'm quoting him exactly." Kate screwed up her face and closed her eyes hard, pondering for a moment. "He said, 'Who the fuck knows?' "

Again they both exploded in laughter.

"A golden tongue has that lad," Gwen said, pride showing in her face. "He'll be a mighty success as a lawyer."

Kate nodded, smiling broadly.

"Let's all go to early mass tomorrow," Gwen said. "We'll both try to beat a little faith into the lad."

It was just a few days till Thanksgiving. Kate and Mike were planning to go to San Francisco for the holiday, their first trip alone together, their first opportunity since the nightmare had ended to get away together and simply enjoy each other. Mrs. Gadarian had agreed to come stay at the house with Jennifer for the three days. She would stay in the room adjoining Jennifer's. Donna's old room.

Kate went into it with sheets and pillowcases to make up the bed. Donna's Bible was still lying on the mattress as Kate and Gwen had left it several months ago. Kate opened it hesitantly, and its broken spine flipped the pages to the Canticle of Canticles. Kate saw the underlined passages, turned a page, sat down slowly on the mattress, and read some more of the underlined verses:

> *I charge you, maidens of Jerusalem, by the spirits and the goddesses of the field: Do not rouse or awaken love until it is ready. . . .*
> *My dove that hides in nests in the cliffs or in nooks on the terraced hillside, let me see your face and hear your voice; for your voice is sweet, your face is lovely.*

And a few pages later:

> *Thou art all fair, my love. There is no blemish on thee.*

Gwen looked into the room.

"What is it, Mary Kate?" She sat down beside her.

Kate bit her lip and handed the Bible to her. Gwen read the underlined passages.

"It does tug at one's heart," Gwen said softly. "What's happened with the girl?"

Kate shrugged. "I don't know." Her shoulders sagged. "God, I feel so guilty."

The next day was the onset of as much winter bad weather as Scottsdale was likely to get. It began with an eastern type of storm, a low, flat, dark gray cloud cover that poured rain from horizon to horizon. It was only fifty-five degrees. Kate had to drive into Phoenix to the diocese to fill out the employment papers.

Gwen called a cab that took her into the flooded roads on the Pima-Maricopa Reservation. She had no idea where she was or where she was going. She didn't know where Donna's home was, and there were hardly any street signs or house numbers. She saw some buildings in the distance that appeared to be different from the rest, new, pink plaster. She told the cabbie to drive toward them. A small sign on the side of the road read, SALT RIVER ADMINISTRATIVE OFFICES. They drove slowly past the police station and the fire department. The third building was the Community Housing Office.

"Here," Gwen said. The cab driver parked, and Gwen walked through the main door. She shook her umbrella off just inside and went up to the desk.

"Do you know where a girl named Donna Alvarez might be livin'?"

"Yah, sure I know her," said the elderly woman receptionist. "She live down dere on Thomas Road, big wood shack all alone. Go down de next street, turn right." She pointed and smiled.

"Thank you very much," Gwen said. She left the building and repeated the directions to the driver. There was a fallow cotton field on the right. On the left they drove slowly by a doorless little shack and saw a larger wooden shack ahead. A woman was sitting on the porch. The cabbie parked, and Gwen walked up to her, holding her umbrella high.

"Are you Donna's mother?"

The bleary-eyed three-hundred-pound woman almost managed to focus on her. "You got money?"

"Are you Donna's mother?"

"Yeah. You got money?"

Gwen ran back to the cab, got a ten-dollar bill out of her purse, ran up on the porch, and handed it to her. The smell of the woman and the fetor coming from the house almost knocked her down.

"I dunno where she went," the woman said. "I dunno. Long time ago."

Gwen went back to her car, having no idea where to search next. She wasn't going to find Donna out there in this anonymous morass of flooded roads. Maybe she was back on the streets downtown. Maybe she was dead in an alley. She shuddered with the thought. They drove down Longmore Road, and there was a small church that looked like a Mexican mission. A sign read, ST. FRANCIS OF ASSISSI.

"Stop here a moment, please," Gwen said.

She went into the church. An Indian woman was on her hands and knees scrubbing the floor. Gwen walked up to her.

"Do you have a pastor?"

The woman looked up, then pointed at a closed door beside the altar. Gwen walked to it, knocked, and walked in. Seated at the desk was a young Indian man in clerical black with no collar.

"Are you the pastor?" Gwen asked.

"No, I'm the deacon."

"Do you happen to know a girl named Donna Alvarez?"

He looked at her a little oddly, then nodded. "You should go talk to Father Oldenham. He's got a small chapel at the end of this road, near the Indian agency." He pointed south. "If he isn't there, he lives about two miles east on McDowell. A little house with a green painted door."

"Thanks," she said.

They drove to the shed that served as a chapel, but it was empty. Then they drove to Father Oldenham's house, easy to find because of the green door. She knocked on it, and a voice called out, "Come in."

He was sitting on a wood slat chair next to a small Formica table. He had an open jar of peanut butter, another of blackberry jam, and a loaf of white bread.

"Hello, Father. I'm Dr. Gwen McLemore, a Sister of Mercy from Boston."

He didn't stand, simply gestured to the other chair at the table. "Would you like some lunch?"

"No thanks, Father." She sat down. "I was just wonderin' where I might find a young woman named Donna Alvarez."

He studied her for a long moment, then laid his sandwich down on the plate. "What is your interest, Sister? Are you a physician?"

"No, a psychologist. The interest isn't all mine. I have a dear friend whom I'm visitin', Mary Kate O'Dwyer, who used to be the girl's foster mother. She's very confused and upset about what has happened."

He contemplated her for a moment. Then he stood up with obvious difficulty and pain, and she noticed for the first time that his knuckles were greatly swollen and his fingers twisted.

"Arthritis," he said. "Come with me. I'll take you to her."

"I have a cab outside."

"You can discharge it. I'll drive. And after you've seen Donna, I'll take you back to Mrs. O'Dwyer's home."

"I'd like you to go with the ladies' auxiliary from the church this Sunday," Gwen said to Kate. "They're scheduled to go out to a little chapel on the Pima-Maricopa Reservation to provide the buffet after the five o'clock mass.''

Kate studied her eyes. "Is this about Donna?"

Gwen nodded, her face uncharacteristically solemn. "Have you seen her?"

Gwen nodded again. "I talked to her for an hour. She's a good girl."

Kate pulled back in surprise. "Is she okay?"

Gwen shook her head.

Kate swallowed. "What is it? You're scaring me. Is she back on the streets? Is she on heroin?"

"I don't mean to scare you, Mary Kate. But this is somethin' you're goin' to have to deal with by yourself. She's at the Health Clinic on the reservation. It isn't anythin' life-threatenin'. I just want you to go to the chapel on McDowell Road and Longmore on Sunday and talk to Father Oldenham. He's a gentle man. Then I want you to do what your heart tells you, and nothin' else."

Kate nodded. "Okay," she said, her voice unsure, her eyes quizzical. "That's all you're going to tell me?"

Gwen nodded and handed her a scrap of paper. "Here's the name and phone number of the president of the ladies' auxiliary."

Kate called the woman, asked her what the buffet at the reservation entailed, and was told that each of the volunteers made one dish, enough to feed about thirty-five or forty people. She was delighted that Kate had called. It was hard to get the decent women of Our Lady of Perpetual Hope to go out to that shack of a church.

"The priest out there got thrown out of Mesa for advocating abortion," she said to Kate confidentially. "None of our ladies really want to go there. And the church? Oh, my heavens. Just an old shed. Dirty and small. You can't even sit down anywhere without getting dirt all over yourself."

Kate thought that it was far preferable to have a therapeutic abortion early in the pregnancy than to murder the newborn baby as Gwen's father had, or to bring it into the arms of a mother who resented it, had no idea how to rear and nurture it, and proceeded to ruin her own life as well as her baby's. But that wasn't any of this woman's business.

"Well, Mrs. Tinsley, I'll be happy to bring some food. What would you suggest?"

"How are you with roasting turkeys and maybe a roast beef?"

"Not such an expert, particularly for forty people, and it all has to be ready for the day after tomorrow. But I'm certainly capable of going over to Cimino's Delicatessen and ordering whatever we need."

"Oh, you needn't go to all that trouble. You can bring sandwich meats, you know, cold cuts, like that."

"It's no trouble, Mrs. Tinsley. I'll bring what? Three, four turkeys, two roast beefs?"

"That would be lovely, dear. I'll be so pleased to have you join our auxiliary."

"Thank you, Mrs. Tinsley. Do I just meet you out there?"

"Yes, dear. Come about five. I've got the truck coming with the tables and some chairs and forks and so forth at that time."

"See you there."

Mike had to go to the law library Sunday afternoon and get ready for his first murder trial. It was beginning on Monday. It was another court appointment, a derelict in a bar in South Phoenix who had been killed by someone with a beer bottle. Ripped his face off. His client was one of the three arrested by the police. One of the three had done it, but who?

It was a good case, "triable" as attorneys called it, meaning that if you did some good lawyering you could win. No technicalities, no motions to suppress, no guilt over getting evidence thrown out on a technicality, no weeping parents wanting to kill you for defending their son's murderer. Just plain and simple good lawyering, a genuine "who done it."

When four-thirty arrived, Kate left Jennifer with Gwen and drove to Cimino's Deli in downtown Scottsdale to pick up the food. It filled the whole backseat of her car.

The day was warm and clear, and the five women from Our Lady of Perpetual Hope church scurried around the long folding tables, covering them with clean white tablecloths and setting up the bowls and platters of food. It took over a half hour.

Indians began filing out of the opening doors of the church. Donna wasn't among these mostly elderly Indians, with whom time and want and desolation had dealt equally harshly. They walked silently by the food on the table, filling their paper plates self-consciously, their eyes downcast, walking away to far corners of the lot to stoop in the dirt and eat without a sound, perhaps the only real meal some of them would have till next Sunday. The priest came last, walking as though his feet hurt, smiling politely at the ladies. The women returned plastic smiles.

Kate said, "Hello, Father. How about a lovely drumstick?" She put it on the plate and looked pleasantly at him.

"Thank you, young lady."

"Father, do you happen to know a girl named Donna Alvarez? She's sixteen, very pretty, tall."

His eyes twitched. He looked closely at her. "And why are you interested?"

"I was her foster mother."

He nodded. "Mrs. O'Dwyer," he said slowly. "Sister Gwen McLemore told me about you."

"Yes, Father."

"Come into the church, Mrs. O'Dwyer. We can talk better."

She looked at him with apprehension, then followed him into the church. He put his turkey leg on a folding metal chair, turned around two others, and pointed. "Please."

Kate sat down. "Is she okay, Father?"

He looked at her with tired, suffering eyes. "Not so good, I'm afraid."

Kate swallowed. Her heart began beating fast. "What is it, Father?"

"There was a fire here, out back by the shed where Donna was living. She dropped a lantern and some of her clothing caught on fire."

Kate covered her mouth.

"She's still at the Health Clinic up on Osborn Road," the priest said.

"How bad is it?"

"Well, it happened several weeks ago, and she actually could be at home, but the ongoing treatment requires the application of things like, uh"—he searched for a word—"poultices, I guess, to some open wounds. This place is just too dirty to come back to. She would undoubtedly get an infection, and that could be fatal. I wish that I could take her home with me, but I have a tiny house with one bedroom, and I'm sure that if Bishop Losiento heard, he would strip me of my priesthood." He looked apologetic. "I'm sorry. I have no home but the Church."

"I understand, Father."

"She needs some plastic surgery, skin grafts, and some work on her face—" His voice cracked.

Kate rubbed tears from her eyes and winced.

"The IHS Health Clinic simply doesn't have a plastic surgeon. They're doing the best they can, but—" He splayed his hands. "Perhaps in your wealthy parish, Mrs. O'Dwyer, perhaps there would be a plastic surgeon willing to donate a bit of time and care to a very sad girl?"

She looked into the priest's bottomless brown eyes and nodded.

"She did not hurt your daughter, Mrs. O'Dwyer,"

he said very softly. "Her soul is as pure as our Mother of Sorrows herself."

Kate broke into tears and pressed her hands to her face. "Yes, Father," she gasped, "I know."

By the time that she came out of the church, the ladies had already left. She drove to the two-story pink plaster Health Clinic on Osborn Road and walked into the waiting room. It was six o'clock, and there were several other people there who looked like they were probably visitors.

"Can you give me Donna Alvarez's room number, please?"

The receptionist was a young Indian woman. She consulted a clipboard, then pointed. "Down there, 117."

Kate walked down the hallway to the room, becoming increasingly apprehensive with each step. She reached it, took a deep breath, and tried to steel herself to what she was about to see. She opened the door slowly and looked into the small room. It was almost dark outside, providing no illumination through the thin-curtained window, and there were no lights on in the room. The television was an old black-and-white, and it was playing, flicking a chiaroscuro of shadows around the room.

Donna was asleep on the hospital bed. Kate tiptoed into the room and closed the door carefully. Donna didn't stir. Her face was lovely, except that there was a quarter-sized spot on the side of her left cheek that was pink, obviously burned, covered with a thick salve. Otherwise, Donna appeared to be perfectly normal, covered in a long, loose white hospital nightgown that buttoned down the front.

Donna groaned in her sleep and her shoulders twitched, but she didn't awaken. Kate tiptoed out of the room and closed the door without a sound. She went up to the reception desk.

"Is there a doctor here I can talk to?" she asked the young woman.

"Yes, Dr. Silverman is making rounds."

"Is he Donna Alvarez's doctor?"

"He's everybody's doctor." She picked up the telephone and made an announcement. "Dr. Silverman, Dr. Silverman, can you come to the front desk, please?" It came weakly out of speakers high on the walls.

A few minutes later, a young man in a white polo shirt and Levi's came up to the desk. He had a stethoscope around his neck. "Yes?" he said to the receptionist. The woman pointed at Kate.

"Yes?" he said.

"Are you Donna Alvarez's doctor?"

He nodded.

"Can I talk to you about her for a moment?"

"Are you her caseworker?"

"No. I was her foster mother."

He looked thoughtfully at her. "I guess I read about that a few times."

She nodded.

"She has a physician-patient privilege," he said. "I'm really not sure I should."

"I'm only trying to help."

He scrutinized her eyes. "Okay, come on over here."

She followed him to the wall, and he leaned against it.

"She's been through a lot. She has third-degree burns on her left breast and the tops of both thighs. Because of her history of addiction, I haven't been able to give her morphine or codeine. She'd be hooked in a minute. So I've had to treat her with only light pain medication. It's been very hard on her."

Kate breathed deeply and nodded.

"She needs grafts for her burns, and I don't have the training for it. I'm treating her traditionally, but she's pretty soon going to need better than the IHS can provide. It's a tragedy that unfortunately repeats itself pretty often out here. If we could afford a good plastic surgeon on staff, she'd have a whole new life. All she needs is a little plastic surgery on her thighs."

"Can she walk?"

"Well enough to go to the bathroom. But it's too painful for her to go much farther. The only reason that we're keeping her here is that she needs a very clean environment to avoid complications, infection, septicemia. She has nowhere like that to go."

Kate swallowed down the lump in her throat.

Mike called Kate at noon the next day. "I just got a severance," he said excitedly.

"Good heavens, Mr. Bobbitt, I hope it didn't hurt."

He laughed. "You're a cute girl."

"What's a severance?"

"The judge just granted my motion to have my murder client tried separately from the other two guys."

"That's good?"

"That's great. It means the guy is probably going to be acquitted."

"Goody for him."

"Goody for me! I did a hell of a job for the guy. Maybe somebody will read about it and hire me."

"Why don't you get a nice, clean job like collecting garbage?"

"That's exactly what I do," he said, laughing.

"You're a cute guy," she said.

"So, you get everything set?"

"Yes, finally. I've been on the phone for three hours."

"No hitches?"

"No glitches."

"No bitches."

"And a wonderful poet, too," she said. "Gosh, what a lucky girl I am."

"I'll be there in forty-five minutes."

*   *   *

Kate knocked on Donna's hospital room door, heard the "Yes?", and they walked in.

Donna opened her eyes wide at them, and her mouth dropped open. Gwen walked up to the foot of the bed and smiled at her.

Mike walked to the bed, put his arms under her knees and her shoulders, and lifted her gently, cradling her in his arms. "We're taking you home," he said.

"Oh, oh, no," she stammered. "My—my mother just sits, and the house is horrible and filthy. I don't want to go home."

"No, I mean *home,* with *us,*" Mike said.

Donna's eyes opened even wider, and she looked at Kate.

Kate walked up to her. "Yes, your little sister is waiting for you. She's very excited."

Donna's tears fell on her cheeks. "But—but I'm all burned, I'm all hurt."

Kate looked at her, her eyes radiant. She bent over and kissed Donna's forehead. "No, no, no," she whispered. *"Thou art all fair, my love. There is no blemish on thee."*